LIBRA'S LIMBO

ZODIAC ASSASSINS BOOK 2

ARTEMIS CROW

LIBRA'S LIMBO

Printed in the United States of America
First Printing, 2018

Print Book ISBN 978-0-9966003-2-3

OTHER BOOKS BY ARTEMIS CROW

Zodiac Assassins series
Lyon's Roar Book 1
Leona's Descent Book 1.5

For my father—the social butterfly with a
pipe and a joke and a tireless helping hand—
the sting of your loss will always be keenly felt.

I T WASN'T A PROPER paranorm party until a troll dropped a steaming pile of dung…or blood was spilled. But the assembled paranorms were not in a celebratory mood.

Poised at the edge between the gloom of the passageway and the light flooding the Great Cavern, Libra pulled his foot back and remained in the comfort of the dark as oily waves of the paranorms' anger and fear coated him. His hands clenched into fists, he forced his pounding heart to slow. He was one meeting away from everything he had longed for: freedom from the life of an assassin.

Sunlight pierced the cold of the paranorm subterranean world, spotlighting the various species enthralled by the spectacle of the Corvus Ward king and Lyon—Libra's fellow Zodiac Assassin and leader—stalking each other inside the circle formed by the crowd's numbers.

Created by the goddess Hecate for persecuted paranorms, the spider-web-shaped subterranean world called the InBetween was vast, and not completely charted. At one time, the species had lived together, but the Twelve's rule had grown predatory and cruel, their grip on the throats of those they were chosen to protect tightening, choking the life out of the relationships they were supposed to be nurturing. One by one, groups of paranorms had left this central hub, the Great Cavern, striking out to create their own territory in the far reaches, and blocking any ingress or egress that they hadn't created themselves to prevent the Twelve from gaining access.

More recently, many of the reclusive paranorms had returned to the Great Cavern seeking help from the Twelve to find their stolen children. But before the mystery surrounding the abductions could be solved, a demon army had been summoned from the depths of the abyss. Punching through the roof of the Great Cavern, the denizens of Hell had erupted into the human world and disappeared.

The Zodiacs and the few paranorms who had chosen to stay in this part of the InBetween had struggled to set their violated home to rights in time for this unprecedented gathering of most of the better-known paranorm groups, species that historically never shared the same square footage.

But history was just that—they had a new future to mold.

Including me.

Libra took a deep breath and released it slowly. His constant struggle to maintain mastery over his dark emotions could be relaxed. Life among humans would never tax him; no demands they might make could faze him. In minutes he would be named the paranorm ambassador to the humans; by tomorrow he would be ensconced in his penthouse in New York while the finest tailor in the city measured him for new suits.

A delicate cough sounded behind him. He jumped then glanced back, instantly regretting his reaction when he saw the arrival's face. His skin chilled, the flesh rising into blizzard-worthy goose bumps.

He had fought for every miniscule scrap of good in him, struggled to hold onto it against the violence and ugliness of his life, the job of assassin foisted on him by familial obligation. The rest was faked, qualities he chose to project, a facade by design. The expensive clothes he wore had become his armor, the manners and insouciance and humor he plied were his shields. Only he knew what it cost him to keep the legacy of paternal rage and maternal hatred shoved deep inside. Only he knew the sliver span on which he walked, or how the dark emotions clawed at him to be loosed. Only he knew that it was his control that kept him from endangering them all.

Only he knew his truth. And how lost he'd been since the rule of the Twelve had ended, when he should have felt free.

And her. She knew his truth; perhaps better than he did. She had created him, after all.

He turned his attention back to the crowd. "Mother."

"Why he was chosen to lead the Zodiacs is beyond comprehension," the woman said low and slow, her gravelly voice as grating as the screech of Kellas Cat nails dragging across slate. "The Beast of the InBetween tamed by a woman and pack of brats—what a waste of raw brutality and rage."

Libra adjusted his tie and brushed his suit jacket, smoothing the non-existent creases to ease the strummed nerves vibrating through him. Predators had a knack for smelling fear, sensing weakness; it was how they survived. But she didn't hunt to fill her belly. No, she fed on the terror, lapped up the adrenaline, rolled in it like a dog in offal, her teeth bared in a grim smile while she devoured her prey.

"His family is precisely why we chose him…and why he wanted to stay here. To protect the family he loves. And any paranorms who choose to live here."

The crowd stepped back from the king and the Zodiac, an en masse cringe in anticipation of violence.

"It appears blood will be spilled, and soon," she said.

"Perhaps. But times are changing. Brute force and savagery can no longer be the norm, not if we want to reveal our existence to the flighty humans and survive." He rolled his neck, focusing on the crowd's rising agitation in an attempt to ignore his own. "It's my job to make them understand that. That's where my talents will best serve the entirety of the InBetween."

The sharp, deep caws of the angry Corvus Ward males punctuated the nasal grunts and growls of the native Kellas Cat tongue. Together they drowned out the hiss of the vibrantly colored, reptilian-humanoid Aspis.

The ethereal, clairvoyant Portends had backed away from the throng, pressing their gossamer-clothed backs against the rough cavern walls, their faces screwed up in pain, cringing away from the anger and fear buffeting their delicate senses.

The lone demon-soul-sucking Innocent Demonica—a haunting, primal species who came in two physical versions: pale white skin with crooked, black cracks in a random pattern over their faces and bodies, and the revered black skin with white cracks—was as far from the rest of the crowd as she could get. That a Demonica had deigned to attend this meeting was singular.

Lyon's face was inches from the Corvus Ward king's. Both men were flushed, the king's ink-black scalp feathers rising out of his long, black hair until they stood straight up. Not a good sign.

Then they bumped chests.

Aw, hell.

Libra stopped fidgeting. His knees bent, his heart rate spiked again—pounding against his ribs as if the organ were demanding he leave, walk away, as if it knew this confab was a bad idea.

Instincts, bah.

He hadn't indulged in instincts or gut feelings since they had been beaten out of him.

Before he could take a step, her hand gripped his forearm. The air swirled around him, reeking of the cloying smell of gardenia that worked hard, but failed, to disguise the rotten-flesh stench of carrion flower nectar. He hadn't seen the woman in years—had hoped he'd never see her again. Perhaps he should have taken up prayer, or destroyed his sense of smell, because in one whiff he was jetted back to his childhood. The sting of her slaps and punches and kicks. The fear that they would never stop; the hope he might die before the next beating.

Adrenaline surged through the shock, obliterating the emotions of the boy he once was, leaving only the numb of a man grown and in strict control. A trickle of sweat formed between his shoulder blades and inched and itched down his back, but he refused to acknowledge the physical betrayal of his body, his emotions. The day he had escaped her, he had sworn no one would ever touch him unless he desired it, hit him without repercussion, or elicit a physical response that he didn't welcome.

Her breath tickled the curve of his ear. "I know why you're here."

He moved his tongue around to wet the desert that was his mouth, but it got stuck in the ridged roof, his lips glued to his teeth. "You know nothing."

"You are just like your father—wanting what you can't have. Taking that which is not yours. Leading the paranorms, advising them, standing as their representative to the human world will take a strong hand, a courageous heart. You have neither, so I'm here to make sure you don't get what you seek. I am here to protect the paranorms from a male so afraid to embrace his greatest gift that he lives a half-life."

Libra took a slow, even breath. He would never let her see how much her words hit home—how they burned like acid on his skin, flayed it, penetrated the crevices to seek out the starving, dark hollows inside him, filling them until they were sated.

"I am nothing like my father, all rage and lack of control, his scale so tipped to the dark that he was chewed up and swallowed by it."

He tugged to pull away from her but she gripped him harder, forcing him to face her. "Before you run away as you are wont to do, the king has a proposal for you."

He studied the sweep of the thick, white hair that covered her shoulders, and the subtle lines around her eyes and mouth. She hadn't aged well; bitterness and anger had eaten away at her once fresh beauty.

Her lips twitched when she realized what he was doing. She bared her teeth for just a moment, the grimace involuntary, her vanity revealed in a blink. Witnessing her weakness should have thrilled him, but it left him hollow. He hadn't been tainted with her malice…at least not fully. Yet.

"I hear that Lyon and his mate stole ten Corvus Ward children." She stood straighter, her lips thinned. "The king wants them back."

Libra crossed his arms. "My compliments to your spy network. Perhaps they can find out why the children were taken in the first place. What purpose does ripping them away from their families and terrorizing them serve? Provide those answers and you may be able to broker a meeting between Lyon, his children and the king." He maintained eye contact with her, refusing to look away. "And to be clear, Lyon and his mate adopted them. That's a far cry from theft. Every child chose to stay—perhaps the king needs to honor their wishes."

"Bah, what do children know?"

He stepped into her, towering over her not-inconsiderable height, his body stiff with uncoiled tension. *They know when they're safe, when they're loved.* He wanted to speak the words, but it would be a waste of breath. She would never understand. He stepped back and forced himself to relax.

She looked up into his face, her eyes roving over it as if searching for something. "I should have known your father couldn't make a man out of you."

Libra grit his teeth and resisted the urge to defend his sire. The man didn't deserve it, nor would he have wanted it.

He turned away. "What is the proposal?"

"Pledge your fealty to the king and he will let Lyon keep the Corvus Ward children. As long as none of them prove to be a royal."

It was all he could do not to snort. Insane. That was the only word that described the ridiculous proposal. First, pledging fealty to the Corvus Ward king would put Libra right back in the muck and mire he had just managed to crawl out of. Another arrogant master who could demand whatever he wanted of him, and, with fealty sworn, Libra would have no choice but to obey.

Second, no one *let* Lyon do anything. "Why would he part with even one Corvus nestling for my fealty?"

"He wants his own Zodiac."

"Then have him approach one of the others. They are much more capable."

He heard her draw in a slight breath and hold it. It wasn't like her to be tentative. She was all sharp angles and pointy ends. Subtle and quick as a paper cut whose sting didn't steal your breath until after your flesh had parted and the blood had welled. He wouldn't spare her by speaking first—he had learned patience, and his control was eternal. He could wait her out.

"The other Zodiacs are strong, yes, but not as strong as you could be."

And there it was—the elephant in the room had finally raised its trunk and trumpeted the truth. A chill stole over his limbs then crept inward until it bottomed out in his gut, freezing him in place. Despite knowing what the king wanted, he had to say it out loud.

"He wants the agent," he said slowly, carefully, the muscles in his belly forcing the air out of his lungs so the words could be released.

"Yes. And it's past time you claimed the role."

"You know that's impossible."

She dug her fingernails into his flesh, anxious, desperate even, an emotion he'd never felt from her. "You could have the power of Aether; you could be its agent.

The quintessence that Chaos herself created to give life to the gods and goddesses of old, their very breath. You could be the spaces between; you could have dominion over matter itself if you would but take it." She hissed and clenched his arm even harder. "The power of the agent should have been mine, but you and your father stole it from me. I will not allow the legacy of my line to die with you because you are a coward."

After decades of estrangement, why had Aubrianna chosen to approach him now?

He was Libra, but living a balanced life wasn't possible for him, not with the piece of demon-king soul attached to his own. The evil inside him longed to be unleashed...always. If he became the agent, if he accepted the curse that his mother considered a gift, he was sure it would be Nether he'd awaken. His scale would be skewed to the dark side and he'd be lost to it forever. He had chosen to live a half-life in the light and made it be enough. There he would remain.

"There hasn't been an agent of Aether for all of recorded history. Only the songs of bards and fools say an Os Mage Mother was ever an agent of Aether, and that, most likely, was wishful thinking." Libra pulled out of her grasp. "Which leaves an agent of Nether, darkness personified, the stealer of breath, the destroyer of life. No." He brushed the wrinkles out of his sleeve. "I will never swear fealty to the Corvus Ward king; my loyalty is to the Zodiacs of the Great Cavern and the paranorms of the rest of the InBetween—all of them. As for Aether and Nether, let them die with me—there is no one and nothing worth activating that power."

2

LIBRA STEPPED OUT OF the dark shadows of the hallway and into the cavern, his stride long and steady. *To get away from my past or to reach my new future?*

He ignored the question and made a beeline for Lyon and the king, desperate to prove himself a worthy ambassador for the paranorms. If they rejected him, he would find another capacity in which to serve as long as it didn't involve swearing fealty to a royal who wanted that which Libra could never give.

He pushed past stiff bodies, ignoring the adrenaline and aggression that flowed over him, his eyes on the two circling alpha males. Finally he broke through the slowly dividing throng and turned in a circle, watching the various species band together into their own kind until they stood back to back, ready for battle.

The Corvus Ward king had balled his hands into fists. Lyon's leonine claws had extended, his canines had dropped, and the gold of his eyes swirled with molten rage. The fight would be on in seconds if Libra couldn't stop it.

"Lyon!" Libra called out, his voice deep and steady. He shoved the men apart then turned his back on Lyon and bowed to the Corvus Ward king. "Highness, please accept my apologies for being late to this meeting. If you would please take a seat, I'm sure we can resolve our differences without drawing blood."

He gestured to the largest chair in the whole place, the throne reserved for Lyon, not only fitting for his place as the leader of the Great Cavern and the Zodiacs, but the only chair that could accommodate his seven-foot, three-hundred-pound frame.

Libra looked back and glared. One of the males had to budge and it needed to be Lyon.

Lyon backed up to Persephone's delicate chair and tried to squeeze his buttocks into the tiny seat. The arms squeaked—the wood and fabric stretched to the limit, threatening to crack and send Lyon to the floor. He huffed, and shifted his hips until they were vertically stacked before settling his bulk down.

Libra would have laughed if diplomacy and saving face weren't perched just as precariously as Lyon's ass. Instead, he exhaled, relieved that Lyon had backed down.

The king smoothed his scalp feathers back until they relaxed and merged with his long, glossy, black hair. "At least someone here understands diplomacy." The man backed into the massive, embroidered, silk chair without looking away, refusing to lose the glaring contest. He ran his fingers along the arms, checked his fingertips, and scowled before rubbing his hands together. "I suppose this will do…after a good cleaning." He snapped his fingers and two servants rushed forward to wipe away the nonexistent dirt.

Lyon growled low and deep in his throat. "My mate cleaned that chair herself just this morning."

The king shoved his servants aside and settled into the chair. "Then perhaps you should have chosen a different mate."

Libra's hackles rose at the insult to Persephone. A sweeter, more caring person could not be found in all of the worlds, and she didn't deserve the king's disrespect. But perhaps that was the king's plan—maybe he was looking to start a fight. The Corvus Wards as a species were antagonistic in all matters, love or hate, peace or war. No one wanted to deal with them, though, as one of the most populous species, they couldn't be ignored.

But the king seemed particularly offensive today. If he was pushing Lyon intentionally, the question became: why?

Libra held a hand up to stop Lyon from rising while studying the Corvus' glittering, red eyes. "Will you join the Zodiacs to rebuild and strengthen the InBetween?"

"Not until *all* of the Corvus children have been returned, starting with the nestlings Lyon stole from us." The king sat back and crossed his arms over his chest.

A growl burst out of Lyon. "And when I don't?"

The king smirked. "Then you're on your own. I will declare you an enemy of the paranorms, and we will take our children back by force."

The king rose and clapped his hands once. One by one, the various species in attendance shifted to stand behind the Corvus Wards, leaving Libra, Lyon, the Fenrir Wolf pack, and a half dozen trolls alone, separated from the rest.

Tension crackled through the giant space. Libra mentally ran through a litany of responses, but he came up short. The succor of cool logic, and the pithy remarks that usually flowed easily, abandoned him—the dark, chaotic ebb and flow of emotions he abhorred choked him, leaving him speechless.

Heat formed in his belly and traveled up his spine. The chance to walk away from his position as an assassin was before him; the one position he'd longed for over the years was beckoning…and he couldn't put together a sentence to salvage the audition.

The hum and hiss of disharmony rose among the king's followers. Lyon growled low in his throat. The Fenrir Wolves prowled to Lyon's side, their hackles standing tall down the length of their spines. The meeting had devolved and was about to go to hell, and Libra was at a loss. Frustration filled him; humiliation found a crack in his control. A wave of energy flowed down his arms and filled his hands until it escaped the tips of his fingers and fell to the floor in streams of shimmering blue.

The ground under him vibrated, the waves soft and slow at first, then increasing. Libra spread his feet to remain standing. The roar of the trolls panicked the

Fenrir Wolves; the creatures slunk in reverse until they came up against the wall, leaving a large, open space around Libra and Lyon save for one—the alpha wolf—a massive, all-black male with glittering, yellow eyes and savage scars that diagonally bisected his head and muzzle. The canid could have been Lyon's twin save for the color of his fur.

Lyon stood. "Brother!"

Libra blinked, Lyon's shout pulling him out of the fugue. He clenched his fists, willing the flow of energy to stop. The shaking ceased but the paranorms remained huddled together, silence reigning until the sharp staccato of stilettos stabbed at it.

The trolls groaned and started to rock. The Fenrir Wolf pack growled and slid farther into the darkest shadows.

Libra's mother emerged from the darkness followed by four muscular males— each more handsome than the last—their heads bowed like supplicants. Libra glanced at her face, expecting to see anger, or frustration, but her cool, composed, smile was more troubling.

She stopped in front of Libra and Lyon, and pulled on the fingers of her elbow-length, red, leather gloves, holding court over the startled paranorms while she removed them at her leisure. "Everyone, please, there's no need for discord." The woman looked at Lyon. "We have not met, though I knew your mother well. My name is Aubrianna."

Lyon crossed his arms over his chest and remained silent.

A hard scowl marred Aubrianna's elegant, composed face for a brief moment, before she schooled her features again and shrugged. "I understand the paranorms need an ambassador. I demand the right to be named such."

Lyon scowled at the imperious woman. "Why should I choose you over Libra?"

"I have been a liaison between the various paranormal species for years." She nodded at several of the paranorms standing with the Corvus Ward king. "At least, the ones in the outer reaches who chose to not claim the protection of the Twelve. I have the experience and the connections, even with some wealthy humans that we could use in the future. You want to have influence outside of your Zodiacs? Then you need to appoint me—not a man with no experience; not a man who could barely stop you and the king from fighting; not an assassin with delusions of grandeur who will lead you to war."

Lyon frowned and stepped close to the woman. "So you have worked for the Pondera Novus Ordo Seclorum and the Bathory Berserkers?" His hulking frame loomed over her. His voice dropped until all that came out was a guttural growl. "How about the Pondera Exemplars? What about the stolen paranormal children? Did you broker that bit of nasty business? Because I would like to understand the why of it."

Aubrianna stood her ground, even leaned in a little. She lifted her chin and looked him in the eye, sending her long, white hair cascading down her back, her pale blue eyes hard and defiant.

"I am the Os Mage Mother," she declared in a low, slow voice before baring her teeth. "You will show me respect."

Libra fought the instinct to shrink away from the energy radiating off her. The Os Mage Mothers were long-lived—dating back to the days when the old gods and goddesses were still worshipped—with powers gifted to them by the primordial goddess Gaia. Each of the four worlds had their own Os Mage maiden who wandered their designated world dragging a bag filled with the lost or abandoned bones of dead paranorms. Without them, the paranormal bones could be used for the darkest magic.

And when an Os Mage died, the Os Mage Mother gave birth to its fully formed replacement within hours. If the Mother died, the oldest Os Mage left her realm to become the new Mother, and bred with a male until, within hours, she gave birth to a new Os Mage for the world she'd left behind.

Palace intrigue played out over four planes of existence. Not much of a surprise that the Os Mage Mothers had to be strong and cautious if they hoped to hold onto their status. Or remain alive.

To Libra's surprise, Lyon did nothing—no growl, no smart retort. The Os Mage Mother was a force no one wanted to challenge, and Lyon was taking heed, keeping his cool.

Libra stared at the woman who had borne him but was never his mother. "She wouldn't use children as political pawns. She couldn't tolerate being around them that long."

She turned to Libra, one eyebrow raised. "Defending me?"

"Just stating a fact."

The Corvus Ward king stood. "Enough talk. Accept the Os Mage Mother as your ambassador, and we will be content to give you time to say your goodbyes before returning our children."

"I don't like being told what to do," Lyon replied.

The king raised a hand. "I'm not done." He walked up to Lyon and stood toe to toe with the much taller Zodiac. He snapped his fingers and pointed at Libra. Two large Corvus warriors grabbed Libra's arms and pulled him over to the king. The royal smirked. "Aubrianna will be our ambassador and yours. You will give us back our children, and, while we wait, we will play host to Libra."

Lyon's canines erupted from his gums for the second time, the long, sharp teeth sliding over his freshly bloodied lips. "No one takes one of mine."

Libra sagged when Aubrianna's mouth curved into a smile—Lyon had fallen into her carefully woven web. Hell, Libra hadn't known the Corvus Wards would work with anyone outside of their own numbers. But that's what had happened here—somehow, Aubrianna had gained their cooperation.

Aubrianna nodded. "Exactly. That is what the king and so many of the paranorms are feeling. Beginning your new relations with the paranorms based on trust and cooperation bodes well for our future together."

"I could have had all of the Zodiacs here backing me, but I chose to send most of them away to demonstrate our *trust* and *cooperation*. Taking Libra is a move too far."

"But you will allow it because you don't have a choice." Aubrianna pointed to the largest passageway.

The paranorms began filing out of the cavern.

"Don't let them do this. You can't trust her, Lyon," Libra said, jerking against the males holding his arms.

"Let me speak to him," Lyon demanded.

The king crossed his arms, his face screwed up in a scowl, but he nodded once.

Lyon strode over to Libra and grunted at the Corvus warriors. "Alone."

They looked at the towering Zodiac then at their king before taking a few steps back.

"This isn't just about the children, is it?" Lyon asked.

"No, at least not fully. The king wants my fealty—and my power, or the potential of my power," Libra whispered.

"*That* power?"

"Yes, he wants me to become Gaia's agent."

"Holy shit. Can he force you?"

"He can try."

Lyon looked past the crowd for a moment. "I can't lose my children, Li."

"I know. This is a damned impossible situation."

Lyon brought his focus back to Libra. "How long can you hold out?"

"Depends on what they do. Weeks, maybe months, if they don't take the torture too far."

"Torture." Lyon ran a hand through his long, blond hair. "Damn."

Libra could feel Lyon's conflict, could see the man quivering with the need to take on all of the Corvus warriors—his bloodlust for a brawl palpable. But the Zodiac was not the Beast of the InBetween anymore; he had a mate and children to consider. No matter how capable he was as a fighter, Lyon couldn't risk harm to them—even if it meant sacrificing a Zodiac.

Libra's nerves settled. He breathed deeply through his nose and exhaled through his mouth. "There's nothing for it, brother. They have to take me."

Lyon's cheek twitched, the muscles along his jaw clenched. "You don't have to do this."

"I'm not crazy about the idea, but yeah, I do. Just, for goddess' sake, get me out before they break me. We both know how bad it could get if I go darkside."

"But you could become Aether, yes?"

"History isn't on my side, so no. Besides, what do you think the chances are that I'll go all sweetness and light under torture? Especially with the demon soul inside me. You know how that feels."

Lyon looked past Libra again, staring at nothing, his memories of dealing with the demon soul and the toll it took on him swimming in his gold eyes for Libra to see. "So you'd become Nether."

Finally, the big guy's getting it. "Yes."

"End of days and all that."

"Exactly. Now, back up, and try not to take a swing at anyone."

Libra smiled to convince the male that he would be okay, but even he could feel how brittle his face was—he must look positively cadaverous if Lyon's pale skin and deep frown were an accurate reflection. Lyon gripped Libra's shoulders and squeezed before backing away.

The Zodiac leader turned his attention to the king. "I will be coming for him, and soon."

The Corvus Ward king smirked again before walking out of the Great Cavern.

"Take him away," Aubrianna snapped with a wave of her hand.

Libra was jerked forward by his brutish guards, his arms in a death grip. No doubt, this was gonna suck ass all the way.

* * *

Lyon watched Libra walk away with his Corvus Ward escort, waiting for the Zodiac to disappear before stalking over to Aubrianna. "This could be considered an act of war against the Great Cavern."

Aubrianna raised a hand and laid her palm on his chest. Her haughty expression changed to one of speculation and she squeezed one of his pecs.

Lyon stepped out of her reach and growled. "Don't."

She held her palm to her nose, closed her eyes, and breathed deep. "Let's consider this an act of…balance." Her eyes remained closed; it was as if she were memorizing his scent. She shook her head, opened her eyes, and pierced Lyon with a look, her pupils so dilated the blue was just a tiny outer ring. "We each have something the other wants. You do your part, and maybe you can keep your children." She donned the red gloves and turned toward the exit.

"What about Libra? Or have you forgotten that the man you've served up is your son?"

She walked away, calling out over her shoulder, "Haven't you heard? Os Mage Mothers don't have sons. Only daughters."

3

TARYN TOOK A DEEP breath as she brushed her hands along the cold stone and lumps of squishy, wet mold clinging to the wall. As soon as she had covered her eyes with the blindfold, her senses had gone into overdrive. A soft hiss flashed past her right ear. She jumped to the left and rolled on the hard-packed ground before rising again. She listened as she backed away, one hand in front, the other behind her. She hit a wall and a whisper of air passed an inch from her nose.

"Shit." She rolled along the wall then pushed off. Her heart pounded, pushing the blood through her ears until the *whooshing* was all she could hear. "Uncle, uncle, uncle."

"Still yourself and find the ley line," her adversary demanded.

"How am I supposed to concentrate with you caning me to death?"

"You need to be able to do more than one thing at a time."

"Like walk and talk?"

"Like finding the ley line while running for your life."

An exhalation sounded close to Taryn's right ear. Her hackles rose and she lifted her arms over her head to block the blow of the gnarled wood staff. It slammed against her forearms, the vibration racing through her body, shaking her to the core.

"Son of a bitch!" She ripped off her blindfold. "Do you have to hit so hard?"

Gemma, the female half of the Gemini twins, lowered the weapon and scowled. "You're the one who demanded we do this. I was happy working in the lab."

Taryn ran her fingers over her aching arms. The swelling had already started; the bruises would be magnificent, hard to conceal and harder to explain.

"I need to find my place," she muttered as she turned away from the woman.

"I thought figuring out what kind of weird science mumbo-jumbo Llewellyn did to the paranorms was your place."

"More like a wicked mix of science and magic. One that we'll never figure out without the primer." Taryn walked to her white lab coat, which was lying in a heap on the ground. A wave of heat raced through her body, followed by a cold sweat—she braced her hand against the wall. The secret training plus all the hours spent in the lab had taken their toll, but add in a lack of sleep and she was sucked dry, hollow. One more blow from Gemma and her exhausted ass would disintegrate into a pile of ash and bone. "I thought my place was on the surface being a human, but that was blown to shit."

"I suppose that would be the case for anyone learning that their mother's not only a witch goddess, but a witch goddess who tried to sacrifice you and your sisters to crack open Hell and release a demon army."

Taryn snorted. "Yeah, and for all her power, I still haven't found a magical bone in my body. God only knows who my father is."

"I'm still convinced your sire is a Corvus Ward."

"If I'm half Corvus, then why can't I feel the ley lines that lace the planet? According to you, there's one running right under my feet. Oh, but I suck at that too because I don't feel a thing." Taryn shrugged into her long-sleeved lab coat. "I have no place. I'm a woman without a country or a purpose."

"Melodrama doesn't suit a descendent of Gaia."

"Gaia?"

"Mother of all? Terra? Mother Earth, in the human vernacular."

"Aren't we all descended from her?"

"True, but very few are so directly connected with her as you and your half-sisters." Gemma closed her eyes and moved her fingers as if counting. "Your great, great, great grandmother, I think."

Taryn pressed on her temples to find some relief from the headache that had plagued her for days. "Okay, so what does that have to do with anything?"

Gemma leaned her staff against the wall and sat on a rock. "Do you know nothing about her?"

Taryn joined the Zodiac. "I didn't know about the paranorm world. Why would I think gods and goddesses were real, much less think that I'm related to one?"

"You've been so worried about the ley lines as it pertains to the Corvus Ward blood you might have, when it's Gaia you should be concentrating on."

"Why?"

"Do you know what a ley line is outside of what you've read in books?"

"Besides being a grid-work of the earth's energy? No."

"It's much more than grid-work. Ley lines and vortices work together to form Gaia's nervous system."

"Vortices?"

"Think of it like the human nervous system. Vortices are her neurons, and ley lines are the axons that carry electrical impulses between the neurons. You need to tap into those electrical impulses to help you feel the matrix itself. Once you learn that, you can tell when someone crosses an axon by the interruption in the impulses. So, next time, visualize neurons and axons."

Gemma stood.

"Why didn't you tell me this before?"

The Zodiac shrugged. "I thought with you having Corvus Ward blood and being a descendent of Gaia, you'd be a natural."

Taryn flinched. "Ouch."

The woman was right to expect Taryn would be a natural given that lineage. But Taryn wasn't sure if the new information helped or would put more pressure on her the next time they trained. She could already feel her failure meter inching toward utter.

Gemma removed a leather pouch from her robe. "The person you should be training with is Libra."

"What? Why?"

"For all your skills in the lab, and with herbs, you haven't even started on what's most important."

Taryn gained her feet and straightened her coat, struggling to contain her irritation. "And that is?"

"Learning who the Zodiacs are and where they come from. Take Libra. He's from a line of women who serve Gaia, created by the goddess with her own blood, just as you were born of the blood of Circe. If there's anyone who could help you find the ley lines, or tap into the power of vortices, it's him."

Taryn wanted to '*humph*' her doubt about Libra teaching her anything. From the first moment they met, they'd been thorns in each other's sides. Too bad spending time with GQ wasn't going to happen; she'd love to ask him questions, but she was realistic. If she asked for his help, he'd say no.

Gemma shrugged then crouched down and dumped two small, glass vials, a small, leather pouch, and a folded piece of paper on the floor.

"Here," she said as she handed Taryn one of the vials, "drink this."

"What is it?" Taryn opened the lid and sniffed. "It doesn't smell bad. Probably tastes like the ass end of a troll."

"I think Lyon's colorful jargon is rubbing off on you."

"Or mine on him."

Gemma threw her head back and swallowed the liquid. "Drink."

Taryn sighed, held her nose, and poured the liquid down her throat. She swallowed quickly, released her nostrils, and cringed, waiting for the inevitable, foul taste to cause a full-body shudder, but her mouth was filled with a sweet, musky flavor, a blend that was unusual but not unpleasant.

"Hmm, not bad. What was that?"

"A blend of horehound to increase our focus and mandrake to empower our visions and use them to manifest the door."

"Manifest a door? What do you mean by that?"

"You'll see."

"Okaaayyy. What next?"

"I'm trying a new spell."

"Magic? You better not let Lyon find out."

"I hide my practice just as well as you." Gemma shook her head. "There's no one in any world who can stop the use of magic. It's all around us, in every stone and tree—in the very sky. It's in you and me. If he expects to defeat Circe and Asmodeus, Lyon needs to embrace magic wholly. They certainly have."

She walked to the nearest section of wall and laid her palm on it.

"Hecate, Goddess of the Thresholds we all must cross,
I ask you to open a door so that we may pass."

She stepped back, took a handful of the contents of the pouch, and blew a blend of dried herbs at the spot where her palm had been. The red mixture landed on the stone then sank into it.

"What was that?" Taryn asked.

"A mix of dandelion and mullein to call the spirits, cayenne pepper to add power to the spell, comfrey leaf to protect us as we travel through the stone, and, last, yew as a call to Hecate specifically."

A tiny pinprick of red light hovered in the air for a moment before expanding over the stone, creating a shimmering circle large enough for Taryn to step through. "Damn, that never gets old." They had almost reached the opening when Taryn grabbed Gemma's arm and stopped her. "Wait, you said 'travel through the stone.' I thought you were opening it."

Gemma laughed. "Not literally opening the stone. That would take a lot of time and spellwork far beyond my ability. What I'm doing is opening our minds, and, with the help of the goddess Hecate, we're traveling *through* the stone."

"Oh, hell no."

"Look, we've done this a few times now. It's safe."

"What's changed then? Because the spell you used before took minutes, not seconds, to work."

"This spell is much faster; we could do it on the run. The other version, the one you weren't paying attention to, was more involved. Trust me, if you're in need of a fast way out, this is it. Now, go, before the spell fades."

"So what's the catch?"

"The opening only lasts for seconds before slamming shut. You get caught inside—instant death."

"And limbs?"

Gemma shrugged. "It's possible you could lose one or two. But you'd survive. Get ready; I've saved the final step. As soon as I speak the word, get through."

"Shit."

She'd learned the first time she traveled via one of Gemma's portals that you better get through quick 'cause it hurt like a mo-fo if it started to collapse on you. But she hadn't given much thought to just how bad it could get.

"Ready?"

Taryn nodded once.

"*Traversus.*" The glowing red circle pulsed and Gemma gave her a small shove. "Go. Now."

4

TARYN JUMPED THROUGH THE shimmering light and landed on the other side of the stone. Her feet slid on gravel—and the momentum carried her forward and into the arms of the Pestilence Fairy girl who had dogged Taryn's steps since she'd started living in the InBetween.

Taryn grabbed her arms to steady them both. "Meri."

Gemma appeared and gasped. "No. Taryn."

Taryn released Meri and stepped back.

"Oh, goddess, look at your hands," Gemma said.

Taryn looked down. Black and blue and green marks bloomed on her fingers before spreading into her palms and up her wrists, the pain breath-taking.

Gemma wrapped her arms around herself to avoid touching Taryn accidentally and leaned close. "It's the pestilence. It has you."

Meri started to cry and backed away. "No, no, no."

Taryn's hands and wrists lost feeling. "It's okay. This has happened before, right, Meri?"

She looked up at the girl and smiled.

"Yes," Meri answered in a rush. "Do you think—?"

"That this will be the same? I hope so."

Taryn bent her knees and plopped on her butt, her back against the wall. Sweat formed on her brow and back; the fever had started much earlier this time. Her body trembled. The sickness covered every inch of her skin then dove deep inside her—so deep it felt like the pestilence was attacking her soul. She leaned to one side and keeled over, the cold stone a blessed relief. At least, this time, she hadn't blacked out immediately, but a righteous faint probably wasn't far away. She closed her eyes and forced her breathing to slow.

Relax. Ride it out.

Meri mewled.

"Go away, you little abomination," Gemma growled. "Or do you enjoy gloating over your kills?"

Meri crouched, her hands in front of her. She hissed, her teeth bared, ready to attack the Zodiac. "I will gloat over your rotting corpse."

"That's enough, Gemma. Meri didn't do this; I fell into her."

Minutes passed before Taryn could sit up and breathe deep. Her lungs cooled, the fire fading away. She pushed her sleeves up and watched the sickness fade, retreat, reverse until the bloom of color hovered on her fingertips for a moment before winking out. The pestilence was gone.

Taryn pushed off the ground and swayed for a minute, waiting for the head rush to stop. "Whew. That was a bad one."

Meri giggled and whooped as she twirled.

Gemma just gaped. "In the name of all that's holy, how did you do that?"

Taryn shrugged. "Haven't a clue, but I'm sure glad it worked again."

"I've never…no one has ever…" Gemma stuttered. "Have you told anyone about this?" She took Taryn's hands and turned them palm up.

"No. And you aren't to either. Not until I understand what's happening."

"But—"

"Not one word. Promise me."

Gemma released Taryn's hands and scowled. "I'll stay quiet. For now."

Taryn nodded then turned to Meri. "What are you doing here?" She leaned closer and took in the fairy's face. "What happened to you? You're covered in bruises." She touched one of Meri's shoulders, careful to touch the fabric of her shirt, not her bare skin, and turned her around. She gasped. "And your wings."

Meri opened her wings to their full, impressive length, each rib stretched, the dagger-like ends in stark relief. Fragile, veined bat wings that shimmered with iridescent color were a source of great pride among the fairies, but the curse of pestilence had riddled the fairy clan's wings with holes and leached out all of the color while leaving the wings functional for flight. Meri's wings, however, were crumpled and torn, the right one hanging down, looking like it was about to fall off.

Meri stared at the ground, her body stiff.

"Who did this to you?"

Meri clasped her hands in front of her and cleared her throat. "I have been very bad. I had to be punished."

"Punished? Why?"

Meri's tears fell. "Maman doesn't want us to be friends."

Taryn squatted in front of her. "Then you need to go back to your room before anyone sees you."

"No more friends?"

"Meri. Look at me."

Meri raised her eyes, her expectation that Taryn would no longer want to be her friend transparent on her face, tears welling in her eyes.

"We will *always* be friends."

Meri's frown blossomed into a smile of surprise and pleasure.

"But we must be more careful, okay?"

"Yes, yes."

"Good girl. Now, go. I'll see you again soon."

Meri jumped and twirled before running down the passage, disappearing into the darkness.

"Immune to a Pestilence Fairy. It's unheard of." Gemma smiled. "Oh, what an experiment that will be."

Taryn started to sweat again, but this time it wasn't the disease. She didn't have a clue how she'd survived the unsurvivable, and, other than being relieved that she'd escaped death a second time, it scared the crap out of her.

"Forget it. I'm not your guinea pig."

"But, if we understood how you did it—"

"No, and not one word to anyone. Got it?"

"I really don't understand why we allow the Pestilence Fairies into the Great Cavern at all. They may be paranorms, but followers of the Pale Horseman shouldn't be allowed to live."

"What do you mean?"

"The Fourth Horseman? Pestilence, famine, and death?"

Taryn held up a hand. "Wait a minute. You mean the four Horsemen, like in the Bible?"

"Yes."

"I thought it was a metaphor, not real."

"It is real, and the pestilence that Meri and her people carry is the plague that the Pale Horseman will use to decimate the human population if he rises again."

"The Horsemen have been here before?"

"Oh, yes. According to legend, when the humans stopped worshipping the gods and goddesses of old, it weakened them. So they protected themselves with spells to hide their location from those who wanted them gone. The Pestilence Fairies didn't always look like that. Not until they betrayed the gods and goddesses to the Pale Horseman, who forced the old ones to fall into Hades. Before returning to Hell, the horseman shared his pestilence with the fairies, cursing them to live isolated, to never be able to touch anyone but their own kind again."

Gemma shrugged a shoulder. "There's another, rather far-fetched myth that the fairies were once fallen angels who served the Horseman and were left behind when he returned to Hell. They say that one day the four Horsemen will rise again, bringing all of the creatures from the abyss with them, including the rest of the fallen angels. The Pestilence Fairies will lead the charge, spreading plagues around the world."

"That's horrible. Poor Meri."

"Why would you pity them? They are betrayers; they deserve to die."

"That's not fair. Meri is just a child, and a sweet one at that, despite what her ancestors did. Would you want to be judged by your kin?"

Gemma glared at Taryn for several moments before shaking her head. "No."

"I'm the first person to survive her touch, and I think she craves more. It's not her fault she was born a Pestilence Fairy, and she deserves our compassion. As for being in the InBetween, she and her kind are far safer here than on the surface."

"Your kindness will be your undoing." Gemma looked down the passage. "We should go."

The two women had just started walking when the shaking started. Pebbles bounced, dirt roiled around their feet, and a dust cloud rose, obscuring Taryn's vision. A loud crack like a baseball bat hitting the sweet spot came from above her head. Her senses told her to run, but her gut overrode the fear. Taryn rested her palms on the walls to keep her balance, hugging the stone and hoping for some protection until everything stopped moving. Earthquakes and tight spaces weren't a good combo, but running blind could lead to injury or worse, and she sure as shit wasn't going to the forever night that way.

Finally, the shaking stopped.

"Taryn?"

"Over here, on the wall."

Gemma's hands found Taryn first.

"Give me a minute, Gemma." Taryn sagged to the ground. "That pestilence hit took it out of me."

They stayed put for a few minutes then Taryn patted Gemma's arm. "Okay, I'm good."

They linked arms and worked their way down the passage until they reached a larger cave. The dust had already started to settle here, the better ventilation allowing them to pick up the pace.

Taryn stopped just shy of the massive Great Cavern to catch her breath and take in the chaos. Small rocks still fell from the ceiling and dust swirled, coating everything. She looked at the hole in the roof, the route the escaped demon army had used to enter the human world. The sky was a blue-green; the few trees still standing around the hole were yellow. The skewed color and shimmering view were the result of a spell that hid the presence of this part of the paranorm world from humans.

It had held despite the frequent quakes, but with each day, the spell seemed to weaken, and Martina, Lyon's former healer and the witch who had wielded the spell, hadn't been able to recharge it on her own. She had left several days earlier, accompanied by Fessa and Hiram from the outpost, in search of other witches who could help strengthen the spell, but they hadn't returned.

A bellowing troll brought Taryn's attention back to the present. Chained to the wall, the huge beast had soiled itself, even as two elves and one flitting fairy scrubbed its grimy skin with soapy push brooms. Persephone had coaxed and cajoled the troll leader into ordering his followers to take a weekly bath for the olfactory relief of everyone in close proximity to the huge beasts. There were, however, a few that didn't want to part with their thick layers of wallow filth, requiring that they be restrained.

The Fenrir Wolf pack cowered against the ground, their hackles raised, their eyes wild and darting around as if searching for the cause of this new attack.

Persephone and Abella emerged from another passageway and joined Lyon in the space before them.

Gemma started forward but Taryn stopped her with a touch on her arm. "You'll keep the training and the fairy stuff between us?"

"Why not tell them the truth? Are you afraid?"

"Absolutely not."

Gemma raised an eyebrow.

"I just need more time, okay? To train and to understand."

Gemma sighed. "Of course. As long as you do the same for me." She jutted her chin in the direction of the group gathered in the cavern. "They think my only interest is science. No one knows about the hours I've put into studying magic."

Taryn looked at her reserved colleague and new friend. "You need more time to train and understand."

Gemma flashed a rare grin, transforming her face, revealing how lovely she was, but it faded as fast as it had appeared. "Precisely."

5

"**W**HAT DO YOU MEAN, GQ has been taken?" Taryn demanded of Lyon, irritated that he was sitting slumped in his King-Of-The-World chair instead of rallying everyone who could carry a weapon and going after one of his own.

"Libra's mom showed up and demanded to be made ambassador," Abella said.

"Oh, I bet he hated that," Taryn said, punctuating her statement with a snort.

"He did, especially when the Corvus Ward king ordered that he be dragged out of here," Abella replied.

"What? The Corvus Wards were here and you didn't tell me? You know I've been wanting to meet the king."

"For what, another of your infernal blood samples?" Lyon asked.

"Yes, and some answers."

Lyon shook his head. "I guarantee, he wouldn't have allowed you anything. Stubborn bastard came itching for a fight and I damn near gave it to him until Libra stopped me. Then Aubrianna showed up and used her own son as a bargaining chip."

"What bargain?" Taryn insisted.

"More like kidnapping," Persephone said, pressing the heels of her hands against her forehead. "Is that why you didn't want us out here, love?"

"The Corvus Ward king is an arrogant ass who has never forgiven the Twelve for not giving him a seat at the dais. I didn't expect him to bring Aubrianna into this business, but he did. Better he took Libra than any of you," he finished with a glance at his inamorata and her half-sisters.

"Do you think you can find him, Persephone?" Taryn asked.

"Lyon has decreed that she can't try to locate him," Abella chimed in.

"Decreed? Really? Has he learned nothing by now?"

"I *am* the leader here, Taryn" Lyon said with a growl. "Duly named, which means I get to decree until the demon army is back in Hell."

Persephone rubbed her temples. Her face grew pale and sweat ran down her face.

Everyone stopped arguing.

The *pat-pat-pat* of bare feet slapping the stone floor echoed in the massive cavern. A girl entered from a hallway, her long, silver hair flying as she ran past the ring of trolls standing guard around the huge hole in the cavern floor. She was followed by the large, loping, black-and-rust Doberman male Finn and, behind him, Blair, the gray-muzzled, red-and-rust Doberman female trotting to keep up.

The girl skidded to a stop in front of Persephone and grabbed her hands. They bowed their heads and touched their foreheads for a few moments.

When Persephone looked up, her color had returned to normal. "Thank you, Candace."

Lyon squatted down in front of Persephone. "Are you okay, my love?"

"I am now." Persephone opened her arms and the little purebred Portend climbed into her lap. "She always knows when I need her."

Lyon touched Persephone's cheek and Candace's head. "This is why I don't want you to practice the sight. You aren't strong enough."

"Libra may need our help. Candace can help me find him without all the repercussions. Please, Lyon, I'm half Portend and half witch goddess—I have this power for a reason. Let me use it to help."

Lyon ran his hand over her barely round belly. "It won't hurt our son?"

She grinned. "Our *daughter* is very healthy, my love, and Fessa swears it's better to use my powers than to ignore them."

"The old woman from the remote outpost? What the hell would she know about it?"

Persephone shrugged her shoulders.

Abella rubbed her forehead with her fingertips as if she had gotten Persephone's headache. "Blood samples and hostages aside, the larger question is what happens if there is a demon attack on the humans. We can't afford to do nothing about Circe and Asmodeus while we deal with paranorm politics. There's no time to waste and we can't afford to be a man down."

"The king threatened to take my…our children, at least the Corvus Wards. That's one reason why he took Libra."

"And what's the other reason?" Abella pushed.

Lyon and Persephone exchanged glances before Lyon answered. "It has to do with Libra's power."

"What power?" Taryn scoffed. "To sniff out the most outrageously expensive suit in a twenty-mile radius?"

"I don't know much about it. He's never consciously used it that I know of— though today he slipped a little and caused a shaker."

"The earthquake from earlier?"

Lyon nodded. "Never seen him do that; the power flowed down his arms and dripped off his fingertips. The ground shook when the drops landed on the ground. It was the damnedest thing. I do know that the power originating from the primordial goddess Chaos was given to Gaia. She, in turn, has passed it down to every Os Mage Mother until Libra. Whatever it is, whatever he can do, there's a light side and a dark side to it, and it's the reason all the Zodiacs have given Libra a wide berth, including me. If the king can force Libra to become an agent of one side or the other, he will be in control of power none of us has seen before."

"It would be very bad," Persephone added.

"It could be good," Lyon said, "though that hasn't happened in a long time, if ever. I don't know how it's decided. But Libra said he was afraid that he would go dark."

Taryn planted her fists on her hips. "So we're going to leave him with the Corvus Wards? Will they torture him?"

"Probably." Lyon frowned. "But what would you have me do? Mount a siege against their stronghold for one Zodiac? When we're trying to establish relations? And what about my children?"

"I'm not suggesting you risk the children, but what about a surgical strike—one or two Zodiacs could break him out. We can't afford to have anyone benched for this fight, and if Libra does go dark side…" Taryn stepped closer to the hulking Zodiac. "A real leader wouldn't abandon his people."

Persephone gasped. "Taryn, no."

Lyon drew a ragged breath before nailing Taryn with a hard look. "A real leader considers the welfare of all of his people. Do you think I wanted this? To have Libra taken without being able to do a damn thing to stop it?" He rose slowly and approached her, his eyes glowing molten gold, a sure sign he was seriously pissed and in need of an epic rant. "Do you understand what has happened?"

Taryn bared her teeth. "Beside abandoning Libra, no."

Lyon paced around her, his hands fisted. "They walked in here, the strongest hold within the paranorm world, and took what they wanted. They did it with barely the lift of a finger, without spilling even a single drop of blood, and I was helpless to stop them."

"I understand the situation, Lyon."

"No, you don't. The Twelve were the biggest, baddest rulers around, and now they're gone—replaced by their sons. Libra said we needed to open a door and invite all of the paranorms to come in, to join us in the coming fight, and I agreed. But instead of cementing a new relationship with us, the Corvus Ward king has turned a bright light on our weakness."

He stopped in front of Taryn. "Even if all the Zodiacs had been here, we wouldn't have had the numbers to defend this part of the InBetween. And I can't attack them to take back Libra." He heaved a sigh and turned away. "In truth, the king is not off the mark. I did take some of his own, and had someone done that to me, I'd do anything to get them back."

"But that's precisely what he's done—taken one of our own at a time when, in your own words, we haven't the numbers."

"Which means we're in a stalemate. He has Libra, and I have ten Corvus Ward children." He raised a hand to stop Taryn when she opened her mouth. "I will never give up my children. Never. If they choose to go and live with their kind, I will let them. Until then, they stay here."

"And in doing so," Persephone said, walking over to her mate with Abella by her side, "the children will be safe and loved, and they will learn one of the most important lessons we could teach them."

Lyon held out an arm and folded her into his chest, his body relaxing as if his anger and frustration were washed away by her touch. "What would that be?"

"That the different paranorm species *can* live together in peace," Persephone said.

Abella nodded, but a frown marred her flawless face. "We need to shore up our defenses, recall the Zodiacs, and figure out how not to get overrun by the paranorms. They know exactly how weak we are. Given time—"

"They could return and take control," Taryn said under her breath.

Lyon nodded.

Taryn paced around the group, ignoring their conversation, until an idea dawned. "So what we need to do is give them something they really want."

Lyon, Persephone, and Abella waited for her to finish.

Taryn threw up her hands. "Oh, come on, it's obvious." She looked at each of them before rolling her eyes. "We find the other children, the ones still lost. That's how we can make an accord happen."

"You think we haven't been looking?" Lyon asked.

"Is that where the other Zodiacs are? Looking for the children?" Taryn fired back.

"Not directly. They're looking as they do other jobs."

Taryn stepped up to him, her head craned back. "We need a dedicated team of people looking for them, not doing it as an after-thought. And we must figure out who took them and why. You saw how bad your children had it in that cave in Texas. Would you really let more children suffer and die for want of trying?"

"Taryn," Persephone said. "That's not fair."

"No, let her get it out."

Taryn crossed her arms, her chin set. "I've said my piece."

Lyon gently released Persephone. "Then let me say mine. There is nothing more important to me than finding the children. Nothing. The other paranorms don't know that, not yet, because they don't know me. All they know is that their babies are gone and they see no proof that anyone is trying to help them. While we stand here and argue, the minds of the parents are being twisted by anyone with an agenda—anyone with the thought of rising to power off the backs of the grieving—until they have no idea whom to trust. The Corvus Ward king has the loudest voice right now, so he's winning them over. Now that he's seen our vulnerability…he knows there's an even greater prize to be won."

"This part of the InBetween," Taryn said, her voice low.

"And more power than the king could ever dream of if he can force Libra to activate it. If he takes the Great Cavern, he takes control of all of the InBetween."

Abella cleared her throat. "But why? What is it about this cave that makes it a center of power?"

"Before the spell that bored a hole through all the worlds and released the demon army, this cavern was the closest section of the InBetween to the surface, and it offered rare deposits of gemstones that could be sold to the few humans who know about this realm. That gave the Twelve great wealth in the human world, which meant access to food and technology unseen and unavailable to the species who broke off from the Twelve and established their own domains. There's also geothermal activity under our feet," he looked at the ground, "as you can see in the death pit. The lava flow may be deep but the heat radiates up, warming this cavern to a survivable temperature."

"How many other species are living outside of here? How do they survive?" Abella asked.

"I'm sorry, Abella, but I want to know more about Libra and this power." Taryn wrapped her arms around her waist and shivered. "How does he 'activate' it?"

"I think he has to kill someone with it."

"But he's killed already," she said.

"By conventional means; never with the power inside him. He's kept it under control, forced it into dormancy, but if he ever kills with it…if he becomes Gaia's agent of Nether, and he suspects that's what would happen because of the demon soul inside him, we're talking destruction on a worldwide scale. He would be the biggest threat, worse than the demon army."

Taryn nodded, itching to race to the lab and find more information about the power Gaia gave the Os Mage Mothers, including how Libra ended up with it.

"Please tell me your ley line ability is improving," Lyon said.

She blinked and looked at the Zodiac. A wave of heat rolled over her.

Her bowels loosened as she struggled to moderate her voice. "Why?"

"Because I need you to be our advance warning. If anyone crosses a ley line near here, you can warn us in time to barricade the entrances. Or run."

"So you're that convinced there'll be an attack? All the more reason to send people out to find the children. Preferably with Libra's help."

"Libra will stay where he is," Lyon said. "He agreed to it and it's our only option for now." His voice dropped so low Taryn could feel the rumble of his chest from several feet away. "That's an order."

Taryn blinked, not sure she had heard him correctly. She sputtered. Oh, yeah, she'd heard him, and his tone made it clear that he'd brook no more argument. Mute with frustration, she marched out of the cavern before she could find her voice and say something she'd regret. No one gave her orders, not since she'd been under the thumb of the foster system that had nearly broken her as a child. She sure wasn't about to start obeying orders now, no matter who issued them, or how reasonable they sounded.

* * *

Abella shook her head. "Oh, man. I wouldn't have said that."

Lyon frowned. "What did I say? Did she grow sweet on Libra when I wasn't looking?"

"Hell, no, she loathes the man, but she hates the word 'orders' more."

Persephone squeezed his arm. "I'm not sure if it was the Libra thing or the children thing."

Lyon grunted. "I don't care what *thing* it was. She better learn to deal with it; this is just the beginning of a mountain of orders to do a rat ton of things none of us wants to do."

THE CORVUS WARD KING and Aubrianna watched the guards punch Libra in the gut and head until they heaved to breathe, sweat rolling down their faces and soaking their shirts.

Libra sagged in the chair, his bindings barely keeping him upright. His muscles trembled from the savage abuse; his face had been turned into a bloody, pulpy mess. But he remained silent, passive, accepting the punishment completely, his only response an occasional, lopsided, split-lipped grin.

"Why hasn't he killed yet?" The king slammed the meat of his palm against the wall. "You said he would break easily."

"He's spent years killing for the Twelve. How was I to know his self-control was this strong?" Aubrianna scowled. "He always was an uncooperative wretch as a child."

"You'd better make him cooperative. I want the power of Aether or Nether."

"Pain doesn't seem to be the key. Perhaps there's something more important to him than relief from the torture. Stop this futile effort and let me try my plan. Unless yours includes killing the man?"

"Feeling maternal?"

"Not in the least. I just don't want you to kill him and lose Gaia's gifts forever."

The king stared at her, his solid red eyes hard, unblinking, not a shred of movement indicating his thoughts. He finally turned away and she exhaled slowly, refusing to betray her unease.

"Fine," he said. "Make the contact. But be warned, if you can't get me the power, you and your son are of no use to me. And I don't suffer the useless to live."

"I am the Os Mage Mother. You can't touch me."

He snorted. "You are defanged; your threats are empty. You bore a son." He turned to watch his guards pummel Libra again. "The power that should have come to you has skipped a generation. You are a disgrace."

She walked to the door of the observation room and opened it, eager to get away from the man before her fury boiled over and she earned her death here and now. As much as she hated the king, he hadn't lied. No matter the circumstance, having a son instead of a daughter was her disgrace. It was a failing she had tried to right, but she'd been stopped.

On top of that, the four Os Mages had become surprisingly long-lived, and restless to supplant her. They didn't dare come at her directly, but if Libra didn't claim his role as agent, she'd have no chance to steal the power from him. Without it, she was vulnerable to the ambitions of the maids serving her.

She would rather die than go back to wandering a realm dragging a bag of bones, a servant of the Os Mage Mother usurper. She'd rather seen the blackest of demons climb out of the abyss and seize the unclaimed bones of dead paranormals scattered across the four worlds, even if they used them for rituals too horrific to be contemplated. She had to find a way to reclaim what belonged to her before it was too late.

She made to leave the room.

"Hear me well," the king said, his voice soft and low. "I will continue as I see fit. I will have his power for my own. If for any reason I can't, I'll kill him with my bare hands, and kill everything and everyone he has ever cared about. Starting with you."

"You can save yourself the trouble," she said, pausing at the doorway. "He has never cared for me. I made sure of that from the day he ripped me open to enter this world."

7

TARYN PACED IN HER room, her emotions driving her in an endless circle. Lyon was proving to be a good leader, but in this he was wrong. Libra locked away? She disliked the arrogant Zodiac, but he was needed for this fight. She felt it to her marrow and she'd relied on her instincts all of her life. If a decision needed to be made, she stilled her mind and waited for the answers to come—they'd never failed her before.

Once the universe, and her gut, provided the answer, she could do anything.

So why was she struggling so much with the ley lines? Why was this different? She'd been so sure that she would master them; she'd felt it in her gut as strongly as with any past decision. She had quivered when the answer had become clear, her path shining brightly for the first time since she had first entered the InBetween.

After being so sure that her place in this new reality was to act as an alarm system against the demons, she was reeling from the failure. Just the thought of ley line twang duty stirred up a hornet's nest of dread, her traitor gut flip-flopping like kids inside a bouncy castle instead of giving her answers. How could she feel a demon coming in time to stop its attack, in time to save lives and limbs, when her ability was nearly nonexistent? Why hadn't she told the others that they couldn't rely on her?

What the hell am I supposed to do?

Climbing into her bed, she curled into a ball and closed her eyes, attempting to get a grip on her fractured thoughts. Abella and Persephone had always been her default, her go-to, but, for the first time, she couldn't bear to tell them the truth.

Persephone had found her place with Lyon, their children, and the Great Cavern. Abella struggled to understand her place in the InBetween, but she made no apologies for her uncertainty. The woman was a rock; self-doubt wasn't in her personal lexicon—Taryn had always envied that about Abella.

Before she could cannonball into a world-class funk, she heard a light tap on the door. Her limbs heavy, she almost covered her head with a pillow. She wanted to yell, "*Go away.*" But hiding wasn't her style.

She rolled up into a sitting position and sighed. "Come in."

Persephone poked her head inside. "You okay?"

"I'm fine," she answered with what little enthusiasm she could muster.

Persephone pushed the door open wide and waited as Candace ran in and lunged at Taryn, her tiny arms wide open.

Taryn caught her and pulled the baby into her lap, her nose buried in the sweet lavender scent of her thick mop of silver hair, the unusual color unique to the purest, most powerful Portends. "Hi, sweetness."

Candace giggled.

Taryn pulled back and forced a smile. How could she not grin back at the cherubic girlie? "How did you know I needed a hug from an angel?"

The little girl squirmed off her lap and trotted around the room, touching photos and Taryn's hairbrush.

"I know Lyon can be…abrasive," Persephone said.

"He certainly has embraced the whole draconian lord-of-the-manor attitude."

Persephone snorted. "His people skills need work, but he's trying."

Taryn sagged, the weight of her argument with Lyon lifting. "I guess I owe him an apology."

The bed bounced when Persephone jumped on it. "He'll get over it. Someone needs to get his blood boiling, or he might stagnate."

"What? He's getting antsy sitting on that ginormous throne?"

"Yep, and I think his butt is getting flatter," Persephone said with a straight face.

Taryn sputtered and choked on the laughter before it escaped her mouth. Persephone joined her and they laughed until tears streamed down their faces.

Candace clapped and danced on her tippy-toes.

Finally, Taryn took a deep breath. "Oh god, I needed that."

She rubbed her eyes, still dry and scratchy, even after the flood of tears.

"Eyes still burning?"

Taryn opened her eyes wide. "Look at them. They're all red." She gasped. "What if it's pink eye? Crap, what about albinism?"

"You don't *become* an albino, you hypochondriac."

"I am not."

"What about that time you thought you had that throwing up disease?"

"Cyclic Vomiting Syndrome."

"Yes, that one, and it turned out to be a stomach bug. Or the time you thought you were a werewolf?"

"I had hairs exploding out of my pores. And it was a full moon."

"One hair. You had one hair on your chin."

"Exploding," Taryn countered.

"Hypochondriac."

They stopped and smiled.

"Maybe it's allergies," Taryn said.

Persephone pointed at her. "Now *that* is a possibility." She reached out and tugged on Taryn's long, thick, curly, black hair. "Candace and I have something for you."

Taryn clenched her fists. The urge to tell Persephone the truth about her fears was stuck in her throat, stealing her breath away. For the first time since they had met as young children, she had a secret, a big one, so big that it could affect not just her but everyone she cared about. Maybe billions more.

"What?"

"Candace has made something for you."

The baby Portend struggled to unfold a heavy sheet of paper, sucking her bottom lip into her mouth as her chubby fingers pulled on the corners, her forehead furrowed. When the paper bloomed open she beamed with delight and presented it to Taryn.

Taryn expected stick figures and a blocky house with a troll or two sitting in the yard, bows on their heads, but a gallery-worthy artist couldn't have done better. The ends of the sprawling, turn-of-the-century gothic building ran off the edges of the paper. In the middle, a five-story entrance towered over the pair of three-story wings. Barred windows dotted the wings, the brick façade crumbling—the child had drawn a haunted house from the scariest nightmare. *Awfully creepy subject for a little girl.*

"This is so beautiful, Candace. Thank you."

Persephone leaned down and whispered in Candace's ear. The girl nodded then folded the paper in half. She closed her eyes for a moment then released the paper and backed away.

Taryn looked down and gasped. The once empty windows were now filled with the faces of children, their mouths opened wide as if crying or screaming.

She brought the drawing closer. "What is this?"

"New one on me," Persephone answered. "She's been drawing that place for days, but each drawing has more and more of the faces. It's as if the house is being filled with unhappy children. Then, today, she nearly pulled my arm out of the socket to get me here—not that I didn't want to come anyway."

"You wanted to come," Taryn observed her friend's strained expression and the shadows under her eyes, "but it wasn't to soothe me. What's got you so worried?"

Persephone's pale skin blanched, no small feat. "I haven't told anyone, so please keep this between us for now."

"Okay. Sure."

"Candace did another drawing of a street in a big city—"

"Which one?"

"I didn't see any markers that I could use to figure that out, only crumbled buildings, abandoned cars, and rotting bodies, all over the street and hanging out windows."

"Jeez. What did Lyon say about it?"

Persephone frowned. "I haven't told him."

"Why?"

"I—" She looked away. "That's not important. Not now." Persephone folded her arms across her chest and sighed. "You think we need to do something about Libra."

"Yes."

Persephone nodded. "I think the drawing of the house and children is real, or a slice of reality. Enough that someone should find out if there are paranorm children being held there. If there are, and any of them are Corvus Wards, maybe the king will reconsider letting us keep our babies." She rose and led Candace to the door. "Go on, sweetheart." She watched Candace take off down the passage before turning back to Taryn. "I can't ask anyone to defy Lyon's orders." She pulled a piece of paper from her pocket and handed it to Taryn. "But Libra may not be hard to find."

She sat on the bed and waited.

Taryn unfolded the paper to find a map of a warehouse district. There was a star marked on one building, and an address scribbled above it. "How did you get this?"

"Not in a vision. This came from one of the Corvus Ward women who chose to stay here with us instead of returning to her people. She used to cook for the warriors when they were in the human world."

"Isn't she afraid someone will find out she gave you this?"

"She's more afraid of what the king is doing to her people. He's ruthless, T, don't forget that. If you get caught, he'll kill you and Libra, maybe all of us."

"Damn, Persi."

Persephone nodded, her hands cupping her still-flat belly.

"But—"

"In this we need to be bold, and fast. Each day that passes with no word of the demon army or Asmodeus or Circe is another day that they have to make plans and consolidate power. I fear that if we don't do the same, we will lose this fight before it even starts."

Persephone stood.

"I think he's rubbing off on you," Taryn said.

Persephone flashed a sly grin Taryn had never seen before. "As often as I can convince him to."

"Ugh, you can leave now."

Persephone walked to the door.

"Wait. What made you think I'd bust Libra out?"

"Lyon is my love, but he's not always right. That, and I know you, sister; your heart is bigger than your head. It has to be you. With your gut instinct and new skill with the ley lines, you have the best chance of getting Libra out and evading the Corvus Wards until you find the children. But please, have a care. Your gut and bravado have served you well in the past, but forces we can't control are buffeting us."

"Control. Ugh, you know how much I despise that word."

"Yes, but, for once, maybe you should embrace a little control, even if only to help me sleep better at night."

"Hah, never!"

Persephone rested a hand on the doorframe. "Whatever it takes, please come home whole and safe."

She left the room and closed the door with a soft click.

Home.

Taryn froze, the word "home" reverberating in her mind. The Great Cavern had become a home without any fanfare or headache. They had destroyed their home in Texas, relieving them of the joyless chore of moving their crap. But that last step before changing locales, no matter how onerous, was necessary to cut ties with the old and knot the new. The weeks following the ritual that had blown a hole in the InBetween and released the demons into all the worlds had been chaotic. No one had had time to contemplate the life-altering, mind-blowing revelations about multiple worlds, paranormal creatures, magic, and trolls.

Taryn shook her head to clear it before pocketing the map and opening Candace's drawing again. The mansion looked familiar but she couldn't quite place it. Excitement gripped her, the adrenaline spike sending her to her feet. She paced her room. First, she needed to help Libra make a great escape. Second, find the location of the building Candace had drawn. And, maybe, somewhere along the way, she would find the help she needed to earn her place. Maybe even from Libra, god help her.

Taryn pulled her backpack from under her bed. She added a change of clothes, the sole magical sachet she had left, a book of matches, and the notebook of spells she'd learned so far, which unfortunately only numbered two. She dropped Candace's drawing on top and zipped the pack closed before dressing to travel. Tired, yet exhilarated, she set her alarm clock for midnight and reclined on her bed to wait.

8

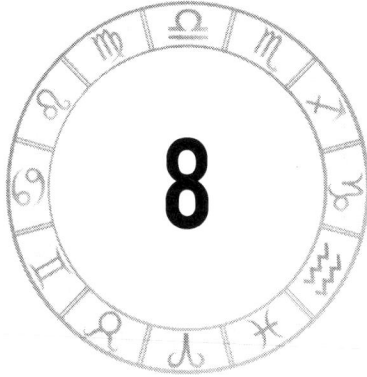

THE DOOR TO HIS cell opened and the burly Corvus Ward guards threw Libra inside. The door slammed just as he crumpled to the concrete floor, the loud bang blessedly hiding the moan he could no longer repress. Goddess be damned, he hurt. Everywhere.

He squinted to clear his vision then flinched. A touch of the skin around his eyes explained why he couldn't see very well; the punches had swollen the lids almost shut. The rest of his face hadn't faired any better. Lumps and bumps covered his normally sharp cheekbones and square jaw; his lips had split under the force of the blows.

He flattened his body onto the floor and pressed the right side of his face against the cold concrete to ease the aches; he was too tired to check the rest of his body for the insults the warriors had dealt the flesh hidden by his clothes.

Libra stared past the bars of the shiny, new cell to the shadow-filled ceiling of the rust- and dust-covered warehouse. He had no idea where they had hidden him, but he was above ground. The air was too fresh for underground, yet there were no smells to help him figure out if he was in a city or the country. No plane, train or car sounds—just cameras and locks and a Hannibal Lector-ish freestanding cell with thick, metal bars that had so far withstood his attempts to bend them.

Who knew the Corvus Wards had spent any time in the human world?

Hulking warriors who could have been mistaken for trolls fed him three square meals a day. Not that the food was palatable—most gray gruels weren't, in his thankfully limited experience. But that dubious joy, interlaced with the torture, made his days perilously close to tedious.

He didn't do tedious.

The torture was excruciating but tolerable; the true pain was the filthy sack-cloth they forced him to wear. He rolled his shoulders against the rough fabric. Unbearable. Who the hell could get away with wearing orange, much less orange covered in someone else's stink?

He watched the valiant shaft of sunlight that had raced across the ceiling disappear, its fight against the earth's rotation lost. *Time for another long night.*

Libra closed his eyes but his mind was too busy trying to sort out what had happened to allow for sleep.

Why had Aubrianna aligned herself with the Corvus Wards? What did she think to gain by becoming the human and InBetween ambassador? She'd ranted more times than he could remember about the paranorm dreck she had to deal with. And, more importantly, what were the Zodiacs doing about getting him out of here?

He shifted—wincing when the itchy fabric of his clothes scraped across his injuries—and pulled the sole blanket off the cot provided him. He covered his body the best he could with minimal movement and closed his eyes. He needed sleep more than the gruel if he was to hold on.

He was sagging, exhaustion leading him into blissful oblivion, when a door at one end of the warehouse screeched open.

Soft footfalls hurried to his cage—definitely not the Cro-Magnon steps of his guards, their knuckles scraping on the ground.

"Come on, grackles. What do you want? Are we starting a nighttime torture schedule?" he asked without opening his eyes, hoping that not looking at them would make them go away.

"Not exactly," a female voice answered.

He opened his eyes and tried to push his chest off the floor until he saw a familiar oval face appear out of the shadows.

He blew out a gusty sigh and settled on the hard concrete again. "Taryn? What the hell?"

"Hello to you, too." Taryn stopped at the bars. "I'm here to break you out."

He studied the frump's cloud of black curls, her long, garish, gypsy skirt, and the white blouse that had seen better days.

He willed his body not to shudder. "Yeah, yeah. You and who else?"

He rolled onto his back and struggled to sit up.

"Just me."

"How did you get in here? A spell? Or did you slay them? Goddess knows that outfit could do the trick. The colors alone could blind a man."

She scowled. "Do you want out of there or not? Because I'm willing to walk out of here alone if I don't start feeling the love."

She wiggled her fingers, beckoning him to declare his undying.

"You've managed to get in here, but how do you expect to get me out of this cage?"

"First, change."

She shoved a garment bag through the bars. He opened it and sighed. She had brought one of his favorite outfits: black slacks and a cashmere sweater, a white, silk, long-sleeved tee, and Tod loafers—comfort and elegance in one combo, but he noted she hadn't brought him any boxer briefs. *Commando?* He wondered if her omission was an admission of her view of undergarments in general. He snorted then banished the thought.

"That's the most inconspicuous set of clothes I could find but don't get used to them. We need to get you dressed in clothes that don't stand out. Work clothes like normal people wear—jeans and tee shirts and a non-descript coat so you don't look like a penguin in a pile of puppies."

"Clothes?"

"Work clothes, preferably used."

He didn't need to hear more, the horror that the word 'used' instilled was enough. "Damn."

He staggered to his feet, turned his back, and unzipped the jumpsuit. But when he tried to shrug out of the sackcloth, his muscles and bones weren't having it. He tried to pull a sleeve off one arm. The agony made his vision swim.

"Son of a—" He rezipped the jumpsuit and closed the garment bag. "That will have to wait. Where are the Zodiacs?"

"Lyon had no choice but to leave you here."

"I don't believe you."

"What did you expect him to do? Your chance of becoming the paranorm ambassador was blown when your mom walked into the Great Cavern. Seems pretty obvious she and the Corvus Ward king planned this, and now she's the ambassador."

"Then why are you here? Does Lyon have a plan?"

"He doesn't know I'm here."

"What?"

His face grew hot—the need to reach through the bars and throttle the woman swelling to epic proportions.

How Taryn got under his skin so easily was beyond him, but she always did. She was the only woman he'd met who was born to tip his scale to the darkside. He'd already deemed her an enemy—her appearance here didn't change that—and this example of impulsive recklessness won her a lifetime membership in his to-be-assiduously-avoided club.

He backed up and sat down hard on the cot. "What exactly were you planning?"

Her cheeks flushed, and she clenched her jaws as if she were grinding her teeth. "Get you out. Learn how to find the ley lines."

"Find them? What the hell does that mean? With a divining rod?" He snorted. "Or maybe you think you have some long-lost ability from your insane, filicidal, witch goddess mother?"

Taryn grabbed the bars of his cell and sneered. "At least my mother has enough passion in her to want to kill me; yours wouldn't lift an anything for you. She shoved you aside and took over the ambassadorship, leaving you here to rot." She waved a hand at his brutalized face. "Or be beaten to death."

Libra's fingers tingled. He clenched his fists and took a deep breath but it didn't quell his rising rage.

"Come now, nothing to say? No smooth comeback meant to put me in my place?"

"Shut it, you little termagant."

"Aw, five-dollar words. You'll have to do better than that."

He charged, his arms raised, his hands open like claws ready to grip her skinny neck and squeeze. His rage tipped over and pulses of blue energy exploded out of his hands. The bars hummed and quivered under the onslaught.

She danced out of reach of his power. "I love it when you lose your temper—makes you positively human—but you might want to step back. My witchy skills are not very developed. I *could* be opening the cell door," she pulled a sheet of paper out of her skirt pocket, "or neutering you." She clucked as she unfolded the page with a snap of her wrist. "Right now, either one would do."

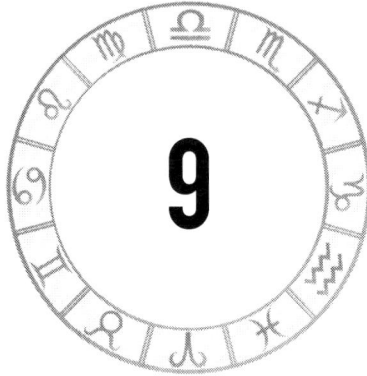

9

"STOP, STOP," LIBRA SAID. "Lyon said no magic, no powers, around the humans. Not until we have an accord with them." He backed away, ignoring the urge to cover his manly bits. "You can't do this. It's not only against Lyon's orders; it'll put a price on your head."

"Like the price you have on yours?"

"At least they want something only I can provide; that's my ticket to staying alive. You have nothing to offer, nothing they want badly enough to stay their hand. Leave while you still can."

She looked up from the piece of paper. Maybe it was the small shaft of moonlight catching in her eyes, but he could swear tears made them glitter, made her look sad, lost.

He'd never felt so small.

"I may be nothing now—" Her voice cracked. She cleared her throat and sniffed, even as she raised her chin in defiance of her softer feelings. "But if we can find the missing Corvus Ward children, that should be enough to buy your freedom and forgiveness for me. Maybe even an audience with the king."

She pressed a palm against the door lock and lifted the paper to the meager light.

"Aperire ostium,
Viam patefaceret.
Aperire ostium,
Viam patefaceret.
Aperire ostium,
Viam patefaceret."

The lock smoked and the door vibrated so hard the entire cell hummed.

"Stop," Libra ordered. "It's not working."

Taryn kept chanting, ignoring the violent shaking.

"Aperire ostium,
Viam patefaceret.
Aperire ostium,
Viam patefaceret.
Aperire ostium,
Viam patefaceret."

The concrete floor buckled and the windows exploded, raining shards on them.

"Aperire ostium,
Viam patefaceret.
Aperire ostium,
Viam patefaceret.
Aperire ostium,
Viam patefaceret!"

"Taryn! Stop!" Libra yelled, his back pressed into the farthest corner of the cell despite the bucking of the metal and the heaving of the concrete beneath his feet.

The woman was a magical menace. Here to rescue him she said, but instead of springing him she was about to kill them both.

She lifted her hand from the lock then reared back and kicked it. As if no stronger than plastic, it snapped into two pieces and fell to the floor. The shaking stopped. A blessed silence fell until the cell door drifted open.

An alarm blared.

Shouts pierced the shriek.

"Are you coming?" Taryn stuffed the paper in her pocket. "A decision before your guards get here would be preferable."

Libra hesitated. Did he really want to sit in a cell and let other people decide his fate? Or did he become a fugitive on the slim chance he could find enough Corvus Ward children to appease the king and Lyon? Hell. Who was he kidding? What Taryn didn't know would get her killed.

"Why are you doing this?" he demanded.

"You're the biggest pain in the ass I know, but your tech skills may be of use finding out where the children are being held. Stay here and take your chances that the Corvus Ward king will activate you, or come with me to find the children. You do that, and it should be enough to earn your freedom…maybe even unseat Aubrianna. You want to prove you are the best choice to represent the paranorms? This is your chance."

Activate him? Damn it.

Lyon must have told Taryn about his power. The question was, how much did Lyon really know about Aether and Nether, and had he shared it with her? Libra wanted to tell her the truth, let her run while she had the chance, before she flung herself headlong into a race for their lives. If his beatings were any measure, the king wanted his power far more than he wanted the Corvus children back, and there was nothing they could find that would change his mind.

Taryn grabbed the bars of the door and wrenched it open. "Well? What are you waiting for? You gonna sit in this cage and wait for them to beat you into submission? Or you gonna show us what you're made of?"

Libra scowled at the termagant with the infuriating grin on her face and lunged.

He grabbed the garment bag and danced across the broken concrete to reach her. She used his irritation to coax him out, but once he was beyond the cell walls, his self-preservation kicked in. There was no going back.

If he were honest, as much as she drove him nuts, he didn't want to see her killed or explain to Lyon and Taryn's sisters the role he played in her demise. And since she hadn't made any effort to hide her face from the cameras, the king would know who had gotten past his guards. Running was their only recourse now. If they managed to find some paranorm children, maybe they could be used to bargain for Taryn's life.

I won't be so lucky.

If recaptured, there wouldn't be a second chance for him. He'd be buried in a dungeon, never to be seen again.

Fists pounded on the door Taryn had used to enter the warehouse, but the metal had warped from the spell, preventing the warriors from opening it.

She grabbed one of his hands and tugged. "Hurry."

He set his feet, whipping her around to face him, and pulled her close, one hand gripping her shoulder. She might have won this round, but he needed to make it clear that he was in charge.

"Hear me true, Taryn. If we do this, we do it my way, all the way."

"You're making demands? Now?" She jerked away from him. "Screw you."

"You made your case. And I do want out. But if I am to help you, you must listen to me."

"Okay."

Libra glanced at the weakening door. Seconds, they only had seconds.

"Spill it before we both get locked up," Taryn said.

"Promise me that you'll do what I say, when I say it. No going off script, no more gut decisions—and no more magic."

"You want to hobble me? I'm just learning how to use magic; I'm not going to bargain it away when we need it most."

The corrugated metal door cracked and screeched. The warriors jammed their arms through the opening and started pulling, caws interspersed between the grunts.

"What you're doing is more like advanced chemistry, not true magic." She tried to wrench out of his grip but Libra held her tight. "Promise me, Taryn. Now. Or we'll sit this fight out."

"Okay, fine, I promise. Can we get out of here?"

He held her for a beat longer, searching her dark eyes for the truth or the lie in them. But they remained clear, unclouded by deception.

"Damn straight then." He released her and hurdled the concrete and glass debris, holding out a hand to help Taryn navigate it, but she slapped it away.

They ran to the farthest end of the warehouse. "How do we get out of here?" Libra said.

She pulled up hard and they slid several inches. She fished a large plastic bag out of one of her bottomless skirt pockets. Inside were five glass orbs containing a golden liquid.

"Magic?"

He hazarded a look back and grimaced. The Corvus Wards were almost through the door.

"Fine, just this once. Then no more."

"Whatever you say." She removed one of the orbs and held it close to her mouth.

Libra leaned close. "What is that?"

"A little hocus-pocus potion. Just needs the magic word."

He leaned closer until his face was level with hers, his curiosity getting the better of him.

Taryn smirked. "Abra—cadabra!"

She threw the glass orb against the metal wall, shattering it—the golden liquid splattered and smoke rose from the contact points. Taryn threw the rest of the orbs against the wall.

A shout rose—two of the warriors had entered the warehouse and were narrowing the expanse between them.

The smoke cleared enough to expose a jagged hole in the metal, as if it had been eaten away.

"What kind of magic is this?"

"Acid. That's magic of the human sort. C'mon." She stepped over the ruined wall and into the frigid silence of the deep night.

Libra followed her. "What about them?"

The rest of the guards had broken through the door, but it was the two largest warriors pounding toward them that posed the immediate threat.

Taryn raised a hand, her palm facing the hole in the wall, but she remained silent.

"What are you waiting for?"

"Quiet, let me concentrate."

The two Corvus raced past the ruined cell—they were only a few feet from reaching the hole.

"Taryn!"

She braced her feet, closed her eyes, and yelled, "*TEGERE!*"

Like the end of a vacuum hose covered by a hand, a sucking *thump* sounded and the ruined wall reformed. The two men slammed into it, denting the metal.

Libra winced. "Oh, man, that had to hurt."

"If you can quit your whining, there are other guards…"

His sympathy for the Corvus Wards gone in a flash, he held out a hand. "Let's go."

Taryn looked at it and snorted her refusal. "Follow me."

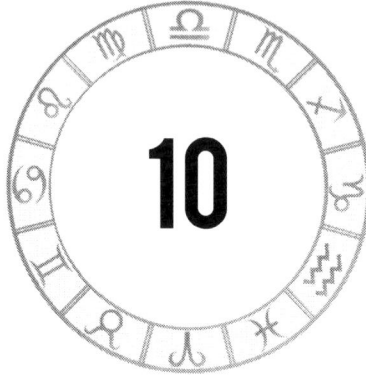

10

TARYN SPRINTED ACROSS THE tarmac for another warehouse, its profile looming in the dark. Any minute now, Libra expected to hear shouting and boots pounding behind them, but the sounds never came. Of course, the hammering of his heart could be blocking any sound the warriors made.

Taryn rounded the corner of the corrugated metal building and slid to a stop. Libra flew past her, hit a patch of gravel, and landed on his butt.

He got back on his feet and swiped at the dust on his coveralls. "Damn it, Taryn, what are you doing? Where's the car?"

She stared at the empty parking lot, but the warriors never appeared.

Strange, but he'd take the good fortune.

"Let's move," she whispered, pointing to the backside of the huge building.

Libra tried to grab her arm to stop her from going out in the open, but she eluded his grasp.

"We don't have the time for me to explain what you'll understand in a few seconds." She trotted away from him and peeked around the corner. "All clear." She raced to the partially open door, glanced inside, and entered the heavy dark.

A soft snort echoed; the grassy smell of manure hit him. The jangle of metal links to his left made him crouch.

"Solidarity," Taryn hissed.

Libra bumped into her back and grabbed her arms to keep them both steady. "What the hell are we doing here? Those warriors aren't stupid. They'll make their way here in minutes."

"We'll be fine," a soft, frail, female voice said from a few feet away.

Taryn jumped beneath his hands. "Are we ready?"

"Yes, little one."

"Ready for what?" Libra ground out.

A tiny, golden glow appeared in front of him, the light coming from an orb floating a few inches from his face. He released Taryn, took a step back, and froze when the glow expanded and brightened, illuminating the circle of painted, draft-horse-drawn caravans. A white-haired woman with sparkling dark eyes smiled at Taryn and took a step forward, her weight supported by a much younger woman—a granddaughter perhaps—who looked none too pleased. Several men had formed a half circle at the edge of the light; women and children peeked out from inside the caravans.

"What's this?" Libra asked.

"This is our ride, our disguise."

"A gypsy caravan? This is a joke, right?" He shot her an incredulous smile. "How are these humans supposed to help us? And how dare you involve them? The moment we leave it'll be a slow roll to our deaths, and theirs."

Taryn scowled. "You ungrateful lout. How *dare* you belittle these people? They're risking much to help us, and you will show them the respect they're due."

"How do you even know them? I thought you and your sisters spent your childhood bouncing from one foster home to another."

Taryn placed her fists on her hips and stuck her chin out. "I met them when I was ten years old and tried to buy a draught from them that would make my foster horrors sleep like the dead. The gypsies refused to sell me the draught but agreed to teach me the healing power of herbal medicine. They are my friends."

Libra was opening his mouth to make another plea for her to return to sanity when the back wall of the warehouse was hit. The solid sheets of corrugated metal vibrated under the attack but held.

"The walls aren't going to last long," he ground out.

All eyes turned to the old woman, clearly the leader of the motley group.

"You going to fortune-tell us out of this?" he asked, unable to stop his derision from punctuating every syllable.

Her thin lips cracked open, revealing a mouthful of beautiful white teeth, discordant with the rest of her appearance.

"Get ready, everyone," she said to the group.

The men ran to the caravans, climbed into the driver's seats and collected the reins. The horses tossed their heads and stomped their huge feet, the chains on their harnesses jingling.

The walls bowed again; the shouts of the Corvus Ward warriors were getting louder.

"Taryn," the old woman said, "take your friend to my van and hide in the front panel."

Taryn grabbed Libra's forearm and dragged him across the space to the last van in the line. She pressed her palms against a long, rectangular, wooden panel painted in wild colors, then pushed hard. A soft *thunk* preceded the panel dropping open, along with Libra's mouth. He bent down and looked inside the dark space.

"Get in," Taryn said.

"Are you kidding me?"

The warehouse walls groaned then cracked. Not enough to let the men inside but a beginning. They only had minutes left before being overrun.

Taryn gripped the ledge at the top of the opening, lifting one leg then the other into the hidey-hole. She worked her way inside until she disappeared.

Libra grit his teeth. "What's the point? We'll be caught inside of minutes even if we manage to escape the warehouse."

Taryn heaved a sigh and waved a hand at him. "Quit whining."

He followed her example and slid into the hole on his back.

"Grab the panel."

Libra craned his neck back and reached for one of the two leather straps attached to the corners of the secret door. Together, they raised the panel.

"Pull gently."

Libra followed her instruction until the panel clicked into place. The caravan dipped and the horses jerked, pulling them forward several feet. Blind in the darkness, sweat broke out on his brow as he tried to divine what was happening, but the sounds gave him little information. He had no control; he was vulnerable to a group of strangers on the word of a woman he had ignored and discounted in the few weeks he'd known her.

"Tell me again why we're doing this?"

The van lurched again, sliding Libra into Taryn. He grabbed her waist and held on.

The metal wall screamed as if alive—the warriors had penetrated its skin. Shouts and footfalls approached in a rush. Libra pulled Taryn close, hanging onto her warmth, drawing on her body for the calm he couldn't muster. His breath caught in his throat as he waited for the van to stop moving and their hiding place to be discovered. But the van didn't stop.

It dipped multiple times, as if the warriors were jumping on. Any moment, they would be found and Libra thrown back in the cell.

"What a fucking terrible plan," he hissed in Taryn's ear.

She dug her nails into his side. "Quiet."

He flinched then forced his body to relax to stop the burning ache of his bruises.

The van stopped rolling. More warriors climbed over the van, their breathing heavy as they scaled the sides and roof.

Adrenaline drove Libra's mild claustrophobia into overdrive; his skin crawled and itched. He needed to move, run, anything to burn off the panic that was creeping in. He gripped Taryn's waist tight to ground himself. The scent of honey wafted up his nose, the warm, rich smell soothing his fraying composure. He breathed deep then exhaled slowly to reclaim his calm.

A deep, male voice barked orders at the others just overhead; booted feet tromped inside the van, loosening dust that coated Libra. His nose twitched and his eyes watered; a sneeze was forming high in his nose. He pinched his nostrils and willed the sneeze away, but it danced past his efforts. He covered his open mouth, hoping to quiet the explosive expulsion of dust and snot when the shouting stopped.

"Leave while you can," the old woman told the men in a clear, strong voice.

The men laughed, dripping with derision.

Not surprising considering he hadn't taken the woman seriously either. What could she actually do? Subdue them with censure?

The sneeze allayed, he sighed and released Taryn, rolling onto his back. He closed his eyes, waiting for the panel to be discovered.

The panel didn't open; instead, a bright, yellow light pierced his eyelids. His eyes watering, he raised his hands to cover them.

What the hell?

11

A LOW WHINE STARTED THEN pitched higher and higher. Libra uncovered his eyes, squinting to block out the extreme light penetrating every seam of the hiding place. The first scream sounded to his left. The sound traveled right as, one by one, the warriors were overcome. Heavy thuds vibrated the floor of the van. Bodies. The warriors were dropping.

Scream. Thud.

Scream. Thud.

Silence.

Seconds later, the panel door opened. The old woman stood to the side while two of the larger gypsy men pulled Taryn and Libra out of the hold.

Libra shrugged the men off him.

"What the hell?" he and Taryn exclaimed at the same time.

The old woman gestured for him to climb onto the van. "Go look."

He climbed up and checked the deceptively large interior. The smell of ozone hit him first, then the metallic scent of blood. Six Corvus Ward warriors had fallen where they stood. Their bodies were sprawled across the floor, the blood that had oozed out of their eyes, ears, and mouths already drying, while the blisters covering their red, raw, exposed skin grew in size.

A gasp close to his left ear made him jump. "Damn it, Taryn."

She ignored him, her pale face and open mouth emphasizing her horror. She backed out of the caravan and stepped down to the warehouse floor.

Libra struggled to make sense of the scene before following her.

"Solange? Did you—? How?" Taryn sputtered, her arms wrapped around her waist.

She was clearly trying, but failing, to stop shaking.

The old woman snapped her fingers and the gypsy men jumped on the van. "Come away while they take care of the bodies. We can't stay here."

"What did you do to them? How?" Libra asked.

"The police will have been called by now. I don't fear their attention but it is tedious." Solange touched Taryn's shoulder but didn't respond when the younger woman jerked away from her. She dropped her arm and clasped her hands together. "I am the leader of the Sol. As my name suggests, I am a kind of sun servant. The 'what' I did to them was shine my light. All of it. At once." She shook her head. "Really quite sad. I'd been saving that up for months. Ah well, I'll just have to start over."

Libra watched Taryn back away from the woman, confusion written on her face. No mistaking it, she'd had no idea her friends were more than human.

"Why didn't you tell me?" Taryn asked, her voice a breathless whisper.

The men joined Solange; the largest one nodded his head.

The old woman walked to her van and climbed up the steps to the driver's seat. "You were not ready for the truth, little one. If I had told you that we were not human, would you have believed us before now? I think not." She looked across the warehouse, her eyes studying the distant wall. "Come with us or not, but you need to decide now."

Libra had opened his mouth to say, "*Leave, I'll make my own way*," when he heard sirens in the distance. The human police wouldn't understand what they saw here, and he had no explanation. They were a headache he couldn't afford.

He mounted the steps and held out a hand to Taryn.

She stared at it, her eyes wide.

"For goddess' sake." Libra jumped down, threw Taryn over his shoulder, and carried her up the steps and into the van. He released her and she bounced onto the bed. "Let's go."

Taryn jumped up and shoved him back. "Never do that again."

Ah, there she is. "What? Save you from yourself?"

"Force me into a decision."

"Like you forced me out of the cell and into this crazy?"

"That was for the benefit of both of us."

"And so is getting the hell out of here before we're found amid a pile of bodies. Or do you want to explain our way into a jail cell or an asylum?"

Before Taryn could respond with what Libra could already tell would be an irrational answer, the van lurched, flinging the pair onto the bed. Libra landed on top of Taryn, snug between her splayed legs. The van lurched a second time, pushing Libra forward. He used his arms and legs to stop his body from sliding, his back hunched in a crude imitation of a thrust.

"Oh my god, get off of me, you perv." Taryn pushed his shoulders with her hands, bending her knees and digging her heels into the mattress to gain leverage.

Their groins met and ground together until Libra grabbed a wooden bar that kept a shelf full of books from tumbling out at the slightest movement. He heaved off her, and landed on his back.

Taryn sat up and scooted off the mattress. She turned to face him.

She glanced down and her face turned red. "Seriously?"

Libra followed her gaze to his tented crotch. "What do you expect when you grind a man?"

He stood and adjusted his jumpsuit, brushing the dirt and dust off the orange material, his legs braced against the rocking of the van.

"Grind you? You sorry—"

He lifted a hand. "Shush."

Taryn opened her mouth, no doubt to spit out a complaint, but nothing came out, her tirade interrupted. She turned to the tiny window fitted into the wall of the van.

Sirens screamed—the noise bouncing off the metal warehouses—the echo heralding the arrival of the police. Libra moved the corner of the curtain and was surprised to see not one, not two, but a dozen marked cars with their blue and red lights blinking, illuminating the rusty, corrugated walls only a few yards from them. He squeezed his body past Taryn's, her unique honey scent flooding his senses, distracting him for the span of a breath until he clamped down his steely control. He stuck his head out of the van.

"How do they not see us?" he whispered to Solange.

"I have found humans can be blind when there's a dead body in the vicinity. Do not fret; the night will hide us."

"No, the dark will get us lost." Libra looked behind the van to see if the police had spotted them.

"The darkest nights let the stars shine the brightest. They will guide our way."

He craned his neck to see where they were headed. The group was descending a slope, the homes and businesses in the valley below illuminated, twinkling like the night sky.

"You always spew that new age crap?"

Solange chuckled. "It's all about balance—give and take. That is not crap, old or new. Just truth."

She turned her attention to the approaching asphalt.

Okay. Conversation done.

Libra stepped back and stared at the small door that led to the driver's seat as it closed without a sound. He rubbed his forehead—gibberish gave him headaches. How many bodies had dropped so they could escape? How many more might fall before this was done?

He shook his head to clear it of questions for which he had no answer then looked back at Taryn. "You got us into this mess. What makes you think we'll have more luck finding the children than the Zodiacs? Now that we're fugitives."

Taryn's face scrunched into a scowl. Her lips thinned as she dug around in a pocket.

She produced a folded piece of paper and threw it into his chest before lighting a lantern and placing it on the floor of the van. "With this."

Libra's lips twitched. The prickly wench was so easy to spark. He held the paper close to the light and opened it. The beautifully drawn building was so large it bled off the edges. Tiny faces crowded the barred windows.

He glanced up. "What's this?"

Taryn leaned a hip against the miniscule sink and crossed her arms over her chest. "Candace drew it."

He held it out to Taryn. "Beautifully drawn, but I don't see how this is going to help us."

Taryn jutted her chin. "Look closer."

He sighed but decided to indulge her. He squinted to see the faces better, their detail and expression. The first thing he saw was fear: wide eyes, open mouths, wrinkled foreheads. Then a single face caught his attention. He took a knee to get closer still to the light and leaned over until the drawing almost touched his nose. The child was taller than the other children in the windows, staring out into the distance. The drawing was so small he wasn't sure if he was seeing a boy or girl, but the long, black hair and the solid red eyes narrowed the possibility of species down to one.

"A Corvus Ward," he whispered. "A royal." Before he could look up, the child's gaze moved—locking onto Libra. He jerked back and fell on his ass, throwing the paper away as if it had burned him. "What the hell was that?"

"I think Portends can do more than read minds or see the future. You didn't know?"

"That they could make a drawing move?" he sputtered. "No."

Taryn picked up the paper and folded it gently, as if she thought the moving children might be affected by the darkness of the closed drawing. "Maybe there's some kind of psychic link…" She opened a long, flat drawer above the sink and tucked the paper on top of the rack of cooking spices. "If you help me find *that* building with *those* children—"

He knew where she was going with this. Despite her not knowing everything at stake here, she might be right. A Corvus royal child as a bargaining chip might carry enough weight to earn Libra his freedom.

"That royal child alone might be enough to excuse what we did tonight."

"What happened to those Corvus warriors…" She closed the drawer and turned toward him, one hand still on the intricately carved wood of the cabinet face as if she needed the support, her gaze lowered. "…there's no way to wash away that amount of blood, but at least we can help the children. Are you with me?" She finally looked at him, her chin set, her stare hard, but behind it he could see the watery shadow of regret. "It's all or nothing time."

Libra pushed off the floor of the van and straightened his coveralls, buying time so he could collect his control and his thoughts, giving Taryn time to contain the tears that had pooled in her eyes and threatened to spill. He waited in the uncomfortable silence until she took a deep breath and her shoulders relaxed.

He didn't agree with her decision to defy Lyon's orders and break him out. He didn't like that she'd risked her freedom and maybe her life unaware of the full truth about why he'd been taken by the Corvus king. But he was grateful to be free. If he could find the Corvus royal…

He nodded, ignoring the voice in his head whispering that his potential power was far more important to the king than ten royal children would ever be. "I'm in. Definitely in."

12

A SEMI TRUCK EASED DOWN the decades-old gravel road, raising dust and breaking off the low-hanging limbs of the overgrown pine and hardwood trees with a loud *crack*. The trucker cursed each screech of the bark scraping the metal of his new rig.

Finally, the old sanitarium appeared, the hulking, brick-and-plaster building his final destination. He shuddered. No matter how many times he'd driven past the abandoned place, it had always creeped him out. So when he'd received a call to come to the place for a job, he'd hesitated…until he'd been told how much he would earn for one trip. More money than he could make in years of driving across the country and back.

Half up front allowed him to buy the new truck outright. Today, he would deliver the load and receive the rest of the money. He bounced over a pothole with a *thunk*. Cries came from inside the shipping container behind him as the truck bounced again and again through a deep rut in the gravel road. He wanted to ignore the sounds, but they had wormed their way into his brain.

He felt around the seat for the bottle he'd been nursing since the container had been hitched to his truck, unscrewed the top, and sucked down the last of the cheap whisky before tossing the empty into the thick vegetation lining the lane.

There goes my oblivion in a bottle.

The road forked. Take the right and he'd end up on the asphalt road that led to the front of the building; the left and he stayed on gravel to the back of the building. He pulled the wheel to the left and slowed, stopping at the loading bay just short of a huge bus with blacked-out windows.

He rubbed his moist palms on his jeans before climbing down. Stretching to ease the stiff muscles, he walked slowly around his rig to warm up his grinding knees until he reached the doors. To his left, an old-style intercom system with some of the numbers missing waited for him to press a button.

He pushed the green one hard and cleared his throat before speaking. "Uh, this is Frank, Frank Miller. I have your delivery."

He released the button and stepped back, the hairs on his neck standing to attention, the sweat rolling down his back despite the cold weather, a warning that he should get out of here, now, screw the money. But he stayed, his need for the payday whitewashing his fear.

A metallic scrape sounded from the other side of the doors. Frank stepped back until his rig stopped him.

The doors opened silently. The shadows inside the bay were too heavy for him to see more than a few feet. But something was inside the darkness, something cold and heavy and alien just standing there watching him, waiting, as if deciding what to do.

Frank removed his crumpled, red ballcap and squeezed the stained bill, his hands at chest level, working it into a tube shape as if his rusty manners would protect him.

He struggled to keep control of his full bladder—peeing himself was not an option. "Uh, ma'am? Sir? I have your container."

A low growl buffeted him. His fight-or-flight instinct kicked him hard in the nuts, sucking them tight against his groin. A disjointed *swish-clomp* approached the line between the shadows and the weak light of the overcast day. Frank pressed his back against the quarter panel, his legs shaking, hot and cold running through him in faster and faster waves.

A foot emerged first. A gaunt, dark-skinned leg with stringy tendons like an insect appeared next, followed by a second. The creature's hips, taller than Frank's six-foot-one-inch frame, appeared in the light. The black flesh slowly morphed—like a chameleon—into a soft gray, the color of the concrete floor.

The trucker dropped his ballcap. He craned his head back as the whole of the creature was revealed. "Wha—?"

The creature ignored the soft hiss of his exhale. It walked toward him, its gait slow, deliberate, and predatory. It raised a light gray hand to Frank's face then grabbed it, covering the whole of the trucker's head with its overlapping fingers.

Urine flowed down Frank's leg, staining his jeans, his muffled pleas incoherent as he sagged to the gravel. His eyes opened; the creature's fingers were spread just wide enough for him to see the horror leaning close.

"Please…"

Before Frank could finish the plea, his head was jerked to one side with an incredible force—the pain was sharp, but darkness took him before he could process more.

* * *

Two distinct sets of footsteps echoed inside the bay, one light and clicking, the other heavy and quiet.

Hanell walked in step behind his lover, waiting for her to express her rage or joy at the scene. She stopped at the line between concrete and gravel and held out her elegant hand. He took it and helped her to traverse the shifting rocks in her high heels until they reached the back of the container.

"Your Creepers don't mess around," he said, staring at the collapsed human.

"My babies are beautiful," she cooed. "Now, open the door. I want to see what new treasures the human brought us."

He lifted the hefty lock and bounced it in his palm, weighing it, judging the level of power he would need to summon to open it without a key. His fingers closed around the thick metal; he closed his eyes and jerked once. The metal snapped and the lock fell to the ground in two pieces.

"You do know killing off the help isn't going to endear you to the neighbors or any other humans we may need to use. What if the man has family?"

She grinned. "I'm finding that greed is the vice most oft found in this time. A vice I can use for as long as I need outside help." She clasped her hands together and rested her chin on her knuckles. "Open the doors, Hanell."

He pulled one door open, the hinges squealing until he pushed it against the side of the container. He rested his back on the door and watched the witch goddess coo over the hunched shapes crowded at the other end of the space. Circe had proven to be far more than he had thought—more ambitious, more far-sighted, more ruthless even than his mother.

Circe waved at the irregular shapes, gesturing at them to come closer. "You must be so cold and hungry. Come, we have plenty of heat and food. And we have beds. So much nicer than the caves you've been living in these past weeks."

One boy with pointed, tufted ears and the beginnings of a navy blue wash of color on his hands and wrists stood, his legs shaking.

The tall, lanky Kellas Cat youth walked slowly to the door and looked down at her, his fierce scowl almost masking the calculation in his eyes. "We want to go home."

Hanell moved to Circe's side, blocking her from potential attack. "Get out here, now! All of you."

The hunched forms turned into children. All heights and ages, the wide range of paranorm species represented in this one load was impressive. A dozen children to add to the others they'd already collected. A total of twenty-seven children with immense potential, living here, waiting for the moment Circe said was coming.

What that moment was still eluded Hanell, and Circe wasn't one to be questioned. Of course, her punishments for his impertinence had proven to be just what he wanted in a woman: harsh pain-pleasure sessions bordering on torture. The real trick was finding the balance between the pleasure and death, each day nudging that thin line closer to that great, yawning forever-dark just to get a glimpse of the beyond without actually being owned by it.

Mother would be so proud.

Hanell waited until the children started filing into the sanitarium before asking the question he always asked. "How many more?"

Circe's back stiffened but she didn't turn; she didn't strike.

Prickly bitch.

Goosebumps covered Hanell's skin, and the electric zing of lust slammed into his groin, making him shiver. Just as love was matched with hate, ecstasy had terror for its mate. He'd found the razor-thin line of her tolerance again; now he needed to see how long he could dance on it without falling into the abyss.

She leaned her head back, her eyes closed, silent for several seconds. "I have somewhere to be." She slid a sharp nail down his cheek, slicing his skin with a shallow stroke. "This game you like to play will have to wait."

13

"**Y**OU MUST BE JOKING." Libra climbed out of the ancient truck Solange had loaned them and stared at the blinking red words. "A motor lodge?"

Taryn snorted. "That's what you're worried about? That it's not a five-star hotel?" She unlocked the room. "Fugitives can't be choosers."

He followed her into the wretched space.

"Quit your scowling. There's a bed, a chair, a little table." She disappeared into the bathroom. "Oh," her hand jutted into view filled with small bottles, "and cute little soaps and shampoos."

"And why are we sharing a room? Don't you want privacy?" Goddess knew he could stand some alone time, even in this dump.

"Lack of green trumps privacy."

"Alright, alright." Libra sank into the lone chair, exhausted. "So, what's your brilliant plan?"

Libra was stunned into silence…but only for a moment. "You? Control? Is that even possible? The sun will rise in the west before you learn control. The heavens will trade places with hell. Fish will walk the land, and humans will go back to the sea."

He sputtered to a stop and laughed.

"No need to get nasty." She looked away and flexed her jaw. "From what I've been told, your connection to Gaia should make helping me easy for you."

Libra jerked backward as if she'd slapped him. "Gaia? Who said anything about her?"

"The original Os Mage Mother was created by Gaia, yes?"

Libra forced himself to take a steadying breath. "Yes."

"So you could help me find her ley lines, the vortices, help me connect with her so I can help protect the Great Cavern."

He sneered. "No. Never."

"Why not? I'm only asking for information."

"Information that will get you killed. No, the farther you are from Gaia the better."

"Why? You care about my wellbeing all of a sudden?"

He leaned forward, his rage icy and tightly contained…but barely. "I don't care about you. What I *do* care about is staying as far away from that goddess as I can. Helping you connect with her—giving Gaia a conduit to work through—would be disastrous."

Taryn bounced off the bed and stalked to the motel door. "Take your shower. Be done by the time I get back. Oh, and if you're hungry, there's a convenience store just down the road. You haven't eaten until you've tried microwaved bean and cheese burritos." She paused and smiled, her head cocked to one side. "Oh, wait. You have had them before…in Texas…with Taurus? When Abella and I kicked your ass?"

Her taunt propelled him forward. "Why, you little—"

Taryn slammed the door just before he reached her.

Libra bounced off it and staggered back, his hands over his throbbing nose. Stars swirled in his vision as he fought to keep the contents of his mostly empty stomach from coming up. He pushed the stiff, plastic curtain aside and watched her slide behind the wheel of the old beater. She wiggled her fingers at him in a silent *toodle-loo* before she drove away.

Libra stuffed a wad of the motel's coarse, thin tissue up his nose to stem the bleeding. Blasted wretch had slammed the door in his face! He shivered as frigid air seeped through the cracks around the window, whistling loudly with each gust of the rising wind, circling him before slithering inside his clothes. It was like Taryn had stolen every bit of warmth from the small space, leaving him alone to mull over what had happened in the last several hours.

He selected 'Hot' on the ac/heater control panel and it wheezed to life. But no amount of heat or five-star accommodations could stop his brooding.

Lyon had planned to leave him with the Corvus Wards. Despite Libra having told the Zodiac that it was okay, he had hoped Lyon would find a way to free him.

He'd struggled to cope with his predicament until Taryn had shown up and offered him freedom. He had bolted his cage regardless of the reason or the means. But, by the goddess, reason and means had certainly brought him to a new low.

He plopped onto the bed and picked at a stiff section on the coverlet before realizing that the source of the crustiness was undoubtedly something he didn't want to touch.

Disgusted, he grabbed the remote control. He flipped through the channels until he reached a station called BZR. He had piled up the pillows and collapsed back on the bed, studiously ignoring the probable filth, when he recognized the landscape behind the news reporter—the distinct profile of the mountains surrounding the main entrance to the Great Cavern and the rest of the InBetween. He increased the volume and listened as the two anchors discussed the unique eruption that had occurred several weeks ago. He sat up when two photos flashed on the screen. The first depicted a black cloud escaping the InBetween; the second showed the cloud splitting apart and flying away in different directions. The reporters listed the various theories floating around: aliens, the end times, locusts, and, last, demons.

Libra flopped back, shocked that some human had filmed the demon army escaping Hell. The station was home to a bunch of conspiracy theorists but, in this case, some of their viewers had made a leap in the right direction. How many others had as well?

The news program shifted to a report of President Nixon's ghost haunting the

San Clemente beach with his dog, Checkers, by his side. Libra turned the television off and stripped. He needed a hot shower; he could mull over this development later.

Grabbing the clean rags Solange had provided, he shut the bathroom door and turned the tub faucet to 'Hot.' He waited for the groaning pipes to stop complaining before stepping into the bathtub.

Pulling the knob for the shower, he yelped when ice-cold water hit him. "Taryn!"

14

TARYN EASED THE CAR into the motel parking lot and released the breath she hadn't known she'd been holding. The moment she'd driven away from Libra, her heart had pounded and her skin had crawled. Her tight grip on the steering wheel had cramped her hands, but she'd made sure not to speed or go too slow. Being stopped by a cop could be disastrous—her driver's license had expired, which might inspire them to do a more extensive search of her record. And the police would have found her fingerprints at the warehouse by now.

Having the Corvus Wards and, perhaps, Lyon after her was bad enough without adding humans to the mix.

She pulled the two bags of clothes she had purchased at the local rescue mission out of the car. They were clean enough, but no doubt Mr. Designer-Duds-Or-Die would have a fit over wearing a stranger's clothes. The thought of his displeasure would normally have made her grin, but not today.

The *plink, plink, plink* of freezing rain and sleet hitting the car and the haunting howl of the icy wind winding around her body had her on edge. March was usually iffy in the weather department, but damn it was cold.

She leaned on the car door for a moment, her instincts triggering her adrenaline, firing up her brain. Time slowed. Her nostrils flared and she took a deep breath. Decayed leaves, the tang of pine needles, oil, and gasoline, laced with the tiniest hint of sulfur, flooded her nose. She closed her eyes and turned in a circle, seeking the direction where the scent of rotten egg was the strongest. There, behind her; on the opposite side of the car.

Taryn opened her eyes and a flash of light made her jump. The streetlight hissed and sputtered for a moment before coming to life, not yet strong enough to illuminate more than the top quarter of the pole upon which it perched.

She looked at the far end of the lot but the spot was filled with shadows from the building next door. Something had triggered her senses but she couldn't make out a lurker. The woo-woo anxiety that would normally make her laugh had grown beyond reason or self-deprecating humor. Knowing about the existence of the paranormal world—hell, being smack dab in the middle of it—had given her a whole new reason to be afraid of the things that went *chomp* in the night.

Taryn ran to the motel door. She fumbled with the key and prayed she wouldn't drop the archaic manner of entry. The door opened. She glanced at the lot corner one more time then jumped into the room and slammed it shut, dropping the bags on the floor. She moved the curtain aside with two fingers and looked out.

The streetlights fought to pierce the approaching darkness but they were too weary; the warm, golden glow they were able to produce was finite. The cold, encroaching darkness ate away at the edges of their humble effort.

The light closest to the corner of the lot winked out, the shadows greedily gobbling up the tiny piece of real estate around the post save for a tall, slim figure. A pale hand extended from a sleeve and pulled back its hood, revealing a head of long, bright red hair.

Circe—her bitch of a witch goddess mother.

As a foundling, Taryn had longed to know her biological parents, but weeks ago she had learned about the subterranean world called the InBetween and that she was not human; she was paranormal. If only she could stuff the Pandora's horror known as 'mommy' back in the box.

Taryn dropped the curtain and spun away from the window, pressing her back against the wall. She reached for a place of calm, but serenity was closed and locked to her.

"Come on. Get a grip."

Taryn peeked outside again. Circe waved and blew a kiss. The window vibrated as if she'd been able to move it from across the tarmac.

Taryn was pressing her palm against the glass to still it when pain exploded behind her eyes, accompanied by a tinny screech. She tried to remove her hand from the pane but it was stuck fast, as if it were glued to the glass. She planted one foot against the wall and pulled. No luck.

"Taryn…" The raspy whisper echoed in her head. *"Look at me."*

"No!"

The screech increased. Blood flooded her mouth and flowed down the back of her throat.

"Look at me, my child. I have so much to teach you, to give you. The world is yours if you come to me."

Taryn fought against the pull of Circe's words, but her will wasn't strong enough. She raised her head and looked out.

Circe waved at Taryn then beckoned someone forward. Two Creepers appeared, their hands gripping the arms of a hooded captive. Tall and skeletal, with jet-black skin that shimmered with iridescent cobalt blue, dark green and dark purple, the chameleon-like creatures stopped next to Circe. She waved a hand and the prisoner's hood slipped off revealing short, red hair and a fierce, *you're-so-dead* stare.

Taryn's hand slipped free and her heart flopped in her chest.

She pressed her face against the glass. "Abella!"

Libra grabbed her shoulders from behind. "Taryn!"

"Circe has Abella."

He eased his grip. "What are you talking about?"

Her hands dropped from the glass, her palms icy cold and her fingertips numb. "There, under the light."

"I don't see anything."

Taryn glanced at him. "They're right—"

She looked out the window, but the lot was empty save for a few sleet-covered cars.

She lunged for the door, ripped it open, and ran into the parking lot, the frozen raindrops stinging her exposed skin. The lamp light flickered as the wind whipped her hair; the frigid blast no competition for the chill inside her. No Circe, no Abella, and no Creepers.

She shook her head and searched the area for any evidence to prove she hadn't lost her mind. "I saw her. Here."

"Her who?"

Taryn spun around. Libra had followed her outside, nothing on but a towel.

"I—I don't—"

Libra sighed and walked back into the room.

Taryn rubbed her face and shivered. She looked back at the lamppost. What had just happened? Had she gone mad? With no evidence, no trail to follow, and a helluva chill battering her, there was nothing to do but return to the shelter and anonymity of the motel room. Taryn jogged inside and softly shut the door.

"I'll ask again. Her who?" Libra insisted.

"Circe."

"Out there?"

"Yes…with two Creepers…and Abella."

Silence flowed over her.

"Outside," Libra said quietly. "Are you sure?"

Taryn nodded.

"I didn't see anyone."

Taryn's gut was tied in knots. She sat on the bed and pawed through the women's clothes in one of the bags.

"What are you doing?"

"Wallet. I need my wallet so I can buy a burner cell and call Abella. See if she's okay."

Libra squatted in front of her and grabbed her hands to still them. "Stop. Take a breath. You know you can't reach her with a phone. A Hermes hawk would be needed and you can't just snap your fingers and have one wing its way over."

"Screw you," she snapped. Logic was not what she needed right now.

"Well, that definitely won't reach her, but it might make *you* feel better."

She looked up and blinked.

Mister Designer Clothes was naked save for a threadbare towel that only kind of covered his manly bits, and a smirk. His furred chest and arms were leaner than most of the other Zodiacs—like a swimmer versus a bodybuilder—but he was still ripped with muscle, his legs long and sleek, perfect for the slim suits and tailored clothes he favored. She focused on his abs, staring at the six-pack to stop herself from looking farther south.

Damn him—he had the body of a god.

Her hands itched to slap him…or hit him with an ugly stick. "You're not dressed."

He looked down. "Appears I'm not. As for leaving the room again, we aren't doing that until we're ready to rejoin your friends." He stood and offered her a hand. "Quick now, get yourself a shower. We need to sleep."

She ignored his hand and stood. "What about Abella?"

"Are you sure it was her?"

Taryn pictured Circe and the Creepers. The hood slipped off the captive's head. Short, red hair, yes. Fashion-model slim, yes. But her face…

She closed her eyes, trying to see the scene again, but the memory was blurred, like water was flowing over the features, obscuring them. She scrunched her face tighter, trying to push past the distortion.

Her breath exploded out of her and she sagged. "I don't know. I can't recall her face clearly now."

She wrapped her arms around her waist.

"Abella wasn't out there when I was standing behind you at the window. I don't think Circe was either; she just accessed your mind to make you think she was here with Abella. The most logical answer is she's messing with your mind. The question is, why?"

"She said she wanted me to join her, that she had things to teach me." Taryn ran her hands over her arms to rub the cold away. "I need sleep."

He sniffed delicately. "You need a shower."

She nailed him with a withering look.

He raised his hands in surrender and backed away, the towel riding low on his hips.

Damn and hell.

She pointed at the second bag of clothes and headed for the bathroom. "You don't like the gypsy clothes? Now you have a choice."

She heard the crinkle of the plastic bag, then a deep grumble.

"Wait—" he called out.

"I've had it with the complaints. And the insults." Taryn threw up a hand, her back to him. "I don't want to hear any more."

Silence—finally.

She slammed the door, stripped, and stepped under the water. "Libra!"

15

"FOR GOD'S SAKE, SIT still, you big baby," Taryn demanded, her hands blue from the healing clay Solange had given her to treat Libra's wounds. "The Corvus warriors did a number on you."

She shifted positions to appease her knees; kneeling before him wasn't comfortable physically or mentally—too damn much like worshipping at his feet.

"Do you have to press so hard? If I'd wanted to be tortured, I'd have stayed in that cell."

She dabbed the clay on the cuts and abrasions on his face, disturbed in no small measure by the rasp of his stubble on her fingertips. Seriously, no man had a right to be this sexy, clean-shaven or not. If only his personality wasn't as grating.

"If you want to heal, I do." She rubbed a dab of blue on his split lips then pulled back and closed the small pot. "So buck up; it's about to get worse."

She rifled through the basket of miracle balms and creams and potions until she found the salve for bruises. They'd returned to the gypsy camp yesterday and after a short night of tossing and turning, they'd hit the road for a very long day. This was the first time Libra had allowed Taryn to minister to his wounds.

"Are we done?" Libra asked. He started to stand.

She placed a hand on his chest and pushed him back on the bed. "Nope, not until I put this goop on your bruises."

"Which ones? I'm covered in them."

Taryn bit the inside of her cheek, desperate not to laugh. He looked like a petulant, little boy who'd skinned his knee, with a requisite lock of chestnut hair falling over his forehead. She itched to use her fingers to comb it back into place, but the man was so prickly he'd probably complain that she had no idea how to fix his 'coif.' That thought sobered up her momentary levity.

Taryn sighed and pursed her lips. "All of them. I need you on your game, so strip."

Libra stared at her for a moment, his expression thunderous...until it wasn't. His lips twitched as he stood.

This does not bode well.

He reached for the hem of the tee shirt she'd bought him and lifted it, refusing to look away, daring her to watch. He pulled the tee over his head, baring his chest and belly to the sunlight streaming inside the caravan.

Oh, good god.

Libra pulled his arms out of the tee, trying hard not to wince, but Taryn caught the pain in his eyes, the slight grimace he couldn't completely hide. The shirt dropped to the floor. He stopped there as if waiting for some maidenly objection, but she'd be damned before she'd admit that she was nearly breathless at the sight of him.

Damn pesky libido.

Taryn swallowed hard but rolled her eyes to give him the impression she was bored by his peacockish display. Anything but the truth—if he'd been a Chippendale dancer, she'd have put all of her dollar bills in his thong.

"Don't stop there. I doubt the Corvus warriors spared you from the waist down."

His perfectly plucked eyebrows rose high.

The gauntlet had been thrown...

He stood and reached for the waistband of his jeans.

…and he was accepting her challenge.

He pushed the button out of the hole then lowered the zipper. With the smallest wriggle, the jeans slid over his hips and fell to the floor, leaving only black boxer briefs that did nothing to hide what was, in theory, supposed to be hidden.

Taryn squared her shoulders and stood to get away from his line-of-sight bulge. Her sole job was to get him battle-ready, in case this mission involved a battle. Leering at him might make her happy for the moment, but it wasn't helpful. She opened the pot and dipped two fingers in the goop.

She stopped when she looked past the pretty and saw his bruised and battered chest. "Jesus, Mary, and Joseph, they did a number on you."

"They tried."

Taryn walked around to his back and gasped. Black and blue and red streaks covered his skin like a painted canvas of pain. Her eyes watered but she refused to let any tears fall. It wouldn't help him, and it would humiliate them both, so she put a kibosh on her sympathy and, with great care, she applied the salve, starting at his neck and working down to his waist.

She didn't speak; neither did Libra. Only the occasional gasp from him and grunt of apology from her punctuated the silence. She finished his sides then walked around to his chest, concentrating as she slathered it.

She kneeled again to study his legs. "They didn't leave any unmarked skin, did they?"

Libra remained silent.

"Will you tell me about your power?" she asked as she ignored his groin, concentrating so hard on everything but that interesting vista that she saw his muscles jerk in reaction to her question.

Yep, a sensitive subject.

He reached down, took the pot from her, and helped her rise. "Go. I'll finish this."

Taryn studied his hard eyes, his implacable expression. There was far more steel in this man than she'd ever suspected. So who was he, really? A ridiculous, narcissistic clotheshorse or…what?

Could he have depths he never allowed anyone to see? And if so, why hide them? She had half a mind to ignore his request and demand answers, but her gut insisted she yield.

Taryn nodded. "Of course."

She gathered his shirt and jeans then opened the caravan door.

"Don't worry about washing those rags; just throw them away," Libra called out after her.

She slammed the door and paused at the base of the caravan steps to take a deep breath.

Odious man.

Before she could descend into a mental litany of his faults, the bustle of the camp distracted her. Thick, gray clouds had rolled in, muting the bright colors of the women's skirts and the men's waist sashes. Laughter rang through the group as they set up a fire pit. The horses, known as Gypsy Vanners, bobbed their great heads and pawed at the ground as children brought them a hot mash to offset the cold.

There was peace to be found among these people; peace was what had drawn Taryn to them many years before.

Solange caught her eye and waved Taryn over. "Come, child, the fire has been started. I need to warm my old bones and I suspect you have questions for me."

Taryn worked her way through the bustling people and sat next to the old woman, Libra's clothes wadded up in her lap.

"You want me to have those clothes washed? They're a mite dirty."

"I might as well throw them in the fire as far as GQ is concerned," Taryn groused, though her heart wasn't in it.

"I don't know what GQ stands for, but I don't think it to be a compliment."

Taryn chuckled. "No, it's not a compliment."

Solange took the clothes from Taryn and laid them on the ground.

She took one of Taryn's hands and squeezed. "You want to know who we are."

"Yes."

"Where should I start?"

Libra interrupted them. "Why don't you start by explaining what you really are and why you befriended Taryn, a human?"

He took a seat across from the women, held his hands to the flames, and waited, one eyebrow raised. He was clothed in another pair of used jeans, an orange Halloween tee shirt with a vampire bat and the words 'Bite Me' printed on it, and a black, down jacket.

Taryn looked at Solange and waited.

The old woman sighed. "We knew from the moment we met you that you weren't human. You may have looked the part, but you radiated energy not of this world." She looked at Libra. "We didn't tell her about the paranormal world because she wouldn't have believed us, and because…she was free of her legacy. Taryn could live as a human and never have to know about us."

"But you kept coming into my life," Taryn said. "Why?"

Solange stroked her cheek with the back of her fingers. "There were whispers. Rumors that someone was searching for Circe. I wanted to make sure you were okay and keep you off the radar of the paranorms. You and your sisters."

"That didn't work very well, did it?" Libra said.

"It didn't work, but she discovered her blood kin, and found strong friends in the Zodiacs. You succeeded in giving her far more than the protection we failed to provide. Something infinitely more precious…a family."

16

A SHOUT RANG OUT ACROSS the camp. Three men and a young woman ran to Solange.

The woman dropped to her knees in front of the leader and bowed her head. "You must hide. There is a murder just beyond the woods."

Taryn jumped up. "A murder? Who? Are there police?"

The woman glanced up, a sneer marring her lovely face. "There are no humans, you ridiculous creature."

Solange rested a hand on the woman's shoulder and stood. "Quiet, granddaughter, no need for that. Come, you two. Let's get you covered up and check it out."

After donning robes and flipping the hoods over their heads, Taryn and Libra walked with Solange and her granddaughter through the thick copse that separated the camp from the country road closest to them. Men, women, and children stood just inside the line of trees staring at the forest on the other side of the tarmac.

Taryn peeked out from under the heavy hood and gasped. A wall of crows filled the trees, with more on the ground.

She backed into the crowd and put an arm out to stop Libra. "Crows."

He scanned left and right. "Shit."

"Do you think they were sent by the Corvus Wards?" Solange whispered.

Taryn nodded. "Most certainly."

"Your damn gut?" Libra said quietly.

She wanted to stomp on his toes for his snide tone. "Common sense and observation. The Corvus crows cluster in large groups like that."

"Everyone knows that."

"But what's not common knowledge is that Llewellyn bred crows for the king. Crows larger than normal with red eyes, not black." Satisfied when his jaw dropped, she pointed straight ahead. "That big bird over there is flashing some red."

Libra turned his back to the feathered blockade. "Suggestions?"

"Use your gifts to convince them to leave," Solange's granddaughter said.

"Gifts?" Taryn asked.

The girl hissed at Taryn, her rancor high, before turning to Solange. "Surely we can drop off the mamón and her lover and make our way. These two are nothing but trouble, and the Nox are waiting."

"Patience, little one, is not your strength."

"Neither is shirking our duty."

Solange stared at her blood kin, not saying a word until the younger woman lowered her head and backed away from her leader.

Solange shook her head. "You both have a tie to Gaia. You, Taryn, with your ability to feel ley lines, and you," she said, glancing at Libra, "with the gift of Aether or Nether, untapped as it is."

Libra's shoulders straightened and he exhaled, hard.

Taryn didn't need to look at him to feel the tension. Hell, the frigid day had just grown several degrees colder.

"Whatever ability I'm supposed to have isn't working. I've tried," she said to break the silence.

"It is inside you," Solange said. "Come with me." She backed away from the tree line until the crows were out of sight. "You too, Libra."

A few of the Sol women followed, leaving the men to watch the crows. They formed a circle around their leader, Taryn, and Libra, and raised their arms, placing their hands on the shoulders of the women on either side, forming a wall of cloth. The crows wouldn't be able to see them unless they were directly overhead.

Solange paced around the circle as if looking for something, then stopped at one spot and closed her eyes for a moment before taking a few steps to the right, then back.

Finally, she smiled. "Here."

She kicked aside the detritus of leaves and pine needles and exposed a narrow crack in the soil that ran alongside a large tree root.

Taryn leaned over and looked at the unremarkable tear in the dirt. "What is this?"

"Slip a hand inside it."

Taryn squinted at the crack and shook her head. "There's no telling what's inside. There could be a snake or bugs."

Her body shuddered at the thought of unknown creepy-crawlies on her skin.

Solange sighed. She lifted her gnarled cane and hit the back of Taryn's knees.

The sharp slap sent her to the ground, more out of surprise than force, only her hands keeping her from a humiliating faceplant.

"Here now," Libra groused at the old woman.

"She needs to do this," Solange countered.

"I'm fine. No need to rush to my defense," Taryn said.

Libra snorted. "I'm not defending you. Just wanted her to know that if she tries that with me, I'll break that stick in half."

Solange cackled. "Bluster. That's a great start."

Taryn had no idea what the old woman thought was starting, but right now, she didn't care enough to ask. "You want me to stick a hand in there. Then what?"

"You'll know."

Taryn made a fist with her left hand before opening it and sliding her fingers inside the crack. "Yeah, you'll know too when I throw the bugs in your face."

Tiny roots tickled her skin; no bugs or snakes…yet. She kept reaching until her palm disappeared. The soil was so icy her fingertips were already numb and stiff. Her wrist disappeared, yet the crack kept going. She stretched out face down on the ground. She wiggled her fingers. In the few inches from her palm to her wrist, the soil had warmed; she could feel her fingers again. They flexed, brushing the wall of the crack. A tingle shot up her arm.

She gasped as it exploded in her chest and behind her eyes. "What is this?"

Solange reached out an arm. One of the women broke rank, the others shuffling in closer to close the gap; she helped the old woman to the ground next to Taryn.

"It is a ley line, child, deep and thick and pure. Out here, there is less interference from the human world, nothing to prevent you from reaching inside Gaia, from tapping into her power."

"Solange. Stop this now," Libra demanded. "There's nothing to be gained by exposing Taryn to Gaia. She's not ready."

Taryn rolled her head to one side and nailed him with a glare. "You refused to help me, so you have no right to weigh in."

He crouched down. "I'm trying to help you now. You don't want to get Gaia's attention; she's hungry to be heard."

"Back off, Zodiac," she threw at him before turning her attention back to Solange. "It tingles, like a nerve that's been struck."

She heard Libra stand and move away, muttering under his breath. What did he expect? That she'd give up because he refused to help her?

"That is what a ley line is. Gaia's nervous system interlaced throughout the planet. You can tap into that energy and manipulate it."

"I don't know how."

"Close your eyes and stretch your arm as deep as you can. Let the energy pull you in. Relax into it. Yes?"

Taryn exhaled, closed her eyes, and pushed her arm as far as it would go. A riotous shades of blue exploded behind her eyes, sparkling, flowing, just as a warm flood of energy filled her body. She struggled to catch her breath. The sounds of the earth, so common she hadn't noticed them until they were gone, were replaced by a humming sound.

From a distance, a distorted voice whispered, "Picture the crows gone and you will make it happen."

Taryn tried to focus her thoughts, tried to see the crows that threatened to betray the camp's location, but the hypnotic humming shifted into a soft song. There were no words, just discordant notes that wound their way through her body and settled in her head, lulling her inward. Like a siren song, it beckoned her to linger and sucked at her body, loosening bone and muscle and sinew, eager for her to stay.

Gaia.

The goddess was singing to her, calling her home.

"Taryn!" a voice cried in the distance.

Male, female, she couldn't tell. She was floating with the current now, her presence an infinitesimal neural impulse among billions, not knowing where she was heading, cocooned in warmth and peace. She was lost in space and time, no fear or feeling of loss for the life she was leaving behind. Becoming one with Gaia was her only need, a craving that increased as she raced along the ley line.

She jerked to a stop. "No!"

She flailed and kicked but the pain increased, her right hand in agony from the cold and pressure. The streams of blue pushed past her, flowing, flowing, as she began to go backward against the tide. She clawed with her left hand, spreading her legs to brace against the force, but the ley line was too wide, too fluid; there was no purchase to be found.

"Taryn!" a loud, male voice thundered.

The blue stream disappeared with a snap and she was left floating in darkness, an inky black with no relief, no up or down or sideways. Her stomach turned; she gagged and heaved, but before she could empty her stomach, light rushed at her. An image slammed into her, a room that she could see but not touch. She floated high, near the ceiling, above the fire in the huge hearth and looked for clues. Clothes were strewn over a bench at the end of the bed—the attire of a young boy—and shoes were tipped over on their sides as if thrown off in haste. A fencing rapier leaned against the large hearth. Books and a collection of old toys were housed haphazardly on shelves over a desk.

Before she could suss out more, the bedroom door slammed open and a tall, slender boy came tripping in. He caught a toe on the throw rug and was sent sprawling onto his belly with a *thud* and a groan. His pants were dirty; his upper body was bare save for the thick, red lines crisscrossing his back and chest. He rolled onto his side and skittered away from the red-faced woman who stalked him.

"We're not done until I say we're done." She raised the long crop in her hand. "You see this blood?" She gestured to the front of her long dressing robe. "This is your fault."

The boy hit his head on the nightstand and raised an arm to block her blow. "Please, no more, mother."

The glow from the fire spotlighted the terror on his young face. Tears traced the angles of his sharp cheekbones and square jaw, stark, heartbreaking. But it was the lock of chestnut hair that fell over his forehead above his hazel eyes that made her gasp.

Libra.

Rage slammed into her—a thick, hot amalgam of dark emotions filling her until she choked. "No!"

The little boy Libra turned his head and looked right at her. No surprise, no fear, his mother forgotten.

"Taryn," he said. "The crows."

The memory of the Corvus Ward crows began to eat at the vision of Libra. She reached for him, desperate to stay, to help him, but the crows crowded him out until they were all that filled her mind's eye. She turned her focus on them and screamed.

17

LIBRA DROPPED TO THE ground next to Taryn. "Damn you, she wasn't ready for this."

"Use your Gaia-given power to reach her. Hurry, before she gets swept away," Solange hissed.

"No."

"I pushed her too deep, but you can help her."

"I can't."

She stepped closer to him. "It is untapped, unreleased, but it is there. Use it."

"You help her," he snapped back.

"I can't."

"You sent her under with no way to help her get out?"

Solange studied him for a moment then crossed her arms. "I have you."

Son of a bitch.

He couldn't let Taryn get lost to Gaia, but he hated being backed into a corner.

The moment she was free, he'd beeline it to the nearest computer, find that blasted building, and put the Sol and Taryn in his rearview.

He snarled at the old woman then gripped Taryn's free hand and pulled. "Taryn!"

Her body vibrated with energy. A blue glow crept up her arm then covered her body before crawling up his arms. In seconds, they were enveloped in blue, deep in Gaia's grip.

The forest disappeared. He was thrown into a black void for a moment, then, in a blink, he was falling. He landed hard on his side, the thick rug under him sparing him a full measure of hurt but still sending hot, shooting pains down his back and chest. His breath hitched and he looked past the bed to the door, bands of fear tightening into terror.

Aubrianna appeared in the doorway, a crop in her hand, the firelight painting her twisted face a flickering, hellfire red.

She advanced on him. "We're not done until I say we're done." She raised the long crop in her hand. "You see this blood?" She gestured to the front of her long gown. "This is your fault."

What was this? How could this be happening? He was caught in a memory of one of the many horrible nights that Aubrianna has chosen to take her rage out on him.

Libra hit his head on the nightstand and raised an arm to block her blow. "Please, no more, mother."

A familiar voice screamed, "No!"

He turned his head. It was Taryn. She was in the memory with him, floating near the hearth, her expression a mix of horror and fury and pity. The memory sucked at him, pulling him deeper into the fear and pain, but he bucked against it. If he didn't stop this and get her out, they would both be lost.

"Taryn. The crows."

She blinked as if lost, unsure where she was, or how important it was that she fight for their lives. She reached out her hands…

His childhood room disappeared and was replaced by the forest and the road and the crows.

…Taryn turned her head in the direction of the crows, opened her mouth, and screamed.

Like the shimmy of hot air rising off tarmac in the summer, vibrating blue rushed out of her mouth in an unnatural torrent that went on for what seemed like minutes. The blue spread wide and high, forming a wall of energy as far as he could see.

Taryn stopped exhaling and took a deep breath. She raised her left hand, squeezed Libra's hands with her right, then shoved the wall toward the crows. As if the energy were solid, it hit the birds and sent them tumbling out of the trees and along the ground. Their cries were deafening, but Libra refused to release Taryn's hand to cover his ears, unsure if this was real or if they were in a shared fugue state that could cause them harm if he let go.

The crows flapped and screeched their alarm but, to a bird, they flew away.

Taryn sagged to the ground but Libra held on; the blue glow still covered their bodies. They were still in thrall to Gaia's power and he had no idea how to get out. He dropped to his knees and pulled Taryn into his chest. She moaned and her body shook as she began to cry.

"No. Don't cry. We're okay."

He tried smoothing her wild curls but they just sprung back, tickling his nose. He looked around for Solange but the forest was empty.

Even the cold didn't touch him.

His breath hitched. No cold. Shit. Where the hell were they? Caught in a memory, a wish? He slipped an arm under Taryn's legs and back and pulled, but he couldn't lift her off the ground. He shifted her weight, spread his feet farther apart, and tried again, but it was as if she were stuck. He lowered her to the ground and searched to see if her foot was caught under a root or her clothes in a vine.

That was when he saw the problem. Her left arm was still caught in the crack in the ground. But he'd just seen her use it to send the crows away. How could it be still caught? He wrapped his hands around her arm and pulled gently, then more firmly.

Taryn moaned, releasing more blue from her mouth, and sagged into the forest floor.

He pulled on her arm again, but the action made her body sink farther into the ground, as though it were quicksand.

Taryn gasped and stopped moving.

Gaia was going to take her if he didn't figure out how to stop it. He dug at the crack, ripping his nails, but he couldn't feel anything but the weight of his growing dread.

Taryn exhaled, the sound soft and finite, a release.

He checked her breathing. Nothing.

He felt for a pulse but it was faint, thready. "Damn it, woman, don't stop fighting now."

He braced his feet against the root and reached down for her wrist. He pulled as hard as he could, more afraid for her life than the probable broken bones he'd cause, but she sank deeper, until all that was left above ground was her upper body.

He felt for the pulse in her neck again, but this time it was gone—her heart had stopped. Gaia's blue tinge had faded, replaced by the blue of Taryn's failing body.

"No!" Libra slammed his fists against the ground. "Gaia! You bitch! You release her; bring her back." He raised his hands above his head and plunged them down into the crack as deep as he could go until they pierced the ley line. "You wanna feel pain? I'll show you what pain really feels like."

He grabbed and clawed at the blue nerve, gouging out chunks and throwing them across the forest. Over and over, blind to anything but ripping and tearing at the goddess, he railed and screamed and demanded until exhaustion stopped him.

Libra fell on his side and heaved to fill his lungs. He reached out and squeezed Taryn's arm.

"Please," he implored, his voice a whisper.

Taryn bucked and gasped, sucking in a deep breath. He curled his body around hers to warm her and closed his eyes.

Several hands touched him, plucking at his clothes.

"What?"

He opened his eyes and held up an arm in defense when Solange's face came into focus.

"Well, boy, it took you long enough."

"What happened?"

"Thought we lost you two, but no."

"The crows?"

"Gone, and I doubt they'll come back. It was a sight."

He released Taryn to the women and struggled to his feet. "I thought we were dead. Taryn was dead."

Solange nodded. "You must have done something right."

"Yeah, I bitched Gaia out and ripped her several new ones."

Solange smiled and patted his cheek. "That's not what brought you back. Think."

He looked at her wizened face, his mind blank for a moment before he recalled his last word.

Please.

Could such a simple word have worked? Was it possible Gaia had really heard him and granted them freedom from her thrall, saving their lives? No, that wasn't it, couldn't be it. The primordial goddess was resolute, even brutal, in her treatment of the humans and paranorms inhabiting the world that was the embodiment of her very being. Entreaties ignored; sacrifices scoffed at. No way in hell would he ever accept any gift from such a cold, implacable force—no, never. Just the memory of this brush with Gaia would haunt him for years.

But even as the thought struck him, a small voice tickled the recesses of his mind. Which would haunt him more—being in Gaia's grip or watching Taryn die?

To his dismay, he had no answer.

* * *

The Corvus Ward king roared and clawed at his eyes. Blood ran freely down his face, not of his own doing but from the damage inflicted on the red-eyed crow by the raven-haired bitch with Libra. Heavy boots ran to him and circled until he was protected from attack.

"No one is here, you dolts." He swatted at the proffered hand of his second-in-command. "Get me Aubrianna. Now!"

His second and two other warriors left the throne room at a run; the others remained on alert around him as he rose to his feet and sagged into the ornate throne.

A wave of blue energy had sent his crow tumbling to the ground. The spell that allowed him to see through the bird's eyes had acted as a conduit for the wave.

His vision returned, but blood still oozed out of the corners of his burning eyes.

Thankfully for his people, none had seen the spectacle or heads would be rolling. Weakness was never tolerated in his species; nothing sparked slaughter like humiliation. He studied the backs of his guards and wondered if their heads would need to be parted from their necks. Before he could decide whether to spill their blood, a woman screeched just outside the double doors. They burst open and the guards marched a flailing Aubrianna to him.

"What is this?" he asked. "Why did I feel what my crow felt?"

Aubrianna wrenched her arms out of the guards' grip, her eyes wide, her smile wider as she leaned forward. "Tell me what you saw. Tell me everything."

The king wiped the blood from his face and scowled at her. "A woman stuck her arm into the earth, so deep she had to lie on the ground. Libra was with her."

"And?"

"She turned blue—"

"Glowing?"

"Yes, then—"

Aubrianna clapped her hands.

The king jumped up. "Enough, woman."

She nodded but still bounced on her toes.

"Libra grabbed her hand and he turned blue. Glowing," he added with a scowl to keep the woman's mouth shut. "They remained like that for minutes before he was able to pull her out of the ground. She turned to my crows and threw a wall of energy at them."

Aubrianna opened her mouth to say something but he cut her off. "Yes, blue and glowing. It knocked all of the crows out of the trees and I ended up bloody. Explain—while I'm in the mood to allow you to keep your head."

"This is much better than I hoped."

"My crows being knocked on their asses pleases you?"

"No. Libra. Gaia. He has gotten a taste of her power. More importantly, she has touched him, even if it was through that woman. She will be hungry for more, eager to bestow her gift on her proxy, so she can once again see the sunlight and feel the earth beneath her feet, let the water slip through her fingers. She knows she can feel alive again through him."

"How does that benefit me?"

Aubrianna stood tall and smoothed her wrinkled robes. "We want him to kill to become Gaia's agent. Now, Gaia will be pressing him to do the same. It'll be an assault on two fronts."

The king relaxed back in his throne. "And you have a plan to make sure it happens?"

"I do, but it entails me leaving here. I need to be in the human world for the next step."

He studied her smug expression, unease making him itch. Suspicion had served him well; it had kept him on this gnarled-wood throne for years, despite efforts by many to unseat him. But the counter-itch of ambition overruled his mistrust.

"You will go…"

She nodded, her lips twitching with a suppressed smile.

"…but I will have two of my guard go with you. For your safety, of course."

Her face remained unchanged, but the wrinkles around her eyes flattened to mere creases. She wasn't pleased, but he didn't give two nestlings for her feelings. She had every intention of betraying him; he had every intention of returning the favor.

Aubrianna curtsied. "Of course."

He snapped his fingers then pointed at two of his fiercest warriors. "Make sure the Os Mage Mother is never out of your sight. We wouldn't want anything to happen to her."

He waited until the men and Aubrianna had departed the throne room before snapping his fingers again. A skinny stripling of a male ran to the king and dropped to his knees before him.

"Are the messages written and the Hermes hawks rested?"

"Yes, sire."

"And what of the hawks of the Great Cavern?"

"The remaining birds are the oldest, slowest hawks, those who have been retired for some time. The hawks you have are the very best Lyon's mews had to offer. They will easily outfly the others." The boy raised his head and dared a look at the king. "But our birds must be released now."

"Then do it. I want the Zodiacs to be in the Great Cavern when I make my move."

The boy remained still, unmoving.

Smart. Someone has trained him well.

"You are dismissed."

The stripling jumped to his feet, bowed low, and ran out of the room.

The king rolled his shoulders and got a whiff of the stench of drying blood on his clothes and skin.

He rose and bellowed at his remaining guards. "Do I have to wait all day for someone to draw me a bath?"

18

LIBRA SLOWED THE VANNER gelding and brought him to a stop. The caravan rocked into place and he sagged. His fingers were frozen into rein-gripping talons, the deep ache punctuated with sharp stabs—just to make life interesting. Dark was falling; it was only minutes away. The snow that had started six hours ago had been merciless to anyone exposed; he'd ceased to feel his toes within fifteen minutes of those three hundred and sixty.

Give me a packed, economy-class plane ride sandwiched between screaming babies over this cold.

He pulled the handbrake, wrapped the reins around the handle, and looked around this next bit of forest Solange had chosen for camp. A blanket of white had touched everything, rendering the still-slumbering trees and vines and the dead-leaf-strewn ground pure, monochromatic.

He turned to the caravan door behind him. Taryn hadn't spoken to him since… the incident. Not a word. Of course, she'd slept most of the time, and, goddess help him, he was relieved to be able to avoid her. The flashback into his childhood had been enough of a horror show without having to talk about it—that was, if she remembered it. The not knowing gnawed at him—was she a witness to his humiliation, or just a figment of his Gaia-fueled nightmare?

He prayed it was the latter.

But as the hours had dragged by his embarrassment had lessened, replaced by gnawing resentment, then fury. The woman was a menace. Jumping into the unknown without regard for her safety or what it might cost those who tried to help her when it went to hell. The only reason he hadn't packed it in and abandoned her and the Sol was they were in the middle of nowhere. There were no towns large enough to either have a computer or any bandwidth for cell reception. And Solange had refused to give him a truck, claiming they would need it for a supply run when the snow slowed. So he was stuck with them for a while longer.

A thump sounded inside the van. Libra opened the door and stepped inside, his head lowered to keep from cracking it on the ornately painted arch.

Her spread legs bare, Taryn sat up, rubbing her rump.

"Fall out of bed?" Libra offered.

She flushed, pushing down the hem of her full-length, cotton slip. "Don't you knock?"

Libra bit back an angry retort. He wasn't even close to forgiving her for dragging him over the cliff, but snapping at her now wouldn't accomplish anything. She was irrational, irascible, impossible. If he wanted to get through to her, teach her anything, he needed to get her focused on their objective: finding the paranorm children. To do that, he needed to clamp down his irritation and power through this mission.

"You've been sleeping like the dead; how was I to know you'd hear a knock?"

"I'm awake now. What do you want?"

"We're camping for the night. Daylight will be gone," he looked at his bare wrist as if checking a watch, "in about five minutes."

Taryn looked around the space. "Where're my clothes?"

"They were filthy so Solange took them. I'm sure there are more in one of those drawers."

She opened the closest drawer, glanced at the clothes, then glanced at him before crossing her arms over her chest. "As sore as I am, I don't need a valet."

Libra smoothed the front of the hair shirt he'd been forced to wear. "Don't you mean lady's maid?"

She waved a hand in the air. "Well, you've certainly got the manners of a maid, but that doesn't mean I need your help."

They stared at each other, the seconds excruciating.

Taryn ran a hand through her hair then sighed, the gust of breath like a release of air out of a balloon: a loud noise followed by full-body deflation. "I haven't had a chance to thank you. Solange told me you saved my life."

Heat climbed up his neck and over his face. His usual response would have been a polite "*You're welcome,*" but the anger that had festered for hours, that he had only moments before decided wouldn't be constructive, bubbled over.

"What were you thinking? Sticking your hand into that ley line."

"Uh, scaring away the crows?"

"You weren't nearly ready, yet you jumped over the cliff. It was reckless and very nearly killed us both." He stepped closer and leaned down until their faces were inches apart. "And, just so we're clear…you did die."

Taryn recoiled. "I died? Solange didn't tell me that."

"The woman seems to be fond of omission. Yes, you died while we were in Gaia's clutches."

She swallowed hard. "I didn't know."

"What do you remember?"

He waited for her answer despite wanting to continue railing at her, the need to dump his dark emotions making him twitch. But, the need to know if she retained the memory of his beating overrode his rage, stealing his breath.

She looked away, studying the clothes in the drawer, a frown marring her gaunt face. "Nothing."

He sagged. He hadn't talked about his past with anyone; having a witness to his abuse, even in a memory, would be too much.

A weak shaft of dying sunlight pushed through a small crack in the curtains, illuminating the blue tinge to her skin. He stepped closer and reached up to cup her cheek, but she flinched away. An infinitesimal movement, but her rejection of his touch was obvious. He dropped his hand.

An awkward silence filled the van.

Taryn chose some clothes and pressed them against her chest. "I need to dress."

Thank the goddess; Taryn had given him the perfect excuse to vacate the caravan posthaste.

"I'll see if I can help set up camp," he said as he backed out.

"Libra?"

He stopped.

"I am sorry you were drawn in, that your life was put at risk. But I'm not sorry that I followed my instincts. That is who I am; risk of injury or even death won't change that."

It was all he could do not to growl. "Then you're on your own. I'll get you to the children, if they do exist, but then we part ways. I won't be party to your foolishness."

She opened her mouth to say something but he closed the door before she could speak.

The frigid gust took his breath away, but he welcomed the cold if it meant he could get away from the foreboding that sucked at him. The world had tilted for both of them, distilling their comfortable antagonism down to a bitter draught that he couldn't swallow. The sooner he got her to the children, the sooner he could leave her far behind. If the woman was determined to risk her life, it wasn't his place—or his desire—to stop her.

"*You don't mean that,*" a woman's voice whispered in his ear.

He whirled around, but no one was near him. He scrubbed his face with his hands then shook his head. Sleep…he must get some sleep.

He wound his way through the forming camp until he found Solange.

"Taryn is awake," he said with none of his normal polite preamble.

"The princess finally stirs," the leader's granddaughter groused.

"Hush, child," the old woman ordered.

"I need to unharness my horse," he stammered, pointing at the Vanner. "I think she's unsettled by what happened. Will you go to her?"

"My grandmother has better things to do than tend to your woman."

"Taryn isn't 'my woman.'"

Solange raised a hand to silence the girl. "Your horse can be ill-tempered. Are you willing to risk a stomp or a kick?"

"Oh, yes."

Libra raised his hands and backed away, eager to divest himself of women in general and Taryn in particular. He needed a hot shower, a soft bed, and his even softer, very expensive, tailored clothes to reclaim his equilibrium.

Tomorrow. He would demand they head to the closest library with a computer. He didn't care if it was a damn Macintosh 128k and slow as hell, as long as he could find the children and go about his merry with Taryn in the rearview.

19

TARYN BUTTONED THE FLANNEL shirt that completed her ensemble before slipping on a ratty but thick, lime-green and brown cardigan. Serviceable was the word of the day, gaudy—and even for her this combo was beyond the pale—be damned. She busied herself making the bed and tidying the caravan, anything to keep her mind off the memory of Libra and Aubrianna and the crows—and the unending darkness that had gobbled her up.

She'd lied to Libra, in part to spare him embarrassment, but also to hide her fear. She remembered everything. The pull of Gaia's power, the need to stay with her, swimming in the energy and euphoria—the thrall had been all-consuming. And knowing she'd died was the crap icing on the cake. For the second time in days—after a lifetime of militant surety—her confidence was shaken to the core. Even her ever-faithful gut had fled, leaving her floundering for direction.

She fisted her hands; it was the only way to stop the shaking. In the short time she'd known GQ, she'd never once thought she'd feel sorry for the popinjay. Stiff, formal, arrogant—he was insufferable—and she'd assumed he'd been raised to feel superior to everyone around him. But the vivid memory she'd been thrust into told a different, horrifying story, one that was way too familiar.

She may not have suffered abuse from a parent, but she and Persephone and Abella had all suffered at the hands of the foster system. It wasn't so much physical abuse as it was the benign neglect—just as painful in its own way. The few adults who had been kind had been so swamped with children who had greater needs than hers that Taryn had stepped out of the way, ignoring her own hunger for affection for the sake of the other kids.

Not that she had been a thorough altruist; she had had her needs met by her friends, and by her study of herbal medicine. The intersection of the arcane and the modern, magic and medicine, had always fascinated her, yet she had never imagined that there was a paranormal world hidden beneath her feet. If only her place in the worlds she now straddled would be revealed.

She'd counted on connecting with the ley line system, perfecting her skills so she could be what the Great Cavern, and maybe even the entire InBetween, needed most: a defense system. Now…there was no way she would connect with Gaia again. She didn't have enough control, and after what had happened, Libra would never help her gain the control she needed to survive another attempt.

Her hands fisted in the down pillow. Hell. Who was she kidding? Like an addict, she might be scared shitless, but she hungered for a repeat. It was as simple as that—and as complicated.

She unfolded Candace's drawing. She couldn't connect with Gaia again, but without that connection, she'd never be able to find and use the ley lines, not as well as the InBetween needed. Outside of ley lines, the only other contribution she could make was to find the children—all of them—and get them back to their families. It wasn't a magical skill, but it would give more back to the paranorm world than reading ley lines ever could.

A soft knock made her jump. "Yes?"

Solange opened the back door and climbed the steps. "I wanted to see how you are faring."

"Libra sent you."

"He volunteered to take care of the horse instead of coming back here. Did something happen while you two were with Gaia?"

"I don't remember anything."

The old woman walked over to Taryn and grabbed her chin, staring into her eyes. "You are lying."

Taryn grit her teeth and kept her mouth shut.

"I sent you into the ley line. It was too deep; you weren't ready."

Taryn stiffened, the hollow in her chest filled with a thick, dark stew of fear. "Killing me was too deep?"

"I didn't think Gaia would try to claim you. I am sorry."

The humble apology shut Taryn down. Solange had always been kind to her; the woman didn't deserve her ire. "As long as I don't have to do that again."

Solange squeezed her shoulder. "Yes, well, despite the dying part, I thought you and Libra did splendidly. The two of you make a great team."

A great team? Taryn's stomach fell into a bottomless pit of longing, pulling tears out of her eyes and dragging them down her cheeks. If only…

If only? Where the hell has this come from?

"Excuse me." Libra stood in the doorway, one hand gripping his upper arm. "I think I'm going to need some of that salve for bruises. And disinfectant." He removed his hand and showed Solange the torn sleeves of his coat and shirt; angry, red teeth marks formed a broken circle in the skin over his deltoid. "That beast is a bastard."

Solange cocked her head and smiled. "Of course, I'll be back."

Libra looked at Taryn, clearly saw the tears in her eyes, and froze. "I'll go with you."

Taryn watched him practically leap out of the caravan to get away. How much had he heard? How much had he seen in her eyes? Could he see her pain? How lonely she was?

"*Splendidly,*" Solange had said. "*A great team.*" *Gah. What a mess.*

Taryn swiped at the tears and heaved a huge sigh.

Sleet clattered against the roof, startling her. Men's voices called out and horses whinnied, the easy pace of the camp set-up changing. She opened the door and climbed down the stairs, her eyes drawn unbidden to Libra's tall form.

He was standing in the middle of the wagons, his mouth open as he watched several new vans roll in. Pulled by elegant, black Friesians instead of Vanners, their wooden sides were painted in cobalt blue and black, and dotted with stars and constellations.

Solange threw her arms in the air, oblivious to the sleet and cold, and greeted the arrivals like old friends.

Taryn walked up to Libra. "Who?"

"Not a clue."

Before her courage failed her, she blurted out quietly, "We need to talk."

He remained silent, staring at the newcomers as the two camps merged.

She sighed and he glanced down at her. "What? Did you say something?"

Taryn shook her head. They did need to talk, but he seemed as reluctant to go there as she was. They could find time later. Or, perhaps, by then, there'd be no need.

20

LIBRA WALKED AWAY FROM Taryn as fast as he could, hopefully without making it too obvious. He'd heard the end of the conversation between her and Solange. *The two of you make a great team.* The line rang in his ears even now. In the moment, he'd been horrified at the thought of them being together in any capacity—this venture was proving to be trying enough—so he had interrupted to avoid hearing what Taryn's response might be before it was released into the universe, or got stuck in his mind.

But as much as he wanted to ignore the idea, or never admit the possibility, he couldn't help but think it to be true. He, the Zodiac who never teamed up with anyone, the male so vastly different from the others as to be an aberration among the aberrant, had found his adrenaline kicking in at the old woman's words. Maybe even the stray desire to have someone in his life who understood the pull of Gaia, and why it terrified him. He stopped and turned back to Taryn, his impulse to return to her and actually talk about what had happened between them overriding his embarrassment, until he saw her laughing…at him.

She pointed at his pants.

He looked down but didn't see anything wrong. He hadn't peed himself and his zipper wasn't down; nothing was hanging out. He reached around. There was a tear in the worn material of the seat and his boxer briefs. His butt was intact, but on display. Goddess damned horse had ripped a hole out of his pants and he hadn't even felt it. Hands covering the hole, he scowled at Taryn and strode to the caravan to change, his interest in the newcomers—and the pursuit of a conversation with Taryn—forgotten.

What the hell had he been thinking? A good team? Never.

* * *

Lyon slouched in his chair, the short message from the Corvus Ward king harsh and breathtaking.

Libra is gone. This is war.

The huge cavern was empty for a change, save for three trolls sitting on the edge of the hole in the center, their thick legs dangling into the dark. The few paranorms who had chosen to make the Great Cavern their home—choosing to follow the Zodiacs over their own kind—had left. They'd scattered after the disastrous meeting with the king.

Now, the small amount of safety Lyon had been able to offer those who remained had evaporated with six little words. A rush of heat left him flushed; perspiration dampened his back and armpits. His muscles jerked with the need to find someone to pummel. The days of fighting in the death-pit matches—the simple act of slamming his fists into flesh, of reveling in the recoil of his opponent's muscle and skin and the crunch of their bone—had narrowed his world to a satisfying clarity. He'd hated the brutality, but damn if it hadn't been cleansing.

"What is it?" Persephone said behind him.

Lyon's heart skipped a beat—his inamorata always had that effect on him, but his fears for the Great Cavern had him too distracted to offer her the pretty words that normally tripped off his tongue without thought. "Libra escaped the Corvus Wards."

"Oh."

His breath caught in his throat. He didn't turn to look at her—he didn't need to see her face to know she'd interfered. The brevity of her response told the tale.

"What did you do?"

She stepped in front of him and raised her chin, her face set in a pleasant smile that didn't quite reach her eyes. "I did what needed to be done."

"Taryn."

"Yes."

Lyon lifted the letter. "Was it worth starting a war?"

Her pale purple eyes scanned the message; her face blanched.

"Was it, my love? Because the Corvus Ward king is deadly serious. They don't joke…no sense of humor."

Her only movement was the thinning of her lips. "I did what I believed to be right."

Lyon had just opened his mouth to demand more answers when Abella walked up.

"You called?" she asked, looking from Lyon to Persephone. "Should I come back later?"

Lyon pushed off the arms of his chair and faced Persephone's half-sister. "Is the house in Texas finished?"

Abella frowned. "Finished enough, despite the vandalism."

"I have two jobs for you. One, I need you to go do what you do best. Play poker. Find the richest sons of bitches out there, take them for everything they've got, and when they're screaming for mercy, you make them a bargain: their money back in exchange for a debt to us, to be called in at any time."

Abella snorted. "Let them walk away from the table with their money? Not bloody likely."

Lyon stiffened. "I'm not finished. Before you do this, I need you to take the children to Texas."

Persephone stepped closer to him. "What are you doing?"

Lyon grit his teeth until he could swallow back the words he would regret and find new ones. "What I believe to be right."

"You can't take them from me."

"I'm not. You're going with them."

"And what will you be doing?"

"I'll be emptying out the Great Cavern."

Abella raised a hand. "Uh, I don't think I have a full hand here. Care to elaborate?"

Lyon handed the note to her without breaking eye contact with Persephone.

Abella read the declaration of war. "Shit. Me."

"You'd let the king take the Great Cavern without a fight?" Persephone asked.

He stepped up to his mate and looked down at her. "You helped Taryn free Libra. What did you think would happen?"

"I—"

"You sent Taryn to free Libra? Are you mad?" Abella groaned. "They'll kill each other."

"I had to. Candace drew a building with children in the windows, paranorm children. I gave it to Taryn. Libra can help her..." Persephone's defense petered out.

Lyon looked away from her. "Abella. Why are you still here?"

"Right. Children, poker, Texas. I'm on it." She trotted away, glancing over her shoulder, a worried look on her face.

Persephone gasped, her focus on a point behind him.

Lyon turned in time to see a doe fall through the concealment spell that shielded the hole in the Great Cavern roof from human view, the panicked animal's slender legs flailing. One of the trolls reached out and caught the terrified creature before she could drop into the hole in the floor that led to Hell. The huge, grayish-green creature pushed off the floor and stood at the edge of the hole. With a gentleness that belied its size and brutish manners, the troll pushed his fist through the spell in the cavern roof and released the doe back into the human world where it belonged.

"You have worked wonders with the trolls, my love." Lyon turned back to her. "But you have jeopardized us all."

She touched his arm. "If they find some of the paranorm children, maybe it will buy us time. Hold off the war."

"Ifs and maybes? It was a risk you had no right to take." He shook his head. "Get packed. I want you and the children gone from here before sunset."

She studied his face for a moment, probably looking for the hard lines to soften, but he wouldn't let her off the hook.

She turned and walked away, her shoulders hunched, her head down.

He hated being so cold, so rigid with her but he was afraid for her, for their children, and for the unborn child in her womb. He had to shield them from harm any way he could.

He rose and walked past the trolls. First, he would send Hermes hawks with a message for the Zodiacs, asking that they go to the new home in Texas and guard Persephone, his children, and any other paranorm women and children who sought shelter there.

Second, he would empty the dungeons. Leaving the prisoners behind would be a death sentence; he didn't need that on his conscience. The Great Cavern would be empty when the Corvus Ward warriors stormed inside, but the loss of this place didn't matter. The only thing that mattered was his family—his people. He would sacrifice all to protect them.

21

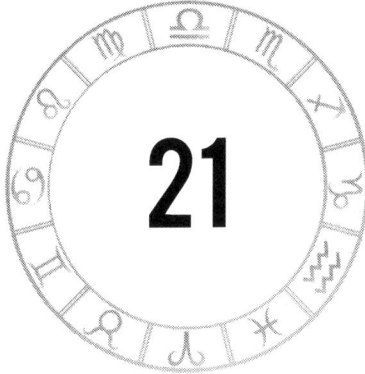

LIBRA FLOPPED ONTO HIS side for the umpteenth time, sighing as he adjusted his pallet of blankets. Horsehair, dander, and itchy wool poked and hived his skin even through the fake silk pajamas Taryn had found in the bargain bin at the shopping hell for used…everything. The marzipan on top of that misery was the embroidered name on the pocket.

"Bubba," he grumbled as he plucked at the thread. He rolled onto his back. "Goddess save me."

The fatigue of the past few days had been almost as torturous as the days in the cell. But at least the cell had been stationary. The car tires and shocks on the van couldn't adequately absorb all the jars and jolts. He was sure his joints would be permanently stiff and achy, an old man before his time. Even the Corvus warriors hadn't caused him this much pain.

He threw off the blanket and sat up. No use fighting it; since he wasn't going to get any sleep, he might as well start searching for the building Candace had drawn.

He pushed off the floor and stood, but the muscles in his lower back cramped when he tried to straighten. He rubbed the offended spot as he shuffled to the back of the van, making his way to the small, folding desk and even smaller stool. Pulling out the smartphone burner the newest arrivals to the camp had brought with them, a people called the Nox, he turned it on and opened the drawing while he waited to get a signal.

The Sol and the Nox had stopped deep inside a forest thick with trees and no sign of humans as far as he could see—no trails other than the lightly trodden paths used by wildlife to access the waterfall several yards from the camp. The old woman had picked the spot and stopped her van, declaring—to his great frustration—that they would be staying for a few days to attend to business, whatever that meant. Seriously mysterious bunch; he really needed to sit someone down and get more of their story.

Libra pushed aside the miniscule curtain that blocked the round window and peered into the darkness. Although nothing could compete with the deep dark of the InBetween or the beauty of its glowworm caves, the thick, remote forest under the new moon had created a black blanket of sky and earth, relieved only by a brilliant spray of stars.

He stared at them for so long they began to move. So slowly at first that he rubbed his eyes to clear them, sure that he was seeing things because of his exhaustion, but when he looked up again, the stars rotated counterclockwise. He swayed, mesmerized, lost to the rhythm of the circling stars. They gained speed until they disappeared, leaving only the cold, lonely black of space.

An itch started in his head, deep in his brain, an itch that turned into a pulsing ache. A pinpoint of blue light appeared in the center and grew larger until it eclipsed the sky. An image of the building Candace had drawn flashed once, starting an impossible slideshow of places he'd never trodden: a dirt road with the building in the distance, an asphalt road that he traveled in reverse, as if on a psychic road trip. The rural road turned into a highway, the highway into an interstate. He struggled to capture just one defining landmark per image but they kept coming so fast, hurtling him backward until nausea threatened. The interstate fell away, leaving the dark forest and the large circle of caravans. The last image was of him, his head back, looking at the sky through the round window.

The glowing blue winked out; the stars reappeared. Libra tilted to one side until he fell off the stool onto the floor, disoriented, everything spinning whether his eyes were open or closed. He breathed deep and exhaled, taking care not to engage his belly muscles in case it triggered an epic vomiting session. A second breath, a third, and his world righted itself. He gripped the edge of the table and pulled himself up until he could stand, his feet wide.

He looked at the phone's still-spinning wheel and shook his head. *Damn it, no more spinning.*

Despite recoiling from the phone, he hadn't missed the time. Fifteen minutes had passed, been lost to a waking sleep. He dropped onto the stool and looked for paper to write on. A small notepad and pen were tucked in a cubbyhole to the left of his head. Grabbing them, he flipped to the first blank page and scribbled what he could remember.

Finally, after four front-to-back pages, he sat back, closed his eyes, and allowed himself to analyze what had happened. Blue, glowing light—son of a bitch, could it be Gaia?

Had the goddess reached out to him a second time? If she had, why would she care whether he found the paranorm children or not? Legend had never painted her as anything but cold and harsh, a big-picture primordial who was more concerned with the planet that was her physical embodiment than the puny creatures that swarmed it like an ant mound.

He scrubbed his face with his hands, groaning with frustration, fatigue, and more than a little fear. He wanted to climb under the blanket and hide, his eyes closed so he couldn't receive anymore visions, but he was too restless, his ears picking up even the slightest sound, especially the blood *whooshing* through his ears. How Taryn slept with all the noise…

Libra heard a buzz, or maybe it started in his head. Darkness descended again, along with a wave of hot exhaustion. He tried to stand but fell to the floor.

* * *

Aubrianna circled the filthy, crouching Portend, stepping over the long, thick chain bolted to the stone basement wall at one end and wrapped around the waist of the captive woman at the other. "Well, did it work? Did you send him the message?"

"Yes, Libra saw the path."

Aubrianna stopped pacing and looked into the darkest corner of the space. The frigid air emanating from the inky depths was far colder than that in the rest of the cold-storage basement room. But the chill was bearable compared to the heavy weight of his presence—oppressively inhuman with a malevolent aura that had stolen her breath and frozen her heart. How low she had stooped to achieve her desires; whom else would she have to consort with to claim her legacy?

The man stepped into the candlelight, his suit rich, his walking stick honed from the black thighbone of a Creeper, the flat expression in his eyes telling his tale. At first glance, he looked like an affluent human male, but his eye color shifted from blue to green to brown to red as if he couldn't decide which color he preferred.

"I still don't understand why you're toying with him," the demon king said. "Why not show him the address?"

"I'm driving him, pushing him into a corner where he'll be trapped. But Libra is smart; if he figures out the game, he'll refuse to play."

"Why not compel him? I have witches who could bespell him."

"Were these the witches who gave you Circe's location?"

"After some convincing, yes. Regrettably, they don't know why the children have been taken or what is to become of them. That nugget—and the identity of those responsible for the reaping before Circe was revived—are yet to be discovered."

He accompanied this statement with a grin and a thousand-yard stare, as if contemplating the lengths he'd go to squeeze the information out of the unfortunate person privy to it.

"Why don't *you* compel him?" Aubrianna countered. "He has a piece of your soul attached to his; surely that means you could force him. Or, for that matter, why not go after Circe yourself? Take her out and stop whatever she's planning."

His smirk flattened into a thin line; his eyes hardened. "That's not how it works. First, my soul was assimilated with his, making it much harder for me to even connect with him—it's the same with practically all of the Zodiacs. The only Zodiac left who isn't assimilated is Scorpio, but he's proving to be quite resistant to my overtures. As for Circe, though I'm loath to admit it, she's a cunning minx. She isn't working alone; we must find out whom she has aligned herself with. Is it the old ones? Have they found a way to reach out from their banishment to Hades to influence the affairs in the InBetween? Or is it the human world…or both? Until I know with certainty, I must wait for her plans to ripen."

"Then we both must wait. Libra can't be tortured into becoming the agent; the Corvus Wards' heavy-handed approach has proven that. And his decision to kill must be his own in order for Gaia to accept him. We can drive him to that decision, but we can't make him kill."

Asmodeus dipped his head in her direction. "Then my Stryx are the perfect solution. Their attack will most certainly be blamed on the witches—their long and well-known association will ensure that—perhaps it will even be thought the work of Circe herself."

"Stryx? How did you find one?"

"Not one, many. Demons weren't the only ones who ascended from Hell. The Stryx who were freed answer to me now, not the witches." He gripped the Portend's chin and squeezed, smiling when she cried out. He threw his head back and groaned. "Nothing sweeter than pain. Really. I can't get enough of it."

Aubrianna wanted to tell him to stop, make him leave the woman alone, but she had made a bargain with the demon king, just as she had with the Corvus Ward king. One of these men would get her what she wanted, and when she had Gaia's power, every humiliation would be worth it. With that power, she could wipe out everyone who'd disrespected her position, discounted her will, and disparaged her failure to become the agent. Starting with the current Os Mages.

"Asmodeus." She bowed her head to offer deference she didn't feel. "This Portend is worth far more than a moment of pleasure."

Asmodeus released the captive. "Hmm. Perhaps you're right."

Aubrianna raised her head to see the man rubbing his hands together, his head cocked to one side.

"What did you do to her to gain her…" he glanced at the captive, "…cooperation?"

Aubrianna relaxed. "Lyon has her child. I promised to reunite them."

"And what? You would release such an asset just because she said 'Please?'"

The Os Mage Mother hesitated to tell him the truth in front of the Portend, but then she caught the look in his eyes. Lying wasn't an option. "She tells me her child is a purebred. That is a commodity too rare and powerful to let slip through my fingers."

The Portend whimpered and sagged to the floor.

Asmodeus squatted next to the collapsed prisoner. "Truth won't set *you* free, eh, girl?" He ran a forefinger down her bare arm then sucked on it. "Emotional agony is quite tasty in its own right. Not as scrumptious as the physical, but still a delicious treat."

He stood and stepped close to Aubrianna. "Betrayal suits you, old girl, but be warned. I know your heart's desire and how far you will go to get it. In that, we are the same." He took a lock of her snow-white hair in his fingers. "I, however, will not tolerate treachery." He wound her hair around his hand and pulled her head down. "Do you understand?"

She hissed but managed to nod. "Yes, of course."

"And you will not harm Libra. I have plans for him."

"No. Never."

He pulled her head down farther then jammed the tip of his walking stick under her chin. "Lying doesn't work for me either."

"I will not kill him, isn't that enough?"

He paused before releasing her. "Good enough. Shall we dine on it? Celebrate?"

Aubrianna straightened.

"Yes, that would be lovely," she said, her voice thin, light.

Asmodeus held out an arm. "My dear."

* * *

The demon king and Os Mage Mother left the cell without a glance at the weeping Portend.

She raised her head the moment the cell door was locked and wiped her eyes. She ached with longing to hold her child again, to bury her face in her daughter's thick hair and breathe deep the scent of innocence and sunshine and sweat and joy that permeated all children.

The Portend species could do many wondrous things: some could predict the future; others could see current events unfolding elsewhere; the rarest of their kind could produce psychic drawings of events happenings around the worlds.

And they could read minds; at least, that's what they had portrayed to the other paranorm species to keep them at arm's length, to maintain a mystique that others feared. In truth, merging with a human or paranorm mind had long ago been proven to be perilous, something to be avoided save for the direst of circumstances. This was especially the case when it came to another Portend, where the power of two psychics linked could cause them to go mad.

So Portends had become experts at observation, using a cold read of a person's body language and facial expressions to wind their way through the maze of the mind. Just as charlatans used cold reads to prove they were psychic, Portends used the same technique to protect themselves from their psychic ability.

As much as she wanted to find her daughter—to look through her eyes and see who had her and if she was safe—she couldn't risk damaging her child's mind. Not even for a glimpse. But she could warn the Zodiac about the Stryx Asmodeus spoke of. Scooting to the wall, she rested on it, crossed her legs, and closed her eyes. This was her talent—looking into the future. She waited, recalling the connection with Libra, exploring his surroundings, seeing what he saw until the interior of the gypsy caravan walls locked into her mind.

She took a deep breath and pushed her thoughts against the vision until, with a mental *pop*, she escaped the walls and fast-forwarded through the future. The forest was dark; there was a fire and many people. She clenched her jaw and pressed on, ignoring the dizzying speed of the future and the piercing cold that had infused her brain. A few seconds more and she released the vision with a gasp, groaning through the agony that racked her body.

Libra's future was about to go very wrong if she couldn't help him.

She closed her eyes again. "Please help me, Chronos, father of time, keeper of the past, the present, and the future."

She pictured the Zodiac's face then dove into the memory of their connection. A troubled soul full of potential, it called to her and she reeled it in until her psychic eye flooded back inside him, filling his mind, soul, and body. Every cell inside her melded with his, her memories and fear for her daughter mixed with the pain and doubt and rage coursing through him.

At this moment, she found herself in the direst of circumstances. She had already touched the man's mind once and had been able to withdraw unscathed. Despite it being a gamble, if she could push him far enough, give him reason enough to defeat his mother, it was worth risking her life, her sanity.

Anything to get her daughter back, the baby now named Candace.

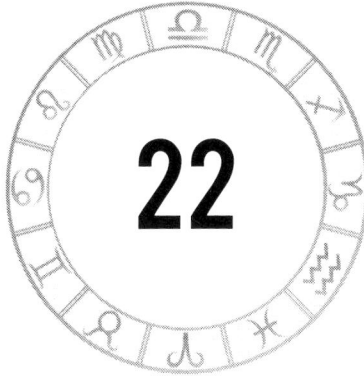

22

$\mathbf{L}$IBRA OPENED HIS EYES and looked at the bed tucked into the back of the van. Taryn. He needed help. The covers were rumpled and very flat—flatter than a body could get, no matter how crappy the mattress. The world spun around him as he crawled to her bed, the air wavering like summer heat radiating off asphalt. He lifted one edge of the quilt then threw it back. Or tried to throw it.

As if the laws of physics had taken a sabbatical, the material hovered and waved like a leaf on the wind for several seconds before landing.

The bed was empty. Taryn was gone.

"What the hell?" he muttered, his words garbled and slow.

This had to be a dream; nothing else made sense. Every movement felt like he was fighting against water, slow, heavy, exhausting. But his dreams never included this much pain. His head pounded harder than his heart; the blood rushing through his ears was deafening.

He fought against the thick air to stand, then stumbled down the van steps and looked around the silent camp for signs of life—a sentry, or others as restless as him—but he was alone. The camp wasn't just silent in slumber. It was empty. The frigid air wrapped around him, his warm breath marked by small clouds that rolled slowly out of his mouth. He pushed through the heavy air to the other side of the van circle, the silence utter and eerie—the lack of a guard was madness.

Libra had worked his way around to the Sol leader's van again when a flicker of light in the distance caught his eye. Fire.

The flames strained for the stars then collapsed back as they burned through whatever accelerant had been used, yet the light was still too bright to make out who had started the fire. Didn't matter; he knew the *who*. The better questions were *what* they were doing, and *why*.

The foreign feel of the dream forgotten, Libra waded his way through the prickly verge, fallen trees, and thick bands of grapevine that strangled the old hardwoods, avoiding sentries until he saw a huge log several feet to his right. He dropped to his hands and knees and crawled to the log, using it to block him from view. He peeked over it and froze.

The Sol camp, men, women, and children, had donned gold robes that shimmered with each movement as they danced clockwise around the fire, the fabric flowing, the women's long hair waving. Weaving counterclockwise between them were the Nox, dressed in glittering robes of obsidian.

The two groups swayed and twirled in slow motion, their arms stretched over their heads or to the side, dancing the ritual in silence. Libra belly-crawled to another fallen log then poked his head up and saw Taryn sitting on the other side of the fire. She was watching the dance, a soft smile on her face, the loose, gold robe hiding her curves. She swayed in time with the undulations; her long, black curls loose down her back and over her shoulders, framing her face. Her wide eyes sparkled. Her pale skin had been warmed by the flames and glowed the same gold as her garb. She looked young and fresh yet timeless, an immortal goddess embodying the feminine.

The silence grew deeper when the figures stopped moving. They dropped to their knees and raised their faces to the sky.

Libra rolled onto his back and looked up, wondering what they were seeing in the stars that he was missing.

A muted crunch of leaves sounded to his left. He rolled his head and sucked in a breath when he saw himself a few feet away—on his back, in the exact same position. Was he dreaming or was this something more?

Libra watched Solange reach down and touch the other Libra's shoulder.

"Shit," he cursed, jerking away from her touch. "That's a good way to get yourself killed."

"You should pay more attention."

"I should *leave*." Vision Libra climbed to his feet. "What are you doing out here?"

Libra watched the Sol and their visitors turn to vision Libra, his voice breaking their fugue state. They rose as one and came to the Sol leader. She touched each man, woman, and child on their bowed head, gold and dark robe alike, until they had all received her gentle, silent blessing. They spread out around the fire creating a solid ring, enclosing the flames.

Solange held out her hand for vision Libra and Taryn. They joined her inside the ring and sat when she sat, folding their legs in an imitation of her.

The real Libra crawled as close to the group as he could, then settled in the hollow of another tree to watch.

The old woman cocked her head and smiled at Taryn, her eyes gentle, knowing. "You have thought us to be Romany."

Taryn pulled her knees into her chest, forming a ball. "And you're not."

"I'm not." She nodded to the group surrounding them. "Nor are the Nox. We aren't Romany, but calling ourselves such has made it easier for us to move freely."

"The Romany are treated like second class citizens. Why would you choose them for a cover?" Taryn asked.

"They are nomads, not connected to any place. They roam, just as we do, giving us the perfect lifestyle for our needs."

"And the persecution?" Libra's vision-self asked.

She chuckled. "The stories of the snake oil salesmen offering great beauty or genitalia enlargement happened in this, the human world. They offered what people most desired then swindled them with sugar water and powerful drugs. We have ways to make the wishes come true, so we are welcomed everywhere."

"Then what are you?" his other self asked when Taryn remained silent. "How are you able to perform such magic?"

She opened her arms, indicating the others. "We are in service to the goddess of the witches, Hecate. Tonight we have come together in Hecate's stead to initiate the Vernal Equinox, to pass the cold mantle of winter to the warm rebirth of spring."

"Sol? Nox?" Taryn asked.

Vision Libra glanced at her. "It means the sun and the night."

The old woman clasped her hands together and smiled. "Yes, very good. He is a smart one, Taryn; I approve. Specifically, we're the Hibernus Sol, also known as the winter sun people. Our friends here are the Fons Nox, the spring night people. There are also the Aestas Sol, of the summer sun, and the Cadent Nox, of the fall dying."

Taryn closed her eyes and frowned. "Please back up. Hecate? Everything keeps coming back to her."

The old woman patted Taryn's knee. "Yes, child. When the goddess Hecate, your grandmother, was trapped in Hades, we pledged our great numbers around the world to keep the seasons coming and going, for years, for centuries. Without us, the seasons would fall into chaos, coming in and out at will, growing seasons and dying seasons appearing randomly, meaning no food for the people and animals. We stand in the way of worldwide starvation and possible extinction."

"Are you witches?" vision Libra asked. "Hecate's coven?"

"We were, but with the passing of the years, and Hecate's absence, we separated from the witches and evolved into more. Focusing our power into one skill until only we could control the changing of the seasons."

"I thought the planet moving around the sun did that."

The old woman cackled. "Yes, it does, but the changing relies on more than this planet spinning around the sun. Humans swallowed that simplistic tomfoolery without question, which has allowed us to work our magic without scrutiny."

"How do you—?" his vision self started to ask, but he stopped when Taryn's body jerked and she rose to her feet, her body swaying like she'd been drinking.

She stared into the darkness around them, first one way then another, as if what she was seeing was moving or, worse, surrounding them. She sniffed the air, still turning in place, seeking for several seconds before shaking her head.

"What is it?" his other self asked.

Taryn rubbed her arms, her shoulders collapsed into her chest. She looked smaller, tentative, like she was wounded or frightened. "I—nothing, it's nothing, I'm tired."

She bent her knees but before she could sit again, an invisible force shoved her. She staggered back several feet, groaned, and fell.

The Sol leader hobbled over, dropped to her knees next to Taryn, and gripped her shoulders. "What is it, child?"

Taryn mumbled but real Libra couldn't make out her words; it sounded like she was speaking Latin or some other obscure language. She rolled to her hands and knees, her body shaking as she dug through the thick mat of pine needles and into the dirt. Arcs of blue light erupted from the ground, wound their way up her fingers and wrists, then traveled over her body until she was enveloped in Gaia's glowing cerulean.

Finally, she spoke words in English—words that Libra knew all too well.

"Hell." She looked at his vision self, and blinked. "Hell is coming."

"What?" the old woman asked as she cupped Taryn's cheek. "Who's coming? Is it the demons?"

"You know about the demons?" Libra asked.

Solange pressed a forefinger to her lips to silence him.

Taryn frowned and shook her head. "No, not demons. Something darker, more dangerous."

"More dangerous than demons?" Libra chimed in.

"There are many creatures hidden in the bowels of Hell who are unknown to us." Solange leaned closer to Taryn. "What direction?"

"I don't know. I need to dig deeper."

Solange rose and beckoned to the Sol and Nox.

Vision Libra gently gripped Taryn's chin and lifted it. He examined her face. "The blue was from a ley line?"

She nodded, her eyes unfocused.

"Stop. Pull your arm out before Gaia gets a good hold on you."

When she didn't answer, he gripped her shoulders and shook her. As if she hadn't heard him, she reached into her pocket and pulled out a small bag and a box of matches. She dropped the bag on the ground, struck a match, and held the flame close to the bag.

Libra grabbed her wrist, pulling her hand away. The match fizzled out. "What are you doing? Magic?"

She jerked free. "I need…want a boost, to feel the ley line better."

Vision Libra's mouth dropped open. "A boost? You want to use magic to amplify it? We've been expressly forbidden to use magic in the human world, and you promised not to use it. You promised to do as I told you, but you seem to forget that at every turn. After what? A few days? Do you have no self-control? Do you have a death wish? Boosting the connection is madness, Taryn. Stop this now."

"That's rich coming from the man who was happy to have me use magic to break him out of that cell. Solange said we make a great team. Take my hand and help me. Together, we can do this."

Vision Libra looked like he'd chewed on a lemon; the real Libra could imagine the snarky response he would have locked and loaded. But before vision Libra could spew forth some withering remark, the ground vibrated, drawing his attention away. Soft and low, but growing stronger with each second until ticklish arcs of blue licked at Libra's shoes. The ley line was reaching for him.

Real Libra placed his palms on the ground and wriggled them until the same blue touched his skin, even though he was several feet away. It was whispering that it had secrets, secrets it wanted to share if only he'd give himself over to it. An ache started in his lower back, hot waves rocking his core, spreading throughout his body.

Despite Taryn's promise not to use magic, he understood her need to figure out where the danger was coming from—in this moment, he felt it too, or at least that's what he told himself to deny the deeper, darker, furtive truth.

The connection to Gaia felt good; it felt right, and despite being terrified of the mere glimpse of the power, it called to him. Every cell in his body ached to reconnect with the goddess, to sink into the blue and never come back, the energy coursing through him a euphoric high. Already the hunger to give himself over was stronger than the first time, a new layer of nacre waiting to be laid down like an oyster creating a pearl, driving him like an addict who needed more, then more again, to find the same buzz. The prickle of need should have frightened him, stopped him, but he did nothing when Taryn struck a second match, the smell of sulfur thrilling him.

Real Libra watched Taryn light the magic bag. She set it on the ground next to her and watched the green flames lap at the cotton until it split open and the burning contents spilled out. Taryn braced herself over the flames and inhaled deeply, over and over, until the flames died. She chanted an 'open' spell, similar to the one she had used to open his cell door, but accessing the ley line wasn't as hard as destroying metal.

Lightening surged out of the ground and danced over her body. Her tie to the ley line had increased, immersing her.

"Taryn?" vision Libra asked, his voice low and close to her ear.

Real Libra's need to show himself—to go to Taryn and grip her free hand and be swallowed by Gaia together—rocked him.

She opened her eyes and her body jerked again, slamming her onto her back. She blinked. "I can't see."

"Release the ley line."

Taryn stared past him. "There's darkness and movement as if I'm traveling through the soil."

Vision Libra leaned closer to her ear. "Stop this."

Real Libra leaned forward too, desperate to take over this vision or dream and connect with her.

"The ground is humming; the soil is vibrating with life and energy." She flinched as if in pain. "There. Up ahead. Light is pulsing. The blue is huge and tumultuous like a river." She moved her head left to right, surveying whatever she was seeing. "The ley line. And there," she raised an arm and pointed, "the vortices." Her mouth formed an 'O'. "It's glorious," she said with a sigh.

Mother Earth's nervous system had been laid bare for Taryn, and based on her rapturous expression she was diving into it. She moaned, her back arched in pleasure.

"Damn it," Libra swore. He gripped the sleeve of her robe, careful to avoid her skin, and tugged hard. "Taryn, if you hear me, pull back. Now!"

Her mouth opened, but her lips and tongue didn't move; no words were formed.

A scream echoed through the woods. The *thump-thump* of heavy wings followed, closing fast just above the trees.

Both Libras looked up.

"For goddess' sake, run!" vision Libra cried.

Before anyone could react to his command, winged creatures appeared out of the darkness and dove at the group.

The Sol and Nox scattered, their cries drowned out by the monsters.

The attackers mowed down men, women, and children, ripping into their flesh as they gripped hold of them and flapped hard to rise back into the sky.

Real Libra watched his vision self lean over Taryn.

The need to protect her tore through him, but he didn't know what the consequences would be if he exposed himself in the vision. He needed to see what was about to happen. Frustration and fear made his heart pound; his head was light from holding his breath too long. Over and over, the birds shredded flesh and severed limbs until blood rained from the sky. Ruined bodies fell to the ground.

The forest floor shuddered beneath him. Libra looked beyond his vision self and Taryn, huddled together. A huge bird had landed a few feet away, its polychromic, red and gold eyes focused on them. It took one step, then another; its head dropped low, bobbing and weaving as it hissed.

There was nowhere to go, no magic to help him fight the beast. The few Sol and Nox who had survived had scattered. His vision self was alone with Taryn with no weapon.

The bird stopped only inches from them. It shook its great head and screeched as if in pain, as if driven by a force unseen. It raised a foot, the talons stained red with blood, then swiped at vision Libra, ripping his back to shreds.

Jumping up, the bird tore Taryn away from him.

Both Libras screamed.

The world went black.

* * *

The Portend fell to the cell floor, her muscles cramping, her mind mush now that the connection had been ripped apart. Blood oozed out of her ears and nose and mouth. She wanted to wipe it away, but her limbs wouldn't cooperate. Didn't matter much. The blood would dry and turn black and blend in with the layers of filth already coating her.

If that wasn't enough to warn the Zodiac, they were all doomed anyway. She curled into a ball and sought the healing sleep she so desperately needed.

23

LIBRA JERKED AWAKE AND threw up his arms to defend himself from the hell-born-bird attack. But nothing happened. He opened his eyes and looked around the dark caravan. He patted his chest and tried to touch his back. No pain—except for a bitch of a headache—no Taryn, no blood-splattered woods, just the quiet of the sleeping camp.

He sat up, grabbed the small trashcan under the tiny sink, and vomited until all he had left was bile. He took a deep breath and felt a tickle on his upper lip and below his ears. He swiped at his nose; his fingers came away bloody. *Damn it.* He grabbed a box of tissues and cleaned up the blood leaking from his nose and ears.

Collapsing on his pallet of blankets, he looked back at Taryn's bed. The covers were rumpled and very flat—flatter than a body could get no matter how crappy the mattress. He crawled to her bed, lifted one edge of the blanket, and threw it back.

Empty.

Just like in his nightmare, only this time there was no slow motion, no muted sound, no muzziness. This had to be real. It hadn't been a nightmare but a vision of the future, this future.

He gripped his head in his hands. "Or this present…or whatever the fuck is going on."

The adrenaline surge nearly made him hurl again. He clawed his way up until he stood then stumbled down the van steps. He looked around the silent camp for signs of life—a sentry, or others as restless as him—but he was alone. The camp wasn't silent in slumber. It was deserted.

"Goddess, no."

The frigid air wrapped around him, his warm breaths marked by small, evaporating clouds. He walked to the other side of the van circle, the silence eerie—the lack of a guard, madness. Libra jogged the outside perimeter until, just a few feet before he came back to the Sol leader's van again, a small flicker of light caught his eye.

Fire.

"No, no, no."

He ran through the forest, his vivid vision proving true with every second that passed. His heart pounded but he couldn't feel his skin. Vines and barbs and branches whipped against him, gouging and scratching and pulling, but he felt nothing but blind panic—the need to get to everyone driving him forward. He broke through the densest part of the forest and skidded to a stop, his *déjà vu* too real, too fresh. He had just dreamed the sight before him.

The Sol camp, men, women, and children, wore the same gold robes that shimmered with each movement as they danced clockwise around the fire. The Nox wove counterclockwise between them, dressed in glittering robes of obsidian.

Taryn was sitting on the other side of the fire watching the dance, a soft smile on her face, the loose gold robe hiding her curves. She swayed in time with the undulations, her long, black curls loose down her back and over her shoulders, framing her face. Her wide eyes sparkled. Her pale skin had been warmed by the flames and glowed the same gold as her garb. She looked young and fresh yet timeless, an immortal goddess embodying the feminine—at least she would for a few more minutes.

Then she would be covered in his blood, trapped in the ley line, torn in two with no way out.

The vision pounded in his head, pushing him forward. "Run!"

The dancers slowed; the music stopped. But no one moved.

He ran into the circle. "I said run! Now!" He pointed at the sky. "They're coming."

"Libra," Taryn scolded. "What's wrong with you? They're in the middle of a ritual."

Solange wove her way through the crowd until she reached him. "What is this talk of running? Take a seat and take a breath."

Libra grabbed her outstretched hands. "There's no time. Please, you must believe me."

Solange and Taryn exchanged looks.

"Okay, fine." He turned to Solange. "You and your people are the Sol." He pointed at the closest obsidian-robed male without taking his eyes off of the Sol leader. "He is a Nox. You all serve the goddess of the witches, Hecate. You're here to initiate the Vernal Equinox, to pass the cold mantle of winter to the warm rebirth of spring."

"Sol? Nox?" Taryn asked.

"The sun and the night."

The old woman frowned. "How—?"

Libra waved a hand to stop her. "You are the leader of the Hibernus Sol, the winter sun people. They are the Fons Nox, the spring night people. The Aestas Sol of the summer sun and the Cadent Nox of the fall dying aren't here."

No one spoke; only gasps surrounded him.

"Come on, people. I know this is crazy but I just dreamed this. Please believe me; it doesn't end well unless you all get out of here, right now."

A cry sounded in the distance.

"That's them; a Hell creature like you've never known. They are coming to slaughter all of us." He held out a hand to Taryn. "Come with me now."

"What?"

"We have one chance to stop this but we must act now."

She frowned.

Her confusion was justified but he couldn't wait for her to make sense of it. He grabbed her hands and jerked her to her feet. He pulled her past the fire and into the woods until he found the ley line from his nightmare.

He dropped to his knees and forced her down. "Here. The ley line is here. Hurry, you must dig down and find it."

"But I don't feel it."

"Damn it." He tugged at her robe until he found the pocket. Reaching deep, he gripped hold of the magic bag and the box of matches. Removing them from her pocket, he held them up to Taryn. "You used this."

"Magic? You're condoning the use of magic?"

"I'm saying you need to grip the ley line tight and if it takes this to make that happen…"

"Okay," she said with a frown. She dropped the sachet on the ground and lit it.

Libra leaned closer and inhaled the sulfurous smoke with her. A deep hum vibrated through his body. He released Taryn's hand and attacked the soil, digging and grunting, his panic growing with each second that passed.

Taryn joined him.

"Libra?" Solange whispered.

He whipped his head around. "What are you waiting for? Get out of here—get all of them out of here before it's too late."

She backed away, her shocked look confirming that she finally understood how serious this was.

"Go! Now! Run!"

The Sol and Nox sprinted away from the fire, scattering into the woods, the smallest children in their arms, the older youths running hand in hand with their parents.

"What about you and Taryn? What did this dream show you?"

He didn't want to answer her, didn't want to speak the words in case it jinxed them, but she deserved to know the truth. "We died."

Solange flinched; her breath hitched. "What can I do?"

"Maybe I can stop it. But if I can't, try to find the children. Help them."

Another scream, this one much closer, sent Solange backing into the shadows. "I promise, but do all you can not to die. Yes?"

He didn't respond; there was no time. His focus needed to be on getting access to the ley line. Just when he thought they'd never connect, Taryn gasped and cerulean tendrils swarmed over her body.

"I feel her." She looked at him, her eyes wide. "Gaia."

"Good. Go deeper, as deep as you can."

She nodded slightly, her eyes already glazing over.

He heard the wings flapping, his nightmare approaching too fast; they would be on them in seconds. "Hurry."

A *whoosh* heralded the birds flying over at high elevation. They would soar in a tight turn and drop down. Seconds—they only had seconds.

"Libra."

Taryn was covered in blue; Gaia's energy had enveloped her. She held out her hand.

He hesitated for a moment then gripped it tight with one hand, leaving the other free. With a sucking sound, the world turned blue. Gaia had both of them in her grasp, and Libra reveled in the seductive power, his fear of her thrall overwhelmed. He raised his hand, looked to the sky, and waited.

24

EVEN THOUGH SHE WAS deep in the ley line, Taryn could feel the creatures, their rage and pain and confusion. They had been bidden to do the work of another, summoned to a world not their own, charged with destruction. A jolt of pain ripped through her head.

A rippling image of a structure came to her. She strained against the building pressure in her head, clearing away the fog until the red bricks and gothic architecture came into focus. It was the mansion Candace had drawn.

Libra yelled some gibberish but Taryn ignored him and pushed deeper into the ley line, struggling to get closer to the vortices. She had to get more information; she had to figure out its location. Her mind traveled to the front door and stopped. She walked up the steps; they felt so real, solid under her feet. She reached for the metal knocker but the carved-wood door opened on its own with a creak, the ubiquitous horror-movie sound that heralded the too-stupid-to-live character was about to get gutted, yet it never seemed to stop them. Movie or dream or hallucination, Taryn wasn't amused at the thought—she understood how people could ignore their fear and walk inside.

To her right lay a small office and counter with a dusty book and pen—a visitor's register so faded by the sun that any hope of reading the letterhead was gone. She drifted through the huge foyer, floating past wood-paneled walls and landscape paintings that ate up the height and breadth of the space. They were meant to be soothing, but the lack of life left Taryn empty. Loneliness filled her, morphing into sadness with each painting she studied. She'd seen the same plains and hills and lakes in the lobbies of the many orphanages she'd been dropped into because she had been too unruly—each place darker, less sun-bright, each with more security for the incorrigibles, less interaction between the staff and the children.

Double doors appeared on her right. She turned the knobs and opened them. Dozens of children lay on rows of beds, legs and arms straight, their eyes on the high, ornate ceiling, offering no acknowledgement of her presence. Could they not see her? Or were they drugged or bewitched to keep them compliant?

Before Taryn could take a step inside the huge room, a woman and a man passed through her body. Nausea gripped her; icy chills made her shudder—the physical reaction unexpected, frightening. She needed to leave, now. She reached for the wall to brace herself but her hand disappeared inside the vision or dream or memory—whatever it was she was experiencing—the wall shimmering until she pulled her hand away.

The woman paused and turned, looking around her as if she had felt the brief connection. It was Circe, her mother.

Taryn staggered back, her heart pounding in her throat, choking her, but Circe didn't see her.

Next to Circe was a young man. Tall, lean, with long, chestnut hair and hazel eyes, he was handsome like an ancient Greek youth: smooth skin, aquiline nose, with full lips that were currently pinched. He was unhappy, shaking his head as he looked at one of the paranorm girls.

Circe cocked her head and studied the exotic, green-gold-skinned Aspis child, and the man frowned, his face paling even as the muscles in his jaw tightened. He grabbed the girl's arm and pulled her toward Circe.

Circe lifted a hand over the girl's forehead.

The girl opened her mouth and screamed, her beautiful skin splitting, liquid-gold blood running down her face.

Taryn stumbled back, away from the brutality, and slammed into a wall. She turned and found herself staring into a mirror, but it wasn't her own reflection staring back at her. Glowing eyes, one red and one gold, studied her, the orbs markedly strange because they had no pupil. A long, gold beak sat in the middle of the monstrous, round face, a network of scars radiating out from the sharp-pointed neb and covering its face and form. Only Persephone's mate Lyon had more scars than the creature in the mirror.

The beak opened. Strings of raw, red, dripping flesh hung from the cracks and chips of its mandible.

Taryn screamed. The image in the mirror melted away and the building faded around her—leaving her suspended in blue.

"Libra!"

* * *

Libra's mouth dropped open. A winged nightmare dove out of the dark, skimming over the ground, and headed his way.

The creature shrieked and kept its beak open, aiming for Libra's chest.

He waited until the last second then shrank to one side, beating the attacker's claws by a hair. The creature's wing tips beat against the ground as it pulled up, fanning the flames of the ritual fire, increasing the light so Libra could see the immense body attached to the head. Red and gold eyes, a cracked and battle-worn gold beak, red feathers, black legs, and each of its two feet missing a toe; the bird-like attacker had been through hell.

The monster used the momentum of the dive to climb above the treetops. Again, the bird attacked and again it missed him by inches, but far fewer than the first time. Next time, Libra wouldn't be so lucky.

The cerulean rippled over his body like a living thing. He concentrated on coalescing the power into his right arm, fear and rage and the need to kill spiking his adrenaline, narrowing his vision to the bird's breast.

The bird dove again, this time skimming the ground, its massive wings tucked in a death run.

"C'mon you bastard." He leaned back against Taryn's still body, blocking her from the bird's approach. "Time for some roasted hell chicken."

"Can't kill it," he heard her whisper.

"Taryn?"

"You can't kill it with Gaia's power. Agent."

Shit. What the hell was I thinking?

The monster rapidly approaching had every intention of making mincemeat of them and he had to kill it to save them, but he couldn't kill it with Gaia's power without giving his mother and the Corvus Ward king everything they wanted.

He waited for the bird to get within yards of them before taking a deep breath and bellowing, "NO."

Gaia's energy exploded out of his mouth, off his skin.

The bird kept coming.

Libra turned his back to the attacker and covered Taryn, the blue light enveloping them both in a bubble.

The bird's claws ripped his back, but before it could lift him off Taryn, Gaia's energy sent the bird tumbling. It jerked to a stop several yards away and lay still for a moment before shaking its head and climbing to its feet. It screamed and the others responded in kind.

The bird swayed on its feet before stumbling like a drunk; its clumsiness would have been funny if not for the situation. It wobbled closer to Libra and took a long look at him before collapsing, black blood flowing out of several wounds.

The other birds circled above, their formation tightening. They arced and dropped down to make a pass at Libra and Taryn.

He tried to raise an arm but the surge of power he'd used to knock the leader back didn't fill him. He shook his hand but nothing changed. Whatever help Gaia had given him moments ago was gone.

Libra covered Taryn and waited for the hot burn of tearing flesh.

The excited cries of the birds stopped suddenly, changing to alarmed screeches.

He looked up in time to see a broad-winged shadow cross in front of the attackers.

The birds pulled up hard, screaming and shaking their heads as if confused before flying away, leaving their leader behind, the shadow chasing after them until they disappeared. Seconds later, the shadow returned, landing a few feet away from them.

It was a Pestilence Fairy, a girl covered not only with her pestilence, but the black blood of the birds.

She jogged over to him and clasped her hands together as she leaned over Taryn. "Is she okay?"

"She'll be fine. Who are you?"

"I am Taryn's friend."

The girl nodded once then, without another word, flapped her ragged wings and disappeared into the darkness.

Libra sagged to the ground, too exhausted to care that he was still deeply connected to Gaia or wonder why the fairy saved their lives.

"Thank you, goddess," he managed to whisper as he exhaled.

In a wink, the blue receded into the ground, leaving Taryn and Libra free.

He pulled Taryn into his chest, spooning for warmth and more than a little comfort. "I don't understand why we were spared, but I'm happy we're alive."

A soft voice called out from behind him. "Libra?" Solange hobbled across to him, two Sol men gripping her upper arms to steady her. "Is Taryn okay?"

"She's unconscious, but alive."

"Get them out of here," Solange ordered.

The rustle of feet filled the silence; within seconds, the Sol and Nox had surrounded them.

"Bring the bird," he managed to get out.

Solange touched his cheek. "Mercy?"

"Strategy," he whispered.

The darkness wound around him and he welcomed the cool relief.

25

"STOP PACING. YOU'RE NEXT," Taryn ordered, her hands blue and sticky from the healing clay she had applied to the injured bird.

The man was impossible, and she was tired of the floor squeaking with his every step.

Libra turned in a tight circle; the bird was taking up most of the caravan's already tiny space. As it was they had had to remove everything but Libra's pallet from the caravan to accommodate the huge, feathered patient. Taryn was stuck bunking with Solange's prickly granddaughter, which had definitely not helped the women's nonexistent relationship.

"I don't need anymore treatments; I'm fine."

"You'll start bleeding again. Just one more and I'll leave you alone."

Libra let the blanket covering his shirtless upper body drop, exposing his chest as he twisted to get a better look. "Fine."

She ignored his beautiful body, ignored the tingle low in her belly, the urge to touch his warm, smooth skin and broad shoulders making her hands shake. The zing of pesky lust had no place between them.

"Stand straight."

Libra faced forward with a huff.

Honestly, the man was a child. The huge predator that had tried to kill them was far better behaved than the Zodiac. It had only been hours since they were attacked, since Libra saved the Sol and Nox from injury and death, and he'd just about whined her to death.

The caravan rocked and rolled through another jarring pothole, rousing the huge bird. It raised its head and cried out, the red and gold eyes glistening; it tried to raise its wings but there was no room.

"No, no. Don't flap your wings." Taryn gently placed her hands on their leading edge and pressed down on the bones. "You'll tear open your wounds."

The bird turned its attention to her voice and touch. The wings dropped and it extended its long neck until it could rest its head on her shoulder. The big body shuddered and its breathing grew labored.

She reached up and stroked its head to soothe it until the bird relaxed under her hand. "Easy now. You mustn't fight this."

As if it understood her, the bird dropped its head into her lap and sagged.

"Helluva pet."

"Not a pet, a living creature who needs our help."

"Why? It could kill you with one blow, but you demanded I not kill it—and, now, hell, you're helping it, keeping it alive."

Taryn packed the last of the wet, blue clay into a broad laceration, and wiped her hands on a damp towel before rising.

"We both know why you didn't kill it; agent of Gaia and such," she said with a flourish of her hands. "But why didn't you have the Sol or Nox kill it once it was down? I was told you demanded they spare the bird."

"I asked first."

She nailed him with a searing glare. She almost gave him a break when he flinched ever so slightly, but his rude behavior didn't warrant her mercy. "When I was tapped into the ley line, just before they attacked, I had a vision of Circe and a man at the building in the drawing. They had paranorm children stashed there."

"And?"

"Just before I broke free, or was released, I saw myself in a mirror. Or, rather, I saw this bird reflected in the mirror. At first, I didn't get it, but now I think I was seeing through this bird's eyes. We were connected for only a moment—" She rubbed her face with both hands; she needed a shower. "I couldn't let the bird be killed. I want to understand how I was able to see through its eyes. Maybe, the answer will allow us to find the location of the house faster."

"You're taking a huge risk, healing it, insisting it comes with us."

She shrugged her shoulders; he wasn't going to like this next part but he needed to understand that his rigid views of the world were wrong. There was more than just light and dark, good or evil. Living a balanced life meant accepting a world filled with shades of gray.

"My gut tells me we need to help the bird, that it won't hurt me."

"It's not just yourself you put at risk."

She crossed her arms, the movement hopefully looking defiant from the outside, though, in reality, it was an effort to protect her heart. Her breath caught in her throat, her confidence rocked. What if he was right? Was her determination to find the building in Candace's drawing clouding her judgment?

Libra stared at her, his chin rigid. Finally, he relaxed and shook his head. "Your gut is going to get people killed."

"What about my question?"

The corner of Libra's mouth twitched. He sniffed once, twice. "I told Solange… it was a strategic decision."

"Could you be more vague? Or dishonest?"

He looked at the resting bird. "How about we skip the dishonest part—neither one of us has a firm hold on the truth here."

"Why can't you just admit that your gut told you to spare him?"

"Because, unlike you, I don't consider flights of fancy a viable tool for making life-or-death decisions. You would have us all go with our gut when that particular part of the anatomy is the most tumultuous, bacteria-ridden, not to mention shit-producing, part of us. For all I know, our lives depend on how much gas you've had any given night." He rose to his feet, the fierce expression on his face driving Taryn back a step. "This is real life, and you don't get do-overs."

Her face flushed. "And what about you? Running to us screaming about monsters from the sky then demanding I connect with Gaia using magic. Where was your real life then? You weigh everything based on your perception of what's light or dark without stopping to consider that what you deem dark may be necessary and right. Who made you the arbiter of good and evil for me, for them?"

He stepped closer and she welcomed it. She threw her head back and bared her teeth.

His nostrils flared. He raised his hands and reached for her neck, his need to grip it and squeeze written all over his face.

Taryn's anger incinerated her caution, but before she could continue blasting him, the bird raised its head and cried out.

Turning away from Libra, her frustration evaporating, she dropped to her knees and stroked the bird's head. "What is it? Are you in pain?"

Libra grunted and lowered himself to the floor. "What's wrong?"

She ran her hands over the creature's neck and breastbone. "Maybe I missed an injury…"

They worked together checking every inch.

"I don't see anything new," Taryn said.

"Maybe we shouldn't argue around him."

Laughter bubbled up from her infamous gut and spilled over. "Yes, daddy, no arguing around the children."

Libra scowled, which only made her laugh harder.

"Do you never take anything seriously?"

"I try not to—" Fresh peels erupted.

His mouth twitched, the corners lifting in amusement—until the bird raised its wings. Taryn fell forward, landing in his arms, the momentum sending them tumbling to the floor.

"Your wounds," she cried as she struggled to push off his chest.

He released her. "I'm fine."

Taryn had just gained her feet when the bird flapped a second time and she fell on him again.

"Okay, that hurt," he managed to get out between groans.

The door opened and Solange poked her head in. "Oh my, should I give you a few minutes?"

"No, no," Taryn said swiftly.

She regained her feet and straightened her clothes, damning the flush she could feel creeping up her neck and blooming on her face. She'd dancing skyclad with abandon under the bright of a full moon, reveled in glorious sex—sometimes under that same moon—and hadn't met a man yet who could shut her down. She could hold her own no matter the topic or situation…so why was embarrassment raising its ugly head now?

She frowned. "What's going on?"

"We've decided to stay here for the night instead of pushing on," Solange said.

"But it's early," Libra said. "I hoped we'd reach the town before nightfall."

"The others have something else in mind for tonight and it will take preparation," Solange said with a wink. "We will get you to civilization tomorrow and you can be on your way." She held out a hand to Taryn. "Come, I have a surprise for you." She nodded at Libra. "You, stay here. My men will tend to your needs."

"My needs?" Libra asked.

The bird raised his head and chuffed.

"My thoughts exactly."

26

THE SUN HAD JUST dipped below the horizon when a knock sounded on the caravan door.

"Enter."

Two Sol and two Nox males stepped inside the tight space, their hands filled with hot and cold pails of water, a small tub for bathing, soaps, towels, and a garment bag. They silently busied themselves creating a bath for Libra, then, without a word, left the van.

The bird had tucked his head under a wing and gone to sleep.

Stripping, Libra stepped into the tub and sat, the fit tight but the hot water soothing. He washed away the sweat and blue clay and scrubbed at his skin hoping to rid himself of the gut-punch feeling that still lingered so long after the connection with Gaia.

He was heading down a path he never could have imagined when he had stood poised in the passageway to the Great Cavern, ready to begin his new life as an ambassador. Hunted by the Corvus Ward king, paired up with Taryn, having a bath in a caravan only a few feet from a monstrosity of a bird who had tried to kill him, yet whom he'd spared for reasons he had yet to fathom. But tomorrow this would end. They would go to town, get a car by whatever means, and follow the breadcrumbs to the building, to the children.

In a few days, he would be back on track. The king would be off his back, the ambassadorship would be his, and he could return to his life in the light. He stopped sponging the soap off his chest, the thought of his designer clothes and an angst-free existence failing to give him the comfort it once did. He shook his head and chuckled. He was tired from the past few days, that was all.

He dried off and opened the garment bag. To his surprise and pleasure, it contained the clothes Taryn had brought to the warehouse. He ran his fingers over the cashmere sweater then hung the bag on a light fixture, eager to feel his own clothes against his skin. But before pulling them out, he hesitated.

This might be their last night with the Sol, and despite wanting a break from the itchy clothes he'd been wearing, he found himself zipping up the bag and turning to the tiny drawer holding the clothes provided by Taryn and his hosts.

He picked his way through the garments, rejecting them until he got to the very bottom. There he found a butter-soft pair of white pants. Underneath them was a shirt with seams that had been hand embroidered with tiny constellation patterns in reds and blues and gold. The stitching must have taken hours. The few repairs made to the outfit had been expertly done, and the clothes smelled of lavender. They were used but someone had clearly loved the former owner.

As much as he wanted to put this dubious adventure behind him, it felt right to don these clothes rather than his own. He quickly slipped into them and ran his fingers through his hair.

He knelt by the bird and touched its head. "Where did you come from?"

Roused from its sleep, it looked into Libra's eyes. Zodiac and predator studied each other for a long moment. What this bird had seen, where it had come from, and who had conjured its presence couldn't be gleaned from its stare, but maybe, when this adventure was over, he could find out.

He shook his head and snorted. "Goddess, what am I doing talking to a bird? Hey, raise a wing. Yeah, like you understand what I'm saying."

He had gotten to his feet when the bird slowly lifted one wing.

"Damn. You understand me?" He stood and watched the bird lower its wing and ruffle its feathers before settling. "Amazing. I definitely need to find out what you are. But not tonight."

He stepped out of the van…and into a fairyland of twinkling lights and a roaring fire. A tantalizing aroma made him salivate.

Instruments had appeared; one man was seated on a box, his fingers and hands beating a rhythm on the front, while three men sat around him playing guitars.

A ring of Nox and Sol had formed. In the center of the ring, a large fire burned, women and men tended to the food cooking over the flames. Curved, wooden panels had been placed on the ground between the fire and the people, creating a ringed floor where children danced and stamped their feet in time to the music.

Most of the camp wore their gold or obsidian robes, but many of the younger men and women were dressed differently. The men wore white pants like those Libra had donned, their tucked white shirts gaping open, exposing their muscular chests and flat bellies. Colorful sashes were tied at their waists, their feet bare.

The women weaving around the men were festooned in flamenco-style dresses: form-fitting through their upper body and hips then flaring at the knees, the backs of the dresses dipping down several inches. Each dress shimmered with different dark-jewel tones: cobalt blue, eggplant purple, blood red, and peacock green, with the ruffles from the knee down banded in black. They twirled and flirted, one moment bending backward as their arms swayed and intertwined, the next standing tall with one hand lifting their skirts to bare their legs.

The audience chattered and clapped, laughing at the children's antics while heckling the dancers to stop their warm-up and begin the dance in earnest.

Libra found Solange. He touched her shoulder.

She turned her head and gasped, covering her mouth with both hands, tears welling in her rheumy eyes. "Where did you find those?"

He looked down at the clothes. "In the caravan dresser." He smoothed the front of the shirt. "Should I change?"

Solange fanned her face for a moment then shook her head. "No, please don't." She patted the bench she sat on, inviting him to join her. "The clothes belonged to my mate." She ran her fingers down the seam of the sleeve. "I embroidered this myself."

"It's beautiful. You have quite a talent."

She smiled softly. "I did once." She lifted her gnarled hands. "These old things can no longer hold a needle."

Solange went back to watching at the dancers.

Libra did the same for a few moments before speaking again. "Where is Taryn?"

Solange nodded her head, indicating a place beyond the fire.

Taryn was picking her way through the milling groups, smiling and nodding at the adults and touching the heads of the children who skipped and danced around her. A billowing, gold robe swamped her, the hem so long she had to hold it up to keep from tripping. Her long, riotous, black curls had been tamed and piled loosely on top of her head—held in place by a circlet of gold wire laced with gold leaves and flowers—her eyes lined with kohl, her lips stained dark red.

The flickering flames highlighted her prominent cheekbones, the soft curve of her full lips, the cream-smooth skin of her face and slim neck. She was a goddess reborn. Fresh, alive, and damnably sexy.

She made her way to Libra and Solange and took a seat between them. "When are they going to serve? I'm starving." She looked at Libra and both eyebrows rose high. "What are you wearing?"

"Not the clothes you sent."

"Didn't like them?"

"Loved them, but this seemed more…respectful."

"Hmm, getting diplomatic, finally?"

He looked at the Sol and Nox. "About time I learned."

Taryn slapped him high on the back, avoiding his wounds. "Well, damn and hell, I'd say yes to that." Her hand stilled and she leaned closer to him. "You smell like lavender."

"It's the clothes."

"It's good."

He took a deep breath. "And you smell like honey. You always smell like honey. How is that?"

Before she could reply, the men and women tending to the cooking began passing out food. Solange and the Nox leader were served first.

Solange tasted the steaming meat and nodded. "Delicious."

The Nox leader bowed her head. The group sighed and the servers bustled about making sure everyone had enough. The feast had officially begun.

27

LIBRA LEANED CLOSE TO Taryn. "What is this feast about?"

"They're celebrating the spring equinox. They started the ritual before we were attacked; they need to finish it tonight."

"So eating and dancing? That's all it takes?"

She snorted and choked back a laugh. "You don't know?"

"Would I be asking if I did?"

She swept her arm across the crowd. "The feast is the beginning, filling our bellies to give us strength for what's to come."

She ended on a low, quavery note like she was narrating a scary tale.

Unwilling to beg her for more information, he crossed his legs and cocked one eyebrow. "Well?"

She whispered in his ear. "Then there's the dancing."

"And?"

"It culminates in the passing of the seasonal baton, so to speak, from the Sol to the Nox. Once that's done, the days should grow warmer like they should."

"Passing the baton—?"

A woman bearing a large platter of food interrupted them.

Solange peered at the pair. "You two will have to share. Not enough plates to go around."

Libra settled the round, wooden platter in his lap. "What about utensils?"

Solange laughed. "Fresh out. Eat with your fingers."

She pinched a piece of meat and slurped it out from between her fingers, chewing with a grin on her face.

Libra looked back at his food for a moment. He was trying to remember if he had washed his hands before joining the group when Taryn elbowed him.

"I'm hungry. Feed me."

She parted her lips and waited, her eyes sparkling with challenge and humor.

He selected a small slice of pulled pork and held it out to her.

She lapped at the dangling meat, pulling it into her mouth with her tongue. She closed her lips around the ends of his fingers and sucked them free of the treat. The jolt of electricity that raced along his fingers and exploded throughout his body caused him to jerk. He blinked and pulled his hand back.

Holy Hades.

He hid his hand from her view and shook it, clenching his fist and opening it several times to get the feeling back in his fingertips.

"Aren't you going to eat?"

Her voice brought him back and, much to his chagrin, made him flush. His body's response to her had been off the charts. He'd bedded many a sexy, inspiring woman but not one of them had brought about such a visceral reaction. It was primal, and most definitely unwanted. Once again, he was reminded this woman was no good for him.

He ate some of the pork and tried the herbed potatoes. "The herbs are good; I don't recognize the flavor."

"Give me some." Taryn opened her mouth and waited.

That way spelled trouble so he moved the platter to her lap.

She laughed. "Coward."

All day long. When it comes to you.

She ate the potatoes and scrunched up her face. "I'm not sure, but they're delicious."

A truce declared, they ate in silence until the food was gone. A Nox woman collected their plate, followed closely by another handing out bowls of cobbler. This time, to Libra's relief, he had his own bowl. He dipped his fingers in the dessert, shoveled it into his mouth, and groaned. Steaming, rich, and thick, the sweet sugar and cinnamon were balanced to perfection by the tart, cooked apple. He gobbled the cobbler down and fought the urge to lick the bowl clean.

Energy surged through him. His skin tingled, and his muscles clenched and relaxed as if preparing for fight or flight…

He glanced at Taryn.

…or fuck. He shook his head to rid himself of the surge of lust and focused on the Sol and Nox, hoping to distract himself from the woman seated all together too close to him.

The feast done, the musicians picked up their guitars and sat on the drum box, tuning softly while the camp shifted their attention from the food to the fire. Children settled next to their parents and the stragglers found seats among their kin.

Libra looked up at the night sky, marveling at the sea of stars.

"Beautiful, isn't it?"

He glanced at Taryn and nodded. "Yes, very."

She scooted closer to him and raised a hand to the sky. "There, do you see those stars?" She outlined three stars that formed a triangle then five others that hung from the corners of the wide base. "That's the Libra constellation."

"You studied astrology?" he asked, impressed that she could find his stars so readily.

She dropped her hand. "No. But I've recently been told that I need to study you." She looked away from him, her face flushing. "I mean all of you. The Zodiacs."

"Ah." He studied her expression, amused by her embarrassment, curious about what it meant. "To what end?"

Before she could answer him, the guitarists strummed a single chord, loud and long, then launched into a fast, complicated, percussive melody, the notes brighter, drier, and more austere than he'd heard in any other music. They sped through the song, the drum driving them, the sounds intertwining until they crashed into the end of the piece to the cheers of the camp.

Without a pause, a single guitar struck up a tune, punctuated by the drum, and one woman dressed for flamenco rose from her seat and lifted her arms, her eyes closed. She swayed and stomped, utilizing the whole wooden floor. She taunted and teased her audience, the beauty of her passionate interpretation of the traditional Spanish dance mesmerizing.

The camp clapped as the guitarist played harder, faster, the dancer lost to the rhythm. The song came to an abrupt stop and the woman opened her eyes. She pointed at the male dancer closest to her and beckoned him to join her. They started a slow, sensuous dance, coming together, then moving apart, barely touching yet still conveying passion, lust, even love with each brief brush of bare and clothed flesh.

The tempo increased and more of the dancers joined the pair, stomping, twirling, writhing, endlessly moving, drawing Libra into a trance. He shifted in his seat, seeking relief from the itch that make him want to jump up and join them—anything to rid himself of the energy building with each passing moment. He needed to dance, needed to pull Taryn to her feet, feel her body brush against his, smell her honeyed scent, touch her hair, tangle his fingers in it. He needed to strip her bare and lay her down…

The music stopped abruptly, jarring Libra out of his thoughts.

He gripped her arm. "What the hell?"

She frowned at his hand.

"You did magic again. Don't lie to me."

She scowled at him, but it was her eyes that caught his attention. Her brown irises were black, even in the bright firelight, the pupils completely dilated.

She jerked away from him, her confusion changing to irritation. "I didn't."

Libra straightened her sleeve. "Sorry."

She turned away from him, her back straight and stiff, his apology not sufficient.

"Is it time?" she asked Solange.

The old woman looked at the sky for a moment then nodded. "It's perfect, but are you sure? You don't have to do this."

"For everything you've done for me, yes, I do."

Libra leaned closer, confused by their exchange.

Solange clapped her hands then raised them high. "Everyone, your attention please. Tonight we have a special treat from one of our own who has recently returned to us after a long time away. She has asked to dance for us tonight, to give herself to the equinox so that we may pass the season from winter to spring."

She clapped as she turned to Taryn, her smile broad, her eyes filled with love and a glint of excitement, perhaps remembering rituals past. Libra couldn't tell.

Taryn stood and the camp erupted with hoots and stomping feet. Two of the dancers ran over and unzipped the gold robe, letting it drop and puddle around Taryn's feet.

Libra gasped and gripped the edge of his seat. Though similar in design to the other dancers' dresses, Taryn's dress was white with the zodiac constellations embroidered in gold.

He ground his teeth.

Her dress didn't stop at mid-back like the others; it dipped all the way down to within a hairsbreadth of exposing the cleavage of her buttocks. He could just see the shadow heralding it. But then his eyes slid down to the curves just hidden by the white and gold. Full, firm, made to be cupped…or spread for pleasure, his pleasure.

His mouth filled with saliva…again, the feast before him far more tantalizing than the food. He swallowed hard. *Goddess damn it.* He cleared his throat and clamped down on his lust. *Control, old boy, remember that?*

Then she turned around.

Aw, hell.

Skin-tight and silk-thin, the dress was a halter, so no sleeves, and the front dipped down just as low as the back did, stopping inches below her navel. Add to that the obvious lack of a bra and the dual slits that exposed both of her legs, and she was essentially naked for all the camp to see.

He jumped up and blocked her from view of the bulk of the camp. "What are you doing?"

She placed her hands on her hips and threw her head back, exposing her long, slim neck and the cleavage that had caused a sweat to break out on his brow. "I'm going to dance to draw down the season."

"Dressed like that? You'll pop out," he choked out, gesturing at her breasts…

her stunning, milky-skinned, nipple-peaked breasts. His palms itched with the need to fondle them.

She glared at him for a moment then her expression changed. She cocked a hip and winked at him as if she had intuited his discomfort and was reveling in it. "That's assuming I'm supposed to remain dressed."

"You wouldn't."

She smirked then stepped away, taking her place on the wooden circle. She stood there alone, her arms hanging by her side, her head bowed. Several of the older women gathered the children and herded them away to their family caravans.

Libra sat down hard. With the children present, he hadn't believed Taryn's jibe to be true; she wouldn't dance nude in front of them. With the children gone…

A single guitar started playing, slow and low, a plaintive melody. Taryn swayed but remained in one place.

Libra slid closer to Solange. "Make her stop. She is not Sol or Nox. This is not her responsibility."

The old woman patted his arm. "She asked for this and we agreed. She may not be Sol or Nox but she is a child of Hecate, making her more closely tied to our goddess than any of us. She is doing us a great honor."

He leaned closer. "She has no skill, no knowledge of Hecate, hell, she barely knows her own mother. She can't find a ley line, much less tap into one, without help. How can she help you with a dance?"

Solange turned to him, a rare scowl on her face. "She has heart. Pure and strong, and she's willing to share it with us. She's not afraid to try, to give of herself, to expose herself to the good and bad in this world in order to feel alive…and find her place. That is very important to her." She looked at Taryn and nodded. "She may not know the steps, she may not perform the dance perfectly, but she will give it her all with no reservation. That is a rare quality. The goddess will be pleased."

Libra crossed his arms and leaned back.

"Perhaps you should take a lesson."

He had given his all to the Twelve, killing to honor his father and his house. But he was free now to do what he could for himself, and sitting here watching Taryn humiliate herself wasn't on that list.

He rose but Solange grabbed his sleeve and pulled him back down. "You will honor her by staying. You will watch her and you will learn what it means to give."

One of the Sol men stepped up behind him, placing his hands on Libra's shoulders and a knee in his back. "He'll stay."

Libra grimaced. "Fine, I'll stay."

Solange smiled and looked away. "Good."

The music shifted to a faster tempo and Taryn raised her arms. She closed her eyes and snapped her fingers as she moved forward, feeling the floor with her feet before taking a step, her hips swaying in a figure eight.

Despite his irritation, Libra was drawn in by her dance, his ire eroding away with each sway of her hips. She completed the circuit and stopped in front of him, opening her eyes and holding out her hands.

He stared at her. He didn't want *her* to dance—there was no way he was going to participate. But before he could refuse her, the male behind him took one of her hands and let Taryn draw him to the floor. He stripped off his black shirt and untied the sash, letting both fall to the ground. As tall as Libra, but with heavier muscle and stronger features, the Nox was handsome enough but coarse. And very eager to sample what Taryn was offering.

They danced in sync, the male's hands on Taryn's hips. He matched her every move, their bodies touching, brushing, pressing, a slow, rhythmic foreplay.

Libra gripped the edge of his seat and leaned forward, his breathing changing to a pant. The world slowed, the edges blurring until all he could see was Taryn and the male groping her. He shook his head to clear it but the fuzziness remained.

The male slid his hands inside Taryn's dress until his arms wrapped around her. He settled his hands on her belly and pulled her bare back tight against his chest, her buttocks into his groin. He ground into her as she lifted her arms. She reached back and slid her fingers through his thick, brown hair then closed her eyes, lost to the slow rhythm.

"Libra?" Solange whispered.

He blinked and looked at the woman.

"Are you okay?" she asked, pointing at his hands.

He looked down. His hands and wrists were glowing blue, Gaia's power dripping from his fingers even as it climbed up his forearms. "Damn it."

He released his grip and shook his hands but the blue kept advancing. He stood, staring at it creeping up his arms.

"Libra?"

Taryn stood in front of him, alone, her partner backing away from the blue energy that had started at her bare feet and was steadily engulfing her.

The crowd murmured, leaning back as if distancing themselves as much as possible without breaking the circle.

"Do you know what's happening?" Libra asked Solange.

"I would say Gaia is speaking quite clearly."

"And what is she saying that is so clear to you?"

Solange nodded in Taryn's direction. "Dance."

28

LIBRA'S BELLY BOTTOMED OUT; icy heat froze and melted his veins. "No. There has to be another explanation."

The men sitting closest to Libra stared at him, their faces darkening with each passing second.

"You asked me what Gaia wants and I told you. Listen to her or don't." Solange crossed her arms and waited.

Taryn walked up to him. "It can't hurt."

"No." He chopped at the air with an open hand. "I won't be manipulated into doing what Gaia wants." He pointed at Solange. "This is how it starts. A little help here, a favor there, then she has you."

"Libra?" Taryn touched his shoulder.

The scent of honey and woman teased him, triggering a battle between his body's desire to drag Taryn away into the dark and his head's logical need to avoid her. There wasn't another woman in all the worlds that could send him careening into his dark side like this. Worse than that, he was afraid she would revel in his dark, writhing and rolling in it like a Kellas Cat in catnip, and make him love it, too.

He pulled away from her. "I've been forced to reach out to Gaia twice now. I've made myself known to her." His belly clenched and he fell to one knee, his body shaking, the stabbing pain in his head nauseating. "I won't be her agent, I won't...I won't..."

He pitched forward. The blue choked him, squeezing the outside of his body. He grabbed his head and pressed on the temples, trying to stop the excruciating waves of pain.

Fingers ran through his hair, smoothing it back. "Come, Libra, open your eyes."

He looked up. Taryn had squatted next to him, a soft smile on her face. She pushed the stubborn lock of hair off his forehead again and cupped his cheek. The headache stopped as fast as it had started.

"Better?" She stood and offered him her hand.

He hesitated, but the relief from the pain was too great a draw to resist. He had to touch her again before it returned. He gripped her hand and let her help him to his feet. They stood staring at each other for several moments, each second dispelling more of the pain until it became mere discomfort.

"What's happening?" he whispered.

"Stop fighting Gaia's call and the pain will end."

He nodded.

She pulled him to the wooden floor. "Dance with me. No fancy moves, no ritual, no Gaia, just us, swaying back and forth under the stars on a beautiful night, surrounded by beautiful people while wearing beautiful clothes. Isn't that what you said you wanted?"

"Your gown *is* beautiful...what there is of it."

Taryn laughed, her genuine amusement infectious.

He grinned and opened his arms. She slid into them, pressing her body against his. The discomfort disappeared, leaving only warmth in its wake. He held out his left hand and she placed her right in it. He placed his other hand low on the small of her back and grinned at her, one eyebrow cocked.

Taryn smiled back. "Yes."

The guitar started again and the tension of the camp eased like a soft wave washing over him. He relaxed into the dance and inhaled the scent wafting off Taryn's skin. He dropped his head to her bare shoulder and pressed his lips to her warm, honey-dust-soft skin.

So sweet, silky.

A pulse of lust rocketed through him. He pulled Taryn's hips into him and pressed against her with a slow, rolling thrust that he couldn't stop. "Taryn."

She looked into his eyes. "I feel it, too."

Libra released her body and cupped her face, leaning close until their lips were a hairsbreadth apart, close enough that they exchanged breath. He inhaled her, welcoming the heat and air and life coursing through her, feeding off it. He pressed his mouth against hers…and was lost. The darkness gripped him, but he was too tangled in needing her to stop.

The Sol and Nox cheered. The music stopped. Several women pulled Taryn away from him. He growled and lunged for her but he couldn't break free of the men restraining him. His hands itched and power built inside him, the need to obliterate anyone keeping him from Taryn almost overwhelming. Twin fires, within and without, heated his body and mind.

Taryn was escorted to the other side of the flames and the music started again. Libra stalked her but she smiled and kept the fire between them, her body spinning so fast her firm upper thighs were exposed.

"Screw this."

Libra tried to catch her but she laughed and danced out of his reach. She beckoned him, daring him to catch her. He lifted his arms and copied her spin, then danced closer to her. The music filled his core. Everything drummed into him about decorum and manners evaporated, leaving him free for the first time since he had become a Zodiac. Free like a child—the child he had been before Aubrianna first lifted a hand to him.

His dark, feral side eagerly filled the vacancy left by the exit of the light. He dropped his head and zeroed in on Taryn, all pretenses gone, all of his masks ripped away, leaving only the base need to capture and mate with her.

Inamorata.

The word filled his head and he smiled. He ripped open the embroidered shirt, sending the buttons flying. The cold air tickled his skin, cooling it, giving him slight relief, but it did nothing to ease the raging heat burning him from the inside out.

The women around him gasped—the men grunted their approval and clapped in time with the music. The rhythm of the drums and guitars slowed, changing from a hard, driving pace to a sensual vine that wound around Libra and forced him to slow.

Taryn stumbled; her eyes widened as she took him in. She stopped dancing and waited as he advanced, white puffs escaping her open mouth.

He stopped in front of her, his body pressing into hers—intoxicated by the feel of her clothed breasts heaving against his naked chest.

Taryn groaned.

The guttural sound was all the permission he needed. Libra ran his large hands into her black hair. He lowered his head until his lips met hers, holding her there for a seeming eternity, teasing, taunting.

She closed her eyes.

He waited.

Their breath mingled, but he waited.

They groaned together, but, still, he waited.

Taryn sagged into him and ran her hands up his back until she reached his shoulders, gripping them tight as if preparing herself for one helluva ride.

The dark lust took control and he plundered her mouth, his hunger fueling hers, matched and equal in their need. He released her head, gathered the knotted halter-top at the back of her neck, and ripped the fabric in two—the delicate panels dropping to her waist. He stared at her full breasts and the swollen, dark pink nipples.

He barely heard the cheer of the crowd, only the music. Taryn lifted her head and squared her shoulders—her breasts jutted closer to him, pressing, begging to be ravaged. He growled his answer, grabbed her buttocks, and lifted her.

Taryn wrapped her legs around his waist and arched her back to give him the access they both desired. He sucked in a nipple and drew hard, over and over, like a man starving. She opened for him, her pelvis thrusting into his in time with his mouth. He slid his hands under her skirt, reveling in her naked thighs, until he reached her core and discovered that she'd gone commando. His knees nearly buckled.

He slid a finger inside her and she bucked against him—natural, naked, and wet as hell. His sex thrummed, his need desperate.

The group roared. Libra glanced around. Nox and Sol clung to one another, their faces fevered, their hands busy ripping clothes, fondling, sucking, thrusting.

As badly as he wanted to seat his sex inside her right here, he wanted Taryn alone. Libra turned away from the fire and carried her into the dark, searching until he found the trailer she shared with Solange's granddaughter. He threw open the door, carried Taryn to the bed, and lowered her half-dressed body. He flipped on a light, then another, until she was exposed to him.

With a pull of the drawstring, his pants dropped to his feet and he kicked them away. He stood next to her, taking in every inch of her delicious curves.

Taryn looked at him with glazed eyes. She covered her breasts. "The light?"

Libra stood over her, his sex bobbing, seeking her—the chill of the night air caressing his engorged flesh. "You got me here. You demanded I dance. I did what you wanted and I bared myself to you. Now, you will do the same."

He climbed onto the bed and hovered over her. He pulled her arms away from her chest, then bent down and lapped at an erect nipple.

She writhed.

"You will moan for me. I want to see you come undone and know that I did that to you. You wanted to see me without my masks. That's exactly what you're seeing now. Don't expect polite or cool. Don't think for one moment that you can avoid giving me your all. You want my darkness? Open your legs and it'll fill you to bursting."

Libra took a deep breath before he continued, praying to all that was holy that she would stop this, stop him. "Or say 'no' and I'll leave."

Taryn's mouth slowly curved up at the corners; her dilated eyes glittered. She pushed her ruined dress over her hips and kicked it off without looking away.

He sucked in air and growled.

She spread her legs as he had demanded and threw her head back. "Do your worst."

He settled between her thighs, his weight sinking into her belly.

Her eyes glazed over and she spread her thighs wider until his sex pressed against her center.

Libra pushed back her hair and nibbled on her bottom lip. He sucked it in and worried it with his teeth before releasing it.

Taryn ran her hands down his back and over his buttocks. She pulled them into her and rocked against him.

Libra palmed a breast then gently twisted her tight nipple. He rocked his hips, sliding his sex along the length of her folds and back. Her core wept for him.

"Do you like this?"

She nodded then shook her head. "I need you inside me."

She reached for his sex and tried to guide it but he eased down her body to escape her grip. He kissed and sucked the skin between her breasts then nibbled down her belly. She arched, ran her fingers through his hair, and pulled.

He growled and flicked his tongue inside her navel before raising his body off the bed. He stayed on his knees at the end of the mattress and pulled her down until her butt hit his belly. He gripped the back of her knees and pushed her legs forward, exposing all of her to his gaze. Beautiful, pale pink flesh changed to dark pink at the heart of her. He spread her folds then leaned down and ran his tongue between them.

Taryn bucked. "Holy mother!"

Libra gripped her tighter and licked again.

She squirmed and clapped her thighs against his head.

He nipped the tender skin of her inner thighs. "Relax."

"Holy crap. How?"

"Get ready." He lowered his head but kept his eyes on her face.

Her thighs jerked. Her hands fluttered around his head for a moment before gripping it and pushing her hips up. He sucked and lapped her in time with the rhythm of the music still playing outside, pushing her closer and closer to her edge then savagely working her as she flew apart beneath him, her wail shoving him into the deepest depths of his darkness.

He rose up above her.

She bared her teeth as if feeling the power and ravenous need inside his body. He paused and cocked his head, giving her one more chance to say no, but desperate for her permission.

Taryn wrapped her legs around his hips and pulled him to her—her demand punctuated by a guttural growl.

He growled back, any pretense of control gone. The dark had pushed away the light and he had fallen. He pressed the head of his sex against her entrance, gripped her hips tight, and looked in her eyes as he seated himself in one thrust.

He threw back his head and roared. He pulled out and slammed inside her again, the slap of skin more of an aphrodisiac than any magical potion.

"Harder," Taryn demanded as she pushed him away then pulled him inside her again. "Don't you dare hold back."

He hissed and stroked harder, faster, adjusting his speed and power to the response of her body, the vehemence of her demands. He grabbed the iron headboard for greater leverage and pounded her small body.

She exploded a second time and he rode her hard through the orgasm, not giving her a moment to rest. She sagged for a moment then lifted her legs, planted her feet against his hips, and shoved him away. He fell off the bed but bounded back, his sex hard, wet, questing. He reached for her but she flipped onto her stomach and lifted her delicious ass high in the air.

"Your turn."

He climbed up behind her and bit her right butt cheek before gripping her hips and impaling her. She groaned, sending him close to the edge. He slowed his thrusts, feeling the wet heat that squeezed him tight, milking him, prepping him for the fall.

Taryn growled loud and long.

His hands tingled with waves of heat. He looked down and gasped when he saw his skin glowing. Gaia's power was flowing out of his hands and over Taryn's body, enveloping her in blue.

She writhed and groaned again. "What are you doing?"

"Shit, am I hurting you? I'll stop."

She looked back at him and scowled. "You stop and I'll kick your ass."

She rested the side of her face against the bed and closed her eyes as she pushed her hips into him. He slid deeper inside then threw his head back when her passage pulsed.

He gripped her hips tighter and concentrated on releasing more power. The glow flowed out of his hands and the middle of his chest, until both of them were inside a cerulean cloud of pulsating energy.

He turned his attention to controlling his release; the need to drag her over with him, to come at the same time, was more overwhelming than just popping his top. He wanted her to understand that she was his. They were dancing in the darkness and she had accepted him fully in this place. But he needed to drive her deeper, as deep as his corruption went, branding her for everyone to see.

Mine, mine, mine.

He repeated the word over and over in his mind until he heard her moan.

His thrusts increased, slapping flesh, the friction engorging his sex to the point of pain. A spasm ran the length of him.

"Now. Now!"

He drove hard into her, frantic, racing against the tightening of her sex that heralded the verge of her explosion.

Pulses rolled the length of him; they were joined in a race to the cliff. His muscles tightened. Her sex clenched around him once, twice, then shoved him over.

They roared as they hovered in mid-air, tight, tense, jerking, thrusting until they dropped into the deepest dark of his soul…together.

29

T HE CAMP WAS SILENT in that time of the deep night where all living creatures slept, even the nocturnal ones. Libra opened his eyes, his senses coming alert. Taryn had snuggled up against his side while she slept, softly snuffling with each exhale. He eased out from under the covers then settled the blanket around her, watching her for a moment before pushing an errant, black curl off her face with one finger. He studied her profile, so relaxed, without a care, his body tingling with unwanted desire.

How had this happened? How had they ended up in bed together? Granted, the sex had been mind-blowing, but why would Gaia push them together? Why would he succumb?

How he'd show his face to everyone who'd witnessed his behavior was a completely different issue that he didn't have the courage or the energy to contemplate right now. His loss of control was unconscionable, disgraceful, and could never be repeated. Hell, he had almost thrown Taryn to the ground and plowed her like a randy dog in front of the whole camp.

Worse still, the woman had been game to be taken. He had felt her body quiver when he had pressed his engorged sex against her belly. He had smelled her honey and musk arousal, inhaled it so deep inside him that it had filled every cell in his body. Damn it, he was still filled with the scent of her and he doubted she would ever be gone from him, no matter how many years passed.

Worst of all, he wanted to wake her and take her again…and again and again… till death did they part, like an inamorata, a mate. He shuddered and backed away, the desire to leave competing with the horror of that urge. Never. It would never happen. After watching his mother and father nearly tear each other apart, he had sworn that no woman could ever be his mate.

A horse snorted and the soft sound of voices drew his attention. He eased out of the van, closing the door gently. The low campfire was the only light in the camp but it was enough for Libra to see the bustle of people and horses.

He grabbed the arm of a passing male. "What's happening?"

"We're breaking camp."

"Were you going to tell me or Taryn? Or just leave us here?"

The male pulled out of Libra's grip. "Just the Sol are leaving; the Nox will remain here as the keepers of the vernal equinox until the summer solstice. I would recommend you leave at sunrise. The Nox don't know you…and they don't want to know you."

He walked away, leaving Libra standing in the middle of the chaos.

The bird cried out. Libra jogged to the van in time to see one side drop down from the roofline, exposing the interior. Solange clucked at the bird, waving raw meat in its face, trying to turn it around, but the beast was too frightened. It cowered into a corner.

"Ah, Libra. Just in time," Solange said under her breath. "Will you help me?"

He climbed the steps. "What are you doing?"

"He is strong enough to fly, but he needs to eat before we send him away." She held the meat out to him. "Will you try?"

Libra took the raw meat from her. "Sure." He approached the bird, watchful of the massive beak as he waved the food closer and closer. "Okay, big guy. Time to eat, without including my fingers, please."

The bird's neck straightened; it cocked its head to one side to eyeball the food.

Just when Libra thought the creature would strike, its beak opened and it waited. Libra tossed the meat and it swallowed it down with one gulp.

"Good job, Zodiac." Solange toed a large bowl with the rest of the bird's meal toward him then backed out of the van. "Finish, will you?"

"Wait. Do you know what kind of creature this is? Where it came from?"

Solange paused. "I thought you knew."

"No, I don't."

"This is a Stryx."

He said nothing because he had no idea what a Stryx was.

"The Stryx are harbingers of war. They've not been seen in this world for centuries. The legend is they fell with the old gods, but instead of landing in Hades, they fell all the way to the abyss."

"Into Hell?"

Solange nodded.

"So these Stryx could have risen with the demons."

"Most likely, if the tales are true."

"That would mean Asmodeus…"

His voice trailed off. The Corvus Ward king, Aubrianna, and now the demon king. How many more players could there be?

Solange nodded and turned away.

Libra eyeballed the bird, who was now very interested in the bowl at his feet. He grabbed a handful of the warm flesh—not sure he wanted to know where it came from—and tossed piece after piece until the bowl was empty.

"Now what?" he called out to Solange.

"Convince him to leave."

"Why are you booting him out anyway?"

"As long as it's with us, the greater chance the rest will return. I can't risk the lives of my people."

Libra couldn't argue with that logic but he had hoped the Sol would keep the bird until after he had rescued the children so he could track it back to its keeper. If he was right and it was Asmodeus who had sicced the birds on them, he needed to find out why and soon. Not to mention, who warned him of the attack?

Wrangling with Taryn over the bird had been difficult enough. Add in some children…yeah, no, he couldn't take the Stryx with him. The bird was a puzzle he would have to let go. For now…

He clapped his hands to get the creature's attention then backed out of the van. The bird followed his movement, turning to face the open wall. Libra backed away, beckoning, hoping the bird was as smart as it had seemed a few hours earlier.

"Time to go, big guy. You're not completely healed but you should be able to fly now."

The Stryx placed its claws on the edge, sniffed the air, then raised its head to the moonless sky. It squawked once, hopped to the ground, and stood tall, its wings extended.

Libra stepped back to give it room and craned his head to take in the immense size of the beast. It had been huge in the van but, now, standing, the thing had to be ten feet tall. Long legged with deadly talons, a massive chest, and a wing span the size of a single-engine plane, the bird was a monstrous and fearsome creature.

Had he been standing against it without Gaia's power and Taryn's help, he'd have been devoured as effortlessly as the meat. He cringed at the thought. The idea that he and Taryn had made a good team sent a shiver through him. They had saved each other with help from the goddess he'd avoided all his life.

Not sure how I feel about that.

Before he could contemplate the topic to death, the bird leaped into the air and flapped its wings. A few hard efforts and it started to climb into the night sky. Within seconds, it had cleared the trees and flown due east.

Libra looked for Solange, but she and the rest of the Sol were already rolling out of the camp…no goodbyes, no great-to-meet-you, and no chance to thank them for saving his life. The Nox leader scowled at him then disappeared inside her van. The rest of the Nox followed suit, leaving him alone. The weight of the past few days descended in the silence. He was exhausted and the morning would bring a new set of troubles, namely Taryn and her determination to fling them into whatever fray was before them.

He slid inside the van and undressed before slipping under the covers. Taryn rolled into him, throwing a leg over his waist and an arm over his chest. She nestled into him, sending his body into lust overdrive.

"For goddess' sake, stop it," he chided his body as he closed his eyes. "That was a one and done."

* * *

Taryn slid out of bed and covered the still-sleeping Libra with the thick comforter. She studied his relaxed, scruff-covered face and messy hair before a twinge in her chest made her look away. Sleeping with him didn't embarrass her—it had been wonderful. What did mortify her was her desperate desire to crawl under the covers and make love with him until they were consumed by Gaia's blue glow again.

He rolled onto his back, his hair standing straight up. She gently smoothed it down until a small voice inside her complained.

What the hell are you doing, Taryn? Falling for the guy?

She clenched her hand into a fist and backed away, nearly tripping over the pile of fabric that was her ruined dress.

She dug through the dresser until she found a fresh skirt and shirt. Topping the ensemble with a thick coat, she escaped the trailer for the fog and overcast sky of the warm morning. The camp was quiet, too quiet. She rounded the corner of the caravan and stopped. Half of the camp was gone. The Sol caravans had left sometime last night, leaving her with the Nox.

The Nox leader turned in her direction, her dark eyes locking on Taryn.

Taryn wrapped her black, puffy coat tighter around her body and closed the distance until she stood in front of the woman. "Where are they?"

"The ritual was completed. There was no reason for them to stay." The Nox leader gestured to the fire pit. "Join me before you go. Solange asked me to make some of that coffee you love so much."

Taryn sat and accepted the mug.

The two women settled by the crackling, dancing flames and sipped the rich, dark brew in silence.

Taryn's heart sank. The warmth that Solange and her people had shared with her wasn't to be found with the Nox. Their leaving without saying goodbye stung like a mother. Perhaps, in light of what had happened last night, it was easier for everyone. But she would miss the loving Solange and the acceptance of her people.

A light, tinkling sound pulled Taryn's attention back to the Nox woman.

She placed a set of keys on the log they were sitting on. "These are to that truck over there. Solange wanted you to have it, for your journey. Everything you need for a couple days is inside."

Taryn palmed the keys and nodded her thanks before sipping her coffee and letting the silence settle between them again. It was time to move on.

30

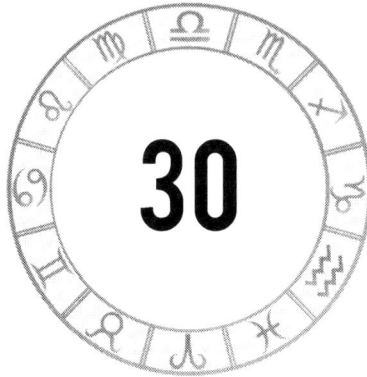

LIBRA OPENED THE DOOR then stopped, surprised by the warm, humid air that slid over his skin. He was overdressed. He pulled the sweater over his head and dropped it on the floor of the caravan. Standing in the doorway, he looked around the half-empty camp. Men and women crisscrossed between black and blue vans, each carrying pots and pans and foodstuffs to the fire while exuberant, colorfully dressed children scampered underfoot. They all looked refreshed, like last night had never happened, or like it happened all the time and they didn't care.

He caught sight of the long, thick, black curls of the woman sitting by the fire, the Nox leader next to her. His heart stopped for a second as a shot of heat and lust rocked him. He walked across the grassy expanse, too focused on Taryn to pay any mind to the people trying to get out of his way, until he stood behind her, watching her sip from a mug. The women sat in silence.

A long, deep roll of thunder rumbled through the camp.

Libra glanced back. Heavy, black clouds had appeared on the horizon, the leading edge a sickly green.

The Nox woman grunted, the sound low and full of disgust. "That storm? You two called down the equinox last night, but no one expected you to bring on such a huge cell."

Libra crossed his arms over his chest against the blast of ozone-rich air that swept over him. "What are you talking about?"

The woman didn't react to the sudden change in the wind. "We are one of a legion of Hecate's children living around the world. After she entombed Circe, the gods and goddesses were angry that Hecate defied her order to kill her daughter and they forced Hecate and Persephone back to Hades prematurely. Crops died, people starved; we all thought it was the end of days. But Demeter saw our suffering and petitioned Zeus to take pity on us. He allowed Demeter to select witches from Hecate's coven. She divided them into four groups, one for each season, and scattered us to every corner of the world. Not long after that, the worship of the old ones was left behind. The people celebrated other gods and we were left on the earth, alone."

"You talk as if you were there," Libra said.

"I was there. I am a queen of spring."

"If you're the queen of spring, why don't you stop the storm?" Libra asked.

"Because whatever you did last night intensified our calling down ritual." She turned to Libra and stabbed him with a milky stare. "That blue glow you two generated? It didn't just happen around you two and it didn't just go away after you found your pleasure."

Taryn choked on her coffee. She coughed and sputtered until she could finally speak. "You saw us?"

"The caravan door was open. We all saw you," she said, "and the whole county heard you."

Libra's face blazed as hot as Taryn's face was red. "Okay, so you witnessed us. What is it you think we did?" He nodded at the clouds. "Looks like you better make it fast."

"The energy you generated didn't dissipate inside you. It surrounded your caravan, then the entire camp. When you found pleasure, the bubble burst but the energy didn't vanish. I felt it fly apart in all directions, still pulsing with power as it soared into the sky to create the coming storm. When it comes down in the rain it will soak into the ground and feed the ever hungry ley lines."

Sleet pelted them. The men and women gathered the children and disappeared inside their vans, leaving the old woman, Taryn, and Libra alone in the storm.

The Nox rose and started walking to her van, her steps slow but sure. "You need to learn to control that energy." She looked back at the pair. "Most importantly, you need to understand how to contain it, reabsorb it, so you don't destroy everything the Sol and the Nox have dedicated their lives to preserving. The planet and all the lives on it."

The sleet changed to hail.

Libra covered his head. "We need to get out of this."

Taryn pointed at a truck and held up a set of keys. "We've been given our marching orders."

She took off.

Libra ran after her, climbing into the passenger side when Taryn took the driver's side. "Why aren't I driving?"

"Do you have a license?"

"No."

"We can't afford to get stopped. At least I have an expired license. You? They wouldn't find you in any system, and who knows what might happen."

"Okay, you drive." He looked back at the camp.

"What about our feathered friend?" she asked.

"Gone, released, flew away last night," he said, staring out the front windshield.

The engine fired and the truck vibrated into life. He belted in and drummed his fingers on the door. At least they were finally on their way to the nearest town and a computer. As vivid as his vision had been, he wasn't going anywhere without researching the route. The way things had gone so far, he didn't trust what he had seen.

Taryn put the truck in drive and eased away from the camp, the hail deafening as it pounded on the roof, the windshield wipers on full speed to clear the glass of rain and ice.

If only he could wipe away his trepidation so easily.

31

LYON STOOD AT THE massive front entrance to the InBetween watching Persephone, Abella, and his children drive away in a large, touring bus—like the ones used by famous singers, Abella had informed him. He had pushed and protested, but the women had refused to be driven away nearly fast enough. A few hours be damned; it had taken him days to get them gone.

He turned on his heel and strode through the hallways, followed closely by the alpha Fenrir Wolf and his pack, until he reached the closest entrance to the dungeon. "I have work to do in the dark." He turned on the canids. "You really don't want to go down there with me." He opened the door. "Stay."

The monstrous, feral wolves whined but obeyed him.

He closed the door behind him and paused, letting the dark and cold and memories wash over him. "Buck up, man."

He rolled his shoulders and started down the worn, stone stairs leading to the cells. Unlike his tenure here, most of the dungeon was empty. Years of torture and pain had left him with no appetite for the punishments the Twelve had meted out so freely, so eagerly.

But, he thought when he stopped at the only closed door remaining, *not everyone deserves freedom after their role in releasing the demon army.* He'd already freed gremlins, Bathory Berserkers, and the other captured offenders, but he'd saved this prisoner for last.

He unlocked the door and opened it wide, searching the dark corners.

"Have you come to kill me?" a woman's raspy voice whispered.

"Come into the light."

Ailith, the Pondera Exemplar spy, walked into the narrow circle of light, her head thrown back, her bright blue eyes snapping with defiance. "So you finally made it to me. Shall I prepare to have my head separated from my shoulders, or will you feed me to the trolls?"

Lyon crossed his arms and held his temper. "They don't like rancid meat."

She stopped. "If you're not here to kill me, then what do you want?"

She pushed her long, brown hair over her shoulders and blew her long bangs out of her eyes.

"I've come to ask you what your plans are now that your cover has been blown. Will you go back to your people?"

She stepped closer. "Why? So if my answer doesn't please you, you have an excuse to throw me in the hole like you did Leona?"

"That's not what happened. She jumped."

"Bullshit."

"How long did you know her? A couple days? And that makes you an expert?"

Ailith came so close her toes touched his. She raised her eyes and jutted out her chin. "I stood this close to her and looked into her eyes. I saw who she was, what she wanted for her life, for the InBetween."

Lyon studied the set of her jaw and the fierce belief in Leona that burned in her gaze. He was sure his sister had had a plan that didn't include suicide; she'd been prepared for a journey. That, and the fact that he'd seen her levitate over the hole for a few seconds before dropping out of sight, had convinced him that she wasn't dead. Not that he would share that with this woman.

"You sound as if you care about her," he said.

Ailith stepped back and looked away. "I cared about her ambitions. And her promises to me."

Hell, the woman looked wistful. Lyon raised an eyebrow. "Promises?"

"I was to be her second, and she promised to make me a Zodiac."

Lyon dropped his arms and sagged. "Hells bells, woman, becoming a Zodiac is the last thing to aspire to. Do you even know how we were made?"

"I don't care."

"You would if you knew the pain."

"I am not afraid of pain."

He closed in on her, cornering her. "I'm not talking about the momentary pain of creation. I'm talking about the daily agony of having such a purulent evil attached to your soul. It is not a curse you want."

"Do not presume to know what I want."

"Fine." He stepped out of the cell and gave her room to pass. "You are free to go."

She moved past him and took several steps down the hall that would lead to her freedom before stopping. "Why are you doing this?"

"Because the paranorms need to work together if we are to survive what's coming."

"And you want to be the great leader of us all." She snorted. "Get in line. There are many leaders ahead of you without the stink of the Twelve on them."

"The Zodiacs are nothing like the Twelve."

She turned on him. "And, yet, no one will follow you. Releasing me will not change that."

They reached the final door out of the dungeon. Ailith stepped aside as Lyon unlocked the door. He opened it and she bounded past him, straight into the pack of Fenrir Wolves.

As one, they stood, their hackles raised and heads low, their growls even lower.

Ailith stopped dead, her hands raised in front of her as if she could placate the creatures. "Call them off."

Lyon waited a couple beats just to make her sweat a bit. He whistled once and the wolves backed away, their hackles still raised.

"You are—" He stopped talking as the ground bucked beneath him.

The earthquake was deep; Lyon could feel the very bowels of the earth heaving. The wolves yelped and cringed as pebbles bounced and dust rained down on them.

"Go that way to get out," he yelled at the woman, pointing to the front entrance. She took off at a clumsy run and disappeared around a bend in the hall.

In the opposite direction, the trolls roared. With no one in the Great Cavern to soothe them, the beasts could stampede or, worse, fall into the huge hole they were guarding.

"Goddess help me."

He took off at a run, the wolves on his heels. With no paranorms to dodge, he only had to contend with the shifting ground, so he made good time. Sliding to a stop at the entrance to the massive space, he looked up and saw the spell hiding the hole in the cavern roof—and hiding the InBetween from exposure to the human world—had failed.

The trolls had rolled away from the hole in the ground and were struggling to regain their feet, their panic increasing their stink exponentially.

Lyon worked his way over to them.

Before he could reach the huge beasts, the earthquake stopped. "It's over. Settle down."

He watched as they righted themselves, but before the trolls could start back to their posts, Lyon heard screams. He looked up and saw two humans fall through the roof. It was a man and a woman, their arms and legs pinwheeling, followed by several pieces of equipment. They fell into the hole in the ground and disappeared, their screams growing softer until they finally stopped.

He walked to the edge and looked down, not expecting to see the humans, but unable to stop himself from trying. There was no sign of them; they were in a long fall, with a *splat* waiting for them at the end. He looked up and saw blue skies, green grass, and brown dirt; there was no distortion of colors from the spell. It had truly failed and it wasn't coming back, leaving them wide open to human eyes for the first time in centuries.

"Well, shit."

* * *

Pisces wiped the water from his face and took a deep breath. "Seriously, Ari, can't you part the waters more than that?"

Aquarius trembled with effort, his feet spread as wide as his upraised arms, concentrating on keeping the aquifer water parted like the Red Sea. "What the hell you want, Pisces? I'm not Moses."

"And I don't have fish gills, I can't hold my breath forever. And the name is Niko—use it or there'll be no more intercourse between us."

"Intercourse? What?"

Pisces grinned, his fists on his hips, and his feet spread wide, looking like a bare-ass naked pirate on a rolling deck. "Yeah, you know, talk."

"Ahh! You and your fucking books."

"You thought I meant sex, didn't you? Admit it, I gotcha that time."

"Damn it, quit fooling around and try again. The Red Cap swore there was a passage to the cave system down there." Ari grunted as he widened his shaking arms. "Why do you care what I call you?"

"What? You think a bunch of children could have been taken under all that water in the pitch dark and to a cave before they all drowned? Hell, even I'm struggling to find it." Pisces shook his head like a wet dog, his dark brown hair sending water flying. "The Twelve are dead and the demon king is loose in the Overworld; I want to use my birth name again."

Aquarius dropped his arms and the two halves of water slammed into each other. The water rebounded, drenching every horizontal surface in the cave, and its interlopers, the force nearly pushing Pisces over the edge and under the waves.

"Sure…Niko."

Pisces sighed and picked up his folded pile of now-soaked clothes. He turned to his fellow Zodiac and shook them in the male's face, his brown eyes flashing his irritation.

Ari closed his eyes and winced. "For goddess' sake, put them on. I've seen enough of your bare ass to last many lifetimes."

"Well, I would, except now they're all wet."

"You're a fish. You love wet."

"I'm a paranorm who happens to be able to hold his breath a long time under water. That doesn't make me a fish." He waved a hand over the side of his neck. "No gills. No fish."

"Cold, scaly…stinky; I'd say that makes you as fishy as any fish living in the water." Ari shook his head. "How the hell do you manage to bed a woman without poisoning her with your spines?"

"My spines are venomous like a reef stonefish; now pufferfish are poisonous, if you eat their flesh. And I can control when they emerge from my skin. Get it straight, brother." Pisces wrung out his pants then his shirt before donning them with a grimace. "As for women, like I said, I can hold my breath a long…long time. The ladies seem to feel the risk is worth the reward."

Ari rolled his eyes and started the climb out of the cave to the surface. "Yeah, I bet you feel right at home down there."

Pisces burst out laughing. "Brother, you have no idea."

"Nor do I want to," Ari called out from above.

"Don't know what you're missing, man."

The two Zodiacs wriggled their bodies out of the tiny shaft and plopped down on the boulder-strewn mountainside.

"The sun feels so good," Pisces muttered.

Ari had opened his mouth to make a snarky remark when the screech of a Hermes hawk brought him to his feet, Pisces right behind him.

"You expecting a message from Lyon?" Ari asked.

"Nope, but maybe it's a call home. We sure haven't found any children."

The hawk drifted on the thermals in a lazy spiral, its glide dropping down with each turn until it made a pass a few feet above their heads. It opened a claw and dropped a small vial.

Ari caught it and removed a tiny scroll of vellum. He read the message and passed it to Pisces while watching the hawk fly away, his eyes narrowed. "Do you recognize that bird?"

Pisces glanced up then snorted. "Like I know every hawk in the mews."

"I know most of them, and that hawk doesn't look familiar."

Pisces folded the note and stuck it in his pocket. "So we're to return to the Great Cavern right away." He looked at the tiny dot disappearing in the distance "You think Lyon united the paranorms?"

"Maybe. But whatever happened, we'd better move it."

"Yes! I am overdue for some breath-holding, preferably with that purple Kellas Cat."

"A cat and a fish? Goddess, you're an idiot."

Pisces trotted down the steep slope. "Yeah, but admit it. You love it, water boy."

"Oh, *hell* no." He shoved Pisces. "Move it. I don't want to be the last ones there."

32

LIBRA SQUIRMED IN HIS seat. "Are we there yet?"

"Hold on, we're only a few minutes out." Taryn frowned at him. "What's the problem? Do you have to go to the bathroom again?"

"No. I don't like not driving. It gives me something to do."

"It's all about control with you, isn't it?" She pointed through the windshield. "Look. The edges of the town."

He sat up and stopped fidgeting. 'Town' was generous. A small, clapboard house flashed by, the structure repaired and clean, but the owner was losing the battle against time and wear.

They passed another house in no better shape, but this one had a picket fence and a couple of small children playing in the dirt while their mother sat slumped in a rocking chair on the porch. She barely registered the truck passing, dark circles under her eyes, her skin sagging from exhaustion or depression.

"You sure there's a library here?" Taryn asked as they slowed to a creep and entered the main body of the town. "There's not even a stoplight."

Libra searched the road ahead until he saw a sign with missing letters that read, 'Sta-ton Li-rar-'. "There, on the right."

Taryn pulled up next to the one-story building. Cracks and chips covered the red brick façade, and the right corner of the foundation was sagging. "They have a computer?"

"They're listed as having one."

Libra opened the truck door and slid out, happy to put his feet on the ground and escape the silence that had reigned over the last few hours. It had seemed the more miles they racked up, the more the distance grew between them. This morning, Taryn had been warm, if a bit distracted by the Nox leader, and he'd hoped to talk with her about last night—more specifically why it couldn't happen again. But as the silence had grown, so too had the chasm between *let's get this conversation over with* and *let's never, ever speak of it*, until the latter won the day.

Finally, he decided to let the matter drop—much easier that way, and less messy.

He held open the door for Taryn and she entered without meeting his eyes or acknowledging him in any way. Freeze out for sure, but it would pass. It always did—or he left town, which was his most common method of letting them down easy. He took a deep breath for the first time since they'd left the Nox camp. That moment was done, gone, over.

So why did his gut flip flop at the thought? Why did he want to lean forward and inhale the scent of her lingering in the air?

Hell and damn.

He stepped inside and let the door close behind him before following Taryn. The small foyer was clean and smelled like lemon. A chalkboard sat on a canting easel, the list of new books filling only a third of the small board. Just beyond it, to his right, was a short hall that led to a large room filled with stacks that took up most of the building's square footage. At the end, there were three doors: one with a restroom sign, the second proclaiming it was the 'office,' the third unlabeled.

He turned his attention back to Taryn and the woman standing behind a counter. Middle-aged, with close-cropped, brown hair, a bright pink polo shirt, jeans, and a huge smile, the librarian was leaning forward, nodding as Taryn talked.

"Li, Ruth here is the librarian."

He offered his hand and the woman shook it vigorously. "Welcome, Lee. Taryn was asking about our computer."

He smiled and turned on the charm. "We are in great need of help."

She batted her eyes, obviously no stranger to laying it on thick herself. "No cell phone?"

"Alas, Taryn's phone is a dinosaur. Internet access is dicey."

"That's interesting since you knew to come here," she said with a smile that didn't quite reach her eyes.

Libra leaned on the counter and smiled broadly. This woman was good. "Just a blip of bandwidth that allowed us to find you, but not near enough to do an extended search. You are the closest place we could find with a computer in this part of the country."

Ruth crossed her arms over her chest. "Uh-huh."

Libra decided to plow on. "So may we use your computer? We'd be happy to make a donation to the library."

She studied him. For a moment he wondered if the woman was a Portend in disguise or a witch. Either way, the hairs on the back of his neck rose. But he held still, his smile locked in place, giving her his most effective I'm-no-trouble look.

Finally, she dropped her arms. "Donations are always appreciated but they're not required to use the computer. Unless, you need to print something." She waved at them to follow her. "Back here."

She led them through the neat, clean body of the library—she obviously loved it—until they reached the third door, the one with no sign. She opened the door and waved them in, following close behind. Three walls had folding tables against them, each laden with microfiche readers, printers, scanners, and, finally, a computer.

"Nice," Libra murmured. "Not too old." He sat in front of the Mac desktop. "Login? Password?"

Ruth leaned over and typed in the information. "How long will you need it?"

Taryn pulled a chair over to Libra. "Hopefully, just a few minutes—"

"—hour," Libra said at the same time.

Ruth snerked. "At least you have your stories straight." She checked her watch. "I lock up at noon for my lunch break. That gives you twenty-eight minutes. If that's not enough time, you can come back after one." She conspicuously left the door open as she returned to the counter, taking a seat facing the room so she could keep an eye on them.

"I don't think she trusts us," Taryn whispered.

"Whispering in my ear isn't going to make her any less suspicious," he countered.

Reaching into his shirt pocket, he removed his notes about his vision and pulled up a maps program.

Taryn slid the paper closer and stared at it. "What is this?"

"That night…the bird attack. I had a nightmare or a vision…I'm not sure, but I saw the building we're looking for and the route to get there."

"Then why are we here?"

"First, because it was shown to me in reverse and very fast. I'm not sure I remember everything. Second, I may be completely nuts. We're here to confirm."

"That you're nuts?"

"That this route is real, smartass."

She leaned back in her chair, crossed her arms, and heaved a sigh. Then she crossed her legs. Bounced her foot. Uncrossed her legs and bounced both legs. She sighed again.

"For goddess' sake, what's wrong?"

"I'm bored."

"Go make nice with Ruth."

Taryn looked over her shoulder then shook her head. "No making nice there." She jumped up. "How about I go explore? We'll need to eat."

Libra entered the first road from his vision, an interstate. The screen filled with options, the damn road crossed several states. He ran a hand through his hair.

"Libra?"

He waved at her without looking up. "Yeah, that's fine. I'm sure there's a book in here that'll keep your interest."

She walked out of the room, her exit punctuated with a heavy sigh.

Libra leaned closer to the screen and ran his finger along the satellite image of the interstate, looking for the highway that intersected it, completely absorbed in his hunt.

33

TARYN PASSED RUTH, IGNORING her raised eyebrows and judgmental stare, and exited the library. There was nothing to the left so she looked right. There was a café several feet down the street and a farm supply store just beyond that, followed by an antique store with a fancy sign covered in shiny, gold scrollwork that seemed out of place in this tiny spot on the map.

She strolled past boarded-up windows, paused to inhale the delicious smell of bacon, eggs, and hash browns pouring out of the café, and ran her fingers along the huge tires of the tractors parallel parked on the street outside the farm supply store. She stopped to study the antique store sign again; it looked brand new, though done in an old style.

She looked at the window displays and gasped, pressing her palms against the glass like a child.

Open books so old that they would have been called tomes in their day leaned against skulls, their pages filled with longhand script detailing what looked like magical spells, tiny print filling the margins. Strewn around the books were apothecary jars filled with herbs and bugs, old lockets, and crosses and pentacles. But in the middle of this spectacular display was a sealed jar filled with a glowing, blue liquid that undulated as if it were alive.

"Gaia."

Mesmerized, she opened the door of the shop, barely registering the tinkling of the bell over her head, her skin tingling the moment she walked over the threshold. The air was cool yet dense, heavy with magic or promise—she couldn't tell which—and it smelled like old paper and incense. She rounded a card rack to get to the display case and reached for the jar, the living blue pulling her.

"I wouldn't do that, young lady," a quiet voice said from the back of the store.

Taryn held her hand over the jar for a moment then backed away. She turned around and saw a wizened man leaning on the counter with both hands, as if they were the only things holding him up. She walked over to him, studying his features. The man looked familiar, but she couldn't place him. By the time she reached him, she realized there was no way she could know him; he was too old.

"How much do you want for the jar?"

"Oh, it's not for sale…to you."

"Why?"

"I can't sell anything in this store without the express permission of the items themselves."

Taryn laughed. "You expect me to believe that the books," she ran her fingers along the necklaces and bracelets hanging to her right, "and these baubles are animate? Impossible."

He nodded in the direction of the front window. "The contents of the jar would beg to differ."

"What kind of store is this? You can't possibly get enough business to survive."

He cocked his head to one side and pursed his lips. "You'd be surprised what is sold and where. But that doesn't change my mind. Nothing in here has picked you yet." He looked around for a moment. "Please, walk through the store."

Taryn walked away, more to escape the odd, little man than to comply with his wish.

"Touch the lovelies. Let them know you," he purred.

The hairs on the back of her neck stood up. "You speak of them like they are alive."

"How are they to choose you if they are not?"

She turned slowly to face him. "Who are you? What is your name?"

The man smiled, baring stained, crooked teeth. He clasped his hands and bowed as low as his bent back would allow. "My name is Mister Medai, and I am but a humble servant to the desire for beautiful things."

"I know someone who's all about beautiful things," she said.

His smile broadened, sending Taryn farther away in the guise of touching more of his merchandise. Gad, he was creepy, but despite her revulsion, she was too mesmerized to walk out the door. She cupped a shimmering pendant in her palm and a zing of electricity shot into her palm and up her arm. She dropped it and stepped back, shaking her tingling hand.

"Ah, I knew it. You came to me for a reason, and this is it." He fingered the heavy, silver byzantine necklace before lifting it off the display hook. He held it up. "May I?"

Taryn opened and closed her hand. "What was that?"

"The stone has chosen you, and very strongly, too."

"Won't it hurt? My palm is still tingling."

He giggled as he unhooked the clasp. "No, no, the stone just wanted to make its choice abundantly clear. There will be nothing but warmth and comfort once it settles around your neck."

Taryn stared at the swaying stone, more enraptured by the shifting colors with each passing moment. The store fell away and all she could see was the pendant. Her skin itched and her shoulders twitched. Her breath hitched with a growing longing.

Puzzled by her reaction but unable to think of a reason why she should refuse the gift, she turned her back to him and waited for him to place the weighty necklace on her.

He reached around her, exposing the inside of his forearms. Thick lines had been gouged into the sagging flesh of his right arm, forming the words: *Come and See.*

Taryn sucked in a breath. *Jesus. That must have been agony.*

The pink and red and white jagged scars were partially healed, as if they'd been made only a few days ago. Had he done it to himself? The crude letters hadn't been carved with a steady hand, and the slant…

Before she could ask him about the phrase, the stone began to hum against her chest, reclaiming her attention.

Medai pulled back and gently lifted her hair to free it from the chain.

She lifted the oval stone and studied it. "What is this?"

"Black opal, very rare, especially in this size. Beautiful, yes?"

"Yes, it is, but I can't afford it."

She reached up to remove the necklace but Medai shook his head to stop her.

"I've had that necklace for many years, and it has never once chosen a patron… until you. That is a rare thing in this store, so it is my gift to you."

She turned the stone over and found writing etched into the silver backing. "*Mors Principium Est*…what does that mean?"

"The words mean: 'Death is beginning,' but do not worry. The words may sound gruesome, but the black opal symbolizes death and rebirth." He tapped the center of the stone resting between her breasts. "There is justice to be found in this, and great protection for the wearer." He leaned close. "Keep it on you always."

Taryn leaned back, as much to get away from the smell of mothballs and sweat as to get some distance from the man eliciting the increasingly dark vibe strumming through her. "And the words on your arm?"

He pushed the sleeve down and frowned. "You'd have to ask the person who put them there."

She studied him for a moment. He didn't want to tell her the story, and a part of her was relieved. She'd already been in the store longer than she'd planned, and she still hadn't asked him about the books.

"Are any of your books about Gaia?" she asked.

"Gaia? That old hag? Why would you want to learn about her?"

She glanced at the bookshelves lining the left wall of the store. "Just point me in the direction."

He smiled, the gentle expression softening his wrinkled face, but it didn't reach his cold, rheumy eyes. There was steel here, and an intensity she didn't understand.

"She's not a goddess to be studied. Or trifled with."

"Reading about her isn't trifling."

He reached for her cheek with a gnarled hand.

She jerked her head away to avoid his touch. "Don't."

His face flushed red, his ire glaring. "Dear child, I have no designs on your flesh. I'm more of a…soul man."

"Well, you can't have that either."

He sighed and shook his head. "Since niceties are being ignored, I'll cut to the chase." His hurt demeanor disappeared and he was all intensity once more. "It's about Gaia."

"I'm getting that."

"Good. Then let me continue by saying you need to stay away from her. Libra too."

"Why? Wait, what? How do you know about him?"

Taryn stopped talking and took a step back. She didn't want to tell the odd, little man that Gaia's help had saved her life once. Of course, Gaia had taken her life once as well, though she was hoping that part was behind them after the successful contact during the bird attack. But how did he know about Libra?

Medai slashed his hand through the air. "None of that is important. Whom I know and don't know makes no difference. Just know that Gaia isn't your friend. The more contact she has with this world, the more she will want. And she already craves a return. So many of them do. That is not good for you, or anyone else whom she has touched. Stay away from her; go back to the InBetween. Find a nice Kellas Cat to mate with and have a mess of kittens." He pointed to the door. "Go, get out."

Her feet propelled her toward the door, almost against her will.

"Wait," she called out over her shoulder, "how do you know about the InBetween? Why warn me?"

But the man had disappeared.

34

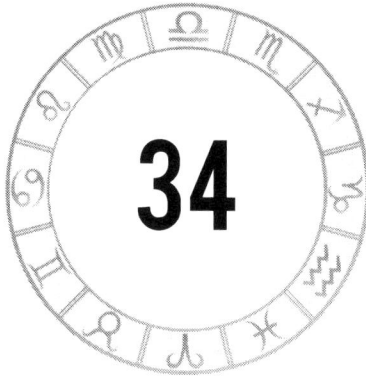

TARYN STOOD IN THE doorway for a moment, confused by the strange conversation. Part of her wanted to go back in, but the rest of her wanted to escape while she could.

She looked at the black opal again then tucked the necklace under her shirt, the stone nestling between her breasts. She stumbled out into the sunshine and blinked, the change in light burning her eyes. She wiped away the tears and saw Libra trotting toward her, a scowl on his face.

"Where the hell have you been?"

"Don't tell me you're already done. It's only been—"

"Three hours. I came out to find you two hours ago and you were nowhere to be seen."

"Three hours? That's impossible; I was only in the store for five minutes."

He stepped around her and looked inside. "There? You were in there? Because I checked it twice and it was just like it is now." He glared at her. "Empty."

She turned back to the storefront and peered through the now-dirty windows. What a moment before had been a fascinating, albeit odd, little antique store was now an abandoned sewing shop. Bolts of dust-covered fabric and a collection of sun-faded bric-a-brac sat in the window. The dark interior held three mannequins and a beat-up counter with two missing legs, which leaned more than Mr. Medai had.

"But...I..."

"Come on, we need to get out of here. The deputy over there has been eyeballing me this whole time. I had to stroll around like I knew what I was doing, not searching for a missing person."

He took her arm, more gently than she thought he would, considering his anger, but then she saw the cop leaning on his patrol car across the street. The man was watching them, his gaze coming back to Libra's hand repeatedly. The deputy pushed off the car and stood with his feet spread slightly, like he was trying to decide if he was going to cross the street.

Taryn leaned away from Libra but he tightened his grip. "Damn it, Libra, you're attracting attention."

"I don't care."

"You will if he decides to ask for I.D."

She glanced back and saw the man cross to their side of the street. "Darn it. Kiss me."

"What?"

"Kiss me, now."

She put on the brakes and locked her knees, bringing Libra around to stand in front of her. She wrapped her arms around his neck and pulled his head down. His eyes widened but she saw the moment he understood.

He slipped his arms around her waist and pulled her close until she was pressed against him from thigh to chest. She looked into his eyes and blinked. The hazel color had almost disappeared, his pupils fully dilated.

She inhaled and was swamped by the scent of sunshine and moonlight. His lips brushed hers, slow and soft at first then the mood changed from seduction to possession. Libra pivoted, placing his back to the cop and her back against the warm, brick wall of the farm supply. He pushed his body against hers.

A growl rose from inside him, vibrating her, thrilling her with the undeniable pronouncement that he had claimed her. Their lips fought for ground, anger and frustration driving them past caring who might stand witness to their public display.

A loud boom rattled the windows on either side; ozone flowed over them. A second, stronger boom preceded an explosion two blocks away.

"Son of a bitch," the cop said.

Libra broke away from her but kept his body pressed against hers. Good thing, since her knees were wobbly and her mind was mush. She looked around him.

The cop had his head back, following something in the sky. He whirled around and ran to his car, pausing to look down the street at the transformer that had caught fire then up at the sky again. He climbed into his cruiser, and radioed someone. Libra and Taryn forgotten, he accelerated into a U-turn and raced past them, his head hanging out of the window.

Libra stepped away from Taryn but kept one hand on her waist, pulling gently. "Not certain what just happened but I'll take the good fortune."

She pointed up. "I think I know what happened."

He tilted his head back. "Shit."

The sky, clear and blinding blue only seconds before, was now filled with dark green and black clouds. A storm had formed—because they kissed.

Taryn allowed herself to be peeled off the brick and leaned into his side as he guided her down the sidewalk and to their truck. Libra opened the driver door and helped her inside before leaning in and kissing her again.

"You don't have to do that. He's gone."

"That was for me." He leaned back. "Are you good to drive? We need to blow out of here before that storm opens up."

"Storm. Right."

Taryn shook her head to empty out her confusion before checking the storm roiling above the town.

Libra jumped in the passenger side and belted up before pointing down the street. "Go east."

She did a U-turn and hustled down the road, glancing in the rearview mirror at the people running into stores for shelter as the lightening storm attacked the tiny place. They were clear of the besieged town in minutes.

Libra drummed his fingers on the door. "So maybe you can explain what really happened back there."

The store? Mr. Medai and his warning about Gaia? That kiss? There were too many things to discuss and not one she could explain.

"No, I really don't think I can."

35

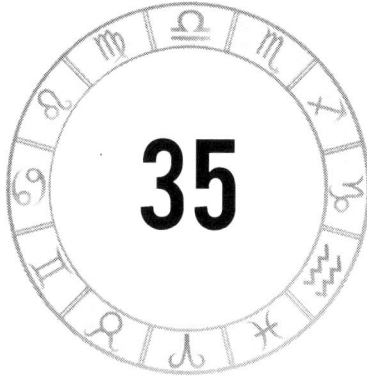

TARYN RUBBED HER EYES and prayed the damn sun would go down already. She squinted against it, using her visor to block as much light as possible, but the glare still brought tears to her eyes. Road fatigue was definitely a thing and it was kicking her in the butt.

Libra had closed his eyes not long after they left town and hadn't stirred since. She wanted to jerk the wheel to jar him awake just so she'd have someone to talk to, but she managed to hold back. She'd be pulling over for gas soon enough and that would surely be enough to wake him.

"Do you want me to drive?" he asked.

Taryn jumped and jerked the wheel. "Holy crap, you're awake."

Libra sat up and stretched. "Not much sleeping to be had with all your groaning and sighing."

"I was not."

"Yes. You were…are." He yawned and rubbed his face. "You ready to talk about what happened in Stanton?"

"There's nothing to talk about."

"You were gone for hours. I think there's a lot to say."

"You wouldn't believe me."

"With all that's happened in the past few days, all the times I couldn't get you to shut up, now you go mute on me?"

Taryn's temper rose hot and fast. "A lot to say? You're one to talk."

"What do you mean?"

She shut her mouth. This wasn't the right time to admit the truth—not that there ever was a good time to confess that you had witnessed a memory filled with so much pain and fear.

"No, really, if you want to get something off your chest then do it."

She glanced at his hard expression and set chin; her anger flared fresh. "Fine. Why don't you start by telling me about your childhood."

Silence fell but she refused to look at him.

"What did you say?" he asked slowly, quietly. Ominously.

In for a penny and all that rot.

"You heard me. Your childhood...your mother."

She heard his breathing increase. *Angry breathing. Silent—not good.*

"So you lied."

She nodded.

"How much?" he ground out through clenched teeth.

"What do you mean?"

"How much did you see? How much do you remember?"

She hesitated. He wouldn't be happy, but she owed him the truth. And if she was honest with herself, she wanted him to go there; he needed to open up and let her in. Why that was suddenly important to her she didn't understand; it just was.

The warning from Medai had rattled her. She needed to understand what was happening—the bigger picture—and she wanted to have that conversation with Libra. His ties to Gaia, and his mother's role, both in the past and with what was happening now, were important; she could feel it in her gut. If pissing him off meant getting him to talk, she'd take the hit. Silence and secrets weren't an option anymore, even if they were an easy refuge.

"I remember it all. The blue light, then floating above your room; you, your mother...the whip...the blood."

Libra rolled down his window.

Taryn risked a glance. She saw only the back of his head and his white-knuckled death-grip on the door.

She looked down the road. "I'm sorry."

"For lying? For forcing me to face the goddess I've so carefully avoided all my life? For last night? Because there's a lot to be sorry for."

Her heart lurched then sank into the vicinity of her gut. "All of it. Except last night; I won't apologize for that." She waited a beat. "Talk to me. Tell me what happened that night. Was what I saw real?"

He sighed. "Yes. It was real."

Taryn's breath caught in her throat. "And the blood on Aubrianna?"

"Not mine, at least, not in that moment. The blood was my brother's."

She waited, trying to be patient.

"Hell, okay, you want to hear the ugly truth? Here it is. I had defied her for the umpteenth time. I tried for years to obey her, to please her, to make her smile, but she whipped and punched and kicked me no matter how hard I tried. So I grew into a perverse, little shit and defied her at every turn." He cleared his throat. "That night I had pushed her too hard. So instead of taking out her rage on me, she started with my little brother to punish me twice. She beat him, whipped him...his screams—" He squirmed in his seat. "So I left the moment I could walk again."

"Why didn't your father stop her?"

"He left early on."

"And your brother?"

"I left him behind. I abandoned him to save myself and ran to my father in the Great Cavern."

"Do you know what happened to him?"

He fell silent again, answering her question without saying a word.

"You didn't have a—"

He slammed his palm against the door. "Don't try to justify what I did or tell me I had no choice. I had a choice and I made the wrong one."

"But—"

"Enough! I told you what happened. That's more than I've told anyone else and I won't discuss it with you again." He took a deep breath. "Your turn. Explain what happened in the store."

She hesitated, trying to figure out the best way to tell him she'd lost her mind. "When I left the library I saw a sign for an antique shop. The sign was bright gold, the scrollwork beautiful and really old looking. So I checked it out."

"For hours?"

"Not hours. I swear I was in there for no more than five minutes. I saw a jar in one of the windows. It had a blue, glowing liquid undulating in it, like I've seen in the ley lines."

"What kind of store would have that?"

"A really old New Age store based on the books surrounding the jar."

"So we're in the middle of nowhere, trying to track down some children while on the run from the Corvus Wards and Aubrianna, and you see a jar with Gaia juice in it and you just walk in? Goddess almighty, have you no sense of self-preservation?"

"I have plenty of it, but I also have a lot of curiosity."

"And that, along with your gut, is gonna get you killed."

"Do you want to know what happened?"

Libra shut his mouth.

"I went inside and met an old man."

"And?"

She shifted in her seat. Boy, oh boy, he was not going to be happy about this; it was better to spit it out quick, like ripping off a bandaid. "I saw antiques, really old, unique books, and jewelry. The man called himself Mr. Medai and he warned us to stay away from Gaia. Then, after I came outside and found you, all I saw was an empty, abandoned store like you did."

Libra sat up in his seat and turned to her, his mouth open. "He knew about Gaia? What the hell, Taryn? Why didn't you say that first?"

"I just told you."

"No, I mean at the store, before we left town." He patted the dash. "Pull over."

"Why?"

"I need you to concentrate on the conversation, not the road." He pointed to a flat spot in the grass, a few feet off the two-lane road. "There."

"Fine." She eased the truck over and put it in park. "I really don't see what the fuss is about."

"What did he say, exactly?"

She almost laughed at his fierce expression but she didn't think he'd appreciate it; she'd already pushed him pretty hard today. "I can't quote him but the gist was we need to go home and leave this alone."

"The children?"

"No, yes, well, only as it pertains to Gaia. He said we need to stop connecting with her because she craves a return."

Libra snorted. "What the hell does that mean?"

"I don't know. He left before I could ask how he knew about the InBetween." She looked down the road. A link in the heavy, opal necklace snagged in one of her curls and pulled. She lifted it out from under her shirt and held it out for Libra to see. "He gave me this. Or, rather, he said the necklace chose me."

Libra palmed the black opal and studied it. "Chose you?"

"Yes." She glanced at him. "It hummed when I touched it."

"Hummed?"

"Hummed, vibrated." She turned the pendant over. "He said these words mean: 'Death is beginning.'"

He stared at the letters. "Did he say anything else?"

"No, but there was one thing that kinda freaked me out." She took the pendant from him, dropped it back inside her shirt, pushed up her right sleeve, and touched her forearm. "He had the words 'Come and See' carved into his skin. Not that long ago either."

"Did you ask him what it meant?"

She shrugged as she dropped her arm. "I did but he brushed me off."

Libra looked out the passenger-side window, his fingers drumming the sill. "Come and see. Come and see. That phrase sounds so familiar." His voice drifted off.

"Uh, can we go now?"

He nodded.

She pulled out and hit the gas.

"If he shows up again, you need to let me handle him. I need to find out who he is and how he knows that much about our world."

Taryn hit the brakes, screeching to a halt in the middle of the road.

Libra glanced out the rear window. "What are you doing?"

She gripped the steering wheel until her knuckles turned white. "Handle him? Like the little woman is incapable? I know you're upset about my omitting the fact that I saw your memory, and maybe I should have told you everything Medai said right away."

"Taryn. The road," he said, checking for cars.

"No, screw the road. There's no one coming and you need to hear me."

He turned on the bench seat and focused on her. "Spit it out then."

"No one 'handles' things for me. Not when I was a child and certainly not now. Do you understand?"

He glanced to his left. "Car."

"Do. You. Understand."

He leaned close and nailed her with a glare. "I understand you are reckless and impulsive." He threw up his hands. "Example, sitting in the middle of the road." His voice rose. "I understand you don't know anything about the InBetween and the paranorms who call it home." His voice dropped into a growl. "I understand that you are so worried about being helpful, as if that's the only way you'll be loved, that you risk everyone around you. Stumbling from one misadventure to another, living by your gut, forcing people to clean up your messes."

A horn blared as a car flew past them, breaking Libra's rant. "For goddess' sake, drive."

Taryn sat breathless for a moment before slowly pressing the gas, her mind too muddled to come up with a stinging rebuke; her normally biting tongue was tied. The engine growled, the transmission jerking her with each gear change, but she barely registered it. How could she care about Libra's opinion? Twenty-four hours ago she would have ripped into him for his attitude and words.

Stupid sex just muddies everything.

What? Had she really thought letting the man climb between her legs would change anything? No, she hadn't; she knew better. So why did she want to cry? She concentrated on the road to avoid answering the question.

"Where are we going?" she asked, her voice flat.

"Eastern Virginia. There's an abandoned sanitarium that matches the drawing perfectly."

"How long?"

"A couple days."

Taryn's gut clenched. Two days with the man. How would she survive the silence?

36

VIRGO AND CAPRICORN CROUCHED in the woods above the main entrance to the InBetween, watching the bloom of humans milling around. They lowered their binoculars at the same time.

"What the hell happened?" Virgo asked, swiping at the gnats buzzing around him.

"Didn't you see the big hole? The mountain top that's no longer there?"

"Don't be a goat; of course I saw that. I'm asking why the spell failed."

Cap leaned back against the tree trunk and sighed. "We knew it would fail eventually; that's why Martina, Hiram, and Fessa left to find more witches. Obviously, they didn't make it back. So what now? I hate to be a pessimist, but we don't have the access cuffs for the remote entrances."

Virgo joined his fellow Zodiac. "We wait until there's a break." A drop of water hit his shaved head and ran down his face. He wiped it away, only to have more hit him. He looked up at the blue sky sans clouds. "Is that rain?"

Cap glanced up. "No clouds. Not possible."

The drops increased until it was drizzling on the two men.

Virgo pressed his back against the pine tree but the needles didn't provide enough cover. "So why am I getting wet?"

Cap crawled to the next tree just a few feet away. He held out his hands and grinned. "Aquarius is here."

Virgo glanced around. "Why do you say that?"

"Because it's not raining on me now."

Virgo moved to join Cap but the rain followed him. "I'm going to kick his ass."

"Aw, poor baby," Ari said as he crawled out from behind a tree, Pisces right behind him.

"You know my black ass doesn't like to get wet," Virgo groused.

Pisces grinned. "That's why it's funny."

Cap grunted. "Stow it. We need to get inside."

Virgo wiped his face dry with his sleeve. "Now that we have Joker number one here, he can make it dump on those humans, chase them away."

Aquarius snorted. "They're here to investigate the weirdness and you want me to make it rain with blue skies?"

A rustling in the undergrowth brought the four Zodiacs to attention. They spun around as one and readied themselves for an attack.

Gemini appeared, crawling on all fours, a grin on his face. "You ninnies are talking so loud the humans are going to hear you."

Virgo looked at the cuff on Gem's wrist. The huge, flat Gemini stone—a stunning, priceless emerald attached to a solid gold band—was glowing. "Gemma?"

"She's in here, but," Gem grinned and nodded toward the entrance, "watch."

They turned their attention to the humans in time to hear a woman's bloodcurdling scream echo from the thick woods to the left. The men paused and turned in her direction. Gemma screamed again, even louder this time, and the humans dropped their equipment and ran for the trees.

"What the hell?" Virgo asked.

"Gemma loves human technology. It's a recording."

"Damn, she's good," Pisces said with a snort.

"Okay, boys, time to hustle," Gem said as he lunged for the downhill slope leading to the InBetween.

The other Zodiacs followed closely, jumping down long sections of the decline then sprinting for the disguised entrance. They entered the quiet, cool dark and closed the doors behind them.

"That Gemma is a jewel," Virgo said between pants.

"You should really let her wear the Gemini cuff," Cap said, pointing at the emerald. "She's got serious skills."

Gemini nodded, his hands raised. "Yeah, yeah, I've heard it all before. But she's no warrior. Screaming won't save you in a fight."

"Don't be a dick, Gem," Virgo countered.

Before the five Zodiacs could continue their banter, the Fenrir Wolf alpha appeared, followed immediately by Lyon.

Their leader slid to a stop a few feet away, his scowl hard enough to break rock. "What the hell are you doing here?"

Virgo gathered his wits first. "You sent for us." He looked at the other four Zodiacs. "All of us."

Lyon clenched his fists. "Nooo!"

Gem ran to the man. "What's wrong?"

Lyon looked down at him, his face red. "I sent you to Texas."

Virgo, Capricorn, Pisces, and Aquarius looked at one another.

"The message said to come here," Pisces said. "What's in Texas?"

"My family. My whole fucking family," Lyon roared.

37

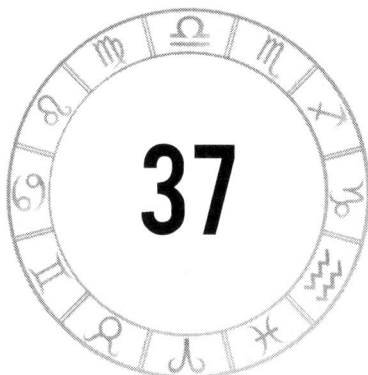

LIBRA LOOKED AT TARYN'S pale, drawn face, the low, artificial light of the motel parking lot highlighting the architecture of her bone structure. A chunk of ice hit his head. The damn storm they'd stirred up in Stanton had followed them all day. They'd managed to stay ahead of it, but each stop for gas or food had eaten away at their lead. Now that they'd stopped for the night, the storm had caught them and parked itself over the motel.

He extended a hand to help her out of the truck. "Come."

Her eyes widened and she flinched as if touching him would cause her pain. After what he'd said earlier that day, and the resultant silence, which had lasted the entire journey, he didn't blame her for avoiding him. He was an ass, but he'd had to tell her the truth as he saw it, for her sake and his.

He sighed. "You're exhausted. Take my hand."

She settled her fingers, but not her whole hand, in his. He pulled on them, supporting her weight as she climbed out of the truck, his concern about facing her after what he'd done with her last night, and said to her this afternoon, suddenly gone. She was afraid and hurt and he couldn't bear to let that stand—the why of it deserving some thought, but not now.

"We need to get inside."

The sleet shifted to hail, pea-sized but growing. Libra tugged on Taryn, but she balked.

She looked at him, her eyes wide, the shadows under them as dark as the thick, swirling clouds overhead. "Did the storm really follow us?"

Another chunk of ice pelted him in the head. "Shit."

This wasn't the place to talk about blame. He scooped her into his arms and carried her inside the room, closing the door against the rising wind before letting her slide down his body to regain her feet.

Taryn backed away from him. The haunted look in her eyes burned like fire in his heart and his gut. *Inamorata? Not likely now.* Not that he had wanted her in his life for the foreseeable future, but that closed door suddenly gave him pause. No, damn it. He was a shit, but if his words saved her life…

She collapsed on the sole chair and drew her knees into her chest. He took a step in her direction but she shrank away from him. He backed up until his legs hit the only other place to sit—the king-size bed. He relaxed back, crossed his ankles, rested his head on his folded arms, and stared at the ceiling.

Hell, what was he going to do now? Since escaping his mother and becoming a Zodiac, he'd had his share of women in and out of his bed, and sometimes as his date, when the mission called for one. He'd found pleasure in their company, while making sure they also found theirs, but he had never sought to know them, never stayed long enough to build a relationship. There'd been no time or desire for more than the give and take of one or two nights.

He wanted it to be the same with Taryn, but the need to share his pain and fears with the woman kept him from walking away, physically and mentally. So what kind of man did he want to be? The same years that had honed his mother razor-sharp had molded him into a man cold and removed from life. His dam was right; he'd lived a half-life. Out of fear or some misguided sense of protecting those around him, the glaring truth was he was more like Aubrianna than he cared to admit. With more time, he would become her.

"I suck at talking about myself." He rolled onto his side, propped his head up with a hand, and studied her face. "But so do you."

Taryn frowned and stared at the plastic curtain. "I thought I was all mouth and gut."

"You are, but I've come to the realization that what comes out of your mouth doesn't really share who you are deep down. You talk a lot, but you're not really saying anything important about the Taryn I've seen."

The motel window shuddered; the wind howled. Hail hammered against the glass and walls, the noise so loud they stopped talking for a moment.

Libra thought about what he'd just said. Who was this woman, really? The need to know filled him with an urgency he didn't understand.

"Tell me about yourself, Taryn."

"No."

"Why not?"

"Because you're asking me to open myself up to you. As soon as this is over, you'll be back to your constipated self—all tight-ass and brittle and cold. You haven't earned the right to know me."

"I'd say last night went a long way toward that right."

She flashed him a fierce go-to-hell look. "We fucked. I owe you nothing."

"That's not what we did."

Her tight expression fell; a tear slid down her cheek.

Goddess damn it, now I've made her cry.

He felt positively withered, but hopeful that the truth could get her to talk. "You asked me about Aether and Nether."

"And you shut me down."

He nodded; she had the right of it. "You've heard of the four elements: earth, air, fire, and water. Aether is the fifth element and Nether the sixth, the ones that were dropped from the element list centuries ago because they were too ethereal, too difficult to see or prove."

Taryn shifted in her chair. Her knees were still tucked up to her chest, but he was making progress, piquing her interest.

"Aether is also known as quintessence," she said.

"Yes. Aether is considered life energy, while Nether is death energy."

"Where did they come from?"

"When the goddess Chaos came to be, it is said that her first exhalation gave birth to the cosmos and all living things. But when she inhaled, she stole some of that life force for herself in order to exhale again. Each exhale and inhale gave to the universe and took from it, setting up the life and death cycle we know today."

"How does that work now? Why does Gaia have those powers and why does she have an agent?"

"History is a bit fuzzier on how Gaia ended up with the power of Chaos, but it's been said that Gaia is Chaos's firstborn. As such, she has been given Aether and Nether so that Chaos can remain neutral, so she doesn't have to weigh in on the affairs of the worlds. Once Gaia and the other gods and goddesses fell out of favor, Gaia created the Os Mage Mother to give birth to the Os Mages. The Mages protect the worlds from the darkest of magic by collecting the unclaimed bones of paranorms."

Taryn released her knees; her body unfolded. "And the agent?"

"With Gaia trapped, she wanted to give the Os Mage Mothers the power to act on her behalf, to protect the Os Mages, and the planet, which is literally Gaia's body. The Mothers haven't had the power of Aether for as long as recorded history—Nether has been the only power passed to the agents, at least until Aubrianna. When she took the role of Mother from her predecessor, I think Aubrianna assumed the power of the agent would be automatically given to her. For some reason, Gaia didn't chose her for either power."

"I'd guess it has to do with her piss poor attitude." Taryn scowled. "And her cruelty," she added under her breath. "How do you know that you would be the next agent—if you chose to be, that is?"

Libra raised his hands, looking at the lines lacing his palms. "It's the blue." He looked up. "The last time Aubrianna beat me—the night I ran away—I was trying to get her to stop when the blue appeared on my hands. I had no idea what was happening, but she did, and it infuriated her. Pushed her beyond any rage I'd seen before. She yelled at me, cursed Gaia for choosing me over her—" His voice lowered to a whisper. "I knew I was going to die…"

The *tink-tink* of the heater punctured the silence that filled the room.

"I didn't ask to be an agent; I don't want to have the kind of power that could corrupt someone, as the promise of it did my mother. I never understood why Gaia would consider giving the power to someone not a Mother." Libra released a ragged breath and shook his head as if to clear it. "Can I ask you a question? If you answer it, you can ask me one."

Taryn cocked her head and studied him like he was a bug before replying. "Any question?"

"As long as you keep answering mine, I'll answer yours. Deal?"

He waited for her to decide.

Her mouth worked like she was chewing on her tongue; her expression said it tasted bitter. "Okay."

"Where did you come from?" he asked before she could change her mind.

"I'm a foundling. Abella, Persephone, and I were dumped at an orphanage in Dallas, maybe by Llewellyn, or under his orders." She leaned forward in her chair. "Why does your mother hate you so much? Aside from the power of the agent stuff."

Libra sat up. "You don't waste any time getting to the rotten core of a topic, do you?"

She shrugged. "Answer the question."

He stared at the floor, the answer swirling around his brain, unable to stop long enough for him to spit it out.

"That's what I thought." She turned away from him and closed her eyes, retreating from him as surely as if he wasn't there.

He felt her absence to his marrow, mentally, emotionally, and it left him as cold as the ice blowing outside. The only one who really knew the answer was his father…his dead father.

Libra had never planned on sharing the horror of his existence, but the need to bring Taryn back from the cold, private place she'd withdrawn to made him coalesce the words. "I wasn't supposed to be born."

He heard her breath hitch but she was a demanding wench. She wasn't going to give him any sway. He'd have to flay his skin, rip his heart out, and cut it open for her if he expected her to do the same.

"The Os Mage Mother only conceives females," he said.

"The Os Mages." Taryn frowned. "Does she do that spontaneously or does she have to conceive them with a man?"

"Conception is required, so she's always surrounded by several males, just in case. When my father fell in love, he convinced her that he would never leave her side, that she could use his seed to create an Os Mage whenever it was needed." He swallowed back his pain and pushed forward. "But he didn't understand, and she didn't inform him, that other than the need to mate to produce an Os Mage, Aubrianna doesn't mate. With anyone. Ever."

Taryn turned to him, her eyes wide—her mouth wider.

"Yeah, that's probably the same look my father had the first time he tried to bed her for pleasure."

"So what did he do?"

Libra grit his teeth and scowled, remembering the first time Aubrianna had spat the truth at him, hoping to hurt him to the core and gloating when she'd seen that she had scored a direct hit. "He tried to woo her but failed time and again. So he did the unforgivable."

Taryn clasped her hands tight in her lap.

Libra took a deep breath and let it rip. "He had a witch bespell Aubrianna, forcing her to lay with him over and over until she conceived me. She was so angry she tried to abort me, but it didn't work. She bore me hours later: a sick, puny, premature baby *boy*—one that grew at the usual rate instead of being born an adult like the females."

Taryn's eyes filled with tears. "That's terrible."

He drew back, the words so true but so hurtful. "That's what she told me, and much worse, from the time I could understand her meaning—but as bad as that was, my father didn't learn a lesson from it. No, he did it a second time and forced her to have my brother, Hanell. He wanted an heir and a spare, and he raped her to get us."

She covered her mouth and shook her head.

Libra jumped up. He looked out at the parking lot, now blanketed in ice. "I was the lucky one. When I ran away, my father allowed me to stay with him. He raised me, convinced me to become the Libra Zodiac, as if that were an honor, as if I could ever want to honor a man who could do what he did. Being a Zodiac wasn't what I wanted, but it gave me the chance to get away from him."

"How does that make you the lucky one?"

"I left Hanell with Aubrianna."

"But you were just a child."

"Yes, but I should have taken him with me. Or gone back to get him before she could poison him with her hatred."

"So all this talk about your scales and the balance of dark and light…"

"I can't allow myself to be like my father. He made a decision to use his darkness, his power, to force another being to bend to his will." He glanced in her direction but didn't meet her eyes. "That same evil is inside me, only it's been supercharged by the demon soul attached to mine. If I let it loose again—" He gestured to the window and the raging storm. "Connecting with Gaia, letting her know who I am, that I exist…" He crossed his arms over his chest to end the conversation, to stop any further introspection.

He heard rustling. Taryn touched his shoulder, then his face.

She pulled his head around then cupped his cheeks, her thumbs stroking his stubbly skin. "You are not evil. Not even close."

She ran a thumb over his lips.

He leaned into her, pressing his forehead against hers, hungry for her warmth to ease the cold that had gripped his body, his soul, his heart. "Last night, I took you hard. I could have hurt you."

"But you warned me; you gave me the chance to say 'no.' You have a dark side, yes, but you are not your father. Just like I'm not my mother, and Lyon is not Llewellyn. You are human, albeit with a little extra thrown in. We all have our own scales—light and dark—that we fight to balance. That's not just a Libra thing. You don't own that struggle, and you sure as hell don't have to have the whole of your life defined by it."

She kissed him softly. No demands, no expectations, just simple acceptance.

He wrapped his hands around her waist, pulled her into his lap and deepened the gentle kiss, nibbling on her plump lips until she opened for him. A hard, hot surge of lust swamped him.

He pulled back and released her. "I…we…can't."

"Blizzard," she said.

"Blizzard."

She laid a hand on his chest. "I think, after that, I owe you some answers."

He looked into her brown eyes and saw strength balanced with tenderness, a gentle core with a tough mantle that he wanted—needed—to explore. "Why are you not mated yet? You're old enough to have had many babies by now."

"My past isn't nearly as hard as yours," she said softly.

"I still want to know."

"It's because of cookies."

"Baked goods are the reason you're not mated? Are they that horrendous?"

Taryn smiled and shook her head. "Wow, you have seriously run out of charm." She looked past him. "There was a time I wanted to open a small bakery. Just cookies, though—at least to start with."

"I'm still not following."

"At the time I was dating the man I thought I'd marry. We had talked about it a lot but he hadn't proposed yet. One day, I went to his office to surprise him with a new recipe. He was busy so I didn't stay, but when I walked past his window, I saw him in a clench with one of his co-workers." Taryn swallowed hard. "They kissed, more passionately than we had in months, then he picked up the plate of cookies, dumped them in the trash, and they laughed."

She glanced at Libra, her smile wobbly. "So the reason I haven't mated is I'm looking for a man who loves my cookies."

Libra pulled her into his arms and hugged her tight against his chest. "That's unfortunate. I hate cookies."

38

TARYN SNORTED THEN COUGHED, before bursting into laughter—Libra joining her—the pain of their stories soothed by their mirth.

"How about we stow the confessions for another time?"

"Oh god, yes. Absolutely." She pursed her lips, deep in thought. "Well, since we're stuck inside, I propose we do some exercises."

"What? Like squats, pushups?"

She led him to the bed then pushed him down. "Sit. Stay."

Curiosity piqued, he obeyed her command.

She unwrapped the motel's plastic cups then placed them in a row next to the television. "You've been afraid of this power you have for so long, you've turned it into the boogie man."

"Not a boogie man. I may have some power but I've never been able to control it. So I don't use it." He looked at his hands. "Mostly it ranges from nonexistent to out-of-control explosive."

"Then you need to learn how to use it, not run from it." She pointed at the first cup. "Knock it over."

"What?"

She grabbed his right hand, pulled his forefinger straight and aimed it at the plastic. "Fire up your blaster and knock over the cup."

"And blow a hole in the wall? No thank you."

Taryn tapped a foot, her irritation almost amusing. "True balance doesn't mean living your life in the light. That's the opposite of balance. You need to work on living in the dark, too. Part of that means mastering your energy waves, when you're angry or horny or scared, and when you're not."

He looked from her to the cup to his finger. The woman was right. Balance, equilibrium; if he wanted to learn it, he had to redefine it in his mind. But to redefine it, he had to find that little boy deep inside and heal him. He couldn't change what his father did, he couldn't forget the constant barrage of his mother's hate-filled words, or fists, but he could choose to put them in the context they deserved. Two people, filled with pain and rage, had lashed out at their son. If he was to become a better man, a balanced man, he had to learn to compartmentalize it.

"You are *not* your father," Taryn whispered, as if she had read his thoughts.

He raised his hand, pointed at the cup, and summoned the energy inside him. Nothing.

Taryn hovered close to him, her gaze swinging from his finger to the cup and back again.

Still nothing. Not a twinge, a flicker, a spark, or even a dribble.

He dropped his hand. "Well, that was—"

Taryn grabbed his face, tilted it up, and kissed him. She opened her mouth and ran her tongue along his lips. "Open for me."

Not one to ignore a lady's wishes, he opened to her questing tongue. Fire and lust rolled through him as they dueled for dominance.

Taryn groaned and straddled his legs.

He pulled her into his lap and rolled his hips, his ridiculous pantaloons giving his sex ample room to swell as he raised her skirt. The heat of her body and the sweet smell of her sex hit him, nearly knocking him flat. He bucked under her, the need to thrust inside her overwhelming, delicious. How the hell could this infuriating woman send him crashing so fast?

Sweat formed on his brow and back; it tickled as it traveled over his flanks. Waves of blue energy filled him; the power had awakened and it was as ready to burst forth as he was ready to bury himself inside her.

Taryn thrust along his length, her sex cradling him through the material. She reached between them, pulled the pantaloons over his erection, then wriggled her backside until she had seated him between her folds. She wrapped her arms around his neck and rose slightly, wetting his sex as she rode the length of it.

"Anything yet?" she whispered in his ear.

Libra lifted his forefinger again and felt energy surge to the tip. He pointed it at the first cup in the line…and blew the plastic apart, opening a small hole in the wall behind it.

"Damn it."

Taryn gasped, then giggled. He growled at her and she laughed until she cried. She wiggled off his lap and stood, her arms around her stomach while she guffawed.

He leaned back on his hands, not caring that his sex had withered or that his lust hadn't been assuaged. "I told you."

Taryn threw the twisted cup away and ran her fingertips over the hole. "Not that bad. Didn't go through to the next room." She pointed at the next cup. "Again."

He raised his forefinger. "It's disappeared. Your laughing didn't help."

"I see it didn't help something else either," she said while pointedly looking at his lap.

Libra pulled the waistband over his limp sex. "Yeah, yeah. What now, genius?"

"We just need to ramp down the sexual energy a bit. Find that spark without igniting you all the way."

She bent at the waist, placed her hands on either side of his hips, and leaned in for a kiss. He smiled and watched her close the gap, then blinked when her lips passed by his and she climbed onto the bed.

She crawled behind him. "Let's try taking your penis out of the equation."

"Good goddess, why?"

Taryn placed her knees on either side of his hips, her groin snug against his back.

225

She wrapped her arms around his chest and leaned down, her mouth by his ear. "Just go with me."

He nodded, his body eager for anything she'd deign to give it.

She pressed her warm lips to his neck then raked her teeth over the sensitive flesh.

Goosebumps raced over his skin. His sex bucked out of its funk, hope reawakened.

She suckled and lathed and nipped a path around his neck, his earlobe. Her clever hands slid inside his shirt, squeezing his pecs and rolling his nipples, pushing his pleasure higher but not once going farther south.

"Try again," she whispered in his ear.

He moaned his frustration, his desire to forget the lesson and get straight to the good stuff just about overwhelming, but he had agreed to try. He raised his shaking hand, squinted to see which cup he was supposed to be aiming at, and released the energy through his finger. The cup hit the wall before rebounding and landing on the floor.

"Woot!" Taryn shoved Libra's back, nearly knocking him to the floor when she jumped off the bed. She retrieved the melted cup and held it up for him to see. "Look at that controlled strike!"

She danced around the tiny space, her glee infectious. He grabbed her waist when she danced past him, lifted her as he stood, then twirled her around and around.

She wrapped her legs around his waist and squealed. "I think we need to anchor that success with a reward!"

He slowed then stopped, but didn't release her. "I don't know what you mean by anchoring, but I'm definitely intrigued by what would constitute a reward."

"Put me down and I'll show you," she answered, her eyes half closed, her voice husky.

Libra set Taryn on her feet. She circled him once, then faced him and removed his shirt. She ran her fingers through the crisp, dark hair covering his chest before following the trail that ventured south between his abdominal muscles and disappeared under his waistband.

"Beautiful," she murmured before grasping the pantaloons and pulling them down to the ground.

"What about the blizzard?"

Libra kicked off the pants and stood before her shaking, exposed, raw, yet filled with power and longing. This woman. He didn't know why she wanted him, but right now he didn't care.

Taryn touched his chest with the tips of her fingers then slid them along his ribs, his flank, his back.

She circled around, her honeyed scent enveloping him. "You afraid of a storm?"

His muscles twitched under her soft touch. "Blizzard be damned; it's the storm raging inside me that should scare you."

She stopped in front of him and gently pressed her warm palms against his chest. "Is it cold and blustery like outside?"

The vibration of her low and raspy voice reverberated through him.

He pushed into her hands and leaned close, nuzzling the black curls until he found the curve of her ear. "Have you felt the power of a lightening strike? Has a scorching sirocco wind burned your skin, heated your blood into molten magma?" He nipped her earlobe then dropped his lips to her neck. "That is what you do to me."

Taryn sagged for a moment. Her body shuddered, but she stepped back.

She raised her chin. "Then undress me. Without shredding my clothes this time, please. Being on the run doesn't allow for much shopping."

Libra grinned. Passion and practicality in the same woman; what a rare find. He made quick work of her shirt and skirt without tearing them, as ordered. He stepped back and looked at her in the light, marveling at her lush figure.

He had once thought her a frump, but she had the body of a goddess: a fertility goddess with full breasts and rounded hips, a flat stomach and bitty waist. A perfect hourglass. How wrong he'd been to consort only with tall, thin women when curves were so delectable.

He touched the silky skin of her shoulders and turned her around to admire her. He ran his fingertips down her smooth back and over her banquet of an ass before pulling her into him.

Her buttocks nestled perfectly into his groin. The urge to bend her over and take her right then was powerful; this woman wouldn't let him remain in control for long, if ever. But his need to take his time stopped him. No rush like last night;

he needed to explore every inch of her. He needed to take hours, days, weeks to discover each swell and dip, each spot that made her sigh or squirm or scream with pleasure.

She spread her feet and gripped his ass as she nestled his sex between her folds—her slow, heated gyration demanding his all until he was nearly undone. Then she arched her back and did exactly what he wanted, as if she had read his mind.

She braced her hands on the bed and glanced back. "Give me the storm. Give me your darkness. Give me your all."

He nodded, his mouth too dry to form words. He ran his hands down her back then up to her elevated buttocks. He parted them and pressed the head of his sex against her passage, holding it there. He wanted to feel everything this time: their combined breathing, that little hitch in hers when he pushed inside a fraction more, her moan when he bent over her and squeezed one of her breasts.

She pressed back and his head slid just inside, but when she rocked back farther he moved with her.

"Not yet, love. You must wait," he demanded.

Taryn growled but acquiesced, her body already quivering as if on the verge of release.

"Very good. Now for *your* reward."

He ran a hand down her belly until he reached her sex. He slipped his fingers through the curls and sucked in his breath when he grazed her hardened nub.

Her back arched again, an involuntary surge that he understood too well but refused to give in to, at least not yet. He dropped his forehead onto her back and concentrated on his middle finger, channeling the energy that had filled him near to bursting already. He closed his eyes and willed a tiny wave to erupt out of him.

Taryn screamed and bucked under him.

He pulled back. "Damn it. Did I hurt you?"

She looked back at him and scowled. "If you stop, I'll kick your ass."

His darkness surged forward, but he was too thrilled by her response to care. "As you wish."

He concentrated on her body and her voice, pushing her to the edge time and again, the energy waves stimulating her until she wept for relief and he had no more will to fight what both of their bodies demanded.

In one stoke, he buried his sex inside her. She pushed against him, grinding until they set up a skin-slapping rhythm. Harder and harder they battled, desperate for the fall but unwilling to go alone. Libra was teetering on the edge, unable to breathe, barely able to think, when, with his last coherent thought, he fired a blast of power through his finger and into her. As if the energy that raced through her sex had ricocheted back into his, his body jerked, and they rode the storm together, screaming their mutual disintegration.

39

LIBRA CRAWLED THROUGH THE thick verge surrounding the huge building Candace had drawn, Taryn on his heels. He eased down onto his belly and waited for her to join him.

"How are we going to get in?" she whispered.

He studied the barred windows and the heavy, wrought-iron curlicue fronting the exterior doors. The building wouldn't be easy to breach but at least the two wings were dark. The only lights were inside the five-story, center building.

"We need to scope out the back. Maybe there's little a less security."

He pushed off the ground, but before he could work his way back, he heard a rustle to their left. Taryn grabbed his arm and squeezed. He settled on his belly again and waited, but though he heard footsteps, and felt the overgrown shrubbery tremble, he couldn't see anyone.

Clouds drifted past the moon; the grounds lit up like a dimmer switch had been turned. The crunch of dead leaves sounded inches from his face.

He stopped breathing.

Taryn's grip tightened.

Midnight-black skin was illuminated by the silver moonlight, highlighting the tendons and bone structure of the massive foot. The Creeper paused and three others joined it. They stood silently, not moving or gesturing but seeming to communicate, maybe psychically. It felt like an age before the four males walked away.

Libra risked shifting forward a few inches, just enough to get a more thorough look at the grounds. His heart sank and sweat formed on his back. There had to be a dozen, maybe more, patrolling the outside of the building. There were probably more inside, in the dark, waiting silently for an intruder or an escape attempt. If there *were* children inside like Candace drew and Taryn believed—that was the question they had to answer before trying to enter.

He waited for the Creepers to go around the corner before signaling to Taryn. They crawled backward until they cleared the shrubs then jogged back to their truck.

Taryn sat on the lowered tailgate. "Creepers. I could have gone the rest of my life without seeing one of those creatures again."

Libra paced past her, his head down. "Creepers being here means it's likely your vision was correct."

"My vision?"

"The one you saw through the bird's eyes. Circe and a man with the children."

"You think that was real?"

"Just as real as this building from Candace's drawing."

"So what do we do? That was a lot of Creepers."

"Too many for us to take on, especially since we don't know if there are more inside." He stopped moving and stared in the direction of the building. "We need to get help."

Taryn jumped off the tailgate. "We don't have time. We're here now; we need to do this."

"We'll get slaughtered in there. That won't help the children."

She planted her hands on her hips. "If my vision was right, that means an Aspis child is going to get skinned alive."

He stepped up to her and looked down. "The Aspis may already be dead. We have to consider all the children."

She scowled. Her expression was fierce, but that only made him want to kiss it away. Of course, the woman would probably bite him if he tried.

"So who would you suggest we ask for help? The Zodiacs? Abella or Persephone? The Corvus Wards? We don't have a lot of friends here."

"And the Sol, if we could find them, would take too long." He stepped back. "Okay, I take your point. But what would you suggest?"

"I think we should finish our recon of the building. Maybe see if we can do a Creeper headcount, maybe even see who's inside." She raised her hands to the sky. "We have several more hours of dark on our side."

He shook his head. "Over the cliff?"

She spread her arms wide as she backed up in the direction of the rear of the building. "For the children."

He took a deep breath. "Why did I even ask?"

They worked their way to the back of the building before dropping to their hands and knees and crawling through the conveniently dense brush. They flattened down and stayed quiet for what seemed like hours to Libra. But the wait proved fruitful. The routine was simple—four Creepers walked the perimeter of the building every fifteen minutes.

Smack in the middle of the main section was a small loading dock, perhaps meant for laundry, food delivery, and more, with a garage door and a side door. If they were lucky, one of the doors would be unlocked or the locks could be picked. The big plus—there were no windows and no bars. They could approach without being seen and leave without being trapped by iron.

Libra rolled onto his back. "As soon as this group leaves, I'm going to make a run at the doors, see if they're locked and alarmed."

"What about me? You aren't going inside without me."

"Your job is to count the minutes and signal me when I'm out of time."

"What am I supposed to do? Holler?"

"I don't know; throw a rock?"

He watched the Creepers round the corner then drew his legs under him. He slowly stood, but before he could step out, she grabbed his ankle. He glanced down, a smile on his face, expecting her to tell him to be careful.

"You go inside without me, I'll kick your ass."

If the need for silence hadn't been critical, he would have laughed. He should have known better than to think this female would give him a loving send off.

He bent down, gripped the back of her neck and pulled her to him. "Give me a reason to come back for you."

"I did that last night. You saying that wasn't convincing enough?"

"A reminder then."

He pressed his lips to hers, gently at first then his need for her surged and the world fell away, leaving only the two of them. Her breath warmed him, her soft lips challenged him, her brash, fearless heart thrilled and infuriated him at the same time, but he hungered for her to his core.

He reluctantly released her and looked at his hands. His fingertips glowed blue. He was ready. With a wink, he worked his way through the remaining brush, paused short of the gravel driveway, and ran to the side door.

Locked.

He checked the garage door but it was locked as well. He held up his right forefinger, concentrating on the tip, and willed his power to collect there. He had returned to the single door, bending over to study the deadbolt when something hit his backside. He stood and looked for Taryn but didn't see her. Listening didn't yield any information either.

He turned his attention back to the door, raised his hand…and nothing. His power had bid a hasty retreat. He shook his hand and tried to concentrate, but he couldn't find the light again. He turned toward the shrubs then flinched when several pebbles hit his face.

Taryn was crouched by the side of the drive, waving both hands frantically. As soon as she caught his eye, she gestured for him to join her, and based on her flailing hands and panicked expression, she meant right now.

He didn't hear anything, but if the Creepers were approaching, the light of the moon would give him away; any surprise they had in their favor would go 'poof.' He had crouched, ready to spring across the drive, when a thick cloud slid over the moon, buying him a moment. He sprung out, his waist still bent, staying as low as possible. Halfway across the drive, twin lights stabbed at the darkness behind him.

Libra dove for the shrubs, grunting as the branches slapped his face and tugged at his clothes. He pulled his exposed legs into his chest and waited for sounds that an alarm had been raised. None came.

Taryn crawled over to him and pulled on his clothes to drag him deeper into the darkness. "That was too close."

"I thought the Creepers were minutes away," he whispered.

She didn't speak, just pointed to the right, down the driveway.

A black sedan eased by them and stopped mere feet away from where they were hidden. The driver door opened and a man climbed out. The cloud obscuring the moon rolled on and Libra looked up. His heart skipped hard in his chest. He knew that face. He hadn't seen the man since he was a boy, but he knew it.

Hanell.

Libra's younger brother stood in front of him.

Hanell looked about the area before walking around to the back passenger side door and opening it. He held out a hand. A slender, pale hand settled in his palm. He pulled gently and helped a woman rise.

Long, red hair flowed down her back, the color like living fire, undaunted by the cool, silver touch of the moonlight.

The woman ran a finger down Hanell's chiseled face then turned back to the car. "Get her, will you."

Taryn jerked.

The shrubs rustled.

Hanell looked up, his eyes narrowed. He studied the shrubs for a moment.

"It's nothing, darling, probably just a little creature running for its life," the woman said. She walked past him to the door, her skintight dress and stiletto heels restricting her normal predatory prowl. "Come now, I'm positively starving."

Hanell reached into the car and jerked a girl out and up.

She hissed and fought him until her hood slipped off. The beautiful, reptilian Aspis child opened her mouth; her fangs snapped into place and she lunged for Hanell's neck.

In a blur of motion, Hanell met the girl's face with his fist, dropping her with one bone-crunching blow. He scooped her up like she weighed nothing, slung her over his shoulder, and carried her to the door. Unlocking it, he held it open for the woman. She rose up on her toes and kissed Hanell deeply. He cupped one of her breasts and she squeezed his groin. They staggered inside, still in a clench, and disappeared, the click of the deadbolt loud and final.

Libra pointed in the direction of the truck and they crawled out again, not speaking until they reached it and climbed into the cab.

Taryn slumped down and groaned, rubbing her eyes. "Oh, man, I didn't wanna be right. Circe. Crap." She looked at him. "What's wrong? You look poleaxed."

Libra stared through the windshield, his hands tight on the steering wheel. "My brother…"

"Hanell?" She touched his thigh. "That man was your brother?"

He nodded slowly. The way his brother had struck the girl…she was small, but it took great force to punch someone so hard that they dropped to the ground. *That kind of power…*

He shook his head. "Yes. Did you recognize the Aspis?"

"Wait. Rewind please. This is huge…and awful."

Libra dropped his head and took a deep breath. He wasn't ready to go there. He could barely process it; talking about it wasn't an option.

"Please, Taryn, I need a minute. Tell me about the Aspis. Was she the same one?"

"Okay, sure. It's hard to tell, but she could be the girl I saw in my vision."

"I think we can safely stop calling it a vision. It was too prophetic for that."

"Like your vision of the attack on the Sol and Nox?"

He sat still for a moment, not answering her question. Twice, he had acted on what he had thought was a dream or vision, not looking too hard at where the information had come from. Add in Candace's map, and it was beginning to feel like they were pawns being pushed across a chessboard, but to what end? Why save them from the bird attack? Why show them the roads to get here? Why show Taryn that Circe and Hanell were together? More importantly, who would benefit from sending them here? What checkmate was in store—and for whom?

He sat back and sighed.

It didn't matter, at least not at this moment. Taryn's vision had proven to be true, which meant there were probably more paranorm children inside, including the Corvus Ward royal. Regardless of the reason they'd been directed here, now that they had found the building, they couldn't leave without the children. And for the first time, Libra had a chance to save Hanell…like he should have years ago.

"What are we going to do?" Her voice caught, the pitch higher than normal.

He heard the tears that had collected; her distress pulled his attention away from what should have been. He held out his arm. She scooted across the bench seat and he folded her body into his.

"Hanell is in there with Circe," he said.

"Yes. So?"

"So maybe that can work for us."

"How?"

"If I can convince Hanell to help us, it might be enough to make this work."

"Whoa, hold on now. You saw what he did to the Aspis. After all these years, you really think you can gain his help in a matter of minutes?"

Libra grimaced, the stab of guilt shredding him. He turned to her and dropped all of his guards, every artifice he'd used for years as a shield from the pain of self-reflection. He let her see his fear and doubt and regret. "I have to try."

Taryn sat completely still as she searched his face for several seconds. She set her chin and nodded once. "So we go in."

He mirrored her nod. "Yes."

"And if you're wrong…if he won't help us?"

"Then you better hope I can control my power…without you having to give me a hand job to do it."

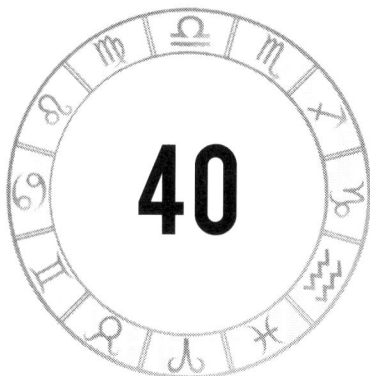

40

TARYN FOLLOWED LIBRA THROUGH the back door, the break in the Creeper patrol giving Libra time to force the lock. A small storage space greeted them along with the sickly sweet stench of death. Libra blocked her with an arm and steered her around the slumped body of a man propped up against the wall to their right, a trucker cap tossed carelessly on his caved-in chest.

"Is he...?" she whispered.

"From the smell, yes."

Her heart skipped in her chest, the gravity of what they were trying to do hitting home. As much as she trusted her gut telling her that this was the right thing to do, it didn't mean they were safe from harm. Going up against her mother so soon after the witch goddess had tried to kill her and her sisters rattled her, but she couldn't forget the vision of the Aspis child being skinned alive.

While she let herself be guided by her gut, that vision was driving her beyond what she knew was safe. But who would she be if she walked away from the children? Left them to Circe and her cruelty? Left Hanell to be warped further by her mother's insanity?

Fear settled low in her belly and she took a deep breath of fresh air as they passed through the door leading from the garage into the interior of the main building. They stopped at the crossroad of two hallways. One ran from the back door to the front of the building, the floors and walls covered in old, slightly warped, hardwood paneling. The other hall ran perpendicular along the back of the building, hardwood continuing on the walls and floors except for the white-tiled kitchen floor and walls on their right.

"Where do you think they are?" Taryn whispered.

Libra pointed to the front of the building. "Let's see how many."

She nodded her head when she really wanted to shake it. Circe, her mother, the woman who had tried to sacrifice her to release a demon army, was in this place. It had been right to make this journey, but now that they were here…

She swallowed hard and took Libra's hand. GQ had become a touchstone, someone to reach out to for reassurance.

He squeezed once and didn't release her hand.

She loved him for that simple comfort. Her heart flopped. She loved him. *Holy crap.*

They hugged the wall as they made their way to the front of the building, Libra testing each floorboard for creaks before putting his weight on it. Stealth was the only way they would survive this. That and the hope that betrayal could be forgiven in record time.

Not that she blamed Libra for leaving Hanell behind when he ran away from Aubrianna. His life had been hell and he'd run to survive. But Hanell might not be so understanding. In a split second, the man would have to choose between the brother who had abandoned him and the woman who had him in thrall.

They reached the expansive, curved staircase and hesitated. Libra released her hand and leaned out to see past the stairs. Taryn followed his lead, looking left then right. Nothing—not a single Creeper. Were they so confident that no one could get inside that their interior security was this lax? Or could it be a trap?

Libra stepped out of the hall and worked his way around the stairs. He stopped at the double doors. They were padlocked.

"Can you open them?" she asked.

"Not with my power; it'll make too much noise," he said as he pulled out a small, black, leather pouch. He unzipped it and showed her the lock-pick set. "Not everything we Zodiacs use is magical. Not when good old human tools will do."

"Why didn't you use those outside?"

"It takes a while."

After what seemed like eons, Libra opened the padlock and eased it off the door handles. He looked at Taryn, his eyebrows raised.

Last chance to back out.

"Do it," she whispered with a nod.

He pushed the doors open.

Taryn stepped into the room and clapped a hand over her mouth to stop her gasp. Circe hadn't quite filled the room but she'd come close. Just like in her vision, cots lined the walls and filled the center of the room, all but a few inhabited by blanket-covered, sleeping children, save for the Aspis who had been placed on the ground, still unconscious.

The sight of the small, crumpled body on the bare floor with no blanket broke Taryn's heart even as it filled the rest of her with rage. Her mother was a monster; she'd figured that out right after meeting her. That Hanell could also be so cruel gave her further pause, and left her wondering if Libra could get through to him.

"I count twenty-six," Libra whispered.

Taryn looked beyond the cots. Tucked into opposing corners of the room, were two tiny cribs, one partially shielded by a curtain. That was new—and heartbreaking.

"Babies."

Libra nodded without glancing at her. "Twenty-eight." He pulled her into the corner to their right.

She took a deep breath. It broke her heart to admit defeat. "We can't do this. There are too many children, and when you add in the babies…"

Libra turned into her and cupped her face, his eyes soft, his jaw clenched, his lips tight. "We're here. We're not leaving without them."

Before she could respond, she heard the *pat-pat* of bare feet. She looked past Libra as he whipped around, blocking her from whoever was approaching.

A gangly, gold Kellas Cat female paused, her eyes wide. She would run if they spooked her.

Taryn pushed past Libra and slowly walked up to the girl. She took in the bruises and open wounds that covered the girl's bare arms, legs, and face. She'd been beaten, repeatedly judging by the varying colors.

"Who are you?" the girl asked, her voice quiet but demanding.

"I am Taryn. This is Libra."

The girl's eyes narrowed. She took a step back. "A Zodiac?"

Taryn held up her hands. "We're here to help you. Are there more children upstairs?"

The Kellas Cat studied Taryn and Libra for several moments. "How did you know about us?"

No doubt the girl had come to distrust adults, but they didn't have time to assuage her fears.

Taryn pulled Candace's drawing out of her pocket and unfolded it. "A Portend drew this. We're here to help you escape."

The Kellas Cat leaned close, peered at the page, and reached for the drawing.

Taryn gave it to her and waited. The girl's mouth dropped open.

"Are there more children upstairs?"

The girl shook her head as she returned the page. "The floors upstairs are rotting and there's no water. They crammed all of us in here."

"Will you help us?" Taryn asked.

The girl nodded. She backed up several more paces before turning away from them. She tiptoed from one cot to another, waking the oldest paranorm children first, whispering so low Taryn couldn't make out what she was saying.

"This is taking too long," Libra said.

He started to move around Taryn but she stopped him with an outstretched arm. "No, let her do this; let them do this. You saw her injuries—she's worked hard to protect the little ones and has suffered for it. These children need to participate in their escape. Trust me, I know. Taking back their power is the best way for them to begin to heal."

To her surprise, he stopped pushing and waited.

The oldest children finished plumping their pillows and covering them with their blankets, then gathered around Taryn and Libra. Taryn sighed with relief when the Aspis girl stirred—they weren't too late. Libra saw the girl too and gave her an almost imperceptible nod.

The Kellas Cat girl walked to the front of the group. "Now what?"

"Is there a Corvus Ward boy here, a royal like in the drawing?" Libra asked.

The Kellas girl walked quickly to another cot and shook the sleeping child there. He slid off the cot, rubbing his eyes as the girl led him over.

Libra squatted. "Sorry to wake you."

The Corvus boy dropped his fists and opened his eyes.

Red. This was the royal from the drawing.

Libra looked up at the Kellas Cat girl. "Before we wake the others, what do you know about the exits? Any hidden ones? Any weaknesses?"

"There's the front door. And the loading dock; that's the way they brought us inside. We haven't seen any others," she answered.

"The front door is closest," Libra said.

"But it has wrought iron on it and a big lock," a tall, thin, auburn-haired Bathory Berserker boy said, followed closely by a limping blue Kellas Cat boy, his left arm in a sling. The Bathory took Kellas Cat girl's hand in his, his expression defiant. "And the Creepers—"

"—patrol the grounds every fifteen minutes," Libra finished, his eyebrows raised high as he stared at the clasped hands.

Taryn elbowed him. Now was not the time to go all slack-jawed over inter-species relations. From what she'd heard and seen, it was about time for some mingling and cohorting.

"So," she said, "back door it is."

Libra grabbed her arm and pulled her away from the children. "How do you propose we get them away from here?" He glanced past her at the large group of children in the room. "The truck won't hold them all."

Before Taryn could respond, she felt a tug on her shirt hem. A tiny, blond Portend stared up at her, the boy's eyes half-closed from sleep.

"Big truck," the child whispered.

Taryn squatted. "What truck?"

The boy spread his arms wide. "Big, big truck."

Taryn glanced up at the older children. "What's he talking about?"

The Kellas Cat girl flashed a grin. "The big truck we came in. It's still here… somewhere."

"Can you show me?" Libra asked.

She glanced at the Bathory boy and nodded once. "He'll go with you; I'll stay. He's shite with the babies."

"Language," Taryn chided.

The Kellas girl shrugged a shoulder and rolled her eyes, just like a human teenager. Some things were universal.

"Taryn?"

"Go, find out what they're talking about. We'll get the rest of the children ready."

Libra waved at the Bathory boy and they slipped out of the room, closing the door behind them with a soft click.

"Your mate is a Zodiac. The stories told say they are incapable of finding an inamorata," the Kellas girl said.

"Libra? My mate? Hardly." Taryn had to stop the laugh bubbling up inside her before it escaped. "But try telling Lyon and my sister that Zodiacs can't find inamoratas."

The very notion was absurd, but the zing that shot through her belied her scoffing tone.

41

LIBRA SLIPPED DOWN THE hallway. He was hugging the stairs to minimize the chance of floor creaks, the Bathory boy on his tail, when he heard a noise directly ahead. He paused, a hand raised to stop the boy and signal him to remain quiet.

A light flashed on in the kitchen, but Libra couldn't see who it was from his position. He hesitated, waiting to see if they would be discovered, but all he heard was the refrigerator opening and closing and the scrape of a chair across the tile.

Damn it, whoever it was had decided to park themselves. If it was a Creeper, he was screwed; Circe, double screwed. But if it was Hanell…this was his chance and he had to take it. He glanced back and mouthed 'stay.'

The boy nodded.

Libra hesitated before taking the first step, his heart pounding, sweat beading on his skin. This was a crapshoot, no doubt, and it probably wouldn't go his way, but he had to try. They needed the help. But what the hell was he supposed to say?

Sorry I left you behind to be Aubrianna's punching bag, bro. Or, *Hey, you know all the abuse you took? Made you man-up, didn't it?*

For fuck's sake.

He rolled his head to pop his neck and strode into the kitchen.

Hanell sat slumped at a stainless-steel prep table, a piece of raw steak pressed to one eye, his free arm wrapped around his ribs as if trying to prevent himself from flying apart. He slowly turned his head and smiled.

Libra stopped.

The brothers stared at each other for several seconds before Hanell placed the steak on the steel and pivoted in his chair.

"Well, what have we here? A reunion?" His smile faded as he waited for Libra to reply.

Hanell looked like hell. Black eye, busted lip, scars twining up his forearms and disappearing under his sleeves. Even the edge of one ear was curled and thickened like a cauliflower. Goddess only knew what scars were under his clothes.

Libra swallowed hard. "It can be."

"Just betray Circe and throw in with you?"

"Yes."

Hanell rose slowly, carefully, and walked over to Libra. "Why would I be interested in that?" He spread one arm wide. "I have it good here."

"I can see that from your face. And your ribs? Bruised or broken?"

Hanell frowned and dropped the arm protecting his ribs. "What do you want?"

"I'm here for the children." Since Hanell was being direct, it was time to put the cards on the table. "I need your help."

Hanell said nothing; he didn't move and barely breathed. "Here for the children? That's rich. Where were you years ago? I would have adored a rescue from that piece of Hell on earth."

Libra rubbed his forehead. *Here we go.* "I was a child. I was scared and I ran."

"No, not then. I'm talking about all these years you've been a Zodiac. Powerful, demon-turbocharged; you could have gotten me away from Aubrianna years ago."

Libra clenched his teeth. He shook his head and looked anywhere but at the hurt face of the brother he should have protected. "You have every right to hate me."

"Well, it's *so* nice to have that cleared up, but you didn't answer the damn question."

Hanell's voice had risen, echoing in the industrial-sized kitchen.

Libra hesitated, not sure how to explain that ignoring what had driven him away from their mother became…a habit. It was easier to keep busy with his life as an assassin, despite hating it, than face his utter failure as a big brother. Maybe that was the answer that Hanell deserved. The raw truth, no matter how much it hurt to speak the words, knowing the pain they would cause.

"I failed you. After becoming a Zodiac, it was easier to pretend it all never happened."

"That I never happened? That I didn't exist?"

Libra nodded. What else could be said?

Hanell sat back down and looked away, his expression an odd mix of angry and haunted. "At least that was honest."

Libra didn't want to press, but if the children stood a chance of getting away from Circe, there was no time to prolong this. "We need your help. I failed you, yes, but I'm here now and I want you to come with us. Start over with us in the Great Cavern, or wherever you want to go. Paranorm world, human world; I have the money to make it happen."

"Do you have enough to buy back my childhood?" Hanell asked in a quiet voice.

Libra swallowed back the gut punch. "You know I can't, but I can give you a new future, away from Aubrianna and Circe."

Hanell finally looked at Libra again, staring for what seemed like forever before nodding. "Okay."

Libra held out a hand.

Hanell stood and shook it.

Libra pulled him into his chest and hugged him. Hanell froze, but submitted for a moment before pulling away, his expression stony.

That Hanell had tolerated his affection even for just a few precious seconds rocked Libra to his core.

"What do you need?" Hanell asked.

Libra cleared his throat. "The children said something about a big truck."

"Ah, that would be the semi we have hidden out back. But it's the bus you want."

"You have a bus?"

Hanell nodded. "Fancy piece of human manufacturing, and huge."

"The keys?"

"Driver visor."

Libra nodded. "Show me."

Hanell walked past Libra and out into the hall. He paused when he saw the Bathory boy hovering in the shadows then moved toward the loading dock. Libra nodded reassuringly at the Bathory and followed closely.

Hanell opened the side door, peeked out, then waved at the pair. "It's clear."

He took off to the right at a jog, a slight limp appearing in his gait.

Libra followed, his relief at Hanell's help tempered by the gut feeling that this was all too easy: visions leading them to this place, the ease of entry, no Creepers inside with the children, and now Hanell's forgiveness and change of loyalty in a nanosecond. Something or someone was driving their good fortune. But he'd take the chance to get the children away from Circe, and if his luck held, he'd have a chance to work on Hanell.

His skin crawled. There would be a price to pay; he could feel it to his marrow. *Taryn's damn gut feelings. I've been infected.*

Hanell turned left down a dirt road then stopped short of the huge semi sitting in the dark. On the other side, hidden by the length of the semi, was a large bus with dark windows.

Libra walked past him and climbed in, taking a seat before pulling down the visor. He caught the keys before they landed in his lap and inserted them in the ignition, turning them just enough to check the gauges without starting the engine. No sense pushing their dubious luck.

Satisfied that the bus had fuel and the battery wasn't dead, he hopped down and walked back toward Hanell. "Let's go then."

The three stopped at the intersection.

Hanell looked at his watch. "Wait."

Seconds later, four Creepers rounded the front corner of the building and walked toward them. Libra and the Bathory sank into the bushes but Hanell stayed still.

246

Here we go.

If his brother was going to betray them, this was the perfect time to do it. Libra held his breath and waited for the skeletal creatures to grab him, but they moved on, continuing their patrol without so much as acknowledging Hanell. If they did, it was silent, nonverbal.

"It's safe," Hanell whispered.

Libra and the boy joined him and they jogged back to the door. Slipping inside, they worked their way to the front room and entered.

The children gasped, their eyes wide. They backed away until they stood behind Taryn.

"Libra?" Taryn said uncertainly.

"Hanell is going to help us. He took us to a bus large enough for all of us. You ready to move?"

"Just waiting for you before getting the babies."

"Then let's do it. Time to get out of here."

Taryn trotted to one of the cribs and collected an infant; when it squawked, the Kellas Cat rushed over, placed a hand on the baby's head, and dropped hers. In a blink, the baby stopped fussing; it cooed quietly. Taryn glanced back at Libra and grinned.

"Amazing," Libra whispered.

"Who is that woman?" Hanell asked.

"A friend."

Hanell snorted. "Right. Friend."

Libra looked at him. "What are you implying?"

Hanell shrugged.

"We need to have a talk about your oratory skills, little brother."

Before Hanell could make some other judgmental gesture, Taryn joined them, the tiny bundle cradled in her arms and a beatific smile on her face.

She pulled back the blanket and leaned forward to show Libra the sleeping baby. "Look at him."

The infant had smooth, solid-ebony skin and chubby cheeks.

Libra covered the baby with the blanket. "He's an Innocent Demonica."

Hanell crossed his arms and shook his head. "Not just a Demonica; he's a

Prime—a baby as important to the Innocent Demonica as a royal child is to the Corvus Wards."

"How the hell did Circe get her hands on a Demonica, much less a Prime?"

Hanell snorted. "What makes you so sure she's the one who procured him?"

Taryn held him out to Libra. "Not important right now. Take him."

Libra held up his hands. "No way, I need my hands free in case there's a fight."

Taryn pushed the baby into his chest.

"Damn it, Taryn," he groused as he took the baby from her.

"We need all hands."

She walked quickly to the farthest corner where a curtain had been pulled closed. She picked up the baby there and walked back to Libra, the children parting like the Red Sea as she passed. The room fell silent. The children's faces were drawn, their eyes wide.

"What's with the fear?" Libra asked Hanell under his breath.

"I could tell you, but seeing for yourself would be better."

"We don't have time for this."

"Take the time, brother. You may think you know everything going on here, but you don't."

Libra met Taryn halfway. "I need to see the baby."

"Really? Now?"

"Look around; the children are terrified. I need to see why."

Taryn shook her head. "Okay."

She peeled back the blanket to reveal pale skin and rosy cheeks; there was nothing out of the ordinary. Libra looked back at Hanell.

"Feel her back," Hanell said.

Libra dipped his free hand under the blanket and slid it around her tiny body to her back. He started at her shoulders and ran down to her butt. "Shit."

"What?" Taryn asked.

He removed his hand and gently opened the baby's lips. "Fuck me."

Taryn looked down. "My god—she has teeth."

"Not just teeth; she has fangs instead of canines." He released the girl's lips and stepped back. "Taryn. Give me the baby."

"Why?"

"Trade with me right now."

She frowned but, for once, she did as he asked. They switched babies.

"Tell me what's going on."

Hanell joined them. "That baby is a Keres."

"What's a Keres?"

They didn't have time to linger longer than they already had, but this was bad and Taryn needed to know. "The Keres are death daemons, agents of the Fates. The wings, the fangs…if the Keres are here, and breeding, that means war is coming."

"There's war all around the planet already."

"I mean the Quietus—"

The sound of footsteps outside the room stopped Libra short.

He waved at the children to follow him then led them to the double doors. He pointed to the walls on either side. They flattened themselves against them and waited.

The footsteps stopped at the door.

Libra shifted the Keres baby to his left arm and tried to call up some power in his right. His hand tingled, but no blue light meant no power. He shook his hand, hard, but nothing came. Before he could make the decision to hand the Keres to Hanell, the person on the other side of the door started to walk away.

Hanell smiled at Libra, the grin hard, his eyes glittering.

A hot knot of fear dropped into Libra's gut. He moved to stop Hanell but the man backed away.

"Oh, Circe!" Hanell called out.

"What are you doing?" Libra ground out.

The double doors flew open, their knobs hitting the walls so hard they cracked the wood paneling. Circe stalked into the room followed by a cadre of Creepers, the moonlight barely tempering the flame of her auburn hair.

The black skin of the Creepers shifted to lunar silver.

Circe twirled, a huge smile on her face, and spread her arms wide. "Daughter!"

42

LIBRA BACKED AWAY FROM Circe and Hanell until he reached Taryn. The children scattered along the wall of barred windows that looked out onto the front of the grounds.

"Hanell?"

"Come on, brother. You think that oh-so-touching talk about being here for me now after all these years is enough to repay me for what you did?"

"No, not even close, but I wanted a chance to make it right. This isn't the way."

"News flash." Hanell leaned forward. "There is no making it right."

Circe clapped her hands. "Children, let us not bicker." She held out her hands to Libra. "Give me my baby."

He backed up, his grip tightening around the Keres. "This isn't your child."

"Well, that's not strictly true. She is a descendent of Nyx, which makes her a cousin of a sort," she rolled her eyes up as if calculating the connection before waving a hand, giving up the attempt, "many times removed."

"That no more makes you this child's keeper than Taryn is your daughter. There may be blood between you, but that's not the only thing that makes family. I'm not handing her over to you."

Circe cocked her head and snapped her fingers. The Creepers fanned out until they formed a semi-circle around the children. "You don't have a choice."

Heat raced through Libra, the rage incinerating his fear, purifying him. *Gaia, stand with me. Now. Please.*

The closest Creeper reached out for the Keres.

"Don't," Libra said, raising his right hand, his palm facing the threat.

Blue light flooded his fingers, pulsing as it spread down his forearm.

"Get him!" Circe ordered.

The Creeper lunged for Libra.

Libra pushed his hand forward and imagined the Creeper being shoved back.

The blue light shot out and struck the Creeper in the chest. The skeletal creature flew across the width of the room and slammed into the wall, cracking the plaster. It slid down until it hit the floor, but Libra could see its chest rising and falling. It was still alive.

He whirled around and handed the Keres to Taryn. "Stay close, all of you."

"Get them," Circe screeched.

The Creepers advanced on the group.

Libra held up both hands. He fought for a few moments, firing at the Creepers, pushing them back until exhaustion stole over him. If he'd been skilled enough to focus the power more discreetly, he could have conserved his energy, but each shot produced a wild cone of force. And with each effort, he weakened. He wouldn't last much longer.

He focused his will on the Creepers, shoving them back again before spinning around.

Digging deep into his reserves, he blasted out the front windows and iron bars. "Run. Now."

A Creeper reached Libra and knocked him off his feet with one blow to his ribs. He slid on his side along the wooden floor, half of his body numb, the other half in agony.

The children screamed.

His vision swam but he could still see the Creepers surrounding the children, reaching for Taryn with their long arms. Libra clawed at the floor with the one hand that still worked, but his body wouldn't respond. He was helpless, and Taryn was in danger.

Gaia.

A Creeper took a fistful of Taryn's hair and jerked her into his chest. It grabbed at the bundled baby in her right arm. Snagging it with long, claw-like fingers, it tossed the infant to Circe.

She cackled as she opened the blanket then looked at the baby's face. "No! It's not the Keres."

She rolled the Innocent Demonica across the floor.

The Creeper grabbed Taryn's throat and lifted her off the ground. She kicked and writhed but he held her tight as he plucked at the other baby in her arms.

Taryn gripped the bundle tighter and screamed.

"Taryn!" Libra answered.

He fought to rise, desperate to save her and the children cowering away from the other Creepers, but all he could do was bend his knees and curl into a ball. No amount of help Gaia could give, even if she chose to, would get him to his feet in time to save them.

A rush of wind passed over him, the hiss too high-pitched for it to just be a breeze. He squinted and scanned the room but saw nothing until the Creeper holding Taryn screamed and dropped her.

A small, dark brown figure clung to its back; thin arms wrapped around the much-larger creature's throat. The Creeper clawed at its skin and staggered back, its breathing labored. The black skin cracked and green pus poured out. The Creeper fell to its knees and the figure jumped down.

It was the Pestilence Fairy, the one who had saved them from the Stryx attack.

Tiny, wearing a troll-worthy scowl, the fairy spread her tattered wings wide. "You will not harm Taryn."

The Creepers stopped; they shifted from one foot to another. They knew what she was, and the risk she posed.

"Meri? What are you doing here?" Taryn asked.

The fairy flashed a smile and waved. "Hi, Taryn. I am here to help you."

Circe growled but kept her distance. "You are alone, little one. You can't hope to kill us all before I kill them. And you."

The fairy whipped her head around, bared her teeth, and hissed at the witch goddess. "You will try." Her wings folded against her back and she crouched, her fingers curled into claws. "You will fail."

Libra took a deep breath. He rolled up onto his hands and knees then pushed off with a great heave of effort. "Taryn, get them out."

She glanced at him and nodded. He scooped up the baby on the floor and staggered over to the trembling paranorm children.

He handed the Innocent Demonica to the Bathory boy. "Take him to Taryn."

He leaned on the windowsill, wanting to help lift the smallest ones but unable to do more than support himself for the moment. The Kellas Cat girl climbed out first, and with Taryn's help, they gathered all the children in the front courtyard.

"Fairy, come," he said under his breath.

"They must die."

"Not by your hand, child. Come now—you did brilliantly. You've saved us all. We'll need your help to get away from this place." He waited, hoping she would listen.

"They hurt the children; they tried to hurt my friend. They must die."

"Look at me."

She glanced at him, her scowl still fierce, the need to destroy everyone in the room glittering in her eyes.

"Taryn needs you to help her now. There's no time to kill them. Okay?"

She rolled her shoulders and backed up to the broken windows.

"Thank you," Libra added as she climbed out.

Her face softened when she acknowledged him. She nodded once then disappeared into the dim light surrounding Taryn and the children.

"You think this is the end, Zodiac?" Circe asked.

Libra glanced at her and stilled.

Her hands were around Hanell's throat, squeezing hard enough that his face had turned dark red, but he made no effort to stop her. He stared at Libra, his expression passive.

"I will take his life if you don't bring the Keres to me. You left your brother behind to suffer Aubrianna's wrath. If you want to help Hanell, if you want to make up for what you did to him, now's your chance. Make a choice."

Libra struggled to breathe. He flexed his hands; the numbness had finally left them only to steal over his heart. "Sorry, brother."

He threw up his hands and willed his power to fly, hoping for one last surge of strength. But all he got was a weak blast of blue that hit the ceiling.

Plaster rained down on them; the Creepers ran toward Circe and jumped.

Libra pushed off the floor and fell out of the building just as a huge *bang* sounded. He looked back and saw the beams in the ceiling give way. The room disappeared under the weight of the collapsing upper floors.

"Hanell…"

He crawled away from the destruction until he reached the Bathory boy and the Kellas Cat girl, his body covered in dust.

Libra stared at the destruction, his heart in his throat. "I killed him."

Taryn reached out a hand. "Libra…"

The children looked between the two adults.

"Help me get to her," he said to the pair supporting him.

They helped Libra walk across the gravel courtyard until he was only a few feet away.

Taryn took a step then stopped, her lips parting as she turned her head.

Before Libra could understand what he was seeing, a huge pair of talons appeared out of the dark. They grabbed Taryn's shoulders, the sharp keratin biting deep into her flesh, and lifted her off the ground. She screamed as the Stryx rose higher and higher.

"No!" he yelled.

He jerked free of the children and leaped, but the Stryx had already carried Taryn well beyond his reach. The two babies fell from her arms; Libra caught them before they hit the ground.

He released them, but before he could rise, he heard the flap of more wings. "Get down."

The children hit the gravel. Their whimpering ripped apart his shock, giving him a burst of adrenaline. He screamed at the birds diving down and fired everything he had through his hands.

Blue light lit up the night sky, Gaia's power flying in every direction, like an upside-down cone. The Stryx screeched when they hit the light but none of them burst into flames or died in mid-air. His power was too tapped out to cause them more than a little irritation, but it was enough to drive them away.

The fairy jumped up and unfolded her wings.

"No, wait."

"I must save my friend."

Libra looked at the pale, wide-eyed children around him. Only hours ago he'd only thought of them as his chance to barter for his freedom. Now, seeing their faces, knowing that they'd suffered at Circe's hands, he couldn't leave them unattended, no matter how he longed to go after Taryn. But an idea came to him.

"What is your name?" he asked the fairy.

"I am Meri."

He placed a hand on his chest. "I am Libra."

Meri nodded once then glanced at the sky, her body quivering like she'd fly apart if she didn't take off.

"How did you find us? Have you been following us this whole time?"

She shook her head. "Taryn is my friend. I have touched her; I know the smell of her blood. I used that to track her."

She shrugged her shoulders; a stark reminder that she was just a child and what he was about to ask of her wasn't fair or right. But he would ask it nonetheless.

"I need you to do something very difficult."

She nodded.

"I need you to follow Taryn. Can you do that? Can you find her?"

She squared her shoulders, her eyes sparkling. "Yes."

"I want you to track Taryn then come back to me."

He looked at the other children. "I know that you've had it bad. I can't say that this trip will be easy, but you are free now. Follow me and I'll make sure you're safe."

The Kellas Cat's frown deepened. "What about our parents? When do we get to go home?"

"First, let's get to safety. Then we'll work on finding your families."

The children shifted their feet and looked at one another before nodding.

He turned back to the antsy fairy. "Meri, will you do this for me, for Taryn?"

"How will I find you?" she asked.

He pulled off his flannel shirt—too exhausted to care about the cold—and handed it to her. "Tie it around your waist and use it to find me."

Her smile was radiant as she spread her wings. She backed into the darkest part of the courtyard. "I will find you."

She squatted then shot off into the night sky.

"Come," Libra said.

The group of children followed him around the back. The front of the bus flickered in the light, drawing Libra's attention back to the destroyed building. A fire had started where the right wing connected to the center. It would spread and destroy this horrible place. Hanell flashed through his conscience, but he wouldn't allow himself to dwell on his brother. The man was misguided but resilient; hopefully, he had survived. If he had, Libra would fulfill his promise and get Hanell free of Aubrianna and Circe. He would help Hanell find a new life without pain and suffering.

But, for now, the children needed him.

He climbed in, pulled down the visor, and the keys fell into his lap. He inserted them and started the engine. Unlike some of the Zodiacs, he knew how to drive. He hopped out and herded the children up the steps. One by one, he helped them climb inside until all that were left were the Kellas Cat and the Bathory boy, each holding a baby. Twenty-eight children total—where the hell was he going to take them?

They disappeared into the bus and Libra slid behind the wheel.

The Bathory boy shoved past the others and claimed the seat behind Libra, a wide grin on his face. Libra put the bus in drive, easing it away from the raging fire and down the gravel road.

The children cheered and clapped.

He looked east, the direction Meri had flown. He hated that he couldn't go after Taryn, but he couldn't track her fast enough with all the children. They needed stability and safety; two things he couldn't provide them on the run.

But as soon as they were settled, he would go into the fires of Hell itself to find Taryn and bring her back.

43

HANELL STOOD NEXT TO Circe amid the crushed bodies of several Creepers, wiping dust and tiny bits of rubble from their clothes. The black blood, however, didn't disappear so easily. The Creepers had jumped on top of the pair, taking the brunt of the weight of the collapsed floors. It had killed them instantly, leaving their masters well and whole.

"What was that power?" Circe asked, her voice quiet, contemplative.

"That was Gaia's power, or a taste of it," Hanell answered, his mouth working like he'd just bitten down on a lemon. "The great prize my mother wants to wrench from Libra."

Circe nailed him with a look. "Explain."

"After you were entombed, but before the old gods fell, Gaia created four Os Mages, one for each world, to collect the bones of paranormals to prevent them being used for black magic. She also created an Os Mage Mother to reproduce more Os Mages if one died. To protect the Os Mage Mothers, Gaia gifted them with the power of either Aether or Nether. Until my mother—Gaia's gift skipped over her for some reason. Libra being the firstborn, he is the next in line for the power of the agent. If he activates it."

"That blue light?"

"It's nothing compared to being an agent."

"And if something happens to Libra?"

Hanell smiled softly. "I am the next in line."

* * *

Abella stood on the deep front porch and studied the hilly terrain surrounding the Texas ranch. It was quiet this evening, like most nights, and the sky was cloudless, which meant they'd get another star-filled show for the next several hours. But her unease ratcheted up with each passing hour. Where were the Zodiacs? Lyon had told her to expect them days ago but no one had showed.

At least Persephone and the children had settled in without incident. Of course, the massive house had only just been finished, so there had been unpacking and furniture arranging to do, which had kept them busy. But now that was done, how the hell were they supposed to keep thirty-three children entertained? The older ones were doing their best, but these kids had barely begun to feel safe when they had had to be uprooted from their home and made to hide out in the human world—a world that had not been kind to them thus far.

"Abella?"

She turned to Persephone and smiled at her lovely sister. The idea of a pregnant woman glowing had never been truer than with Persi. As delicate as always, her beauty had gone from gentle to stunning. Her skin was lustrous, her eyes sparkled with humor and health and love, and her silver hair competed with the radiance of the moon overhead.

"Motherhood suits you."

Persephone plopped down on the sofa closest to the front door and ran her hands over her growing baby bump. "Even when I'm exhausted, starving, and jonesing for a margarita the size of this great state?"

"Two of those can be remedied like that," Abella said with a snap of her fingers.

"But—?" Persephone started to say, her hands patting her belly.

"Virgin margaritas and steak fajitas await us."

"And mounds of guac and cheese?"

"With your favorite tortilla chips flown in from Austin."

Persephone groaned, her eyes rolling back in her head. "You are a goddess."

Abella snorted with laughter. "There was a time that would've been a compliment. Considering the one goddess we've met, I'll pass on that moniker."

Persephone climbed to her feet. "Speaking of Circe, what do you think she's up to?"

They walked down the long hall that ran from the front of the house to the kitchen in the back. Abella pulled out a chair for her sister then set about making a batch of thick, cold, virgin margaritas.

"You don't have to drink a virgin just 'cause I have to."

Abella sat next to her and sipped on the delicious drink. "No, I need to keep a level head no matter how much I want the tequila." She sat back and watched Persephone take a long draw. "As for Circe, I shudder to think what she's doing. But we can't wait much longer to make a move. I'm afraid not knowing what our mother's plans are will get us killed."

"And Asmodeus."

"Him too." Abella returned to the kitchen and started preparing her favorite steak fajita dinner for the two of them. She placed the ingredients for guacamole next to Persi. "Tableside guac, please."

Persi grinned. "Don't forget the garlic."

"Good god, mustn't forget that."

Persi started on the avocadoes. "I know you too well, Abella. You're worried."

"We're both worried."

"Lyon and the other Zodiacs haven't come."

"I don't know why they haven't, but we need to be ready to defend ourselves in case they don't."

"You really think it's that bad? Do you know something I don't?"

Abella placed a platter of steaming, sizzling food in front of Persephone. "Eat first, then I have something to show you."

The pair ate in silence. Once they'd cleaned up, Abella waved at Persephone to follow her.

"The basement has a couple of secrets I haven't shown you yet," she said.

"As big as this house is, I'm not surprised. Why'd you choose this place? When you said you bought land near the caves in Sonora, I figured you bought that horrible house outside of the cave we escaped to."

"I tried to buy it but the town wasn't having it, and the acreage wasn't large enough anyway. So I looked until I found this place. Five hundred acres, remote, quiet, perfect for seeing anyone approaching."

Abella reached the finished basement and turned left. She walked quickly through the cavernous space until she reached double doors leading to an equally large storage room.

After opening them, she turned around to face Persi and walked backward.

"This is grand and very well planned," Persephone said, "but when did you need affirmation for something so…you?"

"Not affirmation, information. Follow me." Abella walked to the shelves at the far end of the space. "Notice what looks like ordinary storage." She waved a hand past the heavily stocked, metal shelves. "But…not so much." She gripped a metal post on the right and twisted clockwise, then twisted the left post counterclockwise. A deep *thunk* sounded behind the shelf. Abella pulled the shelf rack forward and revealed a deep-set, iron door. "The rack is tied into a track in the floor so it's smooth and pretty easy to slide." She pointed at the hidden door. "That leads to a hiding place. You go inside, slide the rack back into place, then shut and bar the metal door."

Persi looked down at the bunched-up rug in front of the rack. "What about the rug? Won't someone notice it was moved?"

Abella pushed the shelf back into position and the rug slid with it. "It's attached." She pulled the rack out again and opened the iron door. "This is a bit harder to open." She leaned into the door and pushed. The hinges were silent, smooth. "But once inside, nothing can get in." She reached for something on the wall and a light flared. "Come on, check it out. This is the real reason why I bought this place."

Persephone entered the crudely carved tunnel, her eyes wide. "Crazy panic room, huh?"

"About twenty yards down this tunnel is a second iron door. Behind it is a bunch of food, medical supplies, clothing, everything you need to last for weeks, and…" She looked away from Persephone, not wanting to see her sister's reaction. But there was nothing for it; Persi would have to deal with it. "…the cave system."

"*The* cave system?"

"It's really the best place to hide. If we need it."

Persephone nodded but remained silent as she left the tunnel. Abella closed the door and replaced the shelf before joining her.

"And the second secret?"

"A bit of a let down since it's the same thing just on the other end of the basement."

"Do they join up or are they separate?"

"They're separate. I didn't want one end to be discovered and lead right to us. One thing to know, I've only been able to chart the tunnels closest to the house, so I have a rope barrier marking where I stopped. No matter what happens, do not go beyond it or you'll get lost. We both know how bad that can get."

Persephone shuddered before nodding. She headed for the stairs. "I need another margarita." She started up then paused. "Lyon better get his butt here pronto."

"I hear you, sister," Abella replied. *And the rest of the Zodiacs better be with him.*

44

"GODDESS DAMN IT, YOU too?" Lyon growled at Sagittarius and Taurus.

The Zodiacs looked at one another, then back at Lyon.

"You called, we came," Taur said, his thickly muscled arms crossed over his massive chest.

The other Zodiacs rounded the corner and stopped when they saw Sag and Taur.

"Yeah, that makes all of us except Libra and Scorpio," Lyon growled again.

Sag rubbed the grime off his face. "We just busted a hump to get here. Not the reception we were expecting. Someone want to explain?"

"Come with us; it'll be easier to show you," Lyon said. He walked away, the Zodiacs trailing behind him until they reached the Great Cavern. He pointed to the hole in the roof. "The spell is gone and two humans have fallen to their deaths."

Before Sag or Taur could speak, Lyon marched out of the cavern and headed down the hall to the aviary. He opened the door and held it ajar.

The Hermes Hawks ruffled their feathers and shifted on their perches.

"Why are we here?" Sag asked.

"Look at the hawks," Lyon answered with a sweep of one hand.

Sag walked up to the first hawk and studied it.

Lyon joined him. "What do you see?"

"He looks tired, ruffled, and he's hunched a bit. So?"

"Check out his leg bands."

The bird had a small, metal band on each leg; one was silver with numbers etched in the metal—the bird's identification; the other band was red with no numbers—the badge that meant the bird had been retired.

"This hawk wasn't meant to be flown again," Sag said. "It shouldn't be here."

"Exactly. Check out the others."

Sag and Taur walked past every hawk in the aviary.

"They're all retired," Sag said.

The men returned to the group.

"What the hell happened to the active hawks?" Taur asked.

"The younger birds are gone." Pisces looked around the aviary. "We've been betrayed."

"Stolen I'd guess," Lyon said. "But the worst part is I had these birds sent to you with orders to go to Texas and protect Persephone and my children."

Sag scowled and shook his head. "Then why are you here? Why didn't you go to Texas yourself?"

"I needed to empty the rest of the Great Cavern before I left. I was about to make a move, but then you all started showing up here."

Pisces frowned. "So where did the other birds go if not back here? The ones with the messages that brought us here? And why didn't your messages find us?"

Lyon clenched his fists. "These birds must not have made it to you. They grew tired, so they returned. Your messages are scattered throughout the human world."

"Why do this?" Aquarius asked.

"Because the Corvus Ward king has declared war on the Great Cavern, on us. I had to get my family out first to protect them. Since then I've been emptying out the dungeon. I released the few prisoners we had so they could run."

Aquarius snorted. "Why bother? A handful of gremlins, a rogue troll...what do they matter?"

"They matter because I was once one of those that didn't matter. I couldn't leave them to be slaughtered."

Sag cleared his throat. "And what about the Pondera traitor? The one who threw in with Leona, who supported her leap into Hell? Did you release her?"

Lyon turned his gaze on Sag, fighting the urge to punch the Zodiac across the room out of sheer frustration and worry. "Yes. She was a traitor to us, but she didn't force Leona to jump; my sister did that on her own. You may not like what I did but it is done."

Pisces held up his hands to stop the blossoming argument. "So why are we still here? Now that Sag and Taur have made it, let's get the hell outta here and go to Texas."

Lyon and Sag stared at each other for a moment longer. The archer had loved Leona for as long as Lyon could remember and he obviously hadn't gotten over her disappearance yet. Not that Lyon could blame Sag for his blind anger, but he needed to be mindful of Lyon's role as leader. Backing down now wouldn't help Sag and it could hurt Lyon's standing with the other Zodiacs. Their bond was still new and tenuous and could break under the strain of the forces mounting against them.

Sag looked away.

Lyon remained still but he heaved a mental sigh of relief. They needed to move. "Now that you're all here, we go."

Without a word, the Zodiacs worked their way back to the front entrance of the Great Cavern. They picked up their waiting packs and stood at the door while Lyon unlocked it.

Sag scratched his backside and grumbled under his breath.

"What's wrong now?" Taur asked.

"I was looking forward to a long, hot bath. With lots of bubbles."

Taur nodded and hummed, his eyes half closed. "Bubbles and a bubble-butted woman."

Pisces laughed. "You better holster that weapon, Taur, before it falls off from overuse."

The bull grunted. "Dedicated use is the only way to keep a muscle hard and strong. Oughta keep that in mind, guppy."

"For goddess' sake," Pisces said, throwing up his hands. "It's Niko. N-I-K-O."

The other Zodiacs stared at him a second before turning back to Lyon.

Lyon pushed open one of the double doors. Sunlight streamed in, blinding him for a moment. His skin tingled, the heat delicious, like the first day of spring when the air was still crisp but the sun warm. But, his goose bumps weren't just because of the sun; they were also because of his desire to see Persephone and hold her again. He'd sent her away for her safety, but it hadn't been a loving departure. With the threat of war looming and now the betrayal with the Hermes hawks, he was desperate to get to his inamorata.

The clearing was empty. He sniffed the cold air. Pine and oak and hickory plus the scent of water hit him. He breathed deep then took a step out of the doorway, followed closely by the Zodiacs.

Once clear, Lyon turned around to close and lock the door and found the barrel of a gun in his face. He looked past the weapon and into the narrowed, green-amber eyes of a woman, her bright red hair nearly blinding him.

A Bathory?

Beyond her was a tall man with pale brown skin and wide, pale green eyes that darted from Lyon to the other Zodiacs, his gun sweeping back and forth as he tried to cover the woman.

She held up the badge hanging from her neck. "FBI. I'm Special Agent Sloane. This is Special Agent Treadwell. Who are you? What do you know about the scientists that have disappeared? Is this a mine?"

Lyon's ire ratcheted up with each question. "I don't have time for this."

He had tensed, preparing to swat away her gun, when a crow cried out. He looked behind him, his gut clenching.

A huge, black bird soared over the crest of the ridge surrounding the entrance. The light reflected off its wings, flashing iridescent blue, black, and purple. But it was the blood red eyes that made Lyon move.

The humans glanced up. Lyon swung his right arm and knocked the gun out of the woman's hands. It fell to the ground and bounced.

Lyon lunged for it.

The other Zodiacs ducked and split apart into two groups, dodging the human male's aim.

Lyon grabbed the woman's gun and threw it.

The weapon struck the male's left hand, spinning him around.

The woman screamed and jumped on Lyon's back, her arms wrapped around his throat, her legs around his waist.

He pulled her arms down just enough to breathe, but held them tight when she tried to adjust her grip.

"Crows!" he yelled, pointing to the ridge.

The Zodiacs looked.

A huge murder of crows flowed over the hill like a black fog, the thick swarm darkening the sky.

Taur ran to the human male and punched him, dropping the large man with one blow. He threw the human over his shoulder and raced to the door, Lyon right behind him, the woman still clinging to his back like a tick.

Sag and Aquarius pulled the heavy door open and waited for the others to stream in before closing and locking it. The screams of the frustrated crows battered the door but they weren't strong enough to cause any harm.

"The Corvus Ward warriors are here," Lyon said softly, his heart shattered. If they couldn't escape the InBetween, Persephone and his children would remain unprotected.

Pisces plucked the woman named Sloane off Lyon's back.

She scrambled over to Treadwell and pulled him into her lap. "If he dies, I will spend the rest of my life tracking each one of you down and killing you."

Sag snorted. "A clusterfuck of grand proportion with death threats to boot." He raised his arms and stretched. "At least now I can take that bath."

45

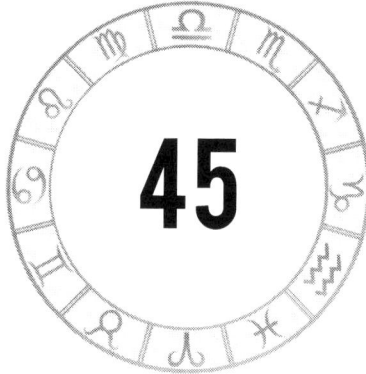

TARYN OPENED HER EYES and took in as much of her surroundings as the dark would allow. *Dank, musty, quiet—could be a basement.*

She tried to sit up but her wrists and ankles were tied to each corner of the bed, her body splayed. At least her clothes were still on.

"You're awake," a man said.

Taryn tried to speak but her throat was so dry she couldn't squeak out any words. The man's voice was familiar but her head was too fuzzy to figure out where she'd heard it before. She waited, listening, her heart banging in her chest, white spots dancing in front of her eyes.

A light flashed on. A man stood with his back to her, the light illuminating a set of stairs covered in dust and cobwebs. He turned to face her. It was Asmodeus, the demon king who had created the Zodiacs with pieces of his own soul and, only a few weeks earlier, had released a demon army into the human world.

She yanked and kicked against her restraints until he held up a hand.

"Please. Let's not have the screaming and crying. It's so tedious. And a waste of energy you're going to need."

She laid her head back and opened her mouth to breathe but she couldn't to get enough air to fill her lungs.

I'm dead.

"It's so good to see you again," Asmodeus said.

Fear swamped her. "You did this?"

Asmodeus pulled up a chair next to her bed and sat. "I warned you about connecting with Gaia. You didn't listen."

"What do you mean? I haven't seen you since the InBetween."

He pulled on the silver chain around her neck until the black opal pendant appeared. "Mr. Medai would beg to differ."

Dropping the chain, he stuck his arm out until she could see the scarified words on his forearm. *Come and See.*

"What?" Her heart sank as she pictured the words carved into the old man's flesh. "You?"

"Clever girl." He crossed his legs and grinned. "It's always a pleasure to converse with an intelligent creature, but apparently you've got a stubborn streak." He leaned close. "Or have I misjudged your ability to reason?"

"I would do anything, align with myself with anyone, to help those children."

"Haven't you turned into a fierce, little thing?"

Taryn forgot about her fear, her anger driving her to stare down the demon king. She sneered. "Perhaps, but your arrogance will be your undoing. The Zodiacs will come for me and when they do, they'll rip you apart and send you back to Hell."

Asmodeus frowned. His hand moved so fast she barely saw the motion before he had her by the throat.

He jerked her as close as the bonds would allow and pushed her hair off her face. "You and your sisters. Your foolish need to save others will be the death of you and the ruin of the Zodiacs. I cannot allow you to interfere with my plans or taint the warriors I've spent years molding."

She struggled against his hold but his fingers tightened, like a demonic monkey trap wrapped around her throat. Her adrenaline spiked. He could kill her easily, or leave her alone here in the dark.

"How could I interfere with your plans? What do you want from me?"

"I'm going to hold you here to protect that which I hold most dear when it comes to you."

He pressed the palm of his free hand against her belly, just above the juncture of her thighs.

She bucked against his hand but couldn't make him remove it. "Gaia can't possibly be worse than you."

Asmodeus laughed. "You may change your mind when you see this."

He squeezed her throat harder. She writhed in his grip, but he held tight. Dark spots danced before her eyes—she would lose consciousness soon. But instead of fainting, a flash of light exploded behind her eyes. When it dimmed, she found herself floating in space. Not actually transported to the deep, dark vacuum—she couldn't have survived that—but in a vision. She turned her head and her body followed until she saw Earth. The big blue ball was stunning, and so far away that she could see North and South America, Africa and Europe at the same time.

With no warning and no sound, the planet exploded into billions of pieces that jetted into the cold, silent abyss of space.

"No," Taryn cried.

Asmodeus released her and she snapped back to the present in the dingy basement.

He leaned so close she could smell his breath, fetid with the sulfurous tinge of hellfire. "There's a darkness coming that is far worse than me, or my demon army, and it will rip this planet apart. You and the humans need me; you need my army to survive. Help me, little gypsy. Stand with me, not against me."

Taryn dry-heaved. What he was asking was against everything she believed. How could she help a monster like him? But what if he was telling the truth? What if the vision wasn't some construct of his but a real vision of the future? How could she stand by and let billions of humans and paranorms die? The very planet?

"Your friends will not find you; I've seen to that. But why would you want to escape when I'm giving you the chance to save us all? You can save the planet from destruction." He spread his arms as wide as his smile. "Just what you want most—a place, a purpose in all the worlds."

Exhaustion washed through her. She opened her eyes and looked the demon in the eye. He was a master manipulator and a liar, but she saw something in his steady gaze, an earnestness that seemed genuine. Was he tricking her? Did demons ever tell the truth? The vision had felt so real. It had felt like all of her cells were exploding along with the planet.

A soft skittering above her head jerked her back. "Demons lie."

"Oh, we most certainly do, and I'm the worst of the lot, but are you willing to risk the entire planet? Now or never, Taryn; what will it be? The short-term victory of fighting me—running away from your destiny—or will you save us all?"

"But you're the bad guy. You must be stopped."

Asmodeus smiled softly like she was an ignorant child. "In this fight, there are no good guys; there can't be any good guys, not if we want to survive what's coming."

"And what do I have to do with any of this? I am no one."

He removed his hand from her belly only to slide it under her waistband and cup her groin. "This makes you so much more than no one."

"Get off me. You must know I would never willingly have sex with you. Or do you intend to rape me?"

The demon laughed again. He released her and leaned back, crossing his legs. "There is a war coming, my dear. I have raised a demon army out of Hell, but I also need to bring my greatest comrades to the human world. I am here to breed them into existence."

Taryn swallowed hard. "As I told you, I'll never sleep with you."

He tsked and stood. "My dear, I wouldn't sleep with you even if you begged." He shook his head. "You are far too pedestrian for my taste. I'd probably perish of boredom before I could spill my seed."

He grabbed her forearm. He ran one of his sharp fingernails along the tender skin, splitting it open two inches before releasing her. He canted his head at her belly.

"I don't want you. I want your womb," he said, before walking away.

Taryn closed her eyes against the pain. She desperately needed to vomit but concentrated on breathing slowly to keep her stomach from heaving.

"Then why cut me? Make me bleed? Isn't that bad for my womb?" she cried out, her voice high and tight.

"You can afford a little blood loss, and my little friends are so terribly hungry. The sooner you accept your situation and cooperate, the sooner I can get on with my plans, and the less damage you'll suffer. You don't need your lips or eyelids or fingers to carry and birth a child; you don't need limbs, for that matter." Asmodeus flipped the light switch off. "The level of disfiguration you can tolerate is really up to you, darling."

He left, locking the door behind him.

Taryn fell into darkness again, tears rolling down her face.

A skittering sound made her gasp. *Cockroaches?* She shuddered. The squeak of a rodent a few feet above her confirmed the source of the sound and ratcheted up her adrenaline. They were attracted to the smell of her blood and she had no way to swat the rodents away. She squirmed against her bonds.

A small body landed on her belly. She twisted her waist hard while arching her back, and flipped the rat off of her. She panted, unable to draw a deep breath. Several squeaks and more skittering surrounded her. Her heart pounded. She gasped for air. She tugged on the ropes binding her, scraping her skin raw. A rat landed on her right foot. She jerked it, unseating the creature.

"Mother of God, help me."

She stilled and reached out with her mind to find a ley line. If there were one nearby, if she could disturb it and signal to anyone close enough to feel it…if, if, if. She clung to the scant hope because it was all she had, but before she could connect with any electromagnetic energy, something scraped then shifted above her head. Wriggling bodies rained down on her. Nails scratched her skin; teeth bit into her lips and cheeks.

She screamed as the rats covered her face and body, and her blood flowed.

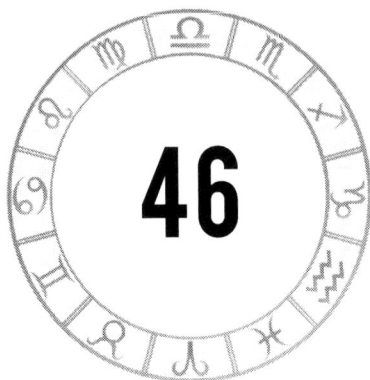

46

LIBRA CLIMBED OUT OF the bus after telling the children to wait inside. No sense in broadcasting his arrival. He looked up at the crumbling exterior of the mansion. Taryn needed him, so it was time to punt, as the humans said.

The Corvus boy slipped his hand into Libra's. "What is this place?"

He looked down into the boy's wide, red eyes and squeezed his small hand. "It's a rest stop. In and out; just one night of sleep."

"Who lives here?"

"The Os Mage Mother owns this house."

"Is she a paranorm?"

"Yes."

"Why does she live here instead of the InBetween?"

Libra had heard about this particular black hole of questioning that drove parents batty, the key word being 'why.' "She lives in many places; she can go to any of the worlds if she chooses to."

"Why would she want to live among humans, in that house? It looks like it's going to fall down."

The boy had mad skills when it came to pointing out the obvious.

"I don't know. Why don't you go back in the bus while I see if she's here?"

The Corvus boy just gripped his hand harder.

That settles that.

Libra adjusted his clothes and ran his fingers through his hair with his free hand before walking up the stairs to the front door, the boy by his side. He looked for a doorbell but only saw a fierce gargoyle knocker. He knocked and waited. And waited. His impatience mounted. He was about to leave when the door creaked open, the sound so creepy it would do a horror movie proud.

Ridiculous drama.

The Corvus boy slid behind him but pressed his head against his flank to watch, both of his hands clinging to Libra's.

A gray-haired, old woman, the witch who'd been in service to Aubrianna for as long as he could remember, poked her head around the door. "No solicitors."

She moved to shut the door but Libra blocked it with his foot. She slammed it and scowled when the door bounced back.

"Ouch, damn it, that hurt."

"Who are you?"

"Nice to see you too, Magda." He stood tall and pushed his way inside. "It's Libra. I've come to speak with Aubrianna."

He glanced around the foyer. The walls were stained with water that had leaked from the holes in the roof. The marble floor was pitted and dull, while the double staircase leading to the second floor sagged in places.

The woman huffed and puffed through her disapproving scowl. "Speak with her, you say?"

The line parents used to scare sulky children popped into his head: 'Your face will freeze that way.' The deep creases in her lined face proved there was truth behind the old adage.

Libra leaned closer.

"Aubrianna," he shouted.

"There's no need to yell," she groused. She clapped her hands twice and the decaying facade around him shimmered then disappeared, revealing the opulence he remembered from his childhood. "She's not here."

He turned his head away to hide his relief. "Good." He waved a hand and the bus door opened. The children streamed out, giddy to escape the confined space. "More room for us."

The old woman sputtered and stomped a foot. "No, no, no. Guests are not permitted when the Mother is away."

"Thank you. A spot of tea would be perfect, with lots of sandwiches and cookies." He pointed to the large parlor to his right. "In there, kids. Magda is going to feed us." He nailed her with a look. "Aren't you?"

She turned and walked down the long hall to the kitchen without looking back.

"And I need you to conjure up some baby formula and diapers while you're at it," he called out.

She waved a hand, her middle finger perilously close to a flip-off. The woman was as cranky as he remembered.

Libra took a deep breath and let it explode out of him, his shoulders dropping, the tension easing as he walked into the parlor. Decorated like a miniature version of the Hall of Mirrors in the Versailles Palace, it was gorgeous, wildly opulent, with a patina that made it look like it had been built in the late 17th century. Which it probably was.

The children stood pressed against one another in the middle of the room, their mouths agape as they looked from one treasure to another. This was as far removed as they could get from their homes in the InBetween. Caves were cold and damp and dark despite the fires that perpetually burned. Here, the setting sun streamed through a wall of windows. A fire burned in the fireplace that took up much of the opposite wall, the large hearth surrounded by a heavy, ornate, marble mantle.

Scattered around the room were settees and couches, armchairs and chaises, all with Tiffany floor lamps standing vigil next to them. The wooden floor was covered with antique Turkish rugs.

The sumptuous space should have made him comfortable—he did so love objects of beauty—but the memories that haunted this room, this house, were ghosts that ate at his soul. He clenched his hands and forced the spirits back down.

His horror of a childhood was behind him, and the children hovering near him needed reassurance.

He waved them over to the closest couch and patted the fabric seat. "It's okay. Sit."

The scrum of children split apart, walking slowly across the rugs, the bravest touching the chairs and lamps and décor, their mouths agape.

He perched his large frame on a delicate French chair close to the fire and wished Taryn could see this…or his mother—goddess, how she would hate the little hands and dirty fingers touching her possessions. The urge to laugh made his gut clench, which, in turn, made his stomach growl.

Magda backed into the room. She turned and stopped cold. "They need a bath."

"As do I, but first we need to eat."

She placed the tray of food on the largest table then planted her gnarled fists on her hips. "I'll not wait hand and foot on you and your horde. If you want food and drink, you can get the rest of the trays." She hobbled out of the room. "And don't you dare stain the furnishings or chip the china."

Libra waited for her to leave before leaning forward. "Let's eat!"

Like a starter's pistol had fired, the children lunged for the sandwiches. The Kellas Cat and the Bathory—the oldest kids and the pair in charge—cleared their throats. The younger children slowed then formed a makeshift line—youngest to oldest—while the food was passed out without a word.

What hell these children must have gone through to have such restraint, to not say a word or laugh or even cry. He waited and watched as the children took their food and sat on the furniture, or in corners with their backs against the wall, or on the floor. The Aspis girl sat next to the fire, the ashen look of her skin blooming into brilliant color as the flames warmed her.

Despite declaring her refusal to serve them, when the last sandwich was carried away, Magda entered with another heaping tray.

She huffed and puffed and tsked as she settled the huge tray on top of the empty one. "I suppose you'll be needing bath towels."

"That would be good," Libra answered quietly. The woman had never been fond of him, but she had bathed his wounds and soothed his fears more than once when he had lived in this house. All without a smile, but the gentleness of her touch had said more than kind words could have done. Maybe it was time to revert back to the charm he'd employed so successfully in the past. "If it's not too much trouble."

She hit him with a withering look. "This is all trouble." She sliced a hand through the air. "It'll take much magic to wipe away every trace of your presence when you leave."

So much for his charm; apparently, Magda was immune. "They'll need a place to sleep. How many beds are there?"

The Kellas Cat girl rose from the ottoman she was perched on, her half-eaten sandwich in her hand, her eyes wide. "We must stay together."

Libra smiled. "I don't think that's possible. There are twenty-eight of you."

Magda humphed, hobbled past Libra, and opened the parlor door. "Come with me."

47

LIBRA SWIPED A COUPLE of sandwiches from the tray and followed the old witch out of the parlor and up the curved stairs. At the top, a pair of ornately carved, gilded doors led to his favorite place, the ballroom. Magda opened one door; he pulled open the other, nodding when she turned on the lights.

Dozens of crystal chandeliers came to life, giving the space a warm glow that chased away the darkness. Honey-colored, oak floors gleamed and dozens of chairs lined the walls, but the dance floor that took up much of the second floor was filled with row upon row of beds.

"This is where she used to keep the males she planned to use as breeders, waiting for the next time she needed to conceive an Os Mage." Magda pointed to the curtains at each end of the room. "Open them."

Libra trotted to one end and opened the heavy brocade curtains. Sunlight filled the room, warming his skin. Fatigue washed through him; he was heavy with the weight of the past few days and his worry about Taryn. Was she in the sunlight or the dark? Was she hungry, tired, in pain? Was she scared? He ached with the need to leave this house, leave the responsibility of the children to someone else—anyone else—so he could scour the country looking for her. But he had made a promise to the children, a promise Taryn would insist he keep no matter where she was or what she was being subjected to. He had to keep them safe and this house was not the place.

He pressed his hands against the glass panes and dropped his head, breathing deep to slow his heart and mind, to ease the pain of his fears for her. *Goddess damn it, this is impossible.*

A touch of a hand startled him and he whirled around.

Magda pointed to the door.

The golden Kellas Cat girl stood in the hall, peering in. "Come quick."

She disappeared down the stairs.

Libra ran across the ballroom and followed the girl into the parlor. The whimpering children were backed into a corner, their arms wrapped around one another, blood running out of their noses and ears. A deep humming ripped through him and a sharp pain stabbed his brain.

The crisp smell of ozone that preceded a rainstorm filled his nose. "What the hell?"

The Keres baby rocked back and forth keening, her arms flailing free of her swaddling. The Innocent Demonica had broken free of his blanket and was lying completely still, his legs and one arm stiff and straight, the other arm stretched out to the Keres, his hand on her forehead.

Libra strode over to the babies and pulled them apart, instantly stopping the humming and the head pain. He rewrapped the boy in the blanket, encasing his arms and legs, while the infant stared at him, calm again, his limbs pliant and relaxed.

"What happened?" he demanded.

The Kellas Cat joined him and swaddled the Keres. "They became upset when you left the room. The Keres began to keen."

"Did she cause the—?" he pointed to his nose.

"The bleeding? Yes."

"What about the headache and the ozone?" he asked.

"The Innocent Demonica."

"What was he doing?"

She shrugged. "We don't know. Soothing her?"

"Has this happened often?"

"Only one other time, when they were first put together in a crib. After that, we kept them apart." She stood and crossed her arms. "I think they got upset because you left the room."

"Me? Why would they care if I left the room?"

She shrugged again.

She had to be wrong. There was no reason the two babies should respond to him in any way. They were babies. They needed food and warmth and shelter and they had that now.

No matter. The paranorms closest to this house, the ones who were immune to the increasingly aggressive politics of the InBetween, were the Pondera Novus Ordo Seclorum. They were the best option for the children. As neutral as the human country Switzerland, the warrior women had one job—to protect the balance between the darkness and the light. From their far corner of the InBetween, located deep inside the Yellowstone caldera, they worked to keep the human and paranormal worlds separate, to maintain a balance that prevented war. Of all the species in the paranormal world, the Pondera Seclorum wouldn't use the children for their own gain.

If he could get them to take the children, even for a short time, he could search for Taryn. He'd get her back and they could take the Corvus Ward royal to the king and strike a bargain—one that let Lyon keep his children and promised Taryn her freedom. Maybe, even his freedom as well. This nightmare would be over and he could go back to his life, hopefully with Taryn by his side.

"Is everyone okay? Have you had enough to eat?" he asked the group.

The children slowly left the safety of their huddle, nodding as they wiped away the blood on their faces with their sleeves.

"Then follow me." Libra picked up the Innocent Demonica and the Keres and led the group up the stairs and into the ballroom. "This is where you'll sleep."

Several children started running toward the beds.

Libra whistled, bringing them to a sliding stop. "Not until you've had a bath."

Magda grumbled under her breath.

"Sit on the floor," she barked at the children. She pointed at four of the older ones. "You, come with me. I can't carry all the towels by myself."

"What about clothes? We still have some here?" Libra asked.

Magda's lips thinned, blanching the flesh. "I have many boxes stored away—your clothes and Hanell's. The children can help me bring them down. You need to stay here with those two," she nodded at the infants, "and keep them calm."

She left the ballroom followed by the four boys she had chosen, but many others followed her as well. The wicked witch as Pied Piper; what a sight.

He sat on the closest chair and opened the blanket to watch the Innocent Demonica sleep. His ebony skin gleamed in the sun, highlighting a dark prism of blue, purple, red, and green within the black. But when he opened his eyes, the white sclera and brown iris had been replaced by a red color that covered the entire eye. Not as bright red as a Corvus Ward royal eye, or the solid black of a normal Corvus Ward or a demon; this was a dark red like congealing blood on its way to turning dark brown.

The baby stared for a long moment as if assessing Libra, memorizing his face, before drifting back to sleep. The Innocent Demonica were just one of many shadow cultures in the paranorm world. They were so secretive that few knew where they lived, or understood their customs. The only certainty was the hierarchy according to skin color, and the physical evidence of their age and power. This child was the most precious and, one day, would be the most powerful of their kind. If there was one way to gain their trust—okay, maybe not trust, but certainly their attention—it was to bring them this boy. No demands, only the hope that they would work with him to help protect the paranorms as their world was introduced to the humans.

But first, he'd have to find them. He sighed as he ran a finger down the sleeping boy's soft, chubby cheek. "Where are your people, little one?"

The patter of feet drew his attention.

The children streamed in. The smaller ones had their arms filled with towels and blankets and pillows; the older ones carried large boxes of clothes. They set them down and Magda joined them, her face not so thunderously dark as before, but not smiling either. She opened the boxes and touched the clothes. For a brief moment, her hard face softened a smidge.

Hanell.

She had loved Hanell, still did, just like everyone had loved his little brother. Even Aubrianna, who loved no one but herself, had had a soft spot for him. She had spared him the worst of her wrath, turning it on Libra instead; at least the most physical manifestation of her anger. He suspected her psychological torture had been reserved for Hanell. It would explain how he had ended up with a woman like Circe.

Magda's wistful moment passed and she growled. "Don't just stand there. Pick some clothes and pick a bed. But make it yourself; I'm not your maid."

The children dove into the boxes; shirts and pants flew into the air. They laughed and argued over which color would look best on them until each one had fresh duds to don.

Magda clapped her hands. "Time for a bath, all of you. Follow me, and bring those clean clothes and towels. I'll not have you running around naked, not in this house."

The children beamed as they followed her instructions, intuiting that Magda was all grouse and no swat, and once again the Pied Piper led them away, the Kellas Cat bringing up the rear with the squirming Keres baby in her arms.

She paused before handing the girl to him. "You'd better take her, too. They've made their preference known."

"You too, Libra, keep up," Magda called out from outside the ballroom. "You stink."

He grunted and got to his feet, an infant in each arm. "Preference? What do you mean, preference?"

48

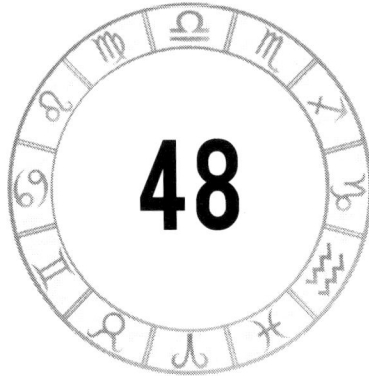

TARYN SHIVERED. THE COLD stiffened her limbs and her clothes, though it also masked the pain of the rat bites that covered her body. A tiny sliver of light escaped one of the windows, giving her a slice of illumination, but it wasn't reassuring. The dingy basement windows were barred. Though it didn't much matter, since her bindings weren't any looser.

She closed her eyes, but the memory of the rodents made her sick. How she had survived being eaten alive wasn't clear. She had been screaming, they'd been biting her, and then she had blacked out. When she'd woken, the rats were gone.

Someone must have helped her. She desperately wished she knew who it was so she could convince him or her to release her.

The basement door opened. A young girl appeared carrying a tray of food. Her red hair and the small, red tattoo on her left upper arm gave away her species. The Bathory Berserker walked up to Taryn's bed and set the tray down.

Her nose wrinkled. "You smell bad."

"Yes, I do. Could I have a bath?"

The girl smirked. "Nice try, but I'm not a fool."

"I don't think you're a fool; you have the power here."

The girl fingered the dagger at her waist as if needing to draw courage from the deadly weapon. "Yes, I do."

"Surely then, you can release me so I can eat and take a bath."

The girl frowned.

"You could always call another Bathory to guard me, if you're worried I could escape."

Taryn stopped talking and waited for the girl to chew through the decision. Sometimes, she knew when to shut her mouth—if only Libra were here to witness it.

The girl looked at the stairs then back at Taryn. She ground her teeth for a moment.

Her face locked into an expression of determination. "I was ordered to take care of you but that doesn't mean I'm supposed to untie you."

"You see the bites? I need to clean them so I don't get an infection. I need to get the dried blood off of me so they don't bite me again. I need a bath and fresh clothes. Surely, whoever ordered you to take care of me wouldn't want me to get sick."

The girl studied her for a long moment before drawing her dagger and pressing the blade edge against Taryn's throat. "Know this: If you do anything I don't like or if you disobey me, I will slit your throat. Do you understand?"

Taryn couldn't stop her tears; she nodded rather than trust her voice.

The Bathory untied her ropes with one hand then stepped back, her dagger at the ready.

Taryn groaned when she tried to move her limbs. Her legs and shoulders burned and the rest of her ached. She rolled onto her side and inched her way up until she sat on the side of the bed. Her head pounded and the basement faded in and out. She scooted forward until her feet touched the floor and winced when they exploded with fire. She looked down—they were swollen and purple.

"Hurry up if you want to bathe; we don't have much time."

Taryn stood and took a step. Pain ripped through her and she almost fell. The

Bathory grabbed one of her arms and jerked it to keep Taryn on her feet. They swayed together for a second before Taryn was able to take another step.

She reached the stairs and grabbed the two banisters. Taking a deep breath, she looked at the top of the stairs and climbed, the girl behind her.

The Bathory reached around Taryn and unlocked the door. She pressed the tip of the dagger against Taryn's back. "Don't forget."

Taryn nodded and walked into the kitchen.

"Left."

Taryn followed the girl's directions until they reached a large window. She slowed then wobbled before falling to the floor.

The girl growled and pulled Taryn to her feet, giving her enough time to look outside. They were in a suburb. The house had a large, well-groomed backyard with a wooden privacy fence, a pool, and a huge pool house with floor to ceiling windows. Through them, she saw the bird who had carried her here. The puncture wounds in her shoulders ached at the memory.

The huge bird filled the window then turned its head and looked right at her. It spread its wings wide and Taryn saw healing wounds on its breast. A screech vibrated the window. This was the same bird she had tended after the attack.

Asmodeus had sent the birds? Why? He'd said she was important, so why risk her life? Would anything ever make sense?

"That damn thing," the girl ground out. "I just got it to shut up." She glared at Taryn. "It seems to like you, or maybe it wants to eat you."

Taryn glanced at the girl bathed in the bright light. She was a child; just a baby. The tiny, red, tribal tattoo on her upper arm declared she'd already killed one person in her short life. A great lump in Taryn's throat threatened to choke her. How could this kind of horror be allowed in the world? How could children be recruited to murder?

"I think the rats have already made their dinner reservation," she choked out, her attempt at humor falling flat.

The girl pushed her and Taryn walked again, hoping there'd be another window showing the front yard this time before they reached the bathroom, but her luck was fresh out.

"The bathroom is the next door," the girl said, her voice low.

Just as she reached for the doorknob, Taryn heard the growl of a garage door. She and the Bathory gasped at the same time.

The girl gripped Taryn's shirt and pulled her back down the hall. "Hurry. If they see you, we're both dead."

"What about your orders?"

"Those women didn't give me the order."

When they reached the basement door, Taryn led the way down, but before she reached midway, she tripped. She tumbled down the stairs and crashed into the concrete floor, the air in her lungs exploding out with an audible *whoosh*.

The girl rushed toward her and waved her hands, her eyes wide. "Get up!"

A door slammed.

The girl pulled on Taryn's stunned body and dragged her to the bed.

Voices called out; feet scurried.

The girl tried to lift Taryn but they toppled over and went down in a heap. She jumped up and wrapped her arms around Taryn's waist.

Finally, Taryn's body began to work. The girl pulled her up and Taryn placed her feet on the floor. She locked her knees. They fell onto the bed.

The Bathory picked up the first rope and her fingers flew, securing the knot. She made short work of the other three.

Taryn was back where she'd started—no shower, no escape route planned, and covered in new aches and pains.

The Bathory pushed back her red hair and wiped the sweat off her brow.

The basement door opened.

The girl hurried to the food tray, filled a spoon with mashed potatoes, and crammed it in Taryn's mouth.

A Bathory woman walked over to them. "What's this? Haven't you finished feeding the woman?"

Taryn's heart dropped. Based on the extent of her tattoos, this woman was one of the top Berserkers. This made her the best of the best killers and, right now, she was none too pleased with the girl feeding her.

Taryn looked from the Berserker to the child. The little Bathory trembled; her face white as a sheet—she was terrified.

Taryn swallowed the potatoes. "That's my fault. My stomach…I can't eat too fast."

Her belly rumbled as if eager to disprove her lie.

The girl cut a piece of steak and held the meat up to Taryn's mouth. "Are you ready?"

Taryn turned her head away from the Berserker and winked before shaking her head.

The warrior stalked over to the girl and knocked the fork out of her hand, sending the steak flying. She hit the end of the food tray and it flipped in the air, landing on the floor.

"Clean up this mess. If she won't eat, then don't give her food." She turned and strode to the stairs leading out of the basement. "Now!"

"I'm sorry, I thought I could help," Taryn whispered.

The girl looked up, her red face and quivering lip negating her hard glare. "I don't need your help."

She picked up the spilled food and marched out, her back ramrod straight. Taryn watched her leave, her need to escape equal to the pain she felt for the child being forced to grow up too fast, surrounded by violence and god knew what else.

"You may not want help but you're gonna get it."

She had shifted in the bed to get comfortable for the meditation necessary to seek the ley line when a flash caught her eye.

The steak knife lay inches from her head.

49

LIBRA OPENED HIS EYES. The house was quiet, too quiet. Not even night sounds filtered past the windows to create the normal ambient noise. He sat up and looked around the ballroom, his senses as slow to catch up as his memory. He was adrift for several seconds before his mind clicked into place.

Aubrianna's house—the horror-show setting of a childhood he'd escaped as a boy. And now he'd run here for help, at least for a day. Just long enough to eat, bathe, and clothe the children before moving on. As soon as the sun touched the eastern horizon, they'd be back on the road, heading north and west to the Pondera Seclorum, where he could leave the children behind.

He pushed aside the bedding and stood, rubbing the itch on the back of his neck, restless when he should have been sleeping. He pulled on his dirty clothes— Magda had none in his size—and padded out of the ballroom, hoping the Keres and Innocent Demonica wouldn't notice his absence. Magda would skin him alive if the children got blood on the sheets or their clean clothes.

The door to the parlor was closed but light seeped out from under it. He opened the door quietly in case the old woman was sleeping, then stopped short, his lungs freezing, the thud of his heart preceding a surge of adrenaline.

Aubrianna sat in a chair by the fireplace, the red-gold light licking over her like the flames of Hell.

She held out a teacup and saucer. "Come in."

He walked over to her and accepted the tea before sitting in the matching chair opposite her.

She took a sip. "What can I do for you?"

He ground his teeth and swallowed back his irrational fear. She was just flesh and blood, and this house, though filled with terrible memories, was just wood and stone.

"Magda," he said flatly.

"Of course she let me know you had arrived. She is *my* servant."

He didn't move, didn't speak. He didn't allow even a flicker of emotion to cross his face to give away what he was thinking.

He placed his cup and saucer on the serving tray and rested his sweating hands in his lap. "I'm passing through. I'll be gone tomorrow."

Aubrianna took a sip of her tea. "What makes you think I'll let you leave? What's to prevent me from keeping you here until you break and become Gaia's agent?"

"Because you know it won't work. I'll never kill for you."

He held her gaze and concentrated on not squirming.

"Oh, I think there are twenty or thirty reasons you'll do as I ask, and they're sleeping upstairs." She smiled, but it didn't reach her eyes—it was more like baring her teeth. "And perhaps one more reason not here."

Libra leaned forward, his temperature rising in a blink. Rage, hot and pure, filled him to bursting, the zing of Gaia's power tingling in his hands. "You know where she is?"

She looked into the fire, her eyes glittering—she was going for the kill. "I do. The question is, what are you willing to do to get her back?"

Anything.

He forced himself to lean back and cross his legs.

"Would you kill for her? This *friend* of yours?"

Absolutely.

The certainty washed through him, cooling his rage and forcing Gaia's power deep inside. That was a hand he dare not let her see, or she would have him.

"You've already made it clear you think I'm a coward," he said. "Why would I lift a finger? She is of no use to you." Libra relaxed. "The only thing you need to know is I have information of great importance to the Corvus Ward king."

He might not be free of her web yet but he had refocused her attention. The less Aubrianna knew about his feelings for Taryn, the safer she would be.

Aubrianna stared at him and he returned the look without unblinking. The tension grew but they said nothing.

She finally took a breath and looked away. "My position as ambassador to the humans is in grave doubt, as is my value to the king since your escape."

He rose. "That's not my problem."

"But the children upstairs are." She stood. "Tell me, son, whom do you have up there?" She looked at the closed door. "Shall I go see? Is it a Corvus Ward royal?" She smiled, the expression predatory. "A boy?"

He backed up toward the door and blocked it. "You'll not touch a hair on any of them."

Aubrianna raised a hand. With a slicing motion, she sent him flying into the corner. He landed on a delicate side table, shattering the wood, sending him to the floor.

She curled her fingers, choking him as she lifted him into the air from several feet away. "You do not tell me what to do. *You* obey *me*."

The room blurred, growing dark in seconds. She would choke the life out of him this time. He called to Gaia for help but she didn't answer. No power surged forward to save him. He clawed at Aubrianna's magical grip, but there was nothing to grab hold of, nothing he could do to wrench himself free.

The room disappeared. He fought to drag in a minute amount of air, but it wasn't enough to sate his lungs, and nowhere near enough to bring feeling back to his limbs.

From a distance, he heard the door burst open—explode really. A scream buffeted his oxygen-deprived brain. He fell to the ground, his body crumpling, but he was so numb he felt no pain.

Another scream jerked him out of his fugue. The room reappeared, his focus not so much, but he could see enough to witness his mother writing on the ground. Blood poured out of her mouth and nose and ears in great gushing rivers of red that splashed on the rugs she valued more than her own sons.

The Keres baby thrashed in the Bathory boy's arms, her face turned toward Aubrianna, her high-pitched screech aimed full-force at her. The Keres' voice rose another octave, like the shrill whine of a banshee.

Libra covered his ears.

Magda shoved her way through the children, grabbed a handful of the Bathory boy's hair, and yanked hard.

He yelled and turned, shifting the Keres away from Aubrianna.

His mother crawled away, putting a settee between her and the child.

"I'll leave. I'll leave," she cried. "But I want something in return."

"Of course you do," Libra panted.

"I want Hanell back."

Libra's first instinct was to tell her that she had pushed Hanell into Circe's arms and that the witch goddess would probably kill him, if the building collapse hadn't already done it. But he held back, stowing away the truth for another time when the information could benefit him. No matter how much that made him like his mother, the need to get Taryn back demanded he do whatever it took, use whomever he must.

"Why?" he spat out. "So you can finish grinding him under your heel?"

"He blames me for your leaving."

"He's right to."

She pressed her body against the back of the diminutive couch, unaware or uncaring that she was staining the fabric with blood.

"Hanell hates me," Libra said. "There's nothing I could do or say to get him to do anything. Why you would think it was within my ability—or think I would subject him to you again—is beyond me."

"Bring him to me. I know you're capable of at least that."

"No."

If he looked at her long enough, he was afraid she'd see a flicker of the scared, little boy he used to be and that was untenable.

"Leave. Now," he shouted, his voice raspy and probably not as loud as it was painful.

Aubrianna winked out of the room with a *pop*.

Libra went down for the count.

50

MERI FLEW OVER THE city marveling at the lights that twinkled like jewels. Red and yellow, green and blue, she wondered why her mother never told her about the sparkle and flash. And why, once she'd reached the human city, she'd lost Taryn's scent. The burning smell of chemicals and myriad scents of the humans below overwhelmed her exhausted, overextended senses.

A *thump-thump-thump* sound beat the air around her, growing so loud that it vibrated in her chest. She flapped her wings more out of reflex, irritation, than a need to gain elevation.

Before she could slow her glide enough to turn, a great roar and *whoosh* washed over the top of her, no more than a few feet above. A great, metal bird passed overhead, its powerful draft pushing her down, collapsing her relaxed wings.

She plunged to the earth, slow to respond to the shock of the attack. The bright lights of a great structure flew by her at such a speed they blended together, mesmerizing her until the loud blasts of noise coming from the moving metal boxes below her pulled her out of the trance.

The ground rushed up.

She only had seconds before she hit.

She flipped out her wings and tensed her muscles to make them rigid. They caught air, but she had waited too long. Arching her spine until she cried out, she swooped down to the black road—just inches from hitting it—before air and arch stopped her downward descent and sent her soaring back up. As soon as momentum peaked, she flapped her wings, beating against the cold, still air, fighting for lift.

A scream shattered the air below her. A woman had pointed at her and flashes of white light sparked. Meri looked away and concentrated on working her way above the buildings, praying she could find the rare thermal a cold night might allow.

But as soon as she saw the first rooftop, she glided over to it and landed in a heap. She'd not slept or eaten since Libra had sent her after Taryn. Her body trembled from the effort. If she could find a warm spot and sleep for a little while…

She staggered over to a door and turned the knob. To her surprise, the door opened. A small pool of light shone on a flat floor and, just beyond it, stairs that disappeared into darkness. Meri crawled inside and let the door shut behind her. She wrapped her wings around her body for warmth—and no small amount of comfort—and curled into a ball. The floor was hard but warmer than the roof. The air was still, the space quiet.

She closed her eyes and sighed. This would do for now.

Tomorrow. I'll find you tomorrow, Taryn.

* * *

Libra woke to the light streaming through the window, blinding him even through closed eyes. He rolled away from the glare and opened them. The sun had risen high in the sky, and dozens of wide eyes surrounded him. The children smiled when he took a deep breath.

"He's awake, Magda," one little girl yelled.

"Let me through, come on, out of the way." She pushed past the little ones and bent low to look at him through squinting eyes. "'Bout time you woke up. You're supposed to be gone from here."

He rolled up into a sitting position and groaned. His throat still burned and turning his head sent a hot bolt of agony through his brain. "I'm still on the floor?"

"What do you expect, being a big, passed-out fella? You think we could move you to a soft bed?"

He rubbed the knots in his aching back. "You could have rolled me onto a mattress on the floor."

"Huh," she said, then paused. "Didn't think of that." She shook her head and waved her hands in dismissal. "But no matter. Just get yourself up and get out of here. I've done enough to earn me much misery from the Mother when next I see her."

She sounded just as gruff as always, but he saw the fear in her eyes.

"I'm getting up." He climbed to his feet with the help of the children. "We need to eat first."

"Eat? These wee ones have about eaten all the food in the house." She grunted. "But I did save some for you." She waved at him to follow her. "Then you go."

She hustled him through his meal and bustled around getting the children ready to travel. She filled a huge, plastic tub with enough food to last them a day or two.

She pointed at it. "There's formula and bottles and diapers in there. And a little money—all I could spare, mind you, so it's not a lot."

The Kellas Cat and Bathory ushered the rest to the foyer in front of Libra then stepped outside. They paused on the porch, hesitating in the bright light as if confused so see their surroundings so clearly. Unlike humans who were afraid of the dark, paranorms found comfort in threat-muting shadows and the deep black of a moonless night. It was daylight's glare and unrelenting exposure to every detail around them that overwhelmed the tentative and bold creatures of his world alike.

Libra stepped off the porch.

"Libra?" Magda whispered.

He looked back at the woman, surprised to see her wringing her hands.

"I had to tell her you were here. There was no way I could wipe away all the proof that you had been in her house."

He nodded once but waited; she obviously had more to say.

She backed up toward the threshold, her body trembling. "I didn't tell her where you're going."

"Come with us," he blurted out before the thought had a chance to rattle around his brain and become a conscious decision.

Her mouth dropped open then snapped shut as fast, her surprised expression shuttering closed. "I'm not free to leave her."

"All you have to do is walk to the bus and climb inside. Leave this place and her behind."

"I can't. I am bound to her as she is to me—damning us both."

"I don't understand, but I won't beg."

She raised a hand. "One more thing." Her voice dropped to a gravelly whisper. "Don't trust the witches."

"You're a witch."

"That's why I'm knowing. The witches. Do not trust them. They are not working for anyone but themselves, and what they want…" She stepped inside the house. "Don't trust them," she repeated before slamming the door.

Libra stood still, the tub of food getting heavier by the second. He hated cryptic messages unless he was imparting them. What the hell was he supposed to do with that? One more vague threat wrapped in a warning.

Gah.

Give him a task, a mission, a direction, a purpose, and he could act. Cryptic just made him dyspeptic.

He grunted and turned back to the mission in front of him. The Pondera. He climbed inside the bus and stowed the tub. In a few hours, maybe before nightfall, they'd be close enough to the Pondera to penetrate their sentry line and get an escort into the InBetween caverns they called home.

51

TARYN PULLED ON THE rope binding her wrist and inched her way toward the steak knife. The sun was setting, ratcheting up her fear. The knife was right there; it had been taunting her all day. Escape—freedom—was so close, but not close enough. She sagged back, tears welling in her eyes—she'd barely made any progress.

The basement door opened and the same Bathory child came down with another tray of food, the light illuminating her swollen, bruised face.

"They beat you."

The girl set the tray down, her jaw clenched, her face flushed red between the black and blue. "Are you going to eat this time?"

"Yes."

The girl stood tall, crossed her arms over her chest, and studied Taryn for several moments, her face stiff, arrogant. Then it softened. Pain and fear swept through her eyes before she caught herself. She leaned over and untied Taryn's left hand.

Taryn gasped. She opened and closed her fingers. "Are you supposed to do this?"

The girl frowned. "Eat before I change my mind." She set the tray on Taryn's lap. "I've already cut the meat."

"Thank you."

Taryn loaded the fork and stuffed it in her mouth. She moaned and closed her eyes. Grilled chicken and fried okra had never tasted so good. She wolfed down her food then glanced over. The steak knife was right there, within reach, but if the Bathory girl took the tray away now, she might see it. Taryn had to get it hidden before then.

"Oh, god, that was good. Can I have more?"

The girl frowned and bent over to take the tray.

Taryn panicked and knocked her glass of water over. It tumbled to the floor and bounced. *Plastic, shit.* She'd hoped for glass that the girl would have to clean up.

The girl growled as she chased after the rolling cup.

Taryn grabbed the knife and looked for the best place to put it. Under the pillow? Too far from her hand. Up a sleeve? No, the knife could slip out. Her heart pounded and she panted, desperate to find the right place.

"You bitch!" the Bathory yelled.

Taryn looked up. The child was staring at the knife.

She lunged and landed on Taryn's belly.

Taryn struggled to hold onto the knife but the girl wiry and strong, and she wrenched it from Taryn's hand.

She rolled off the bed and slapped Taryn hard. "I knew you couldn't be trusted, you half-breed freak."

She retied Taryn's wrist and yanked the knots tight.

"Wait, that's too tight; my hand is already tingling."

The girl leaned close. "You want to feel tingling?" She raised the steak knife, pulled down the neck of Taryn's shirt, and pressed the blade against her flesh. "This is tingling."

The knife pulled on Taryn's skin before opening it.

Taryn screamed.

The girl pushed the knife back up then down again in a sawing motion. "How about I saw off a piece? I can cook it up nice and juicy for you."

Taryn bucked and screamed again, the pain from the dull blade far greater than it would've been from a sharp one.

The girl laughed.

The basement door slammed against the wall.

"What are you doing?"

The Berserker raced down the stairs and tackled the girl.

The woman and child landed on the concrete with a thud. The Berserker raised her fist and punched the girl over and over until she passed out.

"Stop," Taryn said, her yell merely a hoarse whisper.

The Berserker dragged the unconscious girl to a metal pole. She propped her up then looked around before going to a rickety workbench in one corner. She returned with duct tape and secured the girl's hands around the pole. She stood over the child, panting, then wrapped more tape around the girl's chest and ankles until the roll was empty.

The woman picked up the steak knife and looked at Taryn's wound before cutting open the girl's shirt and recreating the wound on her chest.

"No, no, please don't," Taryn pleaded, but it was too late.

The Bathory turned around and snarled. "This is on you, bitch. Whatever you said, whatever you did, she has to pay the price for disobedience. If she's lucky, she'll survive the rats."

Tears and snot ran freely down Taryn's face. "How could you do this to one of your own?"

The Bathory walked toward the stairs. She placed a hand on the banister and paused, looking up at the basement door.

"She is too soft-hearted and if I have to beat or cut or burn it out of her," she pinned Taryn with a glare, "that's what I'll do. No daughter of mine will be a scullion."

She stomped up the stairs but shut the door softly.

Taryn lowered her head and watched the dust motes disappear. The part of her brain that ruled her finer functions shut down—she couldn't fight her way through the fear of the creeping shadows, so apparently her brain had decided to just close shop, leaving only the basest instincts functioning.

Night was almost here and she was no better off than she had been this morning. She looked over at the girl. How could a mother do that to her own child? She closed her eyes— she knew exactly how much pain and terror a mother could and would inflict on her children. Circe had slammed that lesson home.

The sound of skittering cut through Taryn's thoughts. She looked at the pipes above her and saw the flash of dozens of eyes staring down, drawn by the smell of fresh blood and the promise of a bountiful feast. Tears wet her face and the bedding beneath her head in wave after wave of salt-tinged terror.

52

THE SUN HAD DISAPPEARED behind the tops of the forest trees that ringed the entrance to the Pondera Novus Ordo Seclorum realm in the farthest western reaches of the InBetween cave system. Libra crouched and pointed to a deep dip in the forest floor, waiting until the children streamed into it before concentrating on the slit in the rocks several hundred feet away. It was designed like all paranorm entrances: natural design blended with magical reinforcement to hide it from human eyes.

From this distance, the guards looked like two moving dots. He had pressed his hands to the ground to push off and run to the next tree when a whimper echoed. He whipped his head toward the children and put a forefinger to his mouth.

The Kellas Cat shook her head.

The whimper turned into a protest and it didn't take any imagination to work out what would happen if the babies started to wail.

He grunted and turned back to the dip, closing the distance like a scuttling crab before sliding down the steep slope. "What's the problem?"

"They want to be with you," the Bathory boy hissed, his face scrunched into the scowl that only teenagers could manage so spectacularly.

"I can't exactly dash and dart through the forest with two babies in my arms. What if I fall?"

"Oh, for goddess' sake." The Kellas Cat pushed the Keres into Libra's hands and pulled down her voluminous skirt.

"What the—?" Libra barked under his breath.

But under that skirt was another, and under that were a pair of jeans.

"You'll do what women have done for centuries."

She ripped the skirt in half, tied the ends together and draped the circles of material across his chest like bandoleers.

Peeling apart the fabric, she held it open while the Bathory boy settled the Innocent Demonica inside.

"Do the same with the Keres," she ordered.

Libra did as she directed, easing the baby girl inside the makeshift sling.

The Kellas Cat let the material close around them, cocooning them against his chest like peas in pods.

"That will keep your hands free while we travel, and keep them next to you, where they seem determined to stay."

"This is going to be damned inconvenient," he snapped.

Her face fell.

Dammit.

"But it's brilliant."

The girl nodded, not entirely convinced but willing to let it go.

Thank the goddess.

Libra climbed up the slope on his hands and knees, concentrating on adjusting his movements for the extra weight and the shifting babies. When he reached the top, he looked up and saw leather boots. He followed the boots to a pair of legs clad in leathers, a belt with twin daggers, and a leather vest that acted like a chest plate, crossed by a bowstring.

The woman staring down at him smiled. "Well, what have we here?"

Libra looked left and right then groaned. Dozens of similarly dressed women had surrounded the dip. They were well and truly caught.

"Pondera Seclorum by any chance?"

The woman grinned. "Try again."

The babies stirred, probably sensing his agitation.

She leaned closer. "Stand up."

He obeyed her order, willing his heart to slow to keep the Keres from drawing their ire. The Pondera Exemplars were savage in their protection of the balance between the dark and the light.

In his world, Innocent Demonica were the purifiers; they could cleanse a body of demonic possession, literally suck the evil out of you. The Keres were agents of Hell—death daemons—whose sole purpose was the destruction of mankind. Strapped across his chest were the very personification of the light and the dark they sought to control. What they couldn't control, they destroyed.

But when he stood in front of her, she stared. Not at the babies—she didn't even peel back the fabric to look at their faces. No, she stared at Libra, her eyes narrowing the longer she looked.

"You're a Zodiac."

"Libra," he said with a nod.

She reached behind her neck and drew a sword, the rasp of the blade leaving the scabbard echoed by the other Exemplars following their leader. The women closed in and gestured for the children to join them, their silence more concerning than posturing would have been.

"You're coming with me," the woman growled.

"Actually, no, I'm going to the other Pondera, your sisters."

The woman pressed the tip of her sword to his throat. "The one sister I have, the sister with whom I share my blood, is being held captive in the Great Cavern by that pathetic leader you call Lyon."

Libra's mind raced as he tried to recall the name of the woman who had acted as a double agent within the Pondera Seclorum then sold out her sisters to fight for Leona, Lyon's sister. "Ailith."

"Yes, Ailith."

She pushed the tip a little harder, just enough to draw his blood, but he remained still, willing his heart to beat slow and steady. If the Keres decided the women were a threat, she could incapacitate or kill them all just trying to protect him.

Goddess damn it, if it wasn't Gaia's power, the piece of demon soul attached to his own, or the daemon bomb strapped to his chest, it was something else. Couldn't a man get some privacy? How about a break? He was due for one about now, right?

"Let's go. I want them secured before full night."

Well, that's a fuck no.

She removed the sword from his throat and waved him ahead to walk in front of her. Three other Exemplars took the lead; the rest formed a loose triangle behind him and Ailith's sister, the children trapped in the middle, herded forward like sheep. Within an hour, the older children were stumbling, barely catching themselves before doing full faceplants, while the youngest were slung over shoulders.

They reached a cliff face and turned south, then walked several yards to a small crack in the rock.

The leader nodded to three of the women. "Check it out."

They disappeared for a few minutes then returned. "All clear."

"Go," she ordered Libra.

He turned sideways and sucked in his gut to keep the babies untouched as he scraped his back along the rough rock. The crack took a sharp right then opened into a small cave. The warriors lined the entrance and waited for the children to enter before closing ranks, blocking any escape.

"How about some light?" he asked.

The strike of a flint sounded to his left. A tiny ember glowed then expanded into a single flame before igniting the small bundle of kindling.

"Keep it small. The ventilation isn't great in here." She pointed to the ground. "Take a seat. All of you."

The children looked at Libra and he nodded. They crowded around the fire, desperate for warmth, the small children in the laps of the larger ones. He chose a spot farther out. The less light shining on him and the babies, the better.

He settled and looked at the women, studying them. "What are you planning on doing with us? You can't travel with any speed, and the amount of hunting you'd need to do to feed all of us will take up all of your spying time."

Ailith's sister prowled around him in a tight circle, a scowl marring her face. "You Zodiacs. You imprisoned my kin—that was bad enough. Then, you failed to stop the rise of the demon army. Your arrogance or, worse still, your ignorance has created the greatest imbalance this world has seen. If we don't stop you, you're going to stumble your way into loosing the rest of Hell, and all of Hades, including," she said, squatting in front of him, "the pantheon of jumped-up, pissed-off, hungry-for-destruction gods and goddesses trapped there. Evil has been given its greatest foothold in eons, all because of you."

This was the moment. This was why the paranorms needed an ambassador to work on uniting their world before introducing it to the humans. Lyon would have yelled, Scorpio would have flung his scorpions at the women and killed them all without saying a word, and so on down the line. The Zodiacs were just learning to work with one another, trying to form a brotherhood of sorts, but he harbored no illusions about their tempers or their lethality or their willingness to burn it all down.

He dropped his voice and hoped his words would sway her. "Then work with us to restore the balance. We made mistakes, starting with not having the full picture of what Llewellyn, Asmodeus, and Circe were planning. Once we did know, it was far too late to stop it, though many paranorms died trying to help us do just that.

"These children are the start; they are the key to bringing the paranorm world together. Until we move beyond this segregation of the species and learn to work together for the common good, nothing you or I can do will ever be enough. We're not talking just about the demon army, or the cosmic balance you've been charged with maintaining and are now are fighting to restore. We also have to survive being exposed to the humans. Demons and balance won't matter if they slaughter us into extinction."

Her expression remained belligerent, a flush rising with each moment that passed.

He heaved a sigh; she hadn't heard a word he'd said. The Exemplars were far more implacable than he'd heard. Fatigue pulled him down, but he couldn't succumb to his desire to lie down and close his eyes.

She stood and spat on the ground inches from him. "Balance will be restored if I have to kill every last paranorm on this planet."

His frustration welled; he just couldn't stop himself. "And that would make you the greatest evil around, wouldn't it?"

"Then I'll kill myself to make sure the job gets done right." She pulled out a dagger and held it up, the firelight flashing on the shiny, metal blade. "For now, I think I'll start with you."

53

"**I** WOULDN'T DO THAT JUST yet."

The women whirled and crouched, weapons drawn on the hooded figure standing inside the crack.

"Show yourself," the leader demanded.

The tall figure walked past the sentries, paying no attention to the blades only inches away. The hood flipped back and revealed a woman. Haggard and thin, she still projected strength and resolve and a fierce intelligence.

"Ailith?" the leader said.

"Yes, sister."

The sisters stared for a moment before the younger bowed her head. Respect paid, the rest of the women sheathed their daggers and took a knee.

"How are you here?" The leader bared her teeth, the grin malevolent. "Did you break free of the Zodiacs? How many did you kill?"

Ailith looked at Libra as she answered. "None. His leader, Lyon, freed me."

The younger sister beamed. "They didn't break you, this I know."

Ailith placed a hand on the woman's shoulder. "They didn't break me."

The Exemplars murmured their approval.

"Because they didn't try."

Silence fell, as did their proud expressions.

"I don't understand."

"They never laid a hand on me, though I can't say that I would have done the same. They caged me, yes, and their dungeon wasn't comfortable, but they fed me, treated me with respect, and never harmed me."

"What precipitated your release? It wasn't done on a whim."

"Lyon sent everyone away and emptied out the dungeon. I was the last one released. When I left, I saw the woods filled with Corvus Ward warriors." She looked around the cave. "He let me go, emptied out the dungeon, before the Great Cavern was attacked."

No one said a word.

Libra's heart sank even as his adrenaline spiked. The Great Cavern couldn't fall into Corvus Ward hands. There had been too many revelations about what Llewellyn and the Twelve had been doing to the paranorms, and with the humans, in the few weeks the Zodiacs had controlled it. If Gemma was correct, there were years' worth of knowledge yet to learn about magic and breeding and what the Twelve's end game had been. To lose the access to that information would be grievous; to lose what had not yet been discovered, especially if it could be used to fight Asmodeus and his demon army, could mean the end of all of them.

"You must let me go," he said.

Ailith's sister hissed and drew her sword. "You're not going anywhere."

Ailith placed a hand on the woman's forearm and pushed the sword down "What were you doing? Why were you heading to the Pondera Seclorum?"

He would give them the truth. It was time.

"I wanted to leave the children with the Pondera so I could travel to the Innocent Demonica. I hope to gain their aid to help the paranorm world survive."

"They're worse than the Seclorum when it comes to not involving themselves with paranorm affairs."

"True, but this doesn't just involve the paranorm world. The demon army won't only try to wipe us out—they'll kill millions of humans. The chaos they'll sow will plunge the world into a darkness that could take decades to climb out of. If it ever can."

Ailith crossed her arms. "I sense there's more."

Libra hesitated—a dead giveaway, he knew, but telling these women everything could backfire stupendously. Then again, did he really have a choice here?

"I'm also hoping to buy my freedom from the Corvus Wards with that child," he said, nodding at the royal boy.

Ailith snorted. "Freedom?"

Libra grit his teeth before answering. "The Os Mage Mother has teamed up with the Corvus Ward king. They're trying to force me to become Gaia's agent."

That got Ailith's attention.

She squatted in front of him. "*The* agent? The agent of Nether? Or Aether?"

"Nether. Yes. Aether? No one alive has seen an agent of Gaia wield the power of Aether."

Ailith interlaced her fingers and rested her chin on them. "Why are they having to force you? Don't you realize the power you'd have?"

"Oh. I know perfectly well what Nether can do. Why do I sense you want me to become the agent of darkness when your people are all about balance? Can't you imagine how bad it would be with that demon soul inside me?"

"Perhaps, but you, unlike agents in the past, are a known entity. You we can approach, influence, maybe even control."

"Given that, why the hell would I agree to become an agent? You think I want to be controlled by you or anyone?"

"No, I imagine you don't, but you're controlled already, aren't you?"

"What do you mean?"

"You have worked so hard to live your life in the light, you don't even know how to succumb to the darkness. You've flounced and festooned and flouted yourself through life, until no one can remember you being any other way. Fancy clothes, a flippant attitude, and a human lifestyle have kept your scales tipped firmly in the light, at a time when we all need you to be balanced. Light and dark can't exist without each other. You are a living example of everything we have fought for, that we now have to fight against. So don't argue for balance when you are anything but."

"You don't know anything about me."

"I know you because I see you. The Pondera Exemplars and Seclorum know all of you. It's our job to understand those living in the light or in the dark. Those who chose one side or another, and why."

"And I see you," he ground out, disgusted with her hypocrisy. "I see the woman who betrayed her own people to follow Lyon's sister."

The Exemplars stirred.

"I see a double agent who walked away from her mission to help a madwoman rip open the Great Cavern and release a demon army."

"You lie!" Ailith's sister backhanded Libra's face, splitting open his cheek.

He fell to one side, but stopped his fall with an elbow. The babies stirred. The Keres whined.

"Stop, sister," Ailith ordered. She studied the twin slings hiding the babies from sight. "I want to see them."

Libra flinched. "I wouldn't advise it."

She reached for the edge of one sling and pulled back the material. She stared at the Innocent Demonica boy. "Get me a torch."

One of the women lit a torch and held it over the boy's face.

Ailith's mouth dropped open. "You know what he is?"

"He's an Innocent Demonica Prime. That's why I want to take him to them. It's the only bargaining chip that might sway them to help us."

"I thought your plan foolish. Until now." She released the sling and reached for the other. "And what surprise do you have in there?"

"No, don't."

Ailith ignored him.

He tried to scoot back but she pulled a dagger and pressed it to his throat. "Don't."

She reached for the fabric.

"Last chance," he warned.

Ailith sneered at him and applied enough pressure to split his skin. Blood welled then rolled slowly down his neck. She pulled back the fabric.

The Keres' eyes opened and she screamed.

A pulse of energy exploded out of the baby, lifting Ailith off her feet and slamming her into the far wall. The air in her lungs expelled with a loud *whoosh* and she fell to the ground. The other Exemplars ran to the children and grabbed them by the hair, growling as they pressed daggers to their throats. The children cried out in pain; the others clung to each other, whimpering in fear.

"Stop. You're scaring them," Libra shouted.

Ailith heaved and choked for several seconds until her lungs finally fully expanded.

She held up a hand. "Enough, I'm okay." Climbing to her feet, she brushed the dirt off her cloak. "What is it?"

Libra hesitated. These protectors of the balance between good and evil had proven to be absolute in their administration of that duty. Learning that a Keres was on earth could make this situation…sticky. But not telling them wasn't an option either—they'd figure it out on their own eventually. If he and the children were to have any chance of getting released, he had to earn a little trust.

"She's a Keres."

Ailith's eyes widened.

Her sister drew her sword and charged him—the blade raised high—her fierce battle cry echoing in the cave. But before she could split Libra's skull in two, Ailith dropped into a crouch and swept a leg, slamming it into the back of her sister's knees. The woman went down hard inches from him.

He sagged and tried to hide his panting.

"Betrayer!" The sister rolled onto her back, the sword tip pointed at Ailith. "What are you doing? That thing is evil, a spawn of Hell."

The other women released the children and turned to Ailith, their expressions dark, confused.

Ailith rose slowly, her gaze shifting between her sister and the other women. "Your dedication is commendable but shortsighted for two reasons. One, she defended the Zodiac. I barely scratched him and she threw me across the room. Two, this Hell spawn is pressed right up against an Innocent Demonica Prime—*the* Prime that his people have been waiting for these many centuries. The Prime who is the greatest source of good that can be found in any world. She protected him, too."

The women said nothing; Ailith's point hadn't been driven home yet.

"For a Keres, a death daemon, a creature of pure evil, to protect a Prime? Have you ever heard of that happening? Has any elder or text ever said it was possible?" She scrubbed her face with her hands. "For goddess' sake, if the worst of the worst is capable of defending the greatest good, then we have a real shot of bringing the worlds back to balance. That—" she said, pointing at the Keres, "she—can be used to turn the tide against the darkness."

Libra understood what she was saying—and Ailith was right—but he was surprised when his body instinctively curved around the Keres to shield her. Paternal instincts?

I never thought I had them.

Ailith's sister finally nodded.

Ailith held out a hand and helped her up. The women beat their chests twice with a closed fist and the dispute was done.

Ailith looked at each of the Exemplars as she spoke. "We rest tonight. Tomorrow we take them to the Innocent Demonica."

54

LIBRA STOOD AT THE salt mine entrance staring into the sloped shaft, swaying on his feet after driving the bus twenty-two hours straight to north Texas. The sunlight barely illuminated the first five feet of the mine before succumbing to the deepest black.

He looked back at the circle of Exemplars surrounding the children. "You sure this is the way?"

"This is the last place I heard they used," Ailith answered. "It's your best chance, so get to it. I don't want some nosy humans coming by to see what we're doing."

She wiped blood off her upper lip. The rest of the women and the children were too busy cleaning blood from their faces and ears to pay them any attention.

He shifted the twin slings. He had tried to leave the Keres with the Exemplars, thinking that maybe he could get away with it, just this once, but the baby girl had thrown a fit, blowing everyone to the ground and bloodying them up but good. He had a sinking feeling this wasn't a fluke but a real thing. How the hell was he supposed to be an insta-daddy when he couldn't even keep his inamorata safe?

Libra looked past Ailith and saw a chain link fence that had seen better days. Bent and broken from years of weather and falling limbs, the barrier couldn't prevent intruders. The lack of repair said no one cared—official types weren't likely to come—but Ailith was right; the more invisible they remained, the better.

He checked the skies again, but there was no sign of Meri. Going underground wouldn't help her track him but he had no choice. He had to find a safe place for the children so he'd be free to find Taryn.

He took a crude torch from the closest woman and stepped into the shaft, ducking his head to clear a cracked, wooden beam. The ground was pretty clear save for the occasional rock so he was able to make good time, until he reached a fork in the tunnel.

"Which way now?"

He held the torch high and peered down the left fork then the right. Fresh air blew from the right, making the flames flutter. Fresh air was good but it could also mean that the shaft ended at the surface again; not the way he needed to go. He walked left and slid on the rubble covering the steeper slope. His arms pin-wheeled for a second until he could right himself. Taking a deep breath, he bent his knees and placed one foot slowly in front of the other, occasionally stopping to sit and scoot on the steepest sections.

When his legs and butt burned and quivered from the strain, he rested, studying the subtle changes in the walls. At the surface they were the typical brown, but here the brown walls held horizontal striations of color. Reds and greens and blues alternated; the colored lines curved and whorled in a joyous jig.

He pressed on until the shaft ended in a vertical drop with no end that he could see. He lowered the torch and scanned the area. Five feet to his right, a narrow set of hand- and footholds had been carved into the rock. His gut flopped. How was he supposed to climb down with two babies strapped to his chest? The slings were solid but if he slipped…

He wanted to stop, wanted to turn back and find another way. Maybe the Exemplars could be made to see reason. Well, maybe Ailith, but not the others. They'd already done a surprising amount to help him when what they really wanted was to kill him.

He eased the slings over his head and rested the babies on the ground. "Why do you insist that I be the one to carry you? Huh? I could shimmy my way down if you two weren't with me."

"Not if you want to live," a soft voice said behind him.

Libra twisted at the waist to bring the torch around.

A small man stood several feet away, his white skin so covered with black cracks he looked like a jigsaw puzzle that would fall apart with just a touch.

Libra rose and straddled the babies. "What do you mean?"

"It's an illusion, the holes in the wall. They aren't there. If you had tried to use them, you would have fallen to your death."

"Not nice."

"That's what we do to intruders. And it's not nice." He stepped to one side of the tunnel. "Leave."

"Not until I speak with your people."

"There is nothing you could say that we want to hear."

"Take this," Libra demanded as he shoved the torch into the man's hands. He picked up the Innocent Demonica baby boy and peeled back the sling. "You may not want to hear what I have to say, but you *are* going to want him."

The old man leaned close. His mouth dropped open.

He opened the sling farther, exposing the boy's neck and chest. "Great mother earth, is that—? Is he—?"

"A Prime? Yes. There's not a hint of white anywhere on his skin."

The man's hands shook. "Give him to me."

Libra closed the material and slipped the sling over his head. "Not a chance. I've come to talk with your elders." He slung the Keres across his chest and settled her. "The Prime stays with me until then."

* * *

Meri squatted at the edge of the roof, peering down at the metal boxes scurrying along the ground. The rest had done her much good, but her belly rumbled and cramped. She desperately needed food. She closed her eyes and concentrated as she sniffed the air blowing across her body. There was much that smelled bad here, things she'd never smelled before, and she had no frame of reference to give her a clue, but within the foul smells she got a whiff of cooked bird. Her mouth watered and she shifted her position.

Taking a deep breath, she pinpointed the source and launched herself across the roof at a run. She might be weak from hunger but her body felt strong, stronger than she could ever remember feeling. The tough membrane between the bony framework of her wings still had some thin patches and holes, but they seemed to be repairing themselves. It was the most glorious sight; add to that the importance of her mission, and Meri was bursting with joy, brimming with purpose.

The ledge at the building end loomed. She gathered her strength and leaped across the span between buildings. She tucked and rolled the landing—her wings folded tight against her back—then took off at a run for the next building and the next. After five roofs, she reached her destination.

She dropped to her belly on the roof edge and looked down. Steam and smoke rose from pipes in the small building below, filling her nose with the most heavenly scents. She had to get down, but how to do it without drawing too much attention?

"Hey, that's some killer parkour."

Meri rolled onto her back, raised her legs, and flipped her upper body up so she landed on her feet. A girl, maybe her age, stood a few feet away, her clothes loose, her frame gaunt, her brown skin failing to hide the bruises on her face and bare arms.

Meri frowned. "Someone hurt you."

The girl glanced at the hand-shaped bruises that wrapped around her upper arms. She shrugged. "Only on days ending in 'Y.'"

"I don't know what that means."

The human took a step closer. "You homeless or some shit?" She checked out Meri's clothes then studied her face. "You're seriously dirty…almost goopy."

"I am away from my home," Meri said. "And this is what Pestilence Fairies always look like. Goopy."

The human shrugged and rolled her eyes. "Whatever. I don't care."

Meri looked over her shoulder at the long drop down. "I am hungry. But I don't want to fly down. Is there another way?"

The girl's eyes widened. "You take a flight like that and you won't be hungry anymore." She turned toward the roof access door that Meri hadn't noticed before. "Come with me. I'll show you a way down that involves a lot less bodily carnage." She opened the door. "Unless that's your thing, then do what you want."

The door closed before Meri could get to it. Flying among humans in daylight wasn't good, her mother had always said. She opened the door and peeked inside—just like the space she had slept in, there was a small landing, then stairs.

The human had already disappeared.

"You coming?" she called up.

Meri nodded once then stepped inside, letting the door shut behind her.

55

THE OLD INNOCENT DEMONICA scowled but turned around, leading Libra away from the death trap. They walked for several yards before the man disappeared inside a blind wall, so totally disguised that Libra didn't see it even with the torchlight. He ran a hand along the rock until he found the opening. He pushed the torch inside it, saw the old man waving at him impatiently, and scooted through the short passage that led to a much larger one.

The Innocent Demonica trotted off toward a faint light in the distance.

Libra increased his stride but kept to a walk; he couldn't afford to fall and hurt the babies. They reached a narrowed stretch that ended at a steep spiral. Round and round he trod, his arms stretched out to brace himself while the old man skittered ahead of him, his bare feet sure as a goat's.

Within minutes, the slope leveled out. The air was frigid but clean. Libra inhaled deep, reveling in the purity that filled his lungs. Two Demonica had stopped in the hall ahead of them, talking with their hands as much as their mouths until Libra passed them. They hissed when they saw him and fell in behind him.

Every Demonica they passed did the same thing until he had a large following of the reclusive paranorms on his tail. That this was an extraordinary event for them was abundantly clear.

Finally, they reached an opening to a massive cave, one that easily rivaled the Great Cavern. Libra stopped at the threshold and gawked. Salt crystals covered the walls and ceiling, their structure refracting light from the many torches and campfires dotted around the space. The walls winding through the crystals were the same jewel tones he had seen earlier but these shone like they were lit from within. A kaleidoscope couldn't rival the swirls and streaks that painted the cavern, making the primary black and white colors of the Innocent Demonica skin all the more distinct.

High above the crowd were thirteen rock ledges protruding out over the cavern floor like landings, twelve with a single chair and occupant—six Demonica with white skin covered in black cracks, six Demonica with black skin covered in white cracks. The thirteenth ledge held a single empty chair. Behind the chairs were holes in the rock face providing access to the ledges.

Men, women, and children stopped walking, talking, and laughing and turned to the old man. They said nothing, their eyes growing wary as they took Libra in.

"Come," the old Demonica barked.

Libra followed him through the frozen crowd, his hackles raised. If these paranorms decided to imprison him, or worse, there wouldn't be anything he could do about it. Hell, no one even knew more than the very basics about the Demonica. So any kind of diplomatic finesse he hoped he had probably wouldn't help him down here—could even get him killed. But he had to try if he ever hoped to get out of the ever-greater quagmire he was stuck in.

He looked up and found an ancient-looking female staring at him from her seat high above the ground. Her sagging black skin was so covered in white cracks that she could almost be mistaken for white. With each minute stretch of crack representing the consumption of a demonic soul, the number of souls she had ingested had to be in the hundreds of thousands, making her a force to be reckoned with.

She glared down at him and tapped her fingers on the arm of her chair. The synchronized breathing of the Demonica behind him grew louder as he stood there, the increasing pace an unmistakable sign of agitation. They were pissed to have a stranger in their midst, a paranorm who, in their eyes, was unclean, and he couldn't blame them.

They had chosen solitude for a reason, and though he did not know for certain, he suspected, as others did, that it was to shield their numbers from the evil that had roamed the planet with impunity since the gods and goddesses of old had fallen. With no one to protect them, their numbers had dwindled over the centuries. Add to that the lack of a Prime, their most powerful weapon against evil, and they were slowly dying off. If the number of Demonica present in the cavern was all of them, the species was on the verge of extinction.

The man who had led Libra here bowed low to the old woman. "This man has come bearing a great gift."

"And what gift could be so great as to justify him coming into our realm, exposing us to the outside?" She sneered at Libra, her eyes narrowed. She threw one hand into the air as if swatting at him. "Expose us to the evil inside him. Take him away. Kill him and throw his body into the bottomless pit."

"Please, wait," the old Demonica said, his hands clenched together in supplication. "His gift, it is what we've waited for."

The old woman leaned forward and spat, the saliva landing at Libra's feet. "Show me, then take him away."

The old man, still stooped in a half-bow, looked back at Libra and grunted. "Show her before they take him and kill you anyway."

Libra took a deep breath and hoped this punt wouldn't turn into a clusterfuck. He pulled the sling opening back and slid the Prime out, cradling his head in one hand while supporting his tiny body with the other.

The old woman leaned over so far, Libra was afraid she'd tumble off the ledge and go *splat* at his feet. She scowled, then, quicker than Libra would have thought her capable, she disappeared from her ledge, the others following suit.

In seconds, she reappeared in a passageway and marched up to him. She squinted her eyes as she drew close then pulled up the soft shirt the boy was wearing to see his belly. She jerked back with a gasp, and turned to the rest of the Innocent Demonica.

Throwing her head back, her arms held high, she screamed, "Prime!"

One of the other council members rushed forward to take the Prime, but the boy kicked his legs and flailed his arms, his body thrashing when she tried to pull him out of Libra's arms. The woman released him and stepped back.

One of the men stepped up, but he didn't even get his hands on the boy before the Prime howled his displeasure. Libra was staring at the infant, wondering what the hell was going on, when the worst happened.

The Keres woke up.

Her chubby, little arms pushed aside the sling and her eyes opened. She reached for the Prime and touched his head, calming him immediately. The Prime reached out until his hand found her arm. He gripped it and held on, the two connected and suddenly peaceful.

The old woman growled low. "Take it out; show that child to me."

"I don't need to; she's a Keres."

"You dare bring a fully formed daemon in our midst? And you think we'll just let you leave with her? Make her release the Prime. Now! Or we will strike you and her down where you stand."

Yep, I've walked into a serious cluster.

He bounced them and twisted at the waist, hoping to gently jiggle them loose, but they were stuck like burrs in Fenrir Wolf fur. "They don't seem to want to let go."

Several Demonica crept closer, their knees bent like they planned to lunge, scowls marring their cracked faces.

Libra looked around. "I suggest you don't attack. You might kill the Prime if you force this. I've seen the Keres do some impressive damage when she's provoked."

They paused, looking to their council for direction.

The old woman slashed an open hand across her throat and they stopped moving. "Why are you here if it's not to give us the Prime?"

"I came to ask for your help, not for me alone but for all of the paranorms. I thought by giving you the Prime, you might consider it."

She walked close again and circled Libra, her focus on the babies and their connection. "Where did you find him? We would have known if he was taken from us."

"He was with a group of paranorm children I found with Circe, the witch goddess. I don't know how she came to have him or the Keres or the other children."

The women stopped circling. "She had both?"

"Yes."

"What was she doing with the children?"

"That's what we all want to know. All the paranorm species have had children stolen; the reason is still a mystery."

"The Prime doesn't want to be separated from you or the Keres. Why?"

"Honestly, I haven't a clue. I thought that bringing him here, being among his own people, would do the trick. Can you not force him?"

She looked at him like he'd lost his mind. "You don't force a Prime to do anything. Even now, as an infant, he is more powerful than any of us. He doesn't think like you; he doesn't perceive the world like any of us do. He is a creature who feels the balance of good and evil. It's how he measures everything around him, all he comes into contact with. His choices are based on that and that alone. If he has chosen to be with you—to connect with *her*—the Innocent Demonica can not question it."

"That still leaves the need for your help. Will you help the Zodiacs fight the demon army that's been loosed in the world?"

She looked at the other council members. "We will need to confer among ourselves." She waved a couple of women over. "While we talk, I invite you to eat and drink. Feed the babies." She touched the arm of one woman. "Do we have any nursing mothers?"

The much younger woman nodded.

"Fetch two of them," the old woman said, glancing at the still-connected babies, "and nursing bottles. I don't think they'll let go of each other, or the Zodiac, even for some teat."

56

LIBRA NESTLED DEEP IN the straw bedding, a baby under each arm, and closed his eyes. After the Prime and Keres had filled their bellies and passed out, he'd been fed and forced to lie down. Exhaustion had taken a toll, and the Innocent Demonica council was taking its time, so he availed himself of the chance to get some rest. The Exemplars were probably having a fit, but they would wait as long as it took for him to return. With any luck, the paranorm children were running the women ragged.

It seemed he'd just closed his eyes when a sharp poke on one shoulder roused him.

"Made a decision so soon?"

The old woman grunted. "You've been asleep for hours."

He sat up and saw the Demonica that had been bustling around him when he closed his eyes were now asleep, the fires low. "What have you decided?"

"We will not jeopardize our people to aid you in this fight." She held up a hand to stop his protest. "But, because the Prime is critical to our survival, and because he's chosen you to bond with, we are sending our most powerful warriors with you to protect him."

It wasn't what he'd hoped for, but he would take what he could get at this point. "How many?"

"Twenty men and women will stay with you during your travels. They will fight and die to protect the Prime, but they won't do the same for you. Just so you understand," she finished with a sneer. "In truth, your death would greatly benefit us, so watch your back. If you drop, they will take the Prime and bring him here."

Great. Perfect. Clusterfuck deluxe.

"I appreciate the warning. And the guard for the Prime."

"Get up. It's time for you to leave. Your presence has already polluted our realm enough."

Libra struggled to stand, a baby in each arm. "Your hospitality is overwhelming."

The woman gave him a brilliant go-to-hell glance then clapped her hands.

The twenty warriors strode out of the shadows, dressed for battle much like the Exemplars in black leather pants, boots, and thick, red-stained, molded-leather chest-plates that looked like they could withstand a blade, maybe even an arrow. Adequate for the paranorm world, but the thick leather probably wouldn't stop a bullet.

Ten white and ten black, an even ratio of men to women, they were tall and muscular with cold, fierce stares that would wither all but the most hardened warrior. Good for keeping attackers at bay, but not the best predictor of the strength of their tenuous allegiance to him. Scratch that, their only allegiance was to the Prime—Libra was just an obstacle to the Innocent Demonica claiming the boy.

Friendly fire and all that rot.

"One more thing," the old woman said.

One of the female warriors tossed a bundle to him. Libra caught it but couldn't figure out what it was.

"Place it on the ground with the straps down."

He did as she ordered. Once the straps were untangled, he saw immediately what it was. Two long pouches with a hole on top had been sewn together; the straps were for his hips and shoulders. It was a double sling for carrying the babies on his back instead of across his chest.

"We use these when we travel to keep the babies close but our hands free for fighting," the warrior woman said, her words clipped.

Libra placed the Prime and Keres on the ground then slipped them inside the sling. They immediately rested their heads together and fell asleep, not stirring even when he lifted them and made adjustments to the straps.

The old Demonica woman and the warriors watched in silence.

"I don't understand why they have a bond with each other or with you, but a Prime is born with a wisdom and understanding that none of us attain in all our years of life and experience. He has chosen you both." She lowered her voice. "That's the only reason you and the Keres are being allowed to live. But if the Prime loses faith in either or both of you…" She drew a forefinger across her throat, the universal sign for death. "They," she added with a nod to the warriors, "will be watching."

Tired of being threatened with certain death, Libra turned away and walked toward the passage he'd used before, the warriors close behind him.

He paused at the threshold. "Someone want to lead the way?"

A male passed him and lengthened his stride to cover the ground quickly, which was fine with Libra. The sooner he escaped the Demonica the better. Of course, he was walking back into the raging antipathy of the Exemplars, but maybe the paranorm children had worn them down.

One can hope.

Despite the steep climb out of the salt mine, the group made fast time. They reached the final tunnel, the light shining in the distance, sooner than Libra had anticipated. His heart pounded. He couldn't wait to clear the mine and look to the sky for Meri. The moment the fairy appeared, he was off, no matter how many people he had in tow. It could get interesting, though, if Taryn was being held in a city. How he would traverse human urban terrain with decidedly non-human paranorms hadn't come to him yet, but one thing at a time. If only it were All Hallow's Eve…

Yards before the exit, Libra tapped the lead warrior on the shoulder. "You'd better let me go first. Hate to have a fight break out with you and the Exemplars before the first hello."

The male slowed, allowing him to pass. Libra made quick work of the final distance and stepped out into the sunlight with a sigh. The woods around him were quiet. No children or Exemplars anywhere. He glanced up to see if he could spot Meri, but the skies were as quiet as the ground.

"Hello?"

A giggle sounded from his right. The Aspis girl slithered out from behind a tree before trotting over to him, her approach triggering a flood of paranorm children followed by the dour-faced Exemplar women. Ailith in particular wore a scowl that could melt iron, her long hair teased into a rat's nest, her clothes covered in burrs, and her exposed skin scratched and bruised.

"Have fun?" he asked.

She bared her teeth and growled.

The Demonica warriors immediately surrounded Libra, their backs to him, their weapons drawn.

That, of course, enraged the Exemplars. They surrounded the Demonica, their daggers drawn.

"What are they doing?" Ailith asked. "The talks not go well?"

"I'm alive, so I'd say they went swimmingly. Problem is the Prime doesn't want to stay here. He's decided to stay with me. The warriors are assigned to protect the him."

One of the Demonica women glanced at him. "Only the Prime."

Ailith's frown turned upside-down. "I like her already."

"I figured you would."

"So what's the plan?"

"The Stryx headed east so I'm going to head in that direction to find Taryn."

"And if the Stryx changed direction? East could be the wrong way."

Libra growled. "I can't sit here doing nothing."

Ailith crossed her arms. "You're not going anywhere without us."

"You've got the children to take care of. I need to move as fast as the babies will let me, which means the rest can't come."

The Exemplar warriors grumbled.

"I don't want to hear complaining," he ground out. "If you had let me go to the Pondera Seclorum, the children would be safely in their care and we wouldn't have this problem."

Ailith held up a hand, silencing them. "You still think that's the best option? From what I see, you have two babies who won't be parted from you, and a Corvus royal you can't part with."

"You want to go there?"

Ailith remained silent.

"I thought not."

"What's done is done," she said. "We all will travel with you, or you will go nowhere."

The Demonica shifted and muttered, stiffening as if expecting an attack.

Ailith held up a hand. "That's not a threat."

A soft touch on Libra's right hand made him look down.

The Corvus boy hesitated a couple feet away from him, his eyes swimming with tears. "Please don't leave us."

Libra clenched his fists. He took a long, deep breath then let it out slowly. He raised his arm and the boy slipped inside it and hugged his waist.

Libra rubbed the small boy's back. "I need to move fast."

"You have skills in the human world; what would you suggest?" Ailith countered.

"The bus is much too small for all of us."

Ailith smiled, displaying straight, white teeth that were more chilling than her frown. "There are horses not far from here."

"I don't know how to ride," he snapped back.

She snorted. "Then you're going to learn."

The largest male Demonica stepped forward. "There is no need to use four-legged animals to travel. Not when we have buses much larger than that one." He waved a dismissive hand at Libra's wheels, walked past the chain-link fence, and turned around. "Come."

Libra followed the male along a winding path until they reached a rusted storage warehouse, leftover from the time when the mine was active.

The Demonica shoved a wreck of a door out of the way and stepped inside.

Libra was hesitating just inside the gloom, waiting for his eyes to adjust, when he heard a man's voice call out.

"Hey, where we going today? Demons to kill, innocents to save? The buses are all gassed up and ready to go."

A small human man came into view, wiping his hands clean with a red rag. Dressed all in black save for a square of white at his throat, he was too neat for a mechanic. He stepped into a sliver of sunlight, illuminating the cross hanging around his neck.

"A priest?" Libra said.

The human touched the cross and grinned. "Brought some new friends, I see."

The Demonica nodded at the man. "We will need two buses to carry all of us."

"Can anyone here drive besides me?" the priest asked.

"I can," Libra said.

"Saints be praised, come on then. Let's get everyone loaded and you checked out on one of these beasts."

Libra followed the man. "A priest?"

"Close your mouth, son, before a fly gets caught in there. Yes, I'm a priest. Father Harrison."

"How did you come to be here?"

"You don't think the Catholic Church does all those exorcisms by itself, do you?" He snorted then chuckled. "My friends here have been working with us for a long, long time, though most priests don't know about them. Pretty much just me, the Pope, and a few others know about the Innocent Demonica."

"Why are you here?"

"The Demonica saved my sister from possession. Saw it myself when I was a boy and that clenched it for me. Been here since becoming a priest, taking care of their needs, protecting them from prying eyes."

"So you and the Pope and others know about the paranorm world?"

The man stopped and turned around. "What paranorm world?"

Libra could have kicked himself for the slip.

The priest winked. "Ahh, got ya." He clapped a hand on Libra's shoulder. "Sure, son, I know. But it's a very tightly held secret. Gotta stay that way, too, if we're going to keep the lot of you alive." Father Harrison waved a hand at the line of buses that sat gleaming in the dark. "Let's get this done so we can get on the road." He stepped inside the first bus. "Where we headed?"

"East."

"East, where?"

"Just east, for now."

"Mighty vague, but the even good lord himself is mighty mysterious. East it is."

* * *

Meri paused at the door held open by her new friend.

"Come on, I'm starved," the human girl barked.

Meri slipped past her sideways, careful to keep her hands inside the sleeves of Libra's shirt. She looked around the narrow space between buildings and marveled at the sounds and smells carried on the stream of wind blowing past her. Voices and loud beeping buffeted her, tickling her face, setting up an itch in her ears. But she kept her hands hidden, resisted the urge to scratch, lest she make a mistake and touch the girl. Friends were rare in her world; she couldn't afford to kill a single one when she only had two, especially when one of them had offered to help her fill her belly.

"Food?" she said.

The human gestured at Meri to follow her. "You got money?"

"What is money?"

The girl stopped walking and turned slowly, her eyes narrowed. "You're serious with that shit." Her eyes widened and her mouth dropped open. "Damn, you're homely AF."

Meri smiled. "Thank you."

The human blinked, then burst out laughing. "You are batshit, too, but I happen to like that. No money means we're gonna have to do some running. You up for that?"

"I like running almost as much as flying," Meri offered, pleased that the human was amused.

"Alright, Batshit, let's get moving." The girl started down the alley.

"My name is Meri. What is your name?" Meri asked, trotting behind her new friend.

"I go by Grate." She pointed to a metal rectangle in the ground. "You know, everyone walks on me but I'm too tough to bend."

She stopped at the end of the narrow space and pointed to a small box with wheels. Steam billowed out of it every time the man standing next to it opened the lid, flooding the air with the most delicious scents. Meri's belly growled loud and long.

"Come on, Batshit. Follow my lead."

57

AUBRIANNA ENTERED THE CORVUS Ward throne room, pausing for a moment when the men and women surrounding her fell silent. An icy zing of concern started at the back of her neck and flowed down her spine, like snow finding the opening of her collar and chilling her as it slid down her warm skin.

Ruffled feathers—in this case literally—needed to be soothed. She took her time walking up to the king, refusing to look left or right, her will controlling her breathing when alarm demanded she pant. She reached the steps and took a knee rather than curtsying. She didn't consider herself to be inferior to the king, nor was she his vassal, but the decidedly frigid reception warranted caution and a more formal show of respect.

She bowed her head and spread her arms like a bird in flight, the customary Corvus Ward greeting for royalty. "Highness."

"Seize her!"

The audience behind Aubrianna erupted with hissing and chattering teeth as two huge warriors grabbed her arms and yanked her onto her feet.

The frosty chill radiated from her spine; her feet and hands tingled. No one had ever said consorting with mad men wasn't dangerous; they were prone to killing the messenger and all that rot.

"I have come with good news," she cried.

"I agreed to place you in the ambassador position. In exchange, you would get Libra to become the agent so I could take his power. That failed. He escaped and killed several of my warriors in the process. Again you failed. You said let him go; you would push him to give me what I want. Yet, again, for a third time, you have failed. Why shouldn't I kill you right here?"

Aubrianna thought fast. "Because I have something even more important to you and your people than Gaia's power."

The crowd hissed.

The king stood. "My people have fought bravely and sacrificed themselves to protect my kingdom. What could possibly be more important to us than having the power to defeat the demon army?"

The king had a good point. The worlds were in grave danger of being consumed by darkness, and having Gaia's power would put them in a position to destroy all comers. Not that she'd ever planned to let the king take what was rightfully hers.

"The rising of the demons has surely put us all in peril," she said. "And the power of Gaia would not only protect your people, but also unite all of the paranorms under your leadership. That is not a trifle."

The king said nothing.

Her heart thumped hard and a trickle of sweat ran down her spine, but she waited. She had laid out that ego stroke to appease him. Time to see if what she had to offer would be enough to get her out of here alive.

"As for the loss of your men," she continued, "I regret that, but what I have to offer is of great value. In exchange, all I ask is a little more time to achieve our goals."

The king pursed his lips and took a seat again. He flipped a hand in the air. "What do you think is important enough to warrant sparing your life?"

"I have a royal Corvus Ward child."

The audience started whispering behind her.

"A royal boy."

Hisses bounced off the walls. Scalp feathers snapped up, making Aubrianna's skin crawl. She most definitely had their attention.

The king clapped his hands and the two large warriors holding her arms tightened their grip.

The king stood and beckoned the warriors forward. "Bring her. Now."

Aubrianna was pulled out of the throne room and into an antechamber. The king whirled on her, his face bright red, his scowl foreboding.

He gestured to a chair. "Sit."

The warriors pushed but she locked her knees to remain standing. She could have disapparated by now but leaving without coming to a resolution would condemn her to a life of running, a position that was untenable. She willed her heart to slow to stop sweat from beading on her forehead and body. The precarious balance she had to maintain to use the Corvus Ward king and Asmodeus, the demon king, for her own gain came with a healthy dose of fear and anxiety that was foreign to her. But the secret must be kept, or it was off with her head.

The king sagged into a smaller replica of his throne. A crow cawed and flapped its wings beside him.

She stared at the bird, a flicker of concern forming as the king stroked the bird's breast and studied her. She forced her body to relax and pasted a smile on her face.

"I want you to say that again," the king ordered.

"I know where a royal boy is, along with several other paranormal children who were being held by Circe."

The king leaned forward. "Why should I believe you?"

"His eyes are already red."

The king sat back and tented his hands, the tips of his fingers resting on his lips. "Everyone knows that royals have red eyes."

She shrugged. "Yes, but I saw the boy myself."

The king stared at her, the circles he made on the crow's chest slowing the longer he looked. "Where is the child?"

"He is safe." Now was the time for the gambit. "Give me more time and I'll make sure you get the child back."

The candlelight hit the king's red, glowing eyes. He narrowed them and hissed, terrifying the crow. The bird screamed and jumped off his perch, flapping his wings to escape the king's wrath, but his tether kept him from flying loose around the room. The king snapped his fingers and the crow landed on the perch, its feathers puffed up, its beak open.

"What are you playing at?" he asked.

"I'm giving you the one thing you've been looking for these many years."

"And all I have to do is spare your life and give you more time."

"Yes."

"I'll want to see him for myself."

"And I'll be happy to facilitate that, but first I need assurance that you and your people will not harm me. Now, or after you get Gaia's power."

The king nodded. "That is a fair proposal."

Aubrianna stood very still, the fine hairs on her neck rising. Her continued existence could hinge on this.

The king crossed his legs and smiled. "People outside of our kind have always shared rumors—they've told old wives' tales about crows and ravens having the ability find a Corvus Ward anywhere in the world. All that's required is for some-one to have seen them."

Her legs nearly buckled, the panic overwhelming her will.

The king settled back and looked across the room for several seconds, his face blank. "I will share a secret." He dropped his voice to a whisper. "It's true."

The king flipped his hand in the air. "The humans have taken much from us, and the Twelve and now the Zodiacs have done nothing about it. You have promised much and not delivered. I will have the royal back…and I will have Gaia's power, no matter what it takes to get it."

Foreboding gripped her. She'd lost the king's trust and that left only one ques-tion—would she pay the price with her life?

"What do you mean?"

"I will give you one chance to tell me where the boy is," he held up a finger, "or I will make you tell me."

"Let me go now or he's lost to you forever."

Her demand was a last ditch effort. And a futile one. The king nodded to his men.

They grabbed her arms and pushed them behind her back, arching her spine and forcing her onto her toes.

There was nothing for it; she had to escape. She had gambled and lost. But before she could disapparate, they clamped iron shackles on her wrists and ankles, binding her to this place as surely as if she had no power. She was neutralized in a way that no one outside of the Os Mage women was meant to know about.

The Corvus Wards were ruthless with their enemies. They weren't much better with their few allies. That the king would have his men put their hands on her and bind her meant injury to her person was imminent—or death. Most likely one, then the other.

"Get off me." She struggled against the men for a moment then sagged. She scowled at the king. "You dare to accost an Os Mage Mother?"

"There will always be another." He snapped his fingers. "Take her to the aviary."

The males jerked her forward, the shackles forcing her to shuffle her feet to keep up as they led her out of the antechamber and through a maze of passages, the king silent behind them.

"What are you going to do?" she said. "You can't take Gaia's power without me."

"I'm not going to kill you, if that's your worry." He snorted, "Of course, that's your worry."

His tone gave her little relief.

"I'm going to introduce you to my corvids."

"To what end?"

"Information," he said distractedly. "Of course, you'll have to bleed for them to make it happen."

Aubrianna jerked hard against her bonds, willing her body to escape them, but iron imprisoned the Os Mage like no other metal could. It was their one great weakness, and that had never been shared with others. But someone had talked, and with only four Os Mages alive, it wouldn't take her long to suss out the traitor and make her pay dearly.

A dizzying number of hallways later, they arrived at a pair of ancient, wooden doors covered with carvings of crows in flight. The warriors opened them and led the way into the aviary.

Crows, ravens, and magpies cawed and flapped their wings, lifting off their perches until stopped by their tethers, agitated by the sudden entrance of the king and his men.

In the middle of the huge space was a long, wooden table. The males dragged her to it.

The king leaned close to her. "Cut off her clothes."

"What?" Aubrianna asked, her voice a squeak.

She didn't like where this was going but she couldn't stop the males from ripping and cutting her clothes until they fell to the floor in ribbons, leaving her naked.

"Up."

The males lifted her and dropped her on her back on the filthy wood.

"What are you going to do?"

The oldest male smiled, showing off an alarming lack of teeth. "You will see."

She rolled her head and saw thick, black stains. Adrenaline rushed through her. Blood. Old, dried blood. What the hell were they about to do? She swallowed, lay back, and looked up at the slatted ceiling.

The birds flapped their wings harder, their mounting excitement matching her growing dread as the two Corvus warriors freed them.

The old man raised his hands over her and chanted for several moments in a language foreign to her before clapping his hands together once. The crows and magpies dove from their perches and landed on Aubrianna, covering her body save for her face.

The old man laid his hand on Aubrianna's forehead, pressing it down so she couldn't thrash.

"What are we looking for?" he asked the king.

"A royal boy. I want to know what she's seen, where he is."

The old man breathed through his mouth.

The stench of rotten teeth hit Aubrianna; her belly clenched with the need to heave. She bit the inside of her cheek and willed the nausea away.

"The birds will find him."

Aubrianna closed her eyes and tried to ignore the weight of the birds on her while she concentrated on picturing anything that wasn't Libra, her home, or the boy. The corvids seemed relatively calm and they hadn't drawn blood, so she relaxed and pictured herself holding both hands out, the power of Aether in one, and the power of Nether in the other. Anything to distract the birds from finding the memory.

A bird pecked at one breast and she lost the image. "Hey."

The old man snapped his fingers, his amiable smile belied by his cold, glittering eyes.

She tried to rise but the males kept her still; the iron prevented her escape. "What are you doing? Let me go."

The old man placed a leather mask on her face, blinding her. The only openings were the tiny holes at her nose and mouth—barely enough to breathe but she was grateful nonetheless.

"The memory of the boy became one with your blood the moment you saw him. Now the birds will take the memory from you. Humans call them an unkindness of ravens and a murder of crows. Now you will see how they earned those names."

He giggled then clapped his hands twice. The birds jammed their beaks into her skin, pinching and pecking and pulling until they drew blood.

Aubrianna screamed and writhed while the birds feasted on her flesh.

58

THE HELL OS MAGE stood in the shadows of the aviary, a large burlap sack at her feet, watching the Mother getting pecked by the crows. "You didn't kill her."

The king studied her hard profile. Aubrianna had been a formidable ally, or foe, depending on his mood, but this Mage gave him pause. There were moments in the quiet and darkness of the deepest night that he wondered if he'd made a bargain with the devil herself. Between the two women, he'd have to move swiftly and harshly if he stood a chance of claiming the power of the agent before they did.

"She has other information that I greatly desire. Besides, we need to know if Libra has bonded with the woman."

"Because if he has then he'll kill for her…with the right pressure."

"How did you know she had betrayed me?"

One corner of her mouth lifted. "I have stolen a source."

The king crossed his arms. "Must be psychic."

The Os Mage woman remained silent.

The king looked at her. "You have a Portend?"

She nodded once. "I have Aubrianna's Portend." The Mage turned her bald head toward him as if she could see. "Mother shouldn't have betrayed the Portend. Or you."

He flinched away from her empty eye sockets and the many scars that had misshapen her face and the dome of her head. He'd asked her how she lost her eyes; her answer—that she'd gouged them out herself to survive Hell—still turned his stomach.

"And she has agreed to work with you after Aubrianna's lies?"

"*Everyone* has a weakness. She is desperate to be reunited with her daughter."

"And you would release such an asset?"

"Unlike Mother, I always keep my word." She turned away. "There are always more assets to be found."

The king swallowed hard. *Damn and Hell.* "So what's next?"

"We learn what Mother knows about Libra and this woman."

"And then?"

"Then we follow him."

"That's the same plan Aubrianna had and she failed."

The woman smiled, the slight movement highlighting the web of white scars that covered her face. "When they're together…we'll back him into a corner. Once he becomes the agent, we make our move." She glanced at him. "I won't fail."

* * *

"What the hell is going on?" the human woman demanded. She and her partner stood back to back, their fists raised as if just the two of them could hold off all the Zodiacs. "I demand you let us go."

Lyon turned to her. "You're much safer in here with us than out there with the Corvus Wards. They aren't fond of humans."

"Humans," the male repeated. "What do you mean by that?"

Sag crossed his arms. "He means you are humans, and we are not. At least not totally."

The man and woman glanced at each other, their expressions incredulous.

Lyon grunted in disgust. "We'll release you when the warriors are gone, but that may be a while. So here's what you need to know. This place is called the Great Cavern. It is part of a subterranean paranormal world called the InBetween that was created centuries ago by the goddess Hecate for the protection of the species that have been persecuted by humans since recorded history. Several weeks ago, that hole," he pointed up, "was created by a witch goddess named Circe, along with a demon king named Asmodeus, with my father's help. They opened the gates of Hell and released an army of demons into the human world. That's where the black 'smoke' reports came from. Since then, we've tried to hide the hole from humans with a witch's spell, but it failed right around the time two humans fell through that hole and into that other hole in the ground. No doubt, they're dead. Outside, we have warriors who are here to seize the Great Cavern. If we're lucky, they'll just kill us; if we're not, you'll wish for death. That about sum it up?"

The Zodiacs nodded.

The human woman snorted. "If these warriors live in the subterranean world you describe, why didn't they attack from inside? Why attack from outside, from the surface?"

"The InBetween is like a huge, underground spiderweb. The Great Cavern is the center of the web and it extends out in a circle all across this country. The Corvus Wards live in a blocked section of the InBetween—blocked to keep us out. It's much faster for them to travel in the human world."

"Why this cavern?" she asked.

"There is great wealth to be found here and a stronghold that's held for centuries...until recently. We're also close to the surface here. The Corvus Ward king wants this cavern for the power it would give him."

"If you're not totally human, then what are all of you?" the male agent asked.

My name is Lyon. I am the Zodiac Assassin Leo. My brothers are also Zodiac Assassins," he said with a brief nod to the men.

Sloane held up a hand. "Zodiac Assassins?"

Lyon also raised a hand. "Let me finish, then I'll answer your questions."

Treadwell nodded.

Sloane leaned forward, her eyes wide and mouth open. "The Mammoth Cave incident?"

"Yes, and the black cloud that was reported. Those were the demons."

Sloane looked off into the distance. "Where are they now?"

"That's what we're trying to find out, while attempting to introduce our existence to humans without having our world annihilated."

The humans slowly dropped their arms and looked at each other, their faces expressionless for a beat before they erupted into laughter.

The woman snorted. "Right, and the boogeyman is real."

"Well, no," Lyon said. He nodded at the space behind them. "But that troll is."

A gray-green giant lumbered toward the group, its beady eyes darting around the cavern.

"Holy shit," the human male shouted. He pushed the woman behind him and they backed away from the approaching creature. "What kind of trick is this?"

A deep pounding echoed through the cavern.

"You'd better worry less about tricks and more about getting out of here," Lyon replied.

The human male continued backing away from the troll. "Point the way."

Sag and Taur and the other Zodiacs looked at Lyon.

"Hell, if I knew that, we'd already be gone," Lyon growled.

59

ERI AND GRATE RACED from the screaming man, their hands full of what Grate called 'dogs and buns.' They skidded around a corner, laughing at the bellowed insults the vendor hurled at them, and made their great escape into an old warehouse. Grate ran up the rickety stairs and burst out of the door at the rooftop. The door closed behind them and Grate high-kicked a heavy metal bar. It fell across the door so hard it bounced out of metal 'U' that had been welded to the left side of the door.

"We'll get it later," Grate growled. She strutted away, rounding the corner. "C'mon Batshit. I'm starving."

Meri trotted after her strange friend, her stomach burning for food. She turned the corner then stopped dead. Grate had disappeared inside a brightly colored pile of boxes stacked in every imaginable direction. Meri peeked inside the flapping blue sheet that seemed to form the entrance.

Grate had already plopped herself down on a long rectangle of fabric, the food in her arms now piled high on a wooden box in front of her.

She nodded at Meri. "Come on, you got the dogs. Let's eat."

"What is this place?" Meri asked as she poked a soft seat with a finger.

"It's the Taj Mahal, my safe place, my real home." Grate jumped up, all nervous energy and swagger. "Got no television or computer, but we got a couch."

Meri ran her hands over the fabric. "Couch."

"Got a swanky coffee table," Grate added with a kick to the box in front of her, "circa nineteen-whatever."

Meri grinned and touched the box. "Coffee table."

Grate shook her head. "And behind curtain number two is a mattress." She rejoined Meri on the couch and spread out the buns. "Fill 'em up."

The girls ate everything they had stolen until their bellies were distended. They leaned back on the couch and moaned.

"So damn good." Grate opened her mouth and belched. "Better out than in."

Meri opened her mouth but nothing happened.

Grate reached over to push on Meri's belly but Meri lunged away from her and hit the floor.

"Wow," Grate said, punctuating the word with a whistle. "Don't like to be touched, huh?" She sat back again and studied Meri. "That's okay, Batshit. I don't like it much either."

Meri's eyes welled. "I don't want to hurt my friends."

She scuttled backward until she gained her footing then ran out of Grate's home. This human had been so nice that Meri had forgotten for a moment that a simple touch would kill her. It had been fine when she was in the InBetween—the miles of dark nooks and crannies gave the Fairies plenty of opportunity to live a solitary life.

But the revelation that Taryn could survive the sickness had changed everything. Taryn had been warm and gentle and once she had recovered from the sickness the first time, Taryn had never avoided Meri.

The memory of her first hug was Meri's greatest treasure, the sole nugget of hope that filled her with an incessant longing to be touched. It had spoiled her. But she couldn't forget what she was, not for a minute, not around Grate, the first friend she'd made who was her age.

She paced the roof, alternating between wringing her hands and hiding them inside her sleeves. She had to leave; she had to protect Grate. She stopped at the edge and looked down.

"You're not starting with that again are you?"

Grate had walked up behind her, silent as a stalking Fenrir Wolf.

"I should leave."

Grate shrugged her shoulders. "You do you. Makes no diff to me."

"You talk funny."

"And you look funny. So there it is."

"I don't want to hurt you. Touching me would hurt you badly."

Grate held up her hands. "No touch. Cool."

The wind whipped around them. Meri drew a deep breath through her nose and closed her eyes. Rested and fed, it was time for her to continue her hunt. The sun would be down soon and she should go.

"Uh, Batshit? I hate to crash your Zen, but what's going on with your back?"

Meri looked over her shoulder and frowned. Her wings had responded to her anticipation of flight and were trying to rise despite the heavy shirt Libra had given her. She turned toward Grate and shrugged. But before she could explain, she saw five men working their way toward Grate, their knees bent, metal pipes in their hands.

"Grate! Look out!" she yelled as she pointed.

Grate whipped around as fast as any paranorm creature could have done. "Shit." She ran to Meri and stood in front of her, blocking the fairy from the approaching men, her rich, dark skin paling with each second. "Stay behind me, Batshit. This is gonna get ugly."

"Grate, Grate, what did I tell you about stealing in my territory?" The lead male neared, the pipe rising and falling, hitting the palm of his free hand. "You're making me look bad."

"Forcing people to pay you protection money makes you look plenty bad already. At least I'm making you actually work for the money you're stealing."

He stopped a few feet away and waited for the other four to spread out around the girls. "But dogs and buns? Come on, girl."

He shook his head as if he was really pained to have to be there, as if regret would tinge every coming blow.

Grate bent her knees and held up her hands as if she could fight them off. "At least let her go; she only did what I told her."

The man shook his head again. "Nah, can't let anyone off easy, not in this."

He started closing in on Grate, the other men copying his pace, tightening the circle around them.

Meri scanned the men. They had no good intentions; they would hurt Grate, and her. Even their individual scents smelled foul. Not like they hadn't bathed; she could smell the chemicals wafting off their skin that followed a bath. No, this was deep inside them, a foul smell of anger and hate and the need to destroy; pain turned to evil. They would hit and hurt and not feel anything but the rush of adrenaline mingled with their mindless brutality.

That was the way of many in her world. That she'd found it so soon in the human world crushed her.

"Grate, do these men hurt others often?" she asked.

Grate didn't turn. "Oh, yes. And worse."

Meri slid Libra's huge shirt off and let it drop to the ground.

"Grate," she said, spreading her bare arms, "get down. Now."

She shrugged her shoulders hard and her wings flipped out.

Grate hit the ground and glanced up. "What the hell?"

Meri grinned. "Whatever happens, do not touch my bare skin."

The leader of the men laughed. "Who the fuck is this? Batgirl?"

Grate looked at him and sneered. "This is my friend. And her name is Meri. Run if you want to live."

The leader's face flushed bright red. "Get 'em!"

The men raised their weapons and lunged for Meri.

She yelled and spun in a tight circle. The razor sharp tips of the bones in her wings acted like knives, cutting horizontal slices through their heavy coats, baring the tee shirts underneath.

The men jumped back, looked at the destruction of their clothes, then growled in unison. Surprise changed to murderous rage in a blink.

Meri waited, watching. She bent her knees and waited for them to come. The more pissed they were, the more mistakes they would make. Then she would tear them apart.

344

One of the men behind her jumped first, the heavy pipe raised above his head to crush her skull. One step, two steps, and he was one step from striking.

She jumped up at the same time he moved on her, flapping her wings, pulling her over the top of him.

He stumbled forward and Grate kicked him in the back of his left knee, the joint breaking with a sickening *crunch*. He screamed and reached for the leader to break his fall, but the other man stepped to the side and let the injured one crash to the ground.

The leader sneered at his man. "You're no use to me."

With one blow of his weapon, he split open the fallen male's skull.

Meri could see his squiggly brain.

She landed softly, straddling Grate. She pointed at the leader. "You shouldn't have done that."

"Fuck you. What you gonna do about it, Tinkerbell?"

Another man rushed her.

She turned and waited for the sweet spot to get close enough.

"Batshit!"

His arms pulled back.

She waited.

At the apex of his arc, she jumped up again, kicked out her right foot, and hit his throat with all her weight.

His body stopped immediately, eyes wide. The pipe dropped out of his hands, and he fell backward, his hands clutching his broken trachea. He writhed and gagged then stopped moving all together.

The leader howled. "Get her!"

The other two men rushed Meri, coming so fast she didn't have time to jump. A pipe crashed into her right shoulder, sending her to one knee. She reached for the man's leg but he danced out of her reach.

The second man grunted as he swung his pipe, giving Meri warning. She ducked her head. The pipe hit her back, between her wings.

"Meri!" Grate cried.

Meri's body folded over her friend but she kept her skin from touching the human. "Cover your head, hide your hands."

Grate flipped up her hoodie and pushed her sweatshirt sleeves over her hands. Her skin was covered.

Meri spread her wings to block Grate from the men. Another blow to her back and another to her shoulder pushed her down until she was practically lying on Grate. A pipe slammed into her cheek splitting the skin. Blood ran into her mouth, gagging her as stars danced behind her eyes.

She fought to remain conscious; if they knocked her out, it was over.

"Enough," the leader called out. Immediately, the blows stopped and the men backed away. The leader walked up to her and bent over. "You ready to die?" He stood. "Screw that. Ready or not, you're done."

She turned her head to look him in the eye. "This is your last chance. Walk away or I'll kill you and your men."

The pains in her body coalesced, pooling inside her and changing to an anger that swept away the fear.

The leader grinned then swung.

The world around Meri slowed. She could hear Grate's breathing and smell her terror. She watched the pipe arc toward her; she could see the evil in the man's eyes, his hunger for the kill. It was a look she'd seen too many times in her world. Her own life wasn't precious, but there was nothing she wouldn't do to protect her only two friends.

Just as the pipe became horizontal, Meri reached up and stopped it cold. The instant the metal hit her hand the world sped up again.

The leader grunted. He jerked on the pipe but Meri was too strong. He kicked her in the ribs.

She grunted but didn't shift off Grate.

He released the pipe and grabbed Meri by the front of her vest, lifting her into the air. He carried her to the edge of the roof and held her over the side.

His face bunched into an inhuman mask. "You're going to die in a mess of blood and flesh and bone. And every day I pass by your bloodstain, I'm gonna spit on it."

Meri laughed; she couldn't stop the mirth from rising up and bursting out of her. She reached out a hand and grabbed his shirt.

She pulled hard and his shaking arms couldn't stop her from closing the space between them. "The only bloodstain is going to be yours."

She caressed his cheek with the knuckles of her free hand then released him.

He stopped sneering, his face relaxed, his eyes wide.

Out the corner of her eye, Meri saw Grate rise to her feet and slowly approach, while the remaining men stood in place, shocked by either what their leader had been about to do or her nonchalant threat.

The leader took a deep breath and shuddered. Black and green bloomed over his cheek then spread to the rest of his face.

Meri watched her pestilence consume his body in seconds. She tried to spread her wings but one was too numb to obey her demand fully. It wasn't completely useless, but it was hanging at an angle. Flying would be tricky.

The leader staggered; his mouth opened in an 'O' before he pitched forward and tumbled off the roof, Meri's vest still gripped in his hands.

She chopped at his wrists until he released her then spread her wings as much as she could. She began flapping to slow her descent, the male falling away.

She slowed, hovering for a second just a few feet above the mess the human had made on the sidewalk. Ignoring the screams, she struggled to rise to the roof and land.

The two remaining men dropped their pipes and ran.

As soon as they disappeared, Meri collapsed in a heap, not far from fainting.

Grate looked in the direction of the roof access, glanced at Meri, then took off after the men.

Meri sighed and closed her eyes. She didn't blame Grate for running; she hadn't planned on her human friend seeing her like this. Being battered and bruised wasn't unknown to her. She just needed time to rest and then she would go.

She drifted for a moment, trying to push away the pain long enough to actually sleep, when she felt drops on her face. Rain.

Darn it. I'm too tired to move out of it.

A sniff sounded above her and Meri opened her eyes.

Tears dripped off Grate's face and onto Meri. "Damn it, Batshit, don't you die on me."

She lifted the damaged coat she'd taken from one of the dead men and covered Meri with it.

"I thought you ran away."

"Yeah, I did. But who else is gonna put up with your goopy, warrior ass?" She swiped at the tears and sniffed again. "So I locked the door and came back."

Meri closed her eyes. "Good."

"Just shut it and sleep. I'll watch over you."

Meri nodded.

"And, when you're awake, we're gonna have a serious talk about how the hell you did that."

Meri wanted to smile at the demanding human, but darkness slid through her and carried her away.

60

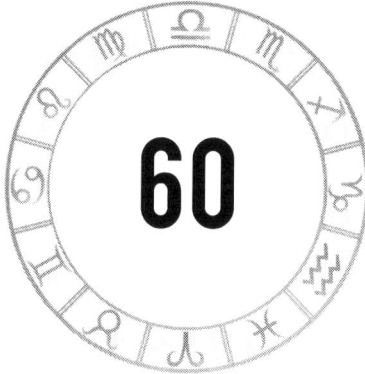

ERI JERKED INTO A sitting position and sniffed. Then the pain washed through her and slapped her back down.

Grate stood a couple of feet away, a long piece of metal in her hand, poking Meri. "Whoa there, girl. Not so fast. You should see your face. Can't imagine how bad your back and shoulder must be."

"You can't touch my skin," Meri said, flinching away from Grate.

The human raised the metal rod then threw it away. "Oh, I got that real quick." She looked over her shoulder and kneeled. "Look, I'm sorry to wake you so soon but folks are pounding on the door to get up here. I'm afraid the cops are gonna send helicopters." She glanced at the buildings surrounding them. "Got a lot of peepers, too."

Meri checked around her. Humans were standing at windows staring at her.

"Can you do that cool, ninja parkour yet? 'Cause we need to scoot."

Meri rolled her shoulders, pushing the jacket off. The pain was still there but the numbness had receded. Her wings flipped out and stretched—not good as new, but serviceable.

"I can run and jump," she said.

Grate jumped up. "Good, let's go."

Meri rose much more slowly than her friend, but she was pleased that her vision didn't swim and her legs didn't buckle. The rest—despite being short—had helped.

The girls trotted to the closest roof edge and studied the distance between buildings.

"Damn. I can't make that," Grate said under her breath.

Meri grabbed the edge of Grate's hood and flipped it up over the human's head.

"Hey!"

"Just stand still, okay?" Meri said, trotting backward. "And don't touch my skin."

She pushed off with her right foot and charged Grate.

The girl's mouth dropped open. "No, no, no—"

She turned her back to Meri and hunched her shoulders. Meri slipped her arms under Grate's and jumped off the roof.

"Shiiiittt!!!" Grate screamed as they fell several stories.

Meri flapped her wings, straining to support both their weights, until the soreness in her body eased and she could take deeper and deeper strokes. They glided past the lower building then began to rise above the city.

"Put me down!"

"We're doing fine," Meri yelled back.

"I think I've shit myself."

"I don't smell any fecal matter," Meri said after a deep sniff.

"You are certifiable!"

Meri laughed. The sweeter air above the city was bracing and she took several long pulls of it. Flying was her greatest joy, second only to being hugged by Taryn. She glided on the thermal, Grate so quiet it almost felt like she was alone.

She was looking for a landing spot, taking one more deep breath, when a memory exploded in her brain. *Taryn.* She drew another breath then glided due east and filled her lungs. The memories of Taryn flooded her. She'd caught her scent again.

"Hey. Put me down."

"No. I have caught the scent of my friend and I have to follow it."

"I didn't agree to that."

"I know, Grate, but my friend was taken against her will and I need your help. These past hours have taught me that." Meri paused. "Will you help me?"

Grate grunted, long and low.

Meri smiled. "Good. Let's go."

She tightened her arms and flapped her wings in earnest until they rocketed east. Within minutes, they were flying over streets filled with large houses and big trees heavy with buds.

"Is this where she is?" Grate yelled. "Freakin' fancy, rich place to be a hostage."

The scent narrowed then dropped precipitously into a white house with a large yard. Meri tilted her body so she could soar above it, confirming that this was the place where Taryn was being held.

The street was quiet—none of the metal boxes moved down the gray-colored streets—but Meri wasn't sure where to land.

"Hey, Batshit, there's a For Sale sign on that house over there so it's probably empty. Land in the backyard and maybe no one will see us."

Meri arched her back and turned in a tight spiral until they were a few feet off the ground. She pulled up hard, her body screaming in protest, and hovered long enough to land on her feet.

Grate grunted when she landed and rolled. She popped up and practically ran backward, her eyes angry and scared at the same time.

She shook a finger at Meri. "You do that again without asking first and I'm gonna kick your ass. I don't know how I'll do it but I'll find a way."

Meri nodded. "Okay."

"Okay, you'll let me kick your ass?"

"No, okay, I'll ask first."

Grate *humphed* and straightened her clothes with a jerk. "See that you do."

She strode toward the front of the house.

"Don't we need to hide?" Meri said.

"No sense trying to skulk among the houses. In this fancy-pants neighborhood, we already stand out. Trying to hide will get the cops called on us." She turned to face Meri and walked backward. "That's if your flying wasn't seen already."

Meri trotted after her, the strong scent of Taryn filling her nose. Her chest puffed out with pride. *I found my friend!*

The sun bounced off the houses and road and trees. The crisp, clean air was so much sweeter than it had been in the city, but nothing could be as delicious as the smell of the woods outside the InBetween.

A dog chuffed softly from behind a window. Birds chittered in the trees.

Two houses down, Meri stopped cold and turned to the large, white house. The windows were so clean the sunlight reflecting off them blinded her. She couldn't see through them but she sure as hell could feel Taryn as if she were standing next to her.

"She's in there."

Grate whistled loud and long. "We could walk right up to it, but I think there's a better way that might make us less obvious."

"What?"

Grate turned around and walked back the way they came.

"Wait. Taryn is in here."

"Sshh," Grate said, one finger pressed to her lips. "Trust me."

Meri sighed and followed her new friend back to the For Sale house.

"We go through the yards until we're on the street behind this one. Then we come at the house through another backyard. That way they don't see us coming. But we gotta stay low and quiet." She pointed to the shirt tied around Meri's waist. "Might want to cover up those wings, too."

Meri pulled the shirt on and let Grate lead them until they reached the next street.

She grinned at Grate. "You are very smart."

The girl snorted. "You brawn, me brains."

"I don't know what that means."

Grate shook her head. "Like I said…"

They found the house that backed up to the one Taryn was in but it was fenced and a dog was on the other side staring at them. Grate chewed on a thumbnail for a second before walking over to the fence of the next house.

She pulled her body up and looked over. "Come on. No dog."

Meri helped Grate reach the top and watched her disappear, then scrambled up and dropped over herself. Flying would have been so much easier but Grate would have fussed. She landed hard, her body protesting. She'd need to eat and rest again soon if she stood a chance of making it back to Libra.

The girls ran to the corner of the back fence and peeked over. All they had to do was get to the top and jump the corner where the four fences met without alerting the dog.

Grate raised a foot and Meri heaved her to the top. The human balanced for a moment then jumped out and over. Simple.

Meri pulled her body up until her belly rested on the points of the fence. She pushed up and kicked her legs. The dog growled once then leaped up and snapped at her arms. She tried to scoot but she was stuck—she needed to swing a leg over to get the leverage to scramble after Grate, but the dog was jumping so high it was a miracle he hadn't bitten her yet.

"Touch him, like you did that bastard."

"No, I won't kill an innocent animal."

"He's trying to pull you down. Not so innocent in my book."

"He's protecting his home, as I would do."

"And making a lot of racket doing it!"

Meri knew Grate was right but she couldn't bring herself to kill the dog.

She looked at him, bared her teeth, and hissed, "Quiet!"

The dog dropped to all fours, his head cocked, his tongue lolling.

"Buster! Stop it!" a voice called out from the house.

Buster looked back at his house, glanced at Meri one more time, then took off.

Relieved to have the opportunity, she kicked her legs, and though it wasn't pretty, she cleared the fence and landed on her back in a shrub.

Grate sighed. "It'll be a miracle if we don't have a whole bunch of cops on us in a lick."

Meri nodded once. "Then we better see where Taryn is and hide."

61

THE PAIR BENT AT the waist and ran along the fence, past a small house next to a body of clean, clear water, until they reached the corner where the fence abutted the side of the house. Meri caught the scent of the bird that had carried Taryn away but couldn't see it.

They collapsed against the white brick, a dirty basement window between them, and waited to see if they heard sirens or yelling, but the neighborhood remained quiet.

"You are the luckiest, Batshit. Did you see that pool house? Looks like a mansion compared to where I've been living."

The sun burst through the branches and lit up the girls. Meri cast off her shirt and held out her bare arms, reveling in the heat warming her skin even as the crisp air struggled to keep her cold. After so many years in the InBetween, she couldn't get enough. She opened her eyes and glanced at the bumps coating her limbs then did a double take.

The normal green-brown cast to her skin had changed. Patches of pink had poked through the pestilence and seemed to be fighting for space with each passing second. She leaned forward and spread her wings to look at the membranes.

"Damn," Grate said. "I'd have thought your wings would be shredded after the fight and flight but they look—"

"Like they're healing."

Grate squinted her eyes as she scanned them. "Yeah, looks like the holes are filling in. That's a good thing, right? You're acting like it's not."

Meri looked up, surprised by her observation. "That's because I've never seen them anything but holey." She held up her arms. "My skin, too. It's…pink in spots."

"We need to converse after we find this friend."

Meri flashed a smile and squatted down. She was reaching for the basement window to clean it off and look through when a sharp, hot zing of energy repelled her arm so hard it whipped her torso around and she slammed face first into the fence. The pain ripped through her and her arm went numb.

"Whoa, what happened? Your arm okay?"

Meri panted through the pain as she tried to turn around. "I wrenched it."

"Is it out of the socket?"

Meri wiggled her fingers; at least they worked. She lifted her hand then slowly brought her arm back to a normal position. "I think it's okay."

"What was that? Some invisible force field?"

"Is that normal in this world?"

Grate shut her eyes and rubbed her temples. "Okay, this is me going with it. Uh, no, that's not normal."

Meri gingerly slid down to her belly and looked inside the recessed well surrounding the window.

Grate mimicked her movement. "It's awfully clean for a window well." She scooted deeper into the well until her upper body was hanging over the edge. She swiped at the sides. "Huh." She wiped away the leaves and dirt. "There's some kind of mark carved in the concrete. Nope, scratch that; there's three squiggly marks here." She lifted her head. "Can you see them?"

Meri inched to the very edge until she could see the marks Grate was talking about. "Sigils."

"What are sigils?"

"They're marks that can keep someone like me out of the house." She pointed to the next window well. "Are there sigils in that one?"

Grate leaned into the well and cleaned the sides again. "Yep." She rose to her hands and knees. "Let me do a check. You stay here."

She crawled around the corner of the house. Several minutes passed before she returned.

"They got a lotta of window wells and all of them are marked."

Meri climbed to her feet and reached for the above ground window.

"Are you nuts?"

"I'll go slower this time." She reached out with the flat of her palm and eased it close to the window until she felt the tingle of energy on her skin. She stepped back. "This is bad."

"Why?"

"The house has been warded to keep out paranorms, probably all paranorms, based on the strength of the energy." She plopped on the grass. "I can't go inside, which means Libra won't be able to go inside. We can't save Taryn."

Grate looked away. "You're a strange girl, but you are my friend. You saved my life."

"You saved mine, too."

"Yeah."

They sat in silence for a few moments before Grate piped up again. "I'll go in."

Meri's gut dropped. "No. No way. Whoever stole her is a paranorm; they'll kill you."

"Then what are we going to do?"

We.

Meri's throat closed; tears welled in her eyes. Weeks ago, she'd had no friends, had never experienced the touch of another person outside of her own kind, and touch between Pestilence Fairies was rare. Then Taryn had touched her by mistake and lived. That had been joy and surprise wrapped up in shock. But then Taryn had hugged her. Not by accident but intentionally. She had reached out her arms, wrapped them around Meri, and held her. Taryn had still gotten sick, but she had recovered again, and faster that time.

After that, Meri couldn't stay away from Taryn, no matter how hard her mother beat her for it. And now, she had a new friend. A human she couldn't touch but who nonetheless had accepted her, a paranorm, in an instant. Her heart was full to bursting.

Meri tugged on the shirt Libra had given her. "I have this to help me find Libra again so I can bring him here."

"Can you take me with you?"

"If I had days and days, yes. But I can't take that long. I'm much faster alone."

Grate's face fell. "I have nowhere to go. I don't know this part of town at all."

"What about that house where no one is living?"

"The For Sale house."

"Is it not empty?"

Grate grinned. "I do believe it is."

"Then come. Let's hop these fences again and go see."

In minutes, they had reached the back of the For Sale house. Grate checked the doors and windows but none were open. She studied the manicured lawn and the shed that matched the house before walking to a flowerpot bursting with freshly planted flowers and grasses. She tilted the pot and looked under it.

Finding nothing, she dug her fingers in the soil until her face lit up. "Predictable." She withdrew a small tube, unscrewed one end, and removed a key. "The house is empty so with any luck their alarm won't be activated." She unlocked the back door and pushed it open. She held up a hand when Meri started to walk inside. "Give it a minute. If the alarm goes off, we run."

Several seconds went by with nothing happening.

Grate walked into the house, Meri behind her, and looked around until she found a white box on the wall. "There's no light, which probably means there's no silent alarm either. But be ready to fly us out of here if any cars pull up."

The girls explored the house for a few minutes until they reached the basement. It was mostly empty, save for a few old pieces of furniture, including a couch that had seen better days. There were some old blankets draped over it.

Grate sat and bounced. "This'll do."

"What about food?"

"I'll figure something out. I always do."

Meri sat on the other end. "Are you sure? I can fly you back to your roof."

"Nope. After what happened, you and me need to stay far away from there." She looked away, her young face pinched into a frown. "I've no real home anyway. After what we've been through, you're more family than those horrors that made me."

"Family. I like that."

Grate flashed her a smile and winked. "Sisters."

Meri nodded. "Sisters."

Grate cleared her throat and looked away. "You better go then; find this Libra and bring him here. I'll keep an eye on the house and see if they've got a routine while I wait for you. Good?"

"Not good…great."

Grate ushered her toward the basement stairs. "Well, go on then. No sense in dragging this out."

Meri walked away but stopped at the top. "Thank you, sister. I'll be back."

62

TARYN ROCKED BACK AND forth knocking rats off her body. Her wrists and ankles burned and bled from her hours-long struggle but her mind was too panicked to stop fighting. The fresh blood had drawn the rodents to her like flies to honey and nothing she'd done had stopped their assault.

She heard a new sound—a tap on a window—and she winced, her gut bottoming out. "What fresh hell is this?"

Tiny, clawed feet scrambled over her. A second tap sounded from another window. Taryn jerked her head to look. The rats screamed and fled.

Then, silence. Not a single tap.

Taryn stopped breathing, waiting for something—please let it be a rescue—but the silence held, tenacious and bleak. She sagged back into the mattress. Her eyes welled with tears that didn't fall—dehydration had taken its due and more. She took a deep breath and willed the dizziness away.

She wanted to stay brave but her courage was waning; the night terrors from her childhood were creeping closer, their hunger for her soul, for her sanity, unabated after all these years. The darkness had shattered her defenses, had torn down the walls she'd built up for so long in just a couple of days.

The only good thing about the dark was that she couldn't see the battered Bathory child duct-taped to the pole—the life that Taryn had taken, not with her own hand, but with her arrogance and disregard. She'd prided herself on living by her gut, jumping off the cliffs she faced, but the cost had always been hers to bear. Now, in this new, violent world, her bravado had grave consequences for other people and she found she couldn't bear it.

She settled into her grief and drifted, her heart so heavy it pressed her down, her breathing so shallow she had to remind herself to fill her lungs fully.

She had almost fallen into oblivion when she heard a faint squeal, similar to nails on a chalkboard but at a higher pitch. She turned her head to the left, trying to find the source of the sound. Soft, blue light filtered into the basement, growing brighter with each passing second—a streetlight, maybe? She lifted her head and blinked. Something or someone was moving just beyond the glass. Her heart skipped, stopped, then pounded.

A soft breath of fresh air passed over her. The window was open. She wanted to call out but she was afraid to wake the house. Her adrenaline spiked; her hope warred with her fear. She had no idea if whoever was coming was friend or foe, but surely she was due some good luck.

A foot appeared, then another, followed by long, skinny legs—a child's legs. Hips, waist, chest, and arms came into view before a girl dropped to the ground and crouched there. When she stood, the light hit her beautiful, fierce face and her head of springy, black curls. The little ninja with a model's features should have been with her family, but instead she was here.

To break me out of Hell?

"Holy mother. Who are you?"

"Quiet." The girl strode to the bed. "You Taryn?"

"Yes."

The girl cut Taryn's ropes. "Wow. You stink."

Taryn wanted to snap some pithy, derisive comment back, but she was beyond caring about insults. Being stinky wasn't even close to being important.

"Taryn," a male voice hissed from outside the open window.

Her mind had to be playing tricks.

"Taryn, it's me."

"Libra?"

"Who d'you think?"

"Not you."

"I'm overwhelmed by your vote of confidence. But I'll admit, I wouldn't have found you if it weren't for Meri. And Grate."

"You better say my name," the whip-thin girl groused.

Taryn rolled up and the girl named Grate pulled on her arms until she could stand. She wrapped Taryn's arm around her shoulders and practically dragged her to the window.

Taryn balked at the sight of the Bathory girl. "Cut her loose."

"She looks dead, lady. Let's go."

"Libra, throw me a dagger."

"We don't have time for her."

"Libra, just do it."

He growled but a blade arced through the window and landed at her feet.

She picked it up and cut the tape to free the Bathory. The girl sagged to the floor.

Taryn tucked the dagger in her belt and pressed her fingers to the girl's throat until she found a faint but steady pulse. "She's still alive."

"For goddess' sake, she's dead weight. Besides, she's a Bathory. What part of that doesn't spell trouble?"

"We can't leave her here. At least let's get her free of the basement so she can make her own choice to stay or go." Without waiting for permission, Taryn grabbed Grate's arm. "Help me drag her to the window."

"Taryn, listen to me," Libra said. "The windows and doors are warded. Even if you two could lift her up, I can't reach down to pull her out. And that's if the wards don't block her from getting out anyway."

"I'm a paranorm; what makes you think I can get out?"

"You probably can't; that's why I'm going to blow a hole in the wall. Once I do it, everyone in the house will come running. There's only going be enough time to get one of you out. You have to choose."

"I won't," Taryn replied. "This girl tried to show me kindness when she had no reason to and she was beaten because of it. I will not leave her."

"You're impossible."

"You two wanna finish this outside when I'm not stuck in hostile territory?" Grate snapped.

"At least gag the Bathory and get her to one side. We have to make this quick," Libra hissed.

Taryn wrapped tape around the Bathory's mouth, but before she finished, the girl woke up and kicked out.

"Stop fighting," Taryn ordered but the girl wiggled and thrashed. "You want to stay here and explain how I escaped while you were free?"

The girl's eyes widened and she stopped.

Grate pushed the Bathory to one side of the basement window. "Get up and cooperate or I'll leave your ass here, you got that?"

"Be ready to jump out as soon as the hole opens," Libra said.

Before Taryn had a chance to reply, a blue light flashed and the concrete blocks burst open with a *boom*. Dust flew, blinding them for a moment, but Taryn pulled the Bathory along the wall until she found the opening with her hands. She guided the girl to the hole and heaved her up until someone took the weight and lifted her away.

She reached for Grate and pushed her. "Go."

The girl didn't need convincing. She was out as fast as the Bathory.

Shouts rang out; footsteps pounded on the floor overhead. They would be in the basement in seconds.

"Taryn!"

Libra's hands appeared through the hole and she reached for them. In one motion, he lifted her up and pulled her out into the cold, sweet, night air.

She fell onto him, the momentum sending them both backward into the grass, her body covering his legs, her head in his lap. She rose to her hands and knees, still straddling him, and grinned.

"Taryn," Libra whispered. He took her face between his hands.

"Oh, no you don't. You're not cuing the romantic, kissy-face music when I haven't had a bath or brushed my teeth in days. *I* wouldn't even kiss me."

362

"You smell like honey?" he countered.

"Nice try, you perv, but there's no time to kiss," Grate said. Her eyes widened when the basement light came on and the shouting Bathory Berserker women flooded into the space. "We gotta go."

The Bathory girl stiffened. Her head came up, her eyes opened, and she screamed through her gag.

"Shut her up," Libra said. "The Bathory know we're here but we don't need to wake up the entire human population."

Taryn and Grate reached for the girl.

The girl ripped the duct tape from her mouth, pulling a chunk of hair out of her scalp with it. She keened, her teeth gnashing and snapping at Grate's hands. Taryn touched her and the girl whipped out a backhand and raked nails across Taryn's chest.

Taryn recoiled—fresh blood flowed down her breast. "How can you possibly have this much energy?"

Dogs barked down the street. A haunting scream rang out from the pool house.

Taryn ran to the corner of the house. "Libra, the bird is in there—the one we saved. Release it."

"Are you kidding me? The Stryx brought you here, and you want to help it?"

"It's as much a victim of all this as we are. Free it, please."

He grunted his disapproval but joined her, raised a hand, and blasted the entire front wall off the frame.

"I see we need to do more practicing," Taryn commented.

"Let's survive your rescue first then I'll be happy to practice all day…and night."

The bird hopped out and looked around the yard before locking eyes on Taryn and Libra. It studied their faces then jumped high in the air and flew away.

Libra and Taryn ran back to Grate.

The Bathory wailed and lunged for Taryn, her fingers curled into talons.

Meri swooped down from the sky, kicked the Bathory's hands away, then grabbed the front of her clothes and held her off the ground. "Do you know what I am?"

The girl nodded.

"You make one more peep, you touch any one of us again, and I'll kill you."

The Bathory girl stilled.

Meri put her down. "Let's go."

"Meri!" Taryn cried. "What are you doing here?"

The fairy grinned at her. "I found you, Taryn."

A dagger flew out of the hole in the basement wall, only just falling short of hitting Libra.

"Damn it, let's go," he said. "We may not be so lucky next time."

* * *

Libra lifted Grate to the top of the wooden fence. As soon as she dropped to the other side, he hoisted Taryn up. He turned to Meri and the Bathory.

"No, I got this," Meri said.

Libra leaped to the top and swung his legs over. "Make it quick."

Meri waited for him to leave before grabbing the girl's clothes again. "We're taking a little flight."

"No, wait. I can't go with you; I'll be hunted for the rest of my life."

"These people are good. You can have a place with them if you want."

"My mother would hunt me down. There would be no rest, no chance to have a life. And anyone I cared about would be a target."

"What are you saying?"

The Bathory girl rolled her shoulders back and raised her chin. "Kill me."

"Oh, I want to after you hurt my friend, but no."

"Then hit me hard, the more blood the better. At least then I will have some honor in their eyes."

Shouts reverberated across the garden; the Bathory were emerging from the basement.

"You have to do it now. They'll be here in seconds," the girl hissed.

Meri saw the pain and fear in the girl's eyes. She knew it well and could understand the need to hide the failure. Goddess knew she'd hidden many such a failure from her mother. She picked up two pieces of concrete and, without warning, walloped one side of the girl's face. Before the girl fell, Meri slammed the second piece into the opposite temple, felling her with the blow.

Hands reached out of the darkness and grabbed the unconscious girl's feet, dragging her inch-by-inch back toward the house.

Meri unfurled her wings and flew over the fence with one flap. She landed in time to see a Bathory Berserker coming from the other direction—a group of them must have come around the other way. The Bathory reared back one arm, her body turned in Libra's direction. The Innocent Demonica warriors raced to protect the Prime strapped to Libra's back.

Without a thought, Meri jetted across the grass and shoved him off his feet. He landed on his hands and knees.

Safe.

She dropped to the ground, the dagger hilt sticking out of her chest.

63

TARYN RAN TO MERI and pulled her into her lap.

"Taryn, no!" Libra hollered.

Taryn yanked the dagger out of Meri and pressed her hands front and back, blood coating them. "It's not bad, baby, come on."

"Drop the girl and come back to the house, or I'll finish off the rest of your friends," the Bathory leader shouted.

Meri's blood tingled where it touched Taryn but she didn't feel a fever coming on, only fear for the girl and rage that the woman would threaten the rest of them. She eased Meri to the grass and stood, her hands still coated in red.

She bared her teeth. "I'll come to you."

"No!" Libra shouted.

He tried to rise, but the Innocent Demonica warriors pushed him down and formed a circle, blocking the Bathory Berserker warriors from getting closer to him, their blades drawn.

Taryn had taken one step when she heard a soft cry. She glanced back at Libra. The Keres bellowed.

Taryn's head exploded with pain. She staggered forward, her focus on the leader while everyone else around her clapped their hands to their ears and fell to their knees.

The Bathory leader raised another dagger and brandished it, trying to fend off Taryn's advance, but Taryn kicked it away and grabbed the woman's face, smearing fairy blood on her bare skin. "That's for Meri."

The woman reared back and screamed as the pestilence raced through her body.

The Keres stopped screaming, leaving only the agonal grunts and gurgles coming from the dying Bathory to punctuate the night.

The other Beserkers stayed on the ground.

Taryn reeled away from the leader and fell to her knees next to Meri. "Come on, baby, stay with me."

She pulled on Meri's arms.

Meri opened her eyes. "Leave me."

Taryn looked up at Libra. "Car?"

"On the street. Come on."

Taryn hoisted the fairy into her arms and they made their way to the road.

A Demonica ran into the street and waved his hands. In seconds, a huge bus with heavily tinted windows pulled up to the curb.

A woman jumped out and ran around to Grate. "Get in!"

The girl ran to the bus. She looked back at Meri but Libra pointed at the bus.

She climbed in but turned so she could watch. "Don't you leave her here. Don't you do it."

Sirens cried in the distance. The neighborhood lights came on and people opened their front doors to see what was happening.

Taryn placed Meri on the front lawn and looked at her hands; the pestilence that had knocked her back hard before had barely affected her this time. She was hot—there was fever—but her skin was barely bruised. She didn't know why she was so unaffected by the pestilence, but maybe…

She raised her wrist and bit down hard. Blood welled in her mouth but it wasn't enough. She bit down harder—groaning through the pain—and this time the blood flowed at a slow but steady pace. They needed to run but only Taryn could touch her and survive, and Meri was fading fast. There was only one chance and she had to take it.

"Keep the cops away, just for a minute," she called out to Libra.

Flashing red and blue lit up the street from both ends; they were close to converging on the house. Libra slipped out of the double sling, set the babies inside the bus, then re-emerged with the Keres' back pressed against his chest. He whispered in her ear and she kicked her legs and pumped her hands. A tiny whimper started and Libra trotted past the bus to face the approaching police cars.

Taryn raised her wrist over the dagger wound in Meri's chest and squeezed her closed fist to encourage the blood to flow. The drops fell into the open flesh.

"Please let this work."

She'd been waiting for what seemed like forever when Meri stirred. Taryn gasped; the wound was closing.

Libra shouted and the Keres cried. The screech of tires and the crunch of metal echoed to Taryn's left.

Meri sat up and rubbed her eyes like the child Taryn sometimes forgot she was. "I feel better."

"Can you move?"

Meri held out her arms.

Taryn got to her feet and pulled Meri up. They staggered to the bus and Meri worked her way to the very back.

"Grate, take shotgun. I can't risk touching you with Meri's blood all over me."

The human girl pushed past the Innocent Demonica standing in a tight ring around the Prime. She climbed into the front, honking the horn to get Libra's attention.

Libra turned around to face the police cars coming from the opposite direction. The Keres bellowed and the cars swerved, crashing into light poles and each other. Police officers climbed out and fell to their knees, clutching their heads.

Libra climbed into the driver's seat and slammed the door. He looked at the Keres then Grate. "You good with kids?"

Grate reached for the infant girl. "Guess we'll find out. Gotta say, though, having a baby in the front isn't a good idea."

"Hang on, everyone." Libra put the bus in gear and gunned it away from the curb. "We'll have to take that chance, at least for a little while."

They raced past the police pileup and through the dark streets until they were miles from the scene.

Libra slowed to the speed limit. "Everyone still with us?"

The joy of freedom, of surviving the Bathory and escaping them, sent Taryn into uncontrollable giggles. Tears rolled down her cheeks, from laughter and relief and the release of the nightmare of the past few days, mingled with the joy of seeing Libra and Meri. She laughed until she couldn't breathe; only then did she shudder to a stop.

"Taryn?" he asked.

She held up a hand and shook her head. "I'm fine. Give me a minute. I'm just so damn glad to see you." She sat on a settee behind the driver's seat and touched Libra's clothed shoulder, careful to avoid the skin of his neck or face. "Thank you."

"What?" he growled. "You thought I'd leave you there? That I wouldn't move heaven and earth to get you back?"

He glanced in the rearview mirror and she saw a flash of heat and rage and frustration in his eyes.

"I—" she sputtered, taken aback at his anger.

"We were terrified that we'd lost you forever. If it hadn't been for Meri…" His jaw clenched and he looked back at the road, his knuckles white from his hand's tight grip on the steering wheel. "I don't know whether to be relieved that you're alive and safe, or furious that you nearly got yourself killed."

"How about relieved?"

He said nothing for a long minute. "I can't take that again. Promise me you'll be more careful."

Grate glanced back at her. "Yeah, you really should. I thought he was gonna bust something over you and I've only known him a couple hours."

Before Taryn could reply, a loud thump hit the roof.

"Son of a bitch," Libra yelled.

Taryn looked to her left. Two Pestilence Fairy women were standing on the side of the road. One pointed at Taryn and elbowed the other. They jumped into the air and disappeared.

"Pestilence Fairies!" she said.

"Meri's people?" Grate asked as she craned her neck to look at the sky.

Two more thumps hit the roof in rapid succession. A blade plunged through the roof and passed millimeters from Libra's nose. It disappeared then stabbed through the thin metal again, this time burying itself in the top of the headrest behind Libra.

"Son of a bitch." He slammed on the brakes.

The fairies tumbled down the windshield and off the hood.

"Holy shit!" Grate yelled.

"My kin," Meri said from the back. "I recommend you go now, Libra, before they get up."

"But I'll run them over."

"Now," Meri said.

Taryn slapped the back of his seat. "Go! Go! Go!"

He gunned it.

The bus bounced just once. Taryn looked back. Only one fairy was on the ground, holding her lower leg; the rest had rolled out of the way.

More bodies landed hard on the roof, denting the metal.

"Holy crap," Grate yelled.

"We have to work on your language," Libra growled as he gunned the engine and swerved across several lanes, cutting off cars.

He slammed on the brakes. Tires squealed and smoked; horns blared.

Fairies fell to the tarmac.

A long, dull blade jammed through the metal roof and stabbed Libra in the shoulder. He cursed, hit the accelerator, and swerved, bouncing off a car on the right and back into his lane. The blade retracted. Libra grabbed his shoulder and leaned over the steering wheel; the bus drifted to the left.

Taryn pounded on his headrest. "Hey, stay awake."

Libra righted the bus but his head lolled.

Meri ran up from the back and grabbed Taryn's arm. "The sword—it was coated with pestilence."

Taryn leaned close to Libra and saw the sweat on his face, the black and blue and green creeping up his neck. "Crap."

She ripped at the slit in his clothes until she could see the wound. It looked like the blade had sliced cleanly through the muscle, but the bleeding was heavy, and the flesh was dark and mottled.

The blade stabbed down again, just touching Taryn's hair.

Grate grabbed the wheel. "Slam on the brakes; get the bitch off!"

Before Libra could respond, a loud screech sounded behind the bus. Huge claws scraped the length of the metal roof, ripping the thin sheet.

"The Stryx," Taryn yelled.

The bird pushed the fairies off the bus, sending them tumbling down onto the road.

Meri and Grate cheered.

Libra sagged against the door and the bus began to slow. He was succumbing to the pestilence.

Taryn had given Meri her blood because she'd suspected it would heal her, but what might it do to Libra? They had no choice. She bit her wrist again, flinching through the pain, until the blood flowed. She spread the edges of his wound and let her blood fill it, her breath caught in her throat as the seconds passed.

Libra inhaled sharply and sat up. The sweat still ran down his face but the color of his skin evened.

He glanced at the wound and turned pale again. "What the hell is in your blood?"

Taryn fell back against the seat and heaved a sigh. "I have no idea; I'm just glad it worked."

Cars honked as they sped around the bus. Libra hit the gas and they roared down the road.

Taryn looked past Meri and out the back window. In the distance, red and blue police lights flared, illuminating the night. The police cars screeched to a halt next to the fairies. Meri's mother landed by an injured fairy and picked her up. She stared at the bus then jumped into the night sky and flew away.

"That's one helluva way to announce your existence," Libra grumbled.

"Where are we going?" Taryn said. She scanned the occupants of the bus, noticed Ailith, and flashed a scowl. "And what's this bitch doing here? I thought she was locked up in the dungeon."

"We're going to Texas. Ailith is a long story."

"Where are we now?"

"Outside Washington, D.C."

"Are you mental? That's at least a couple days away. Why not go to the Great Cavern instead?"

Libra looked at her in the rearview mirror. "The Great Cavern has been attacked by Corvus Ward warriors."

"What? Abella, Persephone…the children?"

Ailith propped her feet on a settee and examined her nails. "They got out before the attack."

"And the children we saved?" Taryn asked.

"See the bus coming up behind us?"

Taryn glanced back and saw another bus just like the one she was riding in. "They're in there?"

Libra nodded. "Yep, our numbers have easily doubled since you were taken. We need a large place to house them until we can get them back to their people. Isn't the house Abella was building finished now?"

"Yes—it should be."

"The house looked huge on the plans; there should be enough room. When you're all secured, I have to get to the Great Cavern."

"You're not going without me."

He glanced in the mirror and caught her eye. "Over the cliff, right?"

"If we make it through this, I'm thinking a little restraint might be in my future."

"Don't go soft on me now, love."

She desperately wanted to climb over the seat, curl up in his lap and show him just how much she was his love.

Instead, she closed her eyes. "Not soft, never soft."

The heavy fatigue of the fading adrenaline pushed her down. She needed to tell Libra about the vision Asmodeus had shown her. Needed to tell him what the demon king had planned for her. She draped her legs across the settee and sagged. The traffic and the city lights flew by, hypnotizing her as the weight of the past few days pulled her under.

Tomorrow. I'll tell him then.

64

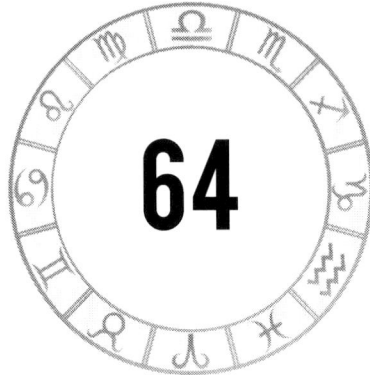

ABELLA STOOD ON A hill overlooking the house and the creek rushing north to south across the property. The night sky had exploded with light; the stars were brilliant and cold, the black of space in between as empty of sound and life as the Texas desert. The slightest creatures had kept away, and even the wind had fled—as had her hope.

She breathed in deep the crisp, clean air then exhaled through her mouth. They couldn't stay here without the Zodiacs. Two women with a bunch of children; despite her planning, the odds weren't in their favor. Even the night seemed to be holding its breath; inertia was a course of inaction they couldn't afford.

She was turning to go when she heard the alarmed yip of a coyote in the distance. Her heart thudded in her chest, but she forced herself to move slowly. She opened her duffle bag, removed the night vision goggles, and trained them south of the house.

Movement.

She dropped to one knee to reduce her profile and pivoted in a circle. "Shit me."

Corvus Ward warriors had ringed the house; their distinctive scalp feathers snapped high on their heads as they stalked forward. They would be at her outer defenses in a couple minutes. She secured the goggles on her head and palmed a remote control labeled with a capital 'A', waiting for the first men in the circle to reach the target area.

They stopped walking. A single male stepped ahead of the line then dropped to the ground. He leaned down until his nose was an inch from the desert floor.

Of course, she wouldn't have done something so obvious as bury explosive charges. That might be what the warriors were looking for, but they had no idea what could be procured in the human world if you had enough money and the right connections.

"Thank you and your horrendous poker face, General Gage," Abella said under her breath.

The warriors advanced.

"Come on, come on. A little closer."

The first line of men crossed the boundary.

She waited.

The second row crossed.

Still, she waited.

The third group crossed.

"Try this, you sons of bitches."

She pressed the remote. Several soft thumping sounds broke the silence.

The men froze and looked around.

"Try looking up," she hissed, her adrenaline spiked almost as high as her blood lust.

She really needed to run to the house, to start the evacuation, but she also needed to see the men die. These men who dared threaten her sister and brother-in-law, who dared terrify the children she had come to love with a ferocity that surprised her.

Multiple lights appeared over the surrounding hills. Their flight path was short—the end result devastating.

She threw the remote in the duffle, zipped it closed, and slung it over one shoulder as she watched the small drone rockets arc over the desert in silence. The warriors finally looked up. They hesitated, unsure what they were seeing, until finally some began to break ranks. But it was too late. The rockets pummeled the earth, the explosions far greater than should have been possible given their small size.

Concussion killed dozens of men in the initial blast, liquefying their brains, dropping them instantly, while dozens more were incinerated by the fireball created by the rocket and the accelerant-rich ring she had created by burying tanks of pure oxygen. When the rockets fired, the oxygen was released around the men. Add in the great fortune of a lack of wind, and it made for a great barbeque.

The screams reached her. She jumped off the small mesa and ran for the house, hoping that Persephone hadn't frozen when the rockets exploded. They needed time to get the children hidden from the warriors.

Abella raced inside the dark house and nearly ran over her sister. "What are you doing? Get the children."

Persephone blinked once than whirled around and ran to the back of the house, her nightgown whipping behind her.

The two women worked in the darkness, waking the children, telling them to dress but remain silent. The older children helped the youngest while Persephone soothed the frightened babies.

They had prepared the group to move when Abella heard a beeping in her jacket pocket. She removed a second remote and ran to the closest window. Despite their losses, the remaining warriors had charged forward.

"Get them to the tunnel," she said.

Persephone nodded then herded the children out of the room, heading for the basement.

Abella waited for them to leave then turned her attention back to the men. The remote had two buttons. She pressed the top button and heard the whirring of hydraulics above her head. When the motion came to a stop with a *thump*, she placed a hand on the windowpane, the cold glass a balm for the heat of her rage. Men and their politics; she would bring them down. And if one drop of her family's blood was spilled—she would destroy them all.

She pressed the second button and watched as the first wave of poison-tipped bolts shot out. Warriors fell to the ground, writhing as the poison made quick work of them.

Thirty seconds later a second round of bolts fired.

More warriors fell to the ground.

A third round fired.

Abella dropped the remote and ran to the basement. The last of the children had entered the tunnel of one of the panic rooms but Persephone stood by the door, a frown on her face.

"Get in," Abella ordered.

"Candace. She's not here. Neither are Finn and Blair."

"The dogs are probably protecting her." Abella tried to push Persephone in. "Go with the children. I'll find her."

"I can find her faster."

"That Portend thing?"

"Yes. Now, go; it won't take me long."

Abella hesitated but Persephone was right; she could find Candace faster than Abella. One needed to go; the other needed to stay with the rest of the children.

"Make it fast, sister; it won't be long before they get inside. I'll close and lock the door, but I'm going to stay here. Knock three times when you get back and I'll open up. Got it?"

Persephone nodded once then took off at a run.

"Son of a bitch, I don't like this," Abella muttered as she locked them inside the escape tunnel.

She waited but heard no knock. Minutes went by and she heard nothing until smashing glass broke the silence.

Growls and yells echoed through the house, followed by the distinct fury of destruction. The Corvus Ward warriors were ripping apart everything she had built as they worked their way through the house: furniture, paintings, lamps... nothing was being spared.

"Persephone, where are you?"

She pressed her ear against the cold metal door, listening for a slight *tap*, any noise that might signal her sister's return, but when the men started in on the kitchen, her heart sank. Even if Persephone hadn't been captured, she was cut off from the basement, from Abella.

A tear ran down her cheek. "What have I done?"

65

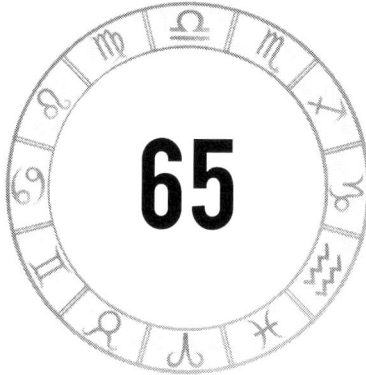

LYON PACED AROUND THE Zodiacs, studying the troll as it studied the humans. The agents had pressed their backs against one wall; the male had one of the floor candelabras in his hands, leaning it forward to block the big beast from getting closer. Not that the gold-encrusted metal would stop the troll if it wanted to get at them. But at least the semblance of protection had shut the humans up.

The pounding at the front door stopped.

Lyon paused; the hairs on the back of his neck stood on end. "That's not good."

"Why?" the human woman asked.

"Because the front door is the strongest physical barrier we have. Now they'll look for another way in."

"There must be more than one way in or out," the male said.

"He has a point, Lyon," Sag said. "What about the lifts?"

"We don't have the cuffs to use them. They've been gone since the battle," Lyon answered absentmindedly as he stared out of the hole in the cavern ceiling.

Gemini joined Lyon. "I think it's time for Gemma to come out. We'll need all hands and she's got all the brains in this duo."

Lyon nodded. "Do it."

Gem rolled his eyes in the direction of the humans. "In front of them?"

"Might as well; they've already had an eyeful and they're going to see more before this is done. Maybe it'll convince them we're telling the truth."

"Okay."

Gemini rolled up his sleeves, revealing his wide, gold cuff and the nearly saucer-sized emerald cabochon in its center. The Gemini constellation was carved in the stone and inlaid with more gold.

He lifted his opposite hand, covered the stone with his palm, and gripped the cuff tight. In seconds, his hand glowed as if a bright light was shining up from underneath. He closed his eyes and mouthed something. His body began to shake. He grunted and gnashed his teeth before throwing his arms and head back. His mouth was open as if screaming in agony, though nothing came out.

A wet, ripping sound filled the room. A yellow light flashed and a woman suddenly appeared next to Gemini.

She crouched and looked around, her hands clenched as if ready for an attack. "What the hell, Gem? Why are humans here?"

Gem gripped her shoulder with one hand and wrapped his opposite arm around his waist. "Stand down. They're trapped here with us. That's Sloane and Treadwell."

Lyon saw Gemma relax and take a long look at the agents. The woman had pressed her back against the rough wall; her mouth was open, her eyes wide as she panted. But the male, Treadwell, had leaned forward, a stunned look on his face. He released his hold on the candelabra, letting it fall to the ground, and ignored the troll as he walked up to Gemma, studying her.

Lyon couldn't blame the man for staring. Gemma was a stunning woman. She was tall and slender, with long, dark, straight hair that hung to her mid-back. Large, luminous, silver-grey eyes were filled with an intelligence that didn't miss anything—yet were haunted with great sadness. Beautiful but complicated, innocent but timeless and wise, Gemma was the type of woman who might want a hero but didn't need one.

From the look on the human's face, he had already thrown his hat in the ring for the chance to change her mind. Ambitious fool.

The agent held out his hand to her face. She remained still, staring deep into his eyes, the pair oblivious to the rest of the people in the room. He touched her cheek with his fingertips, and she covered his hand with her own.

She swayed.

The male grabbed her arm with his free hand to steady her.

"I must ask you to stop manhandling my sister," Gem ground out.

"My word," Sloane exclaimed. "That was amazing. How——?"

"It's the Gemini curse," Lyon answered. "All of us have a curse based on our zodiac sign."

Sloane looked at the other Zodiacs. "I only count ten. Plus her."

Gem cleared his throat. "Gemma and I count as one."

"Libra and Scorpio are out there somewhere." Lyon ran his fingers through his hair. "But our real concern is the warriors outside. We have to find a way out of here."

Pisces stepped closer to Lyon. "I can get out through the underground rivers. Once I clear the cave system, I can try to find help."

Aquarius snorted. "Whom would you suggest? No one's coming to our rescue against the Corvus Wards."

Lyon crossed his arms and nodded. "Ari is right. The other paranorms have bought into the king's bullshit and they fear the warriors. They won't be helping us." He studied Pisces for a moment. "But if you can get out, then go. If one of us is out there, we have a better chance of finding a way to survive this…Niko."

Pisces flashed a smile and a thumbs-up, nodded once, and left the Great Cavern at a run.

"Whoa, whoa," Treadwell said, his attention finally diverted from Gemma. "Are we really talking life or death here?"

Lyon pressed his lips into a thin line. "For us, probably, for you, most definitely. The Corvus Wards hold humans in great disregard."

The conversation fell into a lull. Before anyone could think of something to say, a loud humming noise filled the cavern. The Zodiacs looked up at the hole in the ceiling just as a black cloud of birds blocked the blue sky.

Ravens, crows, and magpies flooded the cavernous space, their caws deafening.

Gemma grabbed Treadwell and Sloane by the arm and jerked them toward the other Zodiacs. The males formed a ring around the humans and Gemma.

The birds flew in a thick line that soared in a downward spiral until they reached knee height. The lead birds broke the circle and flew at the Zodiacs.

The troll bellowed. It backed away from the attack until it reached the edge of the hole in the ground. The corvid cloud formed around the panicked creature, its thick arms pinwheeling and swatting to no avail. The terrified creature screamed as it took a final step back and fell into the dark to its death.

"What do we do?" Sloane yelled above the flapping cacophony.

A loud *bang* penetrated the noise. In seconds, Corvus Ward warriors appeared at the entrance to the Great Cavern, the males fanning out around the Zodiacs until they were surrounded.

"You've nowhere to go," one warrior yelled. "Surrender and you'll be shown mercy."

66

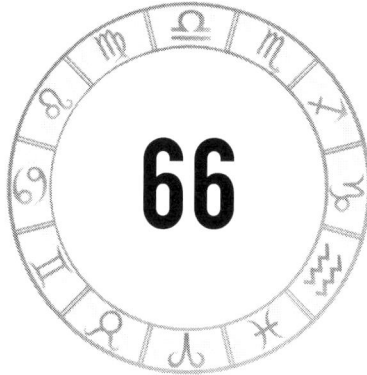

LIBRA CROUCHED LOW AS he ran from one clump of scrub brush to the next, his eyes on the Corvus Ward pair patrolling several yards away. He dropped to his belly and watched the men disappear behind a slight rise before waving at Taryn to join him. The wound in his shoulder still burned like fire, but it did help keep him awake and alert.

He'd been alert enough to stop far short of the long drive that led from the highway to the ranch house, leaving the paranorm children, the priest, and the Exemplars—save for Ailith—with the buses they had used to carry everyone. Ailith and the Innocent Demonica warriors had insisted on coming with him. Thankfully, Grate had turned out to be a better driver than Taryn, though they had had to scoot her seat up all the way so she could reach the pedals and see over the dash. Bloody miracle they hadn't been stopped by cops.

Whether such a large party could escape detection by the Corvus Wards remained to be seen.

"What are they doing here?" Taryn asked, her voice breathless. "How do they even know about the ranch?"

"Good question. How did I get those visions?" he asked.

"Portend?"

Libra nodded. "Someone has a Portend on the payroll."

Several Corvus Ward warriors exited the front door, one of the males gesturing angrily at the others.

"Do you think they have Abella and Persephone?" Taryn asked.

"That male looks frustrated, and look at the barn over there," he whispered. "They're still searching. I think they got away."

A group of crows flew over them on their way to the house.

"Shit," Libra hissed. "We can't stay here. We're too exposed in the daylight, and the nights will be too cold for the babies."

"There's only one other place I know around here," Taryn started.

"The cave in Sonora," Libra finished.

"At least, there, we'd be out of sight. Maybe we can find a way to the house."

"Through that cave system? Are you kidding? It was a nightmare trying to traverse it once, and it was a miracle we got out."

"I didn't say it was a good idea." She rested her chin on her clenched fists. "More wishful thinking than a real plan."

"The first part I like. But we can't meander around in uncharted caves; that'll be no help to us or anyone else." He watched the patrol disappear. "Let's get out of here before our luck dries up."

They crawled their way out until they could stand.

Libra held a hand to his brow to block the sun. "You know the way?"

"Due north from the ranch." She looked around to get her bearings before pointing to his left. "But we better hoof it if we want to get there before nightfall. It gets damn dark out here."

Libra waved at Ailith and the Demonicas to follow before walking by Taryn's side through the rocky, barren terrain.

* * *

The sun was flirting with the horizon when Libra sat down and pulled off his loafers and socks, regretting the fact that he hadn't had a chance to buy more serviceable shoes for all the running and hiking they'd done in the last few days. He tugged on the tattered remains of his clothes—he should have known there'd be nothing at his mother's house that fit him—and wished he'd taken the time to shop. It pained him to admit it, but he missed the simple comfort of the pantaloons and billowy shirt he'd worn while with the Sol. Hell, he'd give anything for a pair of jeans, a tee shirt, and a pair of running shoes right now.

Gad, how far he had fallen; his tailor would be aghast.

"You gonna make it?" Taryn asked, her smile crooked and full of snark.

"You better laugh before you strain a muscle trying to hold it in."

Her lips twitched but she managed to contain her mirth. "Loafers? Really? Is this your normal rescue attire?"

He studied her bemused expression and bit back the smartass remark on the tip of his tongue in favor of the truth. "I was in too much of a hurry to care what I had on."

Taryn's amusement fell away. "I...haven't thanked you properly for getting me out of that house. Or told you what that whole kidnapping thing was about."

Libra removed the sling from his back; the babies were sound asleep. He nodded to the Innocent Demonica warriors. A female trotted up to him and took the Prime and the Keres.

"Give us some time alone," he said softly. If he was lucky, the babies wouldn't wake.

The woman backed away until she was with her fellow warriors and Ailith. The entire group frowned at him, but they edged away until they disappeared behind a small rise in the landscape, giving Libra and Taryn privacy.

"We haven't had time for a proper anything." He pulled her into his lap and nuzzled her soft, warm neck, avoiding the many wounds the rats had inflicted. The hell she had been through was spelled out in her flesh, bite by bite. "I'm sorry that I didn't find you before..." he stroked the skin around one of her wounds. "I'm sorry you were involved in any of this."

She shuddered under his fingers but it didn't feel like pleasure to him, rather pain.

"Not like I gave you an option," she said, leaning closer.

"That doesn't mean I wanted you to get hurt." He reached up and pushed a heavy, black curl behind her ear. "Never hurt."

"That was Asmodeus's doing, not yours." She touched his fresh bruises. "And what about you? What did you do to find me?"

He looked away. "Whatever it took."

Taryn shifted until she could straddle his lap then scooted closer until they fit together. She pulled his face back to her. "Libra. I need to tell you something."

He pressed his lips to hers, heat blooming in his belly and lower. She opened her mouth to him, her tongue teasing and tasting. He slid his hands down her back and cupped her buttocks, pulling her tight against his growing erection.

"It can wait," he whispered in her ear.

Taryn draped an arm over his good shoulder and around his neck and wrapped her legs around his waist.

"Yes. Wait," she replied.

Goddess bless the woman's billowy skirts and gauzy tops. The colors still boggled his senses but...

He slid his hands along her legs and under her skirt, her strong thighs tensing with each inch he traveled. He found her soft, wet core and slipped his fingers inside her, groaning with the need to drop his slacks and replace his fingers with his already throbbing sex.

Taryn rocked against him and moaned deep in her throat. "Where's a bed when you need one?"

Libra opened his eyes and looked around at the Texas desert. Only thing remotely close was scrub brush. "There's not one around for miles, but you have me."

She leaned back to look at him, her eyebrows shooting up.

Her mouth lifted at one corner. "What a difference a few days makes."

He dropped his head and pulled at the edge of her shirt with his teeth. "And starvation."

She shrugged her shoulder and the shirt slid down, exposing a breast. "We ate earlier today."

He wet one nipple with his tongue before covering it with his mouth and sucking.

Taryn groaned and arched, pressing her sex against his.

"Goddess help me, I've been starved for you. I'll always be starved for you."

He reached between them and released his erection.

She rocked against his heat then rose to her knees. "Then let us feed each other."

He spread her buttocks and she wriggled until she'd buried his sex inside her.

They groaned in unison as she set an excruciatingly slow pace.

He tugged on the shirt again, freeing her other breast. Cupping them, he suckled one nipple until the peak was hard and tight, then devoted his attention to the other, pushing her harder, each lusty draw driving her to thrust faster, riding him so close to the edge he could feel the darkness pulling at him, demanding he jump.

"I can't hold on," she growled in his ear.

He reached between them and found her swollen, wet. Rhythmic pulses started inside her passage, squeezing him, sucking at him.

Taryn threw back her head and groaned, long and deep and guttural. A golden glow exploded in the space between them, enveloping their questing bodies.

Her sex clenched around his. He grabbed her hips, leaned back, and slid her back and forth until fire filled his veins and release threw him out into the deepest black.

They rocked together for several moments, milking the last of the waves of pleasure.

Taryn wrapped her arms around him and collapsed against his chest. He held her tight and smiled when he found his breathing matched hers.

She sighed gustily and touched his cheek with the back of her fingers. "What a pair we make."

"A pair indeed."

"Can we stay here for a few hours?"

She grinned with her eyes half shut, like a cat after stealing cream, and rocked her hips.

Still seated inside her, his satiated sex hardened again.

She giggled and rocked again.

He gasped and tried to stop her hips but his sex had other ideas. He grabbed her ass with one hand and the back of her head with the other. Pulling her close, his pressed his open mouth to her neck and sucked hard.

She moaned.

"Maybe it's time for a shift," he growled against her skin.

He rolled slowly to the side until she was under him. She reclined on the ground and spread her legs wide as she pulled up her skirt.

Libra looked down and watched his sex slide in and out of her, his thrusts slow and deep. He needed to feel every inch, possess the very core of her. He looked up at her.

"You. Are. Mine," he declared with each stroke.

Taryn's eyes met his. "You are mine."

The pace slowed and their murmurs softened, tenderness fueling their passion more than lust. Riding the wave together, they gasped and sighed then settled against each other.

Libra rolled onto his side so they could face each other without the weight of his body pressing Taryn's wounded skin into the ground.

"Are you okay?" he asked, wiping the dirt off her back.

She hummed and smiled. "I am deliriously, deliciously great." She reached out a hand and waved it through the cloud of gold that lingered around them. "I guess we're still making magic."

Libra glanced at the clear, blue sky. "No blizzard. I wonder why?"

"Maybe it has to do with this cloud of gold instead of blue."

Libra held out a hand to feel the gold but it dissipated in a wink. "The sun is almost down. Guess we need to get going."

They straightened their clothes and Libra reluctantly put on his socks and shoes while Taryn started walking.

He watched her, his heart full but his gut roiling. If they could find a way to survive the danger surrounding them, he'd have a chance to tell her just what she'd done for him and find the words to convince her to be his mate. But first, he needed to walk to that damned cave in these damned shoes.

"How much farther?"

She pointed to a dirt road a little way down the two-lane highway they had stopped by. "That's the start of the drive, so just a couple miles more."

She held out her hand.

He laced his fingers with hers. "Let's get this over with."

"There's a cold stream in that cave. Great for your feet...and for skinny dipping."

She skipped backward, a wide grin on her face.

"You're thinking about getting naked already? We just—"

She interrupted him with a laugh. "Always."

67

LIBRA'S STOMACH GROWLED, his feet hurt, and the stab wound in his shoulder still burned like hell; the last two miles hadn't helped his recovery. He eased his butt to the ground behind a boulder. If he'd had his way, they'd have stayed in the desert for the night and gotten some sleep, but Taryn would have vetoed that decision even if he'd dangled the incentive of more 'catching up' in front of her. The woman had pushed hard since seeing the Corvus Ward warriors at the ranch house, with no sign of Persephone, Abella, or the children.

"Oh boy, we have a problem," Taryn whispered

Libra ran his fingers through his hair, resisting the urge to rip it out. "What now?"

"Look."

Peering through a crack at the intersection of two rocks, he saw multiple spotlights shining on a volunteer fire truck. A group of humans were pushing gurneys carrying the injured to the multiple ambulances parked across from the narrow cave entrance they needed to access.

"What the hell happened?" he said.

Taryn frowned. "When we came here with Lyon, there was a Red Cap living inside the cave. Frightful little beast, but he was killed by a wraith. Could another Red Cap have moved in?"

"Can't know for sure until we get inside, but it's possible. A huge system like this one, so close to a rich food source like a human town…I'd be surprised if another Red Cap hadn't claimed it."

"Well, there is one good thing."

"What could possibly be good about all this attention?"

She nodded in the direction of the chaos. "Once they're gone, it'll be a while before any human will want to go back inside the cave."

"And if they don't leave it alone?"

"We could try to find the opening out in the desert."

"It would take a miracle to find a random hole in the desert in the daylight. Trying to find it in the dark…" he shook his head. "And, frankly, I'm done. Baked. My feet can't take anymore walking in these shoes."

Before Taryn could fuss at him, sirens flared, and the ambulances and fire truck drove away.

Libra peered through the crack again and watched four men race out of the house with duffle bags in their hands. They climbed into the SUV and gunned it so hard their car fishtailed down the drive.

"That solves that problem."

"Are we going now?" Taryn asked.

He eased down to the ground and leaned back against a boulder. "Let's wait a few minutes to see if there's any sign of life. Then we can slip inside."

* * *

The whimpers of the paranorm children grated on Abella, leaving her feeling impotent in the face of their fear. She dug into the side pocket of her duffle bag and removed a handful of chemical glow sticks.

She snapped one, shook it, and handed it to the nearest child. "Pass this back, so you can see."

She passed out the rest of the glowing sticks, her heart lurching when the ghastly yellow-green highlighted their terrified faces. Persephone would have known what to say; Taryn would have known what to do.

"I know how to play poker, not soothe scared kids," she muttered to herself.

She did know one way to ease their fears, however, with food and blankets and water, and those supplies were only yards away. "Come, it is just a little farther."

The youngest girl whimpered. "I want Persephone."

Abella squatted in front of her. "I do too, little one, but we must go on a little longer. Persephone will be with us soon."

God help her, she couldn't wait for Persephone either.

The older children herded the little ones forward without saying a word. Corvus Ward and Kellas Cat and Portend worked with her to move the group of scared babies to the larger opening in the tunnel where she had stored the supplies they needed for several days. At the opposite end of the cave, rope webbing had been stretched across the tunnel that led deeper into the system, a barrier to block them from entering the unmapped section.

Along one wall, there were stacks of rolled blankets and sleeping pads to protect them from the cold, hard ground. She passed out the rolls until everyone had taken one then walked from child to child, making sure they had what they needed to stay warm until she reached the other side of the space.

Satisfied that they wouldn't freeze, she opened bins containing bottles of water and tins of dried biscuits and passed them to the older children to distribute. "Let them chew on this while I get a fire started. Some heat and light and hot food will help comfort them."

The Kellas Cat girl Arrona touched Abella's arm. "You're doing fine."

Abella started. "What makes you think I needed that?"

Arrona smiled softly. "You are beautiful, smart, and fierce. But your doubt is written on your face."

"Huh. I'm known for my poker face."

"I don't know what that means, but they can see your fear for Persephone and Candace, even though you're trying to hide it. Don't be afraid to let them know. It would make you seem more...like us."

Abella nodded but remained silent. She started the fire and busied herself, pushing aside Arrona's words. Afraid. Yeah, she was afraid. Before learning of the paranorms she had thought she had the world figured out. She'd known who and what she was and how to move among those who wanted something from her. She'd known how to defend herself, known how to read people, and known her limitations. But this new world had rewritten all the rules. The bad guys, the good guys…they were muddled into a blur of the bizarre and brutal.

She'd come to Texas, relieved to get away from the Great Cavern, overjoyed that she could go back to the world she knew so well: designer gowns and poker games, flirtation and fleecing, stealing power by outsmarting the powerful.

Now she was trapped underground with terrified children, wondering how long they had before the warriors found the entrance, and if they could breach it. She shook her head and refused to think about the 'what ifs' until all the children were fed.

Within an hour, the youngest had buried themselves under their blankets and fallen asleep, while the older children sat around the last of the glowing embers, the dark of the cave having nearly won the battle against the light.

Abella sat next to Arrona and sighed. "You should get some sleep."

"You should, too," Arrona whispered.

Abella had opened her mouth to answer when she heard a clatter of rocks from deep in the uncharted tunnel. The noise continued for a few seconds as if the rocks had fallen hundreds of feet down a long, steep slope before coming to a halt.

She jumped to her feet and crouched, waiting for the unknown to rise out of the darkness.

"Get behind me," she said under her breath.

The older children rushed around the sleeping bags, waking the younger. They gathered several feet behind Abella, huddled and totally silent.

How sad it was to know that these babies understood the importance of quiet.

Abella clicked on a flashlight, risking revealing her position in order to see. She scanned the passage, checking the walls, ceiling, and floor.

Before she could find the source of the noise, a deep *bang* reverberated through the tunnel and past the huddled group. The heavy thumps of multiple feet grew close—the Corvus warriors had broken through her defenses. In moments, they would be upon them.

A light bobbed and the first warrior appeared. He stopped and held up a fist. The warriors gathered behind him, their scowls a sign of the pain they would no doubt enjoy inflicting for their aggravation.

"Don't give me any trouble and we'll go easy on the youngest brats," the leader hissed.

"Why the hell would I take your word for it?" Abella asked.

The leader waved the rest of the men into the small cave. They fanned out around Abella and the children, their eyes glittering with malice.

Abella lifted her chin and took a step toward the closest warrior.

"No," the Kellas Cat whispered.

She gripped Abella's arm and pulled. Abella glanced back.

The girl stared at the ground a few feet in front of her.

Abella pointed the flashlight down and saw a black scorpion the size of a dinner plate scuttle toward her. It paused inches from her boot, its tail relaxed; behind it were dozens more. Abella nodded and the scorpion curled its tail, pointing the thick stinger forward.

She turned the beam of light on the leader's face. "I think you and your men should leave here, now, before it's too late."

The men snorted and shifted, waiting for the signal from the leader.

"Take them all," he growled.

The men advanced to Abella and the children.

One warrior stomped a foot. He grunted and swiped at his shin then screamed.

The men stopped for second then, as one, the entire group yelled and danced and fell to the ground writhing, bloody foam running out of their mouths.

Abella spread her arms and crouched in front of the whimpering children. She hated that they had to bear witness to this but...

The last man stopped moving. He fell to the hardpack, dead.

Abella squatted down, placed the back of her open hand on the ground in front of the closest insect, and waited as it crawled into her palm.

"Scorpio."

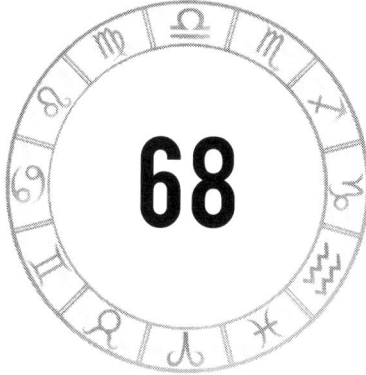

68

PERSEPHONE HELD OUT HER hands in the darkness, trying to feel her way down the crude passage carved out of stone while Candace tugged on her shirttail, leading Persephone as if she knew the path. Finn and Blair padded behind her on silent paws.

"Slow down, darling, before I hit my head on something."

Candace grunted and pulled harder until Persephone's hands landed on rope. She followed the rope by touch until she figured out that it was webbed and strung across the tunnel, blocking them from venturing farther.

Persephone sat with a heavy sigh and rubbed her face. "Candace?"

She reached out with her hands but didn't feel the small Portend. She swept her hands front and back, twisting her waist.

"Candace, this isn't funny. Where are you?"

Nothing.

"Candace!"

A small giggle sounded on the other side of the rope barrier.

Finn and Blair whimpered and paced in front of the webbing.

"Baby, come back," Persephone cried out, choking on the words.

She wrapped her arms around her waist and rocked as the oppressive darkness weighed her down, closed in on her.

"Lyon, you promised." She struggled to breathe. "Never alone in the dark." Tears flowed down her face, her skin itching as her gut roiled. "The dark…"

* * *

Sag crouched, his hands clenched into fists. "Lyon?"

Lyon whirled in a circle, his hands up. They were ridiculously outnumbered and out of options. "Anyone think these warriors are going to let us live?"

Taurus had his arms folded across his chest, his horns slowly growing out of his skull. "Time to go down fighting?"

Lyon looked beyond the belligerent bull and saw an anomaly. A group he hadn't expected to see was standing behind the Corvus Ward warriors, many of their number bandaged and looking worse for some unknown wear. He nodded once and waited to receive the same gesture in return. If he didn't, they were screwed.

To his surprise, the assent came; they were willing to help the Zodiacs. Whether that help included aiding his mad plan was yet to be seen.

Soft growls sounded a few feet away; the alpha male Fenrir Wolf and his pack had taken a stand between Lyon and the hole, their heads low and their hackles high.

"You're going to have to trust me," he said to the others.

"I don't like the sound of that," Aquarius said.

"Bring the humans. And the wolves."

The older Corvus Ward warrior stepped closer. "What's your answer? Surrender or die?"

Lyon dropped his hands and stood tall. "Fuck you. I choose option C."

He took off at a run. He reached down as he passed the alpha Fenrir Wolf and scooped the canid into his arms without slowing.

The other Zodiacs pounded after him, the humans screaming 'no' the whole way, the wolves yelping their surprise as they were grabbed.

The warriors blinked and took a step back.

"Stop them!" their leader yelled.

One, two, three steps…Lyon launched his body into the air and down into the hole leading to Hell, enveloped by a darkness he'd thought he'd never have to endure again without Persephone.

* * *

Hanell stood to one side of the second floor window of the empty house, watching for Libra and Taryn to make their move, while Circe paced in the bedroom behind him.

"When are they going inside?" she whined.

"It'll be soon; he's waiting to make sure that no humans stop him."

"We couldn't have planned that accident better had we tried."

"Doesn't that bother you? Almost seems too easy."

"We don't need much time to get this done, so I don't care."

He glanced back at her. It wasn't like her to be so fidgety. The woman was all sharp angles and strutting arrogance, much like his mother.

"Something bothering you?" he said.

She shook her hands and paced faster, like a junkie needing a fix. "I just want to get this done so I can continue my work."

He turned away from the window. Hell and damn, something was very wrong.

"You haven't been acting right for days." He took a step toward her. "Now that I think of it, you could have blasted Libra and his whore into the next county, but you didn't. Unless…you couldn't."

She flipped her long, auburn hair over her shoulder and stopped moving.

Her face reddened as she stared at him, her body trembling. "Are you challenging me?"

Holy crap.

Hanell raised his hands. "Not challenging. I'm worried about you."

She stalked over to the window and stared out of it. "Save your worry for yourself. I won't forget your insolence."

He had opened his mouth to apologize when she smiled.

She opened the curtain. "There they go. When the moon is high, it will be the perfect time to get me that Gaia juice." She stretched out on the bed and rested her hands on her belly, eyes closed. "We wait for the right moment. Then I'll be back on top."

* * *

Aubrianna sat slumped in one of the human's cars, fighting the urge to scratch at the burning corvid wounds that covered her body. The birds had done a number on her. And they had seen her memories. The king knew the royal child had been at her house, and though his men had returned with the report that the boy was no longer there, the king had been in such a good mood that he had brought Aubrianna with him to Texas.

He hadn't removed the iron bands from around her wrists and ankles, keeping her grounded. There was no way to escape him unless she used the exhausting human method of evasion—running.

Not likely.

The moment she was free of the bands and the bastard, she would run down whoever had betrayed her the Os Mage Mother way and destroy them with her freshly gained power.

Libra and Taryn bolted from their hiding place and ran to the cave entrance, disappearing inside.

The king reached for the car door, a deep frown on his face. "They're inside."

She stopped him with a hand. "Wait."

"It's stuffy as hell in here. I want out."

"We're not the only ones here," she said as she watched a curtain part in an upstairs window.

A light blinked on revealing Circe, then Hanell.

"What are you doing here, son? And with Circe?" Aubrianna muttered to herself.

"That's your son with the witch goddess?"

She didn't answer the king; there was nothing to say. Hanell being here was bad enough—he would surely mess things up for her—but Circe, too? What was she planning? Would she try to steal Gaia's power?

The king grunted. "We need to go, now."

"Not yet," she said as she pointed to the window, "not until they make their move."

"I could call my men and eliminate them."

"And if they alert Libra, he'll be prepared for us. We need him to be off kilter."

The king snorted. "He'll be off kilter when I'm done with him. And he will give me what's mine."

Aubrianna looked out the car window, fury heating her skin and causing a fresh wave of itch to make her squirm. *What's yours? Like hell.*

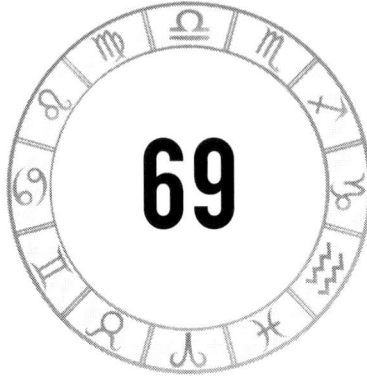

69

LIBRA AND TARYN ENTERED the slim crack that led to the first cave. The few gemstones that had dotted the walls the first time she'd entered the cave had been pilfered, leaving nothing but cold, pockmarked rock.

Taryn gently touched one gouged hole then another. "They've ruined it."

"Probably why they closed it." He paused. "Come, Taryn, we can't stay this close to the entrance. The humans may come back."

"What about the Demonica, Ailith, and the babies?"

As if conjured by her words, the very same slipped quietly into the cave, their black, hooded capes making them undetectable in the darkness. They spread out around Libra and waited.

Taryn followed him through the narrow passage to the second cave, her heart sinking when she saw further evidence of the ruthless harvesting of the precious gemstone crystals that had dotted the walls only weeks ago. Even the glowworm strands were gone, ripped off the ceiling and piled against one wall.

"Death and destruction. Is this all we're capable of?"

Libra looked back at her, fatigue written all over her face and form. "This is what the paranorms fear is in store for them when the humans find out about us."

"There are some who already have."

"And their continued silence has been expensive. A cost I had hoped to eliminate once our existence was known." He started for the last passage to the larger cave, the site of the battle with the wraiths and the death of the girl, M&M, and the Red Cap. "Come, love. Let's get inside and hidden."

She watched him lay the babies on the ground and gently push them through the crack, following closely. Love. He called her 'love.' She smiled as her heart sang with joy. One word she'd never thought she'd hear again; at least not outside of casual flirting. But the way Libra said it—that was not flirting, and not casual, not from him. Who'd have guessed tight-ass GQ could love her? And that she'd welcome his love so thoroughly?

She started after him, her body light, her mind clear. They weren't clear of trouble, not even close to it, but she could see a future with Libra.

Standing in the last cave, she pulled out her mini Maglite and looked around. Libra had crouched by the fire pit and was trying to light the blackened firewood still piled in it haphazardly. A match flared and the tiny flames grew until she could see the whole cave. Ahead of her was the stream, to her left the crevice they had used to escape the wraith attack, and the place that M&M had been taken from them so brutally.

Her gut flopped when she saw the black stain on the ground where the Red Cap had died. The memories of that night were too fresh, too horrible.

She walked over to Libra and touched his shoulder. "This is so open. Where can we hide if the humans come back?"

He stood and pulled her into his arms. "Rocks have blocked the route you used before. Taurus and I removed the stones once, but more must have collapsed." He looked behind them. "But there is another place, a false wall I found." He stepped back and held out a hand. "Come."

They felt along the rock until the wall ended, revealing a hidden opening.

Tall but narrow, Libra tried to squeeze through it but he was too large. "You try."

Taryn took a deep breath and pushed her way through. "It's tight but we can get the babies inside here." She clicked on her flashlight and looked around the space until she saw the ground. "Oh, god, there's old blood in here. A trail. It goes…"

"Taryn?"

"Hold on," she called out.

She followed the blood through a meandering tunnel until it dead-ended, the trail stopping at the base of a wall. She turned around and looked up, but there was no opening, no passage that she could find. Exploring the space more closely, she found evidence that the paranorm children had used this as a safe place for hiding. Ragged blankets and clothes had been tossed aside. A tiny doll made of dry grass had been abandoned. A slight flash drew Taryn's attention. She bent down and poked at a rag with her finger. Black blood covered most of the fabric. Someone had been seriously hurt.

Working her way back to Libra, she reached a hand out. "Hand me the babies so I can get them stowed."

The Innocent Demonica crowded around the crack, studying it. The smallest warrior tried to squeeze through, but she couldn't make it.

She jerked her body free. "No place for the Prime. We can't protect him in there."

"Where do you suggest we hide them then?" Libra asked.

"The Prime stays out here with us. We will make a circle around him."

"I'm not staying in here by myself," Taryn said.

She swept the flashlight in a circle until she found a small pile of wood. She stacked some of the larger pieces and slid them through the opening to the larger cave, then filled her arms with twigs and chunks of what looked like tumbleweed before leaving the smaller space behind.

Libra gathered the wood and dropped it next to the fire pit. "Were there any pans in there? I could get you some water."

"Nothing that can hold water here, but if I remember correctly there were a bunch of pots and pans and other rubbish behind that big rock."

She heard some rattling and cussing before Libra reappeared with a dented pot. He went to the stream to fill it.

"We have water," he called out, "but we have no food. I could go back to the house and see what they have."

She took the pot from him. "No. Rest. We can fill up on water for tonight. Tomorrow we'll figure something out."

After filling her belly with the cold, delicious water, Taryn passed it around.

Libra swayed on his feet.

"Libra?"

He seemed to fight the urge to fall over. Instead, he eased his body into a cross-legged position next to the flames.

"What do we do now?" he said.

Taryn touched his shoulder before settling next to him. "We rest, then we fight."

"Please go back behind the wall and hide. You're too exposed out here."

"We're all exposed, every day. One false wall won't keep me safe. I won't leave you and the babies out here while I cower in the dark."

"It would buy you time."

"To do what? Escape through the walls? Because I didn't see any way out of that cave."

"But you'd be hidden."

"We started this together; we'll finish it together. I won't hide."

"Even if it makes me feel better?"

She smiled. "What will really make you feel better is sleep." She sniffed delicately. "And a bath."

"Too tired for a bath. But sleep…"

Taryn straightened her legs and patted the resultant lap. "Come, sleep. There's nothing we can do right now. Since the Demonica and Ailith aren't here to fight for us, and the Zodiacs are a no-show, we don't stand a chance of getting inside the house and helping Abella and Persephone and the kids right now. But we can get some rest, and then plan."

Libra nestled his head on her thighs and closed his eyes.

* * *

Circe sat up in the bed, the wan moonlight still bright enough to wake her. Hanell sat sleeping in a chair across the room. The boy was wise enough to sense she didn't want him anymore. He'd been a fun toy for a time, but as weakness had crept over her, unassuaged by sex or the sacrifice of the children, her temper had shortened even as her fear ratcheted up.

She rose and kicked Hanell's feet. "It's time to go."

He followed her out of the house, silent, his fear sweat stinking up the sweet night air, until they reached the cave entrance where she allowed him to pass her and enter first. No sense putting herself at risk of stumbling across a booby trap when she had a warm body to do that for her.

* * *

Aubrianna cleared her throat to get the king's attention. "They're inside."

She climbed out of the car and stretched her arms over her head. Her blood raced; her skin tingled. So close. Without looking to see if the king was following her, she walked to the entrance. This was the culmination of years of planning and hoping, making alliances and backroom deals with anyone who could get her to this moment.

The king caught up to her before she entered, at least a couple dozen warriors behind him. He snapped his fingers and two of the largest warriors squeezed through the crack, swords pulled, no doubt carrying a lot more weapons on their person.

"Your men know what to do?"

"They've been told."

"Do they know the whole truth?"

The king grabbed her arm and waited for the warriors to enter the second cave. "They know what they need to know and that's all."

Aubrianna jerked away from the king's tight grip. "Lambs to slaughter."

He leaned close to her ear. "You of all people understand the price of power. Sacrifices have to be made."

He left her to join his men.

Aubrianna quivered, her hands clenched almost as tight as her jaw. "Yes, they do."

70

"LIBRA," TARYN HISSED AS she shook his shoulder. "Someone's coming."

He staggered to his feet. Fatigue washed over him; hunger ate at his fringes.

"Go, Taryn, hide yourself, please."

Her heart ached at his expression. Fear and fatigue, resolve and regret painted his face, the canvas shifting as he sought to find the words to make her go.

"There's nothing you can say that will make me leave your side."

He cupped her face, his thumb rubbing her cheek. "Will you ever listen to me?"

"Only when you make sense."

She picked up a pair of rocks, held her hands in front of her like a boxer, and crouched.

A slow clapping of hands brought her attention to the cave entrance.

The Innocent Demonica surrounding the babies drew their swords with a unified hiss.

Circe smiled at Taryn, a predator having cornered its prey, while Hanell stood a little behind, a frown marring his smooth, handsome features. Circe snarled at him and he stopped mid-clap.

"Our reunion was cut short. We're here to continue that joyous occasion," she said, slithering toward the fire.

"I'm surprised you would risk another round with Libra after he destroyed your building and took the children from you," Taryn taunted. She cocked a hip and studied her mother. "You seem…diminished since the InBetween." She dropped the rocks and took a step forward. "Could you be weakening now that the demons are free and you are alone?"

"I am not alone," Circe cooed as she snapped her fingers.

Hanell walked to her side.

She stroked his head like he was a pet. "I have your brother, Libra. The one you so heartlessly abandoned to your mother. You didn't even bother to save him before collapsing a building on us. You chose others over your own blood. If anyone here is weak, it's the Zodiac standing by you, my daughter."

Libra snorted. "You know, my love, I think you're right. The witch goddess has been shackled by her own hubris."

Hanell stepped in front of Circe. "And what of you, brother? What have you done but cater to your own wants since you were born? You could have taken the mantle of agent long ago, but instead you clung to the notion that you could live in the light, never acknowledging the dark. She twisted me with her poison and you could have saved me." He stepped around the fire until he was only a few feet from Libra and Taryn. "Why didn't you save me?"

"That's a good question," the Corvus Ward king asked from behind Circe.

* * *

Libra pulled his attention away from Hanell and saw the king and Aubrianna enter the cave. Several hooded warriors fanned out on either side of them. They didn't advance but Libra felt truly trapped. There was nowhere for him to go, but Taryn still had a chance.

"Go," he whispered.

She grunted her dissent.

"Then get behind me, please," he begged.

"I will not leave your side."

"And if we fall?"

"We fall together."

Libra grit his teeth. "We'll talk about this later."

"No. We won't."

He risked a glance at her and saw her set jaw. Nope, they wouldn't be talking about this later. If she wouldn't listen to reason, he had no choice but to prepare for a fight. He forced his clenched hands to open and relax, reaching for the energy deep inside him and willing it to well up. Shitty odds, but he would knock out as many as he could and hope he didn't kill any of them.

"Hanell, I want to help you. Come to my side, leave Circe, and let me be a brother to you."

Hanell took a step toward them and turned to face Aubrianna and the king. "I know what you're trying to do, mother. You want to force Libra to kill so he gains the powers of Gaia's agent. But even if Libra does become the agent, Gaia skipped over you. You have been forsaken. Joining with the Corvus Ward king shows just how desperate you truly are."

Aubrianna bared her teeth and hissed. "You smart-mouthed child. Why I was cursed to bear either of you is beyond comprehension."

While Aubrianna slowly crept forward, followed by the king and his warriors, Circe stepped back, away from the rest of them.

Libra watched Circe retreat. *Does she know something is about to happen?*

"All of you, just stop," he said. "You're wasting your time. I'll never accept Gaia's power. It's lost for all time. The sooner you reconcile that fact the sooner we can stop fighting and work to unite the paranorms before humans descend on us and wipe us out."

The king crossed his arms. "That's what I thought you'd say."

He nodded once and two of the warriors raised their arms and threw daggers at Hanell and Libra.

"No!" Taryn yelled as she launched herself in front of him.

408

The dagger meant for him buried itself in her chest and she collapsed to the ground.

Hanell's legs folded under him and he sagged into an awkward sitting position before falling back, a dagger buried in his neck, blood draining down his chest.

Circe crouched, an expression of excitement on her face.

"Taryn!" Libra followed her to the ground, hugging her to him. "No!" He reached for the dagger hilt, but when he saw it moving in time with her heart, he couldn't pull it out. It would mean certain death. "Don't do this, love. Open your eyes; look at me."

The king grabbed the nearest Corvus Ward warrior and threw the man to the ground in front of Libra.

"Kill him, kill him," he yelled, his eyes glittering, mad with lust for murder.

"Libra. No," Taryn whispered.

But Libra's rage and agony deafened him to all but the pounding of his heart and the need to destroy. He panted as power surged through him, filling him until his skin stretched so far he thought it would split.

The king's red eyes widened.

Libra opened his mouth and roared, releasing his hatred in a blinding pulse of white-blue light that hit the king in the chest and sent him flying back until he slammed into the wall.

The king screamed once then crumpled to the ground, a gaping wound in his chest, his heart obliterated by the attack.

Silence fell; the cave filled with a blue glow that turned Hanell's flowing blood purple.

Circe pushed past Aubrianna, placing the Os Mage Mother between her and Libra, but she hesitated at the cave entrance.

"Mother," Hanell said.

He stopped breathing, his lifeless eyes staring up at the ceiling and beyond it.

"No!" Aubrianna started for Hanell but the blue light knocked her off her feet, sending her sliding back with one blow.

A figure appeared and the light that had flooded the cave pulled in until it disappeared inside her.

"Gaia," Aubrianna said, her voice a breathless whisper.

The goddess looked at Aubrianna then Circe. "I am greatly displeased with both of you. I will deal with you later."

Libra focused on Taryn's soft, brown eyes, unable to care about the scene around him. "How am I supposed to protect the woman I love, my inamorata, when she insists on jumping off that damn cliff?"

He pressed a hand around the dagger blade to slow the bleeding.

She smiled softly. "Inamorata?"

"My one and only love. I'll even eat your damn cookies, but you have to stay with me to make them."

A cold touch on his shoulder made him look up. Gaia's form was ghostly, yet partly corporeal, enough so she wasn't transparent, so he could feel her touch.

"You have killed with hate in your heart. I am here to give you the power of Nether."

"I have no desire to be your agent. Aubrianna wants it; give it to her."

"It is too late for her; I have chosen you. And you made your choice when you killed the king."

Taryn reached up to Gaia. "What about the power of Aether? Can he accept that as well?"

Gaia crouched. "He would have to kill with love in his heart."

Taryn turned her head to look at Libra's dead brother. "Can Hanell be brought back to life with the power of Aether?"

"Yes, Hanell is not too far gone unto death. But Libra would have to accept the power of Aether now before death has too great a grip on his brother."

As if on cue, two Memoria Soul-Keepers appeared in the cave. One stood next to the Corvus Ward king, the blue-black butterflies mounted on her head fluttering in anticipation of receiving his soul, joining him with the rest of his ancestors. The second appeared next to Hanell, her hands folded as she waited for him to pass beyond repair.

Taryn looked at Libra, her eyes soft with love. "You must do this."

The realization of what Taryn was asking flash-froze his heart and stole his breath. He shook his head. "No, no, I can't. You can't ask it of me."

"My love, you must. Hanell needs a second chance, and you need to give it to him. You must kill me."

Libra swiped at his tears. "If I do this, if I…" He stopped, unable to say the words. "Can I bring her back, too?"

"No, once you kill Taryn to gain the power of Aether, you can't bring her back with it, just like you can't bring back the king. That is the sacrifice that has to be made for you to become the agent."

Libra shook his head. "Then no, I won't do it." He pulled Taryn closer. "I can get you help; I can keep you alive. I just need you to hang on."

"Libra, no. I cannot survive this." Taryn touched his cheek. "There is no medicine or magic that can heal me in time. But if my dying right now will save Hanell, if it will bestow on you the ultimate balance of power, then my end will have done some good. People like Circe and Aubrianna will go on hurting others if you don't stop them."

"I don't care about other people; I only care about you."

"We both know that's not true." Her hand dropped away. "Kiss me?"

He drew a ragged breath and leaned close, pressing his mouth to hers, warming her cold, blue lips, sharing his breath to give her life. He knew in that moment he would gladly give her any years he had remaining.

He'd never entertained the idea that he could have a woman with such passion and fire by his side. Opening to his dark side had scared the shit out of him. But now? There was no doubt, no hesitation, no limit to his certainty that this woman, the antithesis of what he had wanted, was exactly what he needed. She was his inamorata, his beloved, the woman destined to be his mate, the one woman who had helped him see that true balance could never be found without accepting all of who he was.

And now she was asking him to let her go.

"I can't do this," he whispered in her ear.

"You are so strong and so needed in this world. I will always be there, in the light, in the darkness, always loving you…" She took three rapid breaths, her face bunched in a grimace, her eyes glassy. "You never asked me why I choose to jump off the cliff."

He swiped at the tears on his face. "Because you like to go *splat?*"

The corners of her mouth curved slightly. She closed her eyes. "Because then you can fly."

Libra struggled to draw a breath.

Taryn sighed; her body sagged. Her voice faded to a whisper.

He leaned closer.

"It's time for you to fly, my inamorata," she said, her voice trailing off at the end.

He could feel her heart slow, could feel the coolness of her soft skin turn to cold as the blood slowed. He pressed his palm against her chest, called up his power, and released it slowly. The blue light disappeared inside her chest. He closed his fist and squeezed, imagining he could feel the blue press against her failing heart until it shuddered to a stop.

"I love you, my little gypsy, my fierce angel."

He choked to a stop when she drew her last breath, his grief all-consuming. He yanked the dagger out of her and flung it across the cave, then pulled her lifeless body into his chest and rocked, his keening bursting from deep inside, uncontrollable.

Gaia touched his shoulder again, wrenching his attention away from Taryn.

When she spoke, her voice was distorted, muted, like she was underwater. "Come, stand so I may bestow upon you the power of Nether and Aether."

He slapped her hand away and growled, rabid, enraged. "Give me a damn minute."

"It must be done now," Gaia insisted. "If you want to save Hanell. Once the Soul-Keeper has his soul, you can't use Aether to help him. A life without a soul is the greatest torment to be found in all the worlds."

Libra gently placed Taryn on the ground and pushed her hair off her pale face, struggling to draw air, his body numb. He leaned over and pressed his lips to hers again, desperate to memorize the feel of them.

"Libra."

He looked at the people around him as if seeing them for the first time before rising to his feet. "Get it done, then go."

71

THE GODDESS HELD OUT her hands, palms up, and closed her eyes. As if pulling life force from the earth itself, two columns of light—one white and shimmering like light dancing on a pearl, the other iridescent purple and black like the sheen of oil on water—drained out of the ground and the walls and the water to collect on her hands in growing balls of power.

He swayed as he waited and watched, too raw to care about the rest of his life, only going through with the transfer of power because Taryn wanted it for him.

"It should be mine," Aubrianna screamed. "He is weak where I am strong. It is my birthright."

Gaia opened her eyes and glared at the woman. "You have nothing but hate in your heart. No love, no joy, a vacuum of darkness that destroys everything around you. He has the greatest capacity for light and dark I've ever seen. His love for Taryn, a woman of my blood, is transcendent." She turned her attention back to Libra, her voice dropping to a reverent whisper. "He is the one I've waited for these many centuries."

A scrape sounded to Libra's left.

Circe shoved Aubrianna, sending the screeching woman to the ground. Turning she fled the cave and disappeared.

One of the warriors pushed back their hood. The Hell Os Mage stalked over to Aubrianna and grabbed her hair.

"You? You are the betrayer?" Aubrianna choked out.

"I am the purifier," the woman answered. "And Gaia has ordered a house cleaning."

"I am the Mother. You can't leave the worlds with no way to create a new Os Mage."

The Hell Os Mage laughed. "I am the new Mother. You are the now the Hell Os Mage. Come, let me show you your new home."

Aubrianna shoved the Hell Os Mage away. "Asmodeus, help me."

A robed figure stepped into the cave and threw back their hood. "Aubrianna! Got yourself in a pickle, I see."

Gaia hissed and crouched. "Leave here, demon, before I incinerate you."

He circled around until he was within reach of Aubrianna, then wrapped an arm around her neck and pulled her close. "I suggest you return to Hades and admit defeat. My army is here and more are coming. You and your kind were put in your rightful place centuries ago. You will stay there."

"You demons are foul, loathsome aberrations, and we will destroy all of you."

"We?" He looked around the cave. "I don't see a 'we.' You are alone, and based on your opacity, you are weak." He scowled when he saw Taryn dead on the ground. "You may have won this battle, but how long will it take you to find another agent after I kill him?" Asmodeus raised his right arm. The robe sleeve slid back exposing the words, 'Come and See.'

"You," Libra hissed. "You were in that shop. You gave Taryn the necklace."

"What? Little Taryn didn't tell you already? Truly remiss of her."

Libra sliced the air with one hand to silence the demon king. "You told her that necklace would protect her. You told her that she was important."

"The stone works against this goddess and her kind, yes. Alas, I didn't anticipate her being so foolish as to leave my guardianship and get herself killed by the king— really quite frustrating after I had taken such considerable care choosing her."

414

"Guardianship?" Libra growled. "She was terrorized by rats; she was bound to a bed, her flesh cut to drive the rodents mad."

Asmodeus shrugged. "Demon king."

"Bastard," Libra countered.

"She was defiant and needed to be…marinated, pliant. Couldn't have her fighting me at every turn." The demon sighed. "This explanation has become tedious and it's all for naught. Taryn's dead." He turned his attention back to Gaia. "I shall blow this agent wannabe into little bitty pieces of bone and flesh that no one can put back together. If I have to start over, then it's only fair that you do, too."

He clenched a fist then opened his hand wide, his palm red with fire. He pointed it at Libra.

Aubrianna raised her arms and slammed them down on the demon's arm. The fire hit the cave floor, melting the hardpack and rock into a circle three feet wide. Aubrianna pivoted and backhanded Asmodeus, sending him stumbling back toward the exit.

He staggered a few feet before righting himself. He crouched, his teeth bared in a feral scowl.

Gaia raised both hands and fired.

He jumped to one side, growling, then ran out of the cave, dodging the falling rock.

The Hell Os Mage clapped a hand on Aubrianna's shoulder and the two women disapparated.

Gaia panted for several seconds then raised her arms high, holding them still until the white and black light stopped gathering.

She nodded at Libra. "Come close and place your hands above the light."

He took a stumbling step toward her and lifted his arms, surprised he could make the limbs cooperate. He expected heat or cold but the light was neither of those. Instead it was lukewarm and silky soft. It flowed in a ball under his palms.

Circe lifted her hands until Libra's hands disappeared inside the light. "Do you accept the role of agent of Aether and Nether?"

"Yes."

"Close your eyes and let the power sink into you."

He did as she requested though his heart and soul were screaming in protest.

Nothing—this meant less than nothing to him. If Aether and Nether wanted a recipient, he would accept them, but he would never work for Gaia. This power would never be used to help her, or save her. He would do everything to hinder her, do nothing for her. If these powers had a sentience, a will of their own, then they knew his mind already.

And if you know my mind, you know my will. I will never be Gaia's to control.

And yet the light flowed into him, filled him, as if it didn't care that he was foreswearing his allegiance to the goddess. As if having a body in which to exist was its only desire. With nary a whisper, the power vanished under his skin. No pain, no pleasure, just the feeling that he'd finished a large meal and needed to unzip his pants.

"Is that it?"

Gaia nodded. "One more thing." She removed a silver necklace with a large, black stone from inside her robe and draped it over his neck. "Never take this off. It is black tourmaline and it will protect from you demons."

Libra stood quietly, unable to conjure a protest, his chest burning with the effort to breathe. He looked back at Hanell. A golden orb rose out of his chest, the Soul-Keeper's hand above it.

Libra ran to his brother, dropped to his knees, and removed the dagger.

He touched the bloody hole in Hanell's neck. "I don't know what I'm doing. Is there a magic word or a spell?"

Hanell's soul continued to rise.

"Feel the power within you; it will tell you what to do," Gaia whispered.

He rubbed his hands together and placed them around Hanell's neck. "Come back to me. Give me another chance to be your brother."

The black light oozed out of his pores and covered his hands. It wrapped around Hanell's neck just like Libra's hands, before sinking into his flesh. Libra released him and sat back on his haunches, waiting for signs of life. He watched the soul slow its ascent then come to a stop and hover as if Hanell were weighing his options and hadn't decided whether to return or go.

Libra's heart sank lower with each tick of the second hand until all he felt was regret. What use was Taryn's sacrifice if he couldn't use his gift of Aether to save

Hanell? He had planted his hands on the ground to push off and stand when the soul sank, disappearing inside Hanell's chest.

Hanell sucked in a deep breath and moaned. The blood he had lost traveled back to the stab wound, the skin knitting together until it closed. Hanell reached up with both hands and touched his neck.

"What happened?" he mouthed, his voice gone.

Ignoring his brother, Libra jumped up and turned. If he could bring Hanell back, he had to try to revive Taryn, no matter what Gaia had said. But Taryn's body was gone. The only traces left were a pool of blood and the silver necklace gifted to her, the opal that was supposed to protect her.

Libra picked up the necklace, desperate for anything solid, tangible that had touched her skin, and slipped it over his head.

The king's Memoria Soul-Keeper turned to him. "The goddess took her before I could collect her soul."

"Taryn was a Corvus Ward?" Libra asked.

The Soul-Keeper nodded once.

The king's men gasped.

"I felt the king's blood running through her veins. Her soul called to me; she was ready to join her family's long line."

Before Libra could ask her any more questions, she winked out of sight.

"To hell with that," he muttered.

Taryn may have been part Corvus Ward, but her family was not. Her soul would have chosen to stay. He called to his brother without breaking eye contact with the males.

"Let's go, Hanell."

Libra strode up to the king's body and grabbed the dead man's collar, lifting his shoulders off the ground.

He looked at the males. "You come with me."

The warriors bowed low.

Libra looked back at the Innocent Demonica and Ailith. "Are you coming?"

He dragged the king's body through the caves and out the exit before dropping it at the feet of the waiting warriors. Corvus Ward warriors respected strength;

they might not like that their king was dead but they wouldn't challenge the man who killed him.

"I want you to call off the warriors at the house...now. And if the women or children or dogs have been harmed, I will kill all of you." Libra's voice dropped. "Do you understand?"

They bowed their heads and parted as he walked away from them, Hanell and the others trailing behind him.

72

LIBRA STOOD IN THE front yard of the ranch house, his hand extended to the Corvus Ward royal boy. Corvus Ward warriors surrounded them. Beyond the warriors were several Corvus parents, their arms wrapped around their newly reclaimed children.

"I look forward to working with you in the future," Libra said.

"It is a future none of us would have had if not for you and Taryn," the boy said. "We will honor her as a great Corvus Ward warrior, a daughter of the former king, and my friend."

Libra swallowed hard, afraid he wouldn't be able to hold back the tears if they welled. "All of you fought to survive." He looked around, past the Corvus Wards and to the many other families made whole again: Kellas Cat, Aspis, Portend. "And now we need to keep going."

The Corvus royal released Libra's hand and threw his arms around Libra's waist. Libra held him for several seconds, choking on the pain and joy that warred within his heart.

The boy pulled back. "We will stand ready to help you any way we can."

Libra nodded and watched the boy walk away, surrounded by his people. He turned around and sighed.

Though several children had been reunited with their parents, there were two or three times as many adults crowded together, different species standing shoulder to shoulder, bonded by their shared fear for their still-missing babies.

He walked up to them and touched the shoulder of an Aspis male. The multi-colored scales that covered his body shimmered under the warm, spring sun.

"Please," the male whispered as he held out a piece of thick paper, "this is our daughter. Have you seen her?"

Libra took the portrait from him and glanced down. "I'm sorry, no."

He held the page out to the male to return it but the Aspis shook his head.

"Keep it. Find her. I beg you."

"I'll try."

Libra looked at the rest. The paranorms surged forward, handing him portraits and locks of hair and the occasional name.

An Elven female handed Libra a book. "This is a complete list of the Elven children who are missing."

Libra opened it and sucked in a breath. There had to be a hundred children listed. "So many?"

The female bowed her head. "Yes, and I fear that there as many, if not more, missing from each of the paranorm species."

Hundreds of children. Missing. His heart sank. How many would die before he could find them? How could he even hesitate in the face of such a tragedy?

He grit his teeth and raised his head. "Give me everything you have. Every name, every picture, anything I can use to find them."

The rest of the crowd swamped him, their chatter and pleas drowning out any other sounds.

After what felt like hours, weighed down with a huge stack of paper, his pockets burgeoning with wrapped hair and more, he was finally done.

Abella waded through the dwindling crowd and took some of the stack. "Come, you need a break."

He followed her into the blessedly empty family room. Setting the papers on a desk, he collapsed on a leather sofa next to the picture window to watch the flurry of Sol and Nox activity that struck up once the dust trail retreated behind the Corvus Ward warriors and the royal boy.

In many societies, a young boy would not rule without the aid of a council. But this royal boy had been in full command the moment the warriors saw him. He had ordered them to send crows to the Great Cavern and call off the attack; the Corvus Wards would join forces with the Zodiacs to ensure the survival of the paranorm world.

After the Corvus warriors at the house had retreated with their dead, Abella and Persephone and her children had been found in the bolt tunnels none the worse for the experience. Abella had been babbling about Scorpio saving the day, telling them that she'd held one of his scorpions in her hand before it jumped off and disappeared into the tunnel.

"Are you sure you won't stay?" Persephone asked as she joined him. "We plan to go back to the Great Cavern to find Lyon and the others."

He couldn't look at her. He could still barely speak for the lack of breath that had been his continual condition since Taryn had died. And he couldn't stand to see his grief reflected in her purple eyes, knowing the part he'd played in putting it there.

"I have to find the rest of the missing children," he said. "The Corvus Wards have promised to leave you alone; they shouldn't be a problem for you."

"Getting the royal back did soothe their ruffled feathers."

"Hopefully, like the Corvus Wards, the other species will work with us once we return their missing children."

"What you did today got us a lot closer to that end—they would welcome you as the ambassador. Lyon will want one of the Zodiacs to speak for us."

Libra shook his head. "Then you'll need to find the others. I won't be the InBetween ambassador or its spokesman. After what happened today…all those joyous parents, and so many more grieving ones." He paused to take a breath. "Finding the children is what Taryn would have done, and it's what she would insist I do if she were here. So I must go if I am to honor her." He finally turned to her. "They need help. I will be the one to give it to them."

Her eyes filled with tears and she nodded. "Taryn would be proud."

"I would rather her be here than proud of me."

Persephone broke their gaze and looked out the window again.

Libra felt her pain; no doubt she felt his as well.

"But for all this, we are no closer to figuring out why the children were taken," she said. "It was easy to blame Circe, since she had some of them, but many were lost before she was reawakened. Someone started all this and we don't have a clue who."

He picked at a tiny burr stuck in his jeans. "One thing is for certain. Asmodeus and Gaia are not friends. The way they acted, I'd guess there's a war brewing. And, somehow, witches are involved," he finished under his breath.

Twin shadows crossed the courtyard, drawing his attention. Meri and the bird were doing barrel rolls and loops in the cloudless Texas sky. He could hear the fairy giggle with each twist and turn.

"What about them?" Persephone asked.

"I tried to convince her to go to the Great Cavern with you but Meri insists that her job is to watch over me as Taryn would have wanted. And that bird is infatuated with Meri, follows her like a puppy."

"Interesting thing, she can touch it without infecting it," Persephone said.

"Like she could with Taryn. I wonder why that was."

"Interesting to see the changes in her, too. Her skin and wings…it's like they're healing."

Abella joined them. She sighed and wrapped her arms around her waist. "I wish we could have said goodbye, buried her."

She sat on the other side of Libra without touching him or looking at him. She had withdrawn from the world, from all of them. She didn't blame him for Taryn—she'd made that clear—but, like him, she was too raw to draw comfort from anyone.

"We should go, Persephone," Abella said. "The children are fidgeting so much my teeth are on edge."

Persephone nodded. "Don't even think about passing out the Benadryl. We are not drugging them with antihistamine."

"Oh, come on. It won't hurt them. How about margaritas? They'd love the sweet."

"Abella."

"For god's sake, okay." She sighed with gusto. "It's gonna be a long couple of days."

Without a word, Libra followed the women outside and helped them board the huge bus they'd arrived in. With curtains blocking the heavily tinted windows, and a toilet, the vehicle was a blessing for traveling such a long distance with children that were distinctly not human.

Persephone took a seat but Abella stood at the door and eyed the children Libra couldn't see. "All right then. This is going to be a long trip. I want no yelling or crying. Laughing should be kept to a minimum. In fact, if you can sleep the whole way, I'd be ever so grateful."

"Abella," Persephone fussed under her breath.

Abella ignored her. "Do you understand?"

Silence.

"All right then, we're off."

A rousing cheer ricocheted around the bus, the joy and excitement stinging when it washed over him.

Abella threw up her hands and rolled her eyes before sagging into the driver's seat and starting the engine.

Libra watched them pull away, dust rising up as they eased down the gravel drive. He waited until he could no longer see the evidence of their passing. Minutes ticked by and he stood there watching the horizon, the great emptiness gaping inside him just as harsh and barren and monochrome as the landscape.

"Libra?" a soft, feminine voice said behind him.

He turned to Solange, the leader of the Sol.

"Are you ready to go?"

Her wrinkled face looked harsher in the bright light. Like him, she was still lost, her grief pinching her features severely, just as the pain of Taryn's loss had pinched everything about him.

"Your people don't have to make this journey with me."

She walked closer but stopped short of reaching out to him.

Some needed the touch of others to muddle through, but not him, and she seemed to sense his need to be untouched, at least for now, for which he was grateful.

"With the Nox in charge of the season, we can devote months to your journey. It is the one way to honor Taryn and her love for you and the children she saved." She watched with a smile as one of the young men wrestled to get a halter on a young foal while avoiding the nips of its protective mama. "We also want to protect you from those hoping to steal your power or imprison you to control it."

The shadows passed over the ground again.

"Seems I have a lot of protectors for this journey," Libra said.

"A Pestilence Fairy and a Stryx. Who would have thought it possible that two such dark species could find happiness in the light?"

"I think the Stryx rose with the demons. Makes me wonder what else came along for the ride."

She shrugged and craned her head back to watch the pair. "Those are mysteries for another day. Perhaps it is good to just take a moment and watch their simple joy."

Libra raised a hand to shield his eyes from the sun. Joy. That emotion would be a stranger to him for a very long time.

Meri led the Stryx on a wild chase on the thermals, her fairy wings nearly healed; the pestilence that had covered her really did seem to be dissipating. Were the Pestilence Fairies born that way or were they cursed to be pestilent? There were rumors about the fairies and one of the Four Horsemen, but no one knew for sure. Maybe one day he would ask the girl, when he was able to breathe deep again, when he didn't dread the rise of the sun and the set of the moon and every agonizing minute between them.

Libra dropped his hand and turned.

Several yards away, Hanell sat in the driver's seat of his caravan, pale and subdued but still here, the reins controlling the golden-dappled Vanner in his hands. To Libra's surprise the horse adored Hanell, following him around like a besotted pet, which was good for Hanell and even better for Libra.

Ailith sat next to Hanell, her arms crossed over her chest, one foot bouncing. She and the rest of the Exemplars had decided to stay with the Prime and Keres, along with the Innocent Demonica, each species sure that only they were fit to guard the babies from all comers. It made for the kind of tension that Libra hoped wouldn't flare into arguments, but it was a start, and one that was needed throughout the paranorm world.

Libra walked to his caravan. Instead of the golden-dappled menace, the Nox had gifted him a pair of black Friesen stallions, for pulling or for riding.

He climbed onto the driver's seat.

Grate grunted as the van dipped under his weight. The human had planted herself firmly in his and Meri's life—the two girls vastly different but bonded harder than sisters—and refused to return to her 'crappy nonexistence.'

Zodiac and girl waited in silence for the last of the Sol to finish getting ready. They'd decided to head north and west until they reached the Pondera's part of the InBetween in the Yellowstone caldera. There they could rest and make plans to find more of the children the paranorms parents were now counting on him to rescue.

Getting the Exemplars and Seclorum to work together again could be the hardest part of the entire mission, but there was no place for old animosities. He wouldn't call himself an ambassador; that was a lofty title wrapped around a lot of politics for which he no longer had any stomach. But being Gaia's agent gave him power formidable enough to make the paranorms listen. And they would listen even if he had to knock their heads together.

The group pulled away from the ranch house and eased down the long drive. Turning onto the highway, they hugged the lane-wide shoulder and began their long journey into his new reality. But before they managed to get a mile down the road, Libra heard a muffled noise inside the caravan.

He stopped the horses and set the brake before easing his body through the small door into the interior. "Stay there, Grate."

He turned around and pulled up abruptly when he saw a woman. "What the hell are you doing here?"

Gaia had reclined on the settee and was busy checking her nails. Her ghostly appearance from only days ago had solidified somewhat; she was more opaque than translucent.

"Get out. Leave. I will never be your agent; I will never use the power you gave me."

She sighed and turned her attention to him, a resigned expression on her face.

"I can see you're serious and that distresses me. Truly. So I've decided to give you a gift to appease you, to convince you that there's no reason to hate or fear me. But, I must warn you, my gift is slightly damaged." She cocked her head. "Like scratch and dent."

"Leave. Now, before I do something rash."

"My, how you've changed, Libra. So controlled, so levelheaded, and yet you threaten to do something impulsive. Bravo." She raised a forefinger and waggled it in his face. "But I suggest you see my gift first, then decide if you want to return it."

She waved him to the bed and pulled back a curtain.

73

CURIOSITY PULLED HIM TO the bed.

"Taryn," he whispered, the surge of adrenaline mingled with such hope and fear and longing that it threatened to send him to the floor.

He lunged for her, desperate to touch her to make sure she was real. He ran a hand over her black curls and they sprang between his fingers. Her cheeks were pink and her skin soft and warm—no rat bites, not even the tiny scar on her throat where Circe had tried to kill her so many weeks before. She looked normal, alive, but her eyes were closed.

"What is this?"

"She is sleeping and won't wake unless I let her."

"Do it. Now."

"You have a choice to make first…a promise."

"What do you want?"

"I am not your enemy, Libra. I want what we all want: to exist, to feel," she took

Taryn's limp hand in hers and stroked it, "to love and be loved. I want to rise again and feel the sun on my skin, dance skyclad under a full moon, the light caressing my naked flesh. I want to be filled with the devotion of my worshippers. But I can't do that without you."

"Get to the point."

Gaia's lips twitched; her eyes narrowed. The woman was irritated by his lack of manners but he didn't give a troll's ass.

She released Taryn. "You will be my agent. You will do what I want, when I want. In exchange, you can use the power of the agent to rescue children, and kill or save whomever you want." She crossed her arms. "But you will answer my call and do my bidding."

"If I do this?"

"Then I awaken your inamorata."

"And if I don't?"

"Then I take her with me. I will destroy her body and her soul so you'll never see her again, in this life or any other."

"What did you mean by scratch and dent?"

Gaia cocked her head and pursed her lips. "I'm not feeling the love from you, so I have leverage. If you agree to be my agent, I will wake her. But she will not remember you." She pulled a chain out from under her gown and revealed a vial filled with a gold liquid that shimmered and danced. "If you want her memory returned, be there when I call. If you ever fail to answer, I will take her from you, and there will be nothing you can do to make me return her."

Libra looked at Taryn's serene face. There was no question; he would do anything to get her back and Gaia knew it. "Wake her up, then go."

Gaia nodded, her smug smile grating. She touched Taryn's forehead with the fore and middle fingers of her right hand, and closed her eyes for several seconds.

She backed away. "I will see you very soon, Libra."

"Why? What do you know?"

She placed a hand on his forearm and leaned close to him. "The Quietus is quickening." Releasing him, she backed away. "Don't forget—I own you now."

She disappeared as soon as she finished her taunt, as if sensing he was ready to blast her with coarse language.

Which he was.

He took a deep breath, the rush of hate flowing out, to be replaced by hope. Memories or not, Taryn was back. He'd been lucky enough to stumble into her love once; this time he would do better. He would win her heart.

Taryn opened her eyes and looked at him, her face blank.

She turned her head and clenched her hands in the comforter under her. "Oh, I'm sorry. Is this your bed?"

"Taryn," he whispered.

He leaned over to gather her close, the need to touch her pushing Gaia's words out of his mind, until his sudden movement made her flinch and squeak.

He forced himself to stand up and drop his arms. "I'm sorry, Taryn, I didn't mean to scare you."

She relaxed but her eyes were still wide, her breathing ragged. "Why are you calling me that?"

"Because it's your name. Taryn Rose, that's your name."

Her face remained as blank as his mind felt. Son of a bitch, had Gaia taken more of Taryn's memories than she'd said?

He sat down hard on the bed and looked away from her, trying to relax to ease her fears. "Do you remember anything about who you are, or who I am?"

"No, nothing."

"Do you remember anything at all?"

"I was somewhere very dark. There was crying, a young baby, I think, but I couldn't see who it was. Then that woman brought me here. She told me to lie down and close my eyes, so I did."

The reality of the loss hit him; the cruelty of Gaia's leverage rocked him to the core. What should he do now? He was desperate to hold her, touch her skin, but he would have to woo her and hope that he could control fate, bend it to his will, and make Taryn love him again.

"So why am I here?" she asked.

"Let's start with my name. It's Libra."

"That's a funny name."

He grinned. "Yes, it is."

He was scratching his head, trying to figure out what would convince her to stay with him, when he realized the truth would work best. The unadulterated truth—no matter how scary—was what she needed from him.

"I think you're here to help me. There are children who've been taken from their parents, and I'm going to find them."

"Like these two babies?"

She pointed to the cribs bolted to the side of the van.

"Yes, just like them."

"May I see?"

Libra pulled back the netting tented over the cribs. He looked down at the sleeping Keres and Innocent Demonica Prime.

Taryn ran a finger down their plump, content faces, a soft smile relaxing her strained expression. "They are beautiful."

Libra opened one of the long, narrow drawers tucked under the bed, the drawings and journals with faces and names nearly overflowing. "These are the missing children; I hope this is all of them."

He looked from the evidence of the parents' hopes and fears to Taryn's fading smile.

Reality had hit.

"I could really use your help. With these babies, and with the rescue."

She glanced up, her eyes filled with trepidation. "I don't know."

He crossed his arms. "I had a friend who loved taking chances; she called it jumping off a cliff."

Taryn nodded, her expression of uncertainty changing to contemplation. "I think I've heard that before. I like that idea, taking chances."

He desperately wanted to smooth her frown with a stroke of his thumb; he wanted to kiss her concerns away, nestle his nose into the smooth, warm skin of her neck and inhale her honeyed scent, but that would have to wait.

He held out a hand, not caring what Gaia might ask of him as long as he had Taryn by his side. "You think you could jump off the cliff with me? For the children?"

She studied him for a moment, then placed her hand in his and smiled.

The End

ACKNOWLEDGEMENTS

The best things in life aren't created in a vacuum. Whether it's a book or a song, a poem…a child, we are all influenced and aided, sometimes abetted, by the people and animals and the world around us. It's that need to be a part of a whole that keeps us together, working for a better today for everyone and everything around us, while hoping to leave behind a better future for those generations we will never know.

This book, this author, had help from many hands and many minds, so many talented people who dared me to push forward, to take the time needed to make this as good a book as it could be. I want to acknowledge those people.

To my former editor Jen Blood, thank you for taking the original manuscript of this book and challenging me to rework it, to make it more true to the series as a whole, and for reminding me that the heart and soul of this, and any story, is our connection to each other. As difficult as it was to essentially start over, the result is a story that I can be proud of, and the one I think you were hoping to see.

To my new editor Sara Litchfield from the land of Mordor, thank you for being willing to take on the challenge of what will be a large series, at the second novel, rather than at the beginning. You picked up the gauntlet and ran with it, pushing me not only to make it a good read but a consistent one. I look forward to working with you on this journey of many years!

To Jane Dixon-Smith, thank you for taking up the formatting challenge at the last minute and doing an amazing job! Also, thank you for your infinite patience; you are a goddess!

To the wonderful writer Deborah Dorchak, thank you for reading all my books to date and giving me such supportive feedback at a time when I really needed it. You told me it's better to take your time and write the best book you can, rather than rush it. I took that advice and spent the time I needed to bring Libra and Taryn to life.

As always, thank you to Derek Murphy for his beautiful covers. I've had many compliments on your work and I hope we work together for the entirety of the series.

To my many friends in the Doberman rescue world, thank you for participating in the name game benefiting Decker McKee Doberman Rescue Assistance. The two Dobermans that Lyon rescued in *Lyon's Roar* will appear throughout the series and now, in Libra's book, they finally have names.

Thank you to Patricia Bertka Buchner and Rebecca Hensarling Burcham for naming the huge, black and rust, male Doberman Finn, after a loving, funny, goober boy who will always own a piece of Patricia's soul.

For the feisty, senior, red Doberman girl, Ellen Berry offered the name Blair, after her rescue dog, the love of Ellen's life. I personally knew Blair, and I can attest that she was a once-in-a-lifetime dog.

In real life, Finn and Blair were loved and cherished, and I'm honored to have them immortalized in print!

To my beta readers Bryn Donovan and Laura McCarthy, thank you for taking the time to read through a not fully polished copy and for giving me the feedback I needed to make this book even better!

Finally, thank you to my family, especially you, my dear husband, for always believing in me. I've been a Jane-of-all-trades, searching for that one thing to stick, and writing was it. Through every venture, you have supported me, encouraged me, and never doubted that I could do anything I put my mind to. You have enriched my life beyond measure; you're the precious inspiration behind each love story.

AUTHOR'S NOTE

Toward the end of writing this book, I learned of a young Piscean living in Florida, fighting a type of blood cancer. His continuing battle inspired me to sign up with the organization, Be The Match. I have submitted a cheek swab to see if I could be a bone marrow match for this young man, or for someone else in the country in dire need of a bone marrow transplant.

To honor his fight, I have given my Zodiac Assassin Pisces the name Niko.

Please consider signing up to see if you, too, could be a match.

Be The Match

www.bethematch.org

92013702R00239

Made in the USA
Columbia, SC
24 March 2018